SPELL-BOUND WIZARD

"Let the slave bastard Dheribi be seized and slain, along with his mother the witch Pelkhven."

As they surged toward him, Dheribi raised the staff.

Focus.

He shouted out the spells that would free the Sterkar powers within the staff and bring down destruction on his enemies. Even as he spoke, he felt the Sterkar leap and twist, sensing their freedom. And he felt magic course through him, filling him with a terrible energy.

The Sterkar poured forth, a shimmer of pale blue against the autumn sun. But in the same moment, something else left the staff and wrapped itself around Dheribi's neck—an entity he did not know, a being of malice.

He gasped and began a Sending to drive it away. But he could not speak. The entity had taken his voice—and with it his power to utter spells!

By Crawford Kilian
Published by Ballantine Books:

The Chronoplane Wars:
    THE EMPIRE OF TIME
    THE FALL OF THE REPUBLIC
    ROGUE EMPEROR

EYAS
GRYPHON
GREENMAGIC

GREENMAGIC

Crawford Kilian

A Del Rey Book
BALLANTINE BOOKS • NEW YORK

A Del Rey Book
Published by Ballantine Books

Copyright © 1992 by Crawford Kilian

All rights reserved under International and Pan-American Copyright Conventions. Published in the United States of America by Ballantine Books, a division of Random House, Inc., New York, and simultaneously in Canada by Random House of Canada Limited, Toronto.

Library of Congress Catalog Card Number: 91-93147

ISBN 0-345-36140-7

Manufactured in the United States of America

First Edition: April 1992

Cover Art by Romas

Maps by Claudia Carlson

For Mary Johnson, with love

Contents

Cantarea
in the age of the
Five Kingdoms

N
W   E
S

Vesparushrei (West River)

Aishadan
(Burning Stone)

• Staldhuno
(Steel Town)

Ner Kes

Nemarei (Blood River)

Bayo Bealar
(Underland)

Ghrirei

Ghrirei (Green River)

Halamor
(Holy Lake)

Tanshadabela
(Two Stream Village)

Dragon
Lands

Kormannalendh
(Brave Men's Land)

CLAUDIA CARLSON 1991

Prologue

Drunk and giggling, the raiders lurched down the trail toward the meadow.

The long summer evening was almost over; the sun was far behind the mountains to the northwest, and even the highest clouds had turned from pink to gray. The great river, Vesparushrei, was a dark noise to the south, beyond the lodgepole pines that lined its banks. To the north, the forest extended indefinitely around the feet of enormous mountains. The woods sang with mosquitos, but the raiders ignored them.

Albohar, less drunk than the others, led the way. He had not unsheathed his sword, and he walked with what he knew must seem a casual air. They were deeper into the country of the Menmannar, the mountaineers, than any raiding party had ever gone, so far west that Sneghibi and Slibakh half-joked about bringing back a baby dragon or two instead of mountaineer slaves. But Albohar reminded himself to show no anxiety, not even excessive caution: he was the son of the Aryo, after all, with a reputation to build and maintain.

Vulkvo stumbled over a root and swore. Albohar ignored him. They had all needed a few quick cups of medh to stiffen their courage before leaving the boats and venturing ashore. But Albohar had offered it to them as a simple ceremonial toast to success, and he had drunk little himself.

He paused, hearing the whinny of a horse. The meadow must be close. He had glimpsed it just before dawn, on his first reconnaissance from the boats, but the twilight made distances confusing. Not far beyond it, he knew, was the mountaineer village, a big one. They would have to cross the meadow, slip into one of the nearest houses, and seize a few of the inhabitants. It would be a dangerous business, kidnapping people and es-

1

caping in the dark to the boats. Let one of the mountaineers cry out, let anyone stumble in the woods, and all ten raiders would be dead men.

Holding up a hand, he stopped the others; then he ventured forward. The trees thinned out, and shards of evening-blue sky glowed between their trunks. Albohar could smell horse dung; for a nervous moment he wished he were home in Aishadan, hanging about the stables.

He cursed in his thoughts: the meadow was not deserted as he had expected at this hour. A single pale horse stood in the meadow now, and a single person: a woman, calling in song to the horse as she walked through the grass. Albohar stood very still beside a lodgepole, watching horse and woman. The horse was to his left, not far from the riverbank, and the woman was crossing from his right.

Her presence was not a setback, he realized, but a gift of the Firelord himself. They would not have to enter the village after all. It would be an easy matter to cut the woman off, trap her against the riverbank, and overpower her. The bank was steep here, three times Albohar's height, and at its foot was swift water running shallow over rounded stones. She would have no escape.

He liked the way she moved. She was wearing a mountaineer smock of bleached-white hide, and even in the gloom he could see that it had been richly worked with beads and feathers. Like most mountaineers she was tall and slender, with a long and easy stride. Confident bitch. He'd teach her to walk in the crouching scurry of a slave, to speak Badakhi instead of singing in her rude mountaineer tongue. She'd be more than a prize: she'd be the proof that he'd led the other youths farther into the mountains than even the bravest war parties had ever dared. His father would grant him new slaves, a compound of his own within the Arekaryo Kes, and a retinue of tough fighters as a bodyguard. When the warriors planned new forays, he would sit in their councils.

The mountaineer woman was calling again to the horse, but it only flicked its tail and stepped a little farther away. *Good horse*, Albohar thought. His left hand reached down to grip the steel and waxed leather of his scabbard, to keep it from rattling. His right beckoned the others forward.

Drunk or not, they were young Badakhar: warriors with the wits to move as silently as shadows. In a murmur he told them what they must do, and heard their whispered assent. Then he turned and sprinted out into the meadow.

His deerskin boots made little noise in the thick grass, though his breath seemed to thunder in his ears. She was a long stone's throw away when she heard him and turned.

He grinned at the thought of what they must look like to her: ten demons from the Black World, bursting out of the trees in search of souls to eat. Their wargear was all black, their faces were shadowed by their helmets, and their steps made a rhythmic susurration as they glided through the grass.

Or had the stupid bitch even recognized them for what they were? She turned and went on walking slowly toward the horse, which had paused to stare nervously at the intruders. Albohar heard her singing to it, with only the faintest shimmer of fear in her voice, and he grinned again. No, she was no fool: had she bolted for the horse she would only have driven it farther away, and on foot she had no chance of reaching the security of the darkening forest. And she was no fool to stand and gape at her fate either; she had seen her choices and instantly taken the wisest.

He slowed a little, letting Slibakh and Vulkvo go on ahead to cut off her escape, and turned directly toward her. A good loud Badakhi war cry would send the horse galloping, but it would also alert the village. Ten Badakh boys would be no match for a hundred Menmannar warriors.

The woman was smart not to scream either; she must realize they would not kill her unless they had to.

He was closer, closer—and she stood beside the horse and swung herself lightly up onto its back. It snorted and plunged forward, straight at Albohar.

Pivoting, he turned out of the way and then reached up to grasp the woman's leg. She was wearing buckskin trousers, easy to grip, and she herself could hold on to nothing but the horse's mane. She came down heavily onto him, knocking him to the ground while the horse galloped away into the darkness.

His nostrils were full of the strange scent of her, and her loose black hair blinded him for a moment. She struggled free, got to her feet, and fell again as he tripped her with one outstretched leg. Albohar sat up and launched himself forward, pinning her beneath him. Her elbows smashed into his ribs; he casually gripped her hair and yanked her head back.

"*Si eslisi talom,*" he hissed. "I'll kill you. *Sisima.*"

She obeyed his command to be silent and relaxed with a shudder. Albohar relaxed a little also; he had feared that mountaineers this far west might not even speak the same language as their enslaved cousins in Aishadan. His father was wise: "Know the slaves' language, and you know the slaves."

Without easing his grip on her hair, he got to his feet and pulled her up with him. The others clustered round, gawking at his captive.

"*Skeiar!* Stupid shits!" he growled. "Keep a lookout. The first person to see that horse will rouse the village. Let's get back to the boats."

From a patch pocket on the left leg of his trousers he drew a thong; it bound her wrists behind her. She was whispering something in her own crude dialect—a prayer to their gods, perhaps, or a plea for mercy. From another pocket he drew a knitted wool scarf and tied it over her mouth as a gag.

"Now you'll ride a different mount," he chuckled to her and bent over to put his shoulder against her belly. The scent of her made him a little dizzy, but he stood up with her slung over his shoulder. Holding her to him with his arm tight across the backs of her thighs, he set off toward the trail.

The others had regained some sense of discipline now, and formed guards to front and rear and flanks. They let him set the pace, a steady stride.

The forest had seemed threatening before; now it welcomed them into its protective darkness. Albohar drew Sneghibi in front of him and, with his free hand, held the boy's shoulder. Now he could anticipate the ups and downs of the trail. The woman's weight was slight. They would be back at the boats before long.

In a way, he thought, the raid was almost a disappointment: six nights' travel upriver, the last three through unknown mountaineer country, a long day ashore without being detected, and now a brisk, businesslike slavetaking. They would be all home without a scratch. He had planned things well. He always did. His father would be proud of him.

Tilcalli shivered as the raider carried her through the darkness. She wished she could go into trance, enter the Open Dream, and abide there with her great-grandmother Calihalingol and the other great spirits of the Siragi Aibela until this night was over.

The air reeked of the Badakhar: sweat and shit and medh and fear. When Dragasa and the others came, they would be able to follow the raiders' track as if it had been set with burning torches. But they would come too late, too late.

To talk about this in the silent, eternal sunshine of the Open Dream was one thing; to allow it to happen, here in the darkness, was very different.

We should tell Dragasa, she had said to her great-grandmother. *It would only be fair.*

The old woman Calihalingol, sitting beside on the bank of the Silent River, had smiled toothlessly and chuckled.

He is a good magician, but he is also a man. He would not let you go. Leave him to us.

So she had returned from the Open Dream to the world of Sotalar, had sought the herbs her great-grandmother had told her of, had brewed and drunk a tea, and had gone to her young husband's bed. She had wept a little in his arms, and reassured him that all was well, and then while he slept she had lain awake in the short summer night. She had traced his features with her fingertips, held his breath in her hands. He was so beautiful, and he made her laugh as no other man ever had.

When he comes to you, tell him I have not betrayed him, she had asked Calihalingol. *Tell him I have gone to help Cantarea and to make Callia stronger, as your dream foretold.*

We will tell him, but I do not know if he will listen.

She could tell him herself, of course, if they chanced to meet in the Open Dream. But she dreaded the thought, dreaded what she would read in his eyes when they met under the endless noon while the ancestors of the Siragi Aibela, the clan of magicians, danced and sang the future and the past.

The raiders crashed through the branches of a dead tree and down a steep slope. Tilcalli had no idea how long they had been traveling. She was dizzy and nauseated, and her bound wrists were agony. The noise of the river was louder now, and she could glimpse a few stars in the upside-down sky. Boots clashed on loose pebbles. Without warning, the raider dumped her from his shoulder to the ground. He groaned and laughed, and the others laughed also in boys' braying voices. They must be as frightened as she.

Now they spoke urgently together in their guttural tongue. The one who had carried her seemed to contradict another one, then raised his voice in command. His companions muttered; they sounded disappointed. Tilcalli lay on her side, breathing in quick sobs through her nose and wishing the gag were gone.

Dread seized her. Casting a spell on a human soul was the

hardest, most uncertain of all magic. She would never have dared try it on her own, but Calihalingol had rehearsed her, time after time, until the words were as natural as breathing. But what if she had not properly focused when she cast the spell? What would befall her then?

The raiders' voices rose again in dispute, and again the one who had carried her ended it with a short word. Yes, he was the leader; that much the downriver witches had seen, and Tilcalli had guessed that he would personally seize his prize.

He rolled her onto her back, so that her bound wrists dug painfully into her spine. She felt his hands grope at her waist, pull down her trousers, and slide over her buttocks. The stink of medh on his breath made her stomach heave, and he chuckled as one hand moved to her groin. When he entered her she gasped and then lay silent, holding her breath as he thrust himself deeper. He grunted in her ear, finished, and withdrew while his companions giggled.

One of them spoke again in the same demanding, querulous tone, and Tilcalli knew what he wanted, what they all wanted. Now she would know if her spell had worked.

The leader pushed himself off her, got to his feet, and turned away. She could see him, and the others, dark outlines against the last light of evening. With a casual grace the leader swung out and struck another man. She heard him squawk and fall onto the stones. The leader spoke again: *"Dasha kven beikab maina!"*

The others stood silently. Tilcalli allowed herself to roll onto one side and at last to weep. *Kven*, she knew, meant woman, and *maina* meant mine.

Alo tal eastan zio, she thought coldly. And you are mine.

The spell had worked.

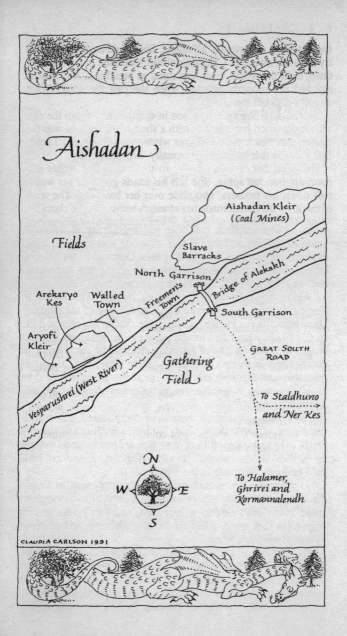

One

The squadron had been training all day in the fields south of the river, charging and wheeling and charging again until the horses were lathered and even Demazakh, the training officer, was tired and sweaty. The early spring sun was warm, even as it sank toward the distant mountains.

"Form up by twos," Demazakh rasped. The squadron obeyed, leaving only Dheribi alone at the rear of the column. He sat erect in his saddle, ignoring the dust in his eyes and the stink of horse dung and unwashed men. Tonight was Seventh Night, the eve of a day of freedom. Tonight he could bathe in peace, sleep in a clean bed, and wake to spend First Day with his books and focusing exercises. Tomorrow night he would be back in barracks for another week, but tomorrow night was still a long time off.

"At a walk—advance," the trainer commanded. The squadron moved off the training field, harnesses jingling and helmets bright even under their film of dust. Slender lances stood straight up in their saddle sheaths, spearheads gleaming and red-and-gold pennons fluttering in the wind.

No one spoke. Demazakh had long since imposed that simple discipline, and many others as well. Dheribi had no urge to speak to his fellow-riders in any case, and they spoke to him only when they must. After six months' training, he had come to enjoy being left alone.

His right forearm ached. Blaidakh, one of the other trainees, had beaten him in a practice duel and had slashed the dull edge of his training sword across Dheribi's arm. "A real blade would have taken your arm off," Demazakh had snarled, and Dheribi had not argued. He blamed himself; he had not been paying

8

attention, and Blaidakh had only seized the advantage of his opponent's distraction.

Soon they reached the road to the bridge and followed it northeastward along the south bank of the Vesparushrei. Here and there, slaves tending gardens dropped their hoes and spades to kneel to the riders as they passed. Other slaves, dragging driftwood from the banks of the swollen river, hastened out of the riders' way.

Tired as he was, Dheribi still looked around to enjoy the beauty of the late afternoon. Off to the right, an apple orchard was already a breeze-blown cloud of blossoms above its brick wall; to the left, the gray river humped itself over Gembh Rock, creating eddies and skiffs of foam. Crocuses clustered along the riverbank, splashes of white and gold and purple among the new grass.

And across the river stood Aishadan. Its slate roofs marched down from the citadel, Arekaryo Kes, to the walled town to the freemen's town and then ended with the squat bulk of the garrison at the bridge's north end. Beyond the garrison's yellow-gray walls stood Aishadan Kleir, Burningstone Hill. It was a long, low ridge scarred and scoured by a century of digging. Slagheaps spilled down its slopes, past mineshaft entrances and the narrow footpaths of the miners. Along the base of the hill stood the slave barracks, built of crudely mortared stone and broken bricks.

Even a sunny and windswept day like this one could not make Aishadan lovely, Dheribi thought. But at least the city was stripped of its eternal smoke, and the flags of the Aryo stood out: each put its golden swastika on a red field against the blue spring sky.

Those flags were streaming out to the northeast, he saw: dragon's wind they called it, the warm wind that broke winter's grip and hastened summer. It would blow sometimes for weeks, until the snowmelt from the mountains filled the riverbed to its banks and spilled into the low-lying fields to leave a thin crust of silt behind. Then the slaves would march out to plow and seed, while the warriors rode away to the summer's wars.

And this year it will be my turn, he thought. He looked down at the two swords strapped to his saddle. One was a mere trainer, a strip of iron with a cushioned edge, but the other was a fine steel saber with a handguard of gilded iron and a lump of uncut amethyst set into the pommel: a gift from his royal father, a rare acknowledgment of their relationship: "Bring it back blooded in honor," the Aryo had said, laying it gently in Dheribi's hands.

Since then he had scarcely drawn it from its gilt and leather scabbard. In the barracks he kept it beside him when he slept, but only because each warrior must; Dheribi would have been glad to lock it in a closet and forget it forever.

The squadron quickened its pace to a trot as it approached the village near the south end of the bridge. A smaller garrison stood here, defending the approach to the Bridge of Alekakh, and Demazakh always wanted his trainees to look smart under the eyes of the garrison veterans. Dheribi kept up without difficulty; he was a good rider, one of the best in the squadron, and his horse Gheli came from the Aryo's own stables. But he looked away from the stained brick walls of the village and the garrison, south and east across the prairie.

Cantarea, his mother's people called it: Big Prairie, their ancient homeland. Now they lived far to the west, in the mountains where the sun would soon set, but still they called themselves Cantareans. They knew the old names for every plant and flower, every bird and animal that made the prairie its home. They knew the deep names too, the names by which magicians could call upon the Powers that infused all things that lived or had simple being. They recalled the names of towns burned to ashes a century or more ago, sang the ancient songs, and worshipped Callia though she had been driven from her home along with them.

He wondered what the Cantareans would think of it now. At the far horizons, the low hills lay scarred by gullies; bunchgrass made scattered spots of green on the dun land. Once, the old people said, the pastures had stretched unbroken and nourished great herds of horses and flocks of sheep. Now only the wealthiest of the landowning upermannar, those who had fenced in their meadows, could still keep livestock within half a day's ride of the city.

Within a league of the river, though, endless toil had kept the land fertile. Here and there, a carefully tended orchard flourished behind walls topped with spikes, and the walled fields would soon turn green with new wheat. But these were the property of the Aryo, and their crops would benefit only his court. To feed the warriors' families, and the freemen's, and the thousands of slaves who labored in the mines and forges, Aishadan must draw on its provinces.

As the squadron reached the south end of the bridge, a caravan blocked its way: a hundred wagons laden with grain, with iron ingots, with barrels of salt beef and with fearful slaves. Its escort was fifty warriors, veterans who glanced with genial contempt at the apprentice cavalry lined up behind Demazakh. The caravan would soon reach its destination, a market in the walled town or freemen's town. A few days from now the caravan would go out again, its wagons empty save for armor, spearheads, coal, and hides. That freight would help support the upermannar, who owed fealty to the Aryo. And in return they would pay still more tribute in food and iron and slaves.

The bridge was clear at last, and the squadron rumbled out onto its thick planks. It rose three times a man's height above the river, its pilings driven deep and well secured by boulders and spells; it had outlasted many floods since the Aryo Alekakh had built it sixty years past. The riders kept to the left, allowing a steady traffic of slaves and freemen to jostle along. Most were moving north, back to their homes in the city. An occasional freeman glanced up at the riders, but the slaves kept their gazes fixed on the uneven planks of the bridge. Meeting a Badakh warrior's eyes could cost a slave his own.

Dheribi's hands tightened on Gheli's reins as he looked at the slaves. They were ill-clad in coarse wool tunics or kilts, and showed plenty of scars. Most were pure Cantareans, tall, lean, and dark of hair and skin. A few had the sturdier build and fair hair that meant a Badakh father or grandfather.

Like me, Dheribi thought. *Though I might as well be all Cantarean.* He was black-haired and brown-skinned, slim and long-limbed and wiry. His father had named him: Little Dark One, it meant, though now he was a head taller than the Aryo. Dheribi had often looked for similarities to his father, and found few: an impatience in their strides, a harshness in their laughter.

But he had his mother's eyes, and coloring, and moods, and something else that she did not have but seemed to have given him also: a pleasure in trees and flowers, an ear for music, a sense of absurdity.

And his mother was a slave. By rights, he too should be walking on this bridge in a gray tunic, showing the weals of his last beating. He should be keeping his gaze from the proud faces of the warriors, and thinking not of a hot bath and a good meal but of a lump of oil-soaked bread and a straw mat in his master's stables.

Somehow, though, the old Aryo's heir had treasured his captive from the mountains, kept her in a fine apartment with slaves of her own. When Albohar had himself become Aryo, he had raised his half-breed son to the ranks of the warriors.

He should have paid me no notice, Dheribi thought. *Perhaps I would have been happier as a slave.* He shrugged off the thought; his mother had little tolerance for self-pity, and that also she had given him.

The cavalry barracks was just outside the walls of the citadel; as trainees, Dheribi and the others were obliged to stable their own mounts. The sun was down before Demazakh had finished his inspection of the horses and dismissed the men. They fell at once into convivial knots of four or five, guffawing as they argued over how to spend their evening. Loudest of them was Blaidakh. He was the son of one of the great upermannar families, a powerfully built, red-faced youth with drooping yellow moustaches and cold eyes.

Dheribi did not stay; he walked up the cobbled lane to Second Gate, where the sentries let him pass.

This was Arekaryo Kes: Kingsguard Fortress, a great jumbled pile of stone and brick. The main walls and the Inner Keep were over a century old, built by Kvosedakh when he first brought his people into this land to found his own kingdom. His dynasty had added to it haphazardly, a tower here, a palace there. It sat on the upper slopes of Aryofi Kleir, thought Dheribi, like a helmet on a giant's skull.

For all its gray walls and dark corridors, it was home—a redoubt within which he found as much safety as his royal ancestors had. He had roamed it all his life, from the beer cellars to the hearing rooms and armories.

His route took him up the east face of the hill, past the great reservoir and across a grassy terrace. Slaves and guards acknowledged him—the slaves with a bent knee and perhaps a shy smile, the guards with a surly nod. Dheribi raised his hand in his father's perfunctory greeting.

He soon came to a compound of whitewashed brick houses with steep slate roofs. Two Cantarean slaves stood guard at the entrance to the compound; they carried truncheons that were purely ceremonial, a compliment from Albohar. They knelt as Dheribi passed brusquely through to the inner garden.

Other slaves swarmed around him, took his helmet and cloak, and murmuringly escorted him to a steaming bath in his room. He sank into it gratefully, letting the water soak away the aches.

"Pelkhven awaits you for dinner, sir," one of the slaves told him after he had almost dozed off in the tub.

"I will attend her at once." He hoisted himself from the wooden tub, and walked dripping across the tile floor to a slave with a towel. Dry and dressed in a wool tunic, he strapped on sandals and drew a bone comb through his long black hair. He rubbed his chin: no whiskers there. He was as beardless as the mountaineers, while his fellow-trainees, no older than he, were as hairy-faced as bears.

Well, it could not be helped. He left his apartment and walked across the little garden to his mother's rooms. A slave bowed and admitted him to the dining hall.

"Good evening, Son."

"Mother."

To others she was Pelkhven, Black Woman; to him and no one else she had told her Cantarean name, Tilcalli, Small Beauty. She was seated in her usual chair, at the table beside the hearth. As usual, her dress was a simple white gown that set off her brown skin and black hair. A lamp hung from the low ceiling, throwing a dim light across her face. Dheribi thought she looked tired. He took his seat across the table from her and gratefully lifted a mug of beer to his lips. Just in time he caught the alarm in her dark eyes.

"Thanks to the Gariba Sotalara, the Powers of Earth, for this gift," he murmured, and his mother relaxed.

"Never forget. They give us life itself."

"Yes. But other people don't give thanks each time they pour themselves a cup of beer or medh."

Tilcalli smiled. "I'm not responsible for other people's ignorance—only for yours. How was the training?"

"Much as always. Demazakh knows his business and works us hard."

She looked at the darkening bruise across his forearm. "Are you any more reconciled to a warrior's life?"

He put his tankard down and took up a silver skewer for his meat. "I can do it. I enjoy the riding, and the swordplay. When I see Demazakh's tactics, I marvel at what the old man knows."

"You haven't answered my question."

He spiked a lump of stewed beef. "It's all still play. I would have to know real combat, with a real sword. When I was little I used to dream about serving my father as a great warrior—"

"I remember well."

"—but now I wonder. I will never rise high in his service. I'll be just another horseman with a sword, fighting his battles until I'm killed or crippled."

Tilcalli nodded, dipping a crust of bread into her stew. "Most young men think that a fine life."

"For most it is. The others will earn some honor, some booty, enough to win a wife and start a family. Who'd have me but a Cantarean slave?"

Her dark eyes flashed in the lamplight. "Mind your tongue. I too am a Cantarean slave."

"I apologize, Mother." He looked around the room, as if seeking some better way to express himself. "I know how lucky I am. But I know also I have no place here."

"Nor did I when I first came here. I was a trophy, something for your father to show off. But I made a place, and not a bad one, you'll admit."

"We could lose it any moment," he replied quietly. "Some day Ghelasha will strike at us, and Father's protection will not be enough."

"The Aryasha does not love us, I know. But she is the true wife of the Aryo, and her son is heir to Aishadan. No one questions that, I least of all. I have never even hinted that Eskel should not succeed his father."

"Mother, you know Ghelasha would sleep better if both of us were dead."

She frowned. "You are dreadful company this evening, Dheribi. I ask you how the day went, and you only complain. Have you meditated today? Have you focused?"

"No."

"You would feel better if you did."

He said nothing, knowing his mother was right. He had consoled himself all day with the thought of spending tomorrow morning in a long focus. But the skills of thought and perception she had taught him were Cantarean, barbarous practices no self-respecting Badakh would engage in. They even seemed something like the strange trances that magicians put themselves into, when they became even crazier than usual.

Once or twice, when she had first taught him focusing, he had wondered if Tilcalli herself were a magician, but the idea was absurd. Men, not women, had the talent for magic, and paid for it with madness. His mother was eminently sane, more so than most people.

Still, what she had taught him only made him feel yet more out of place, and now she only encouraged him in that feeling.

Irrational anger flooded him. Whom could he talk to about

his worries, his disappointments, his fears, if not Tilcalli? And if she would not listen, who would?

"I would feel better after a few more tankards, down in the freemen's town," he growled, and stood up. "Good night, Mother."

Her eyes looked up at him, unreadable. "Good night, Dheribi. We will talk again soon."

He strode back to his own apartment, snapping at the slaves who drew a cloak around his shoulders and buckled his sword to his belt. "May we escort you, sir?" asked Andho, the compound's senior slave.

"No. Be off with you all, see to my mother and leave me in peace!"

A breeze had sprung up, and lightning flickered far off to the east. Dheribi walked rapidly down the paths and steps to the gate, and on into the city. His hooded cloak both revealed and concealed him: the broad brown-and-white stripes proclaimed him a novice warrior, while the hood kept his face in darkness. His training sword was back in his apartment, but the good one he wore as he must. In the torchlit streets he strode without stepping aside for anyone, his hand on his sword's pommel.

The walled town had few taverns, and those were jammed with upermannar and their retinues carousing on their visit to the capital. Dheribi passed them by, and went down by narrow lanes to the freemen's town. He knew a beer hall off the fountain square, a favorite of cavalrymen. No doubt he would see some of his fellow-trainees there, but they would have the grace to leave him alone.

The hall was a narrow room, roughly walled in brick and with a low ceiling. Halfway down the right side of the room was a fireplace, throwing heat from a pile of glowing coals. Candles burned at some of the tables, illuminating blond-bearded faces. The place smelled of smoke and beer and vomit, and the noise was a cheerful deep roar of men's laughter and argument.

Dheribi sat himself at a table; a slave hastened over with a burning taper to light his candle and take his order. When it came, he remembered to thank the Powers of Earth. Odd how the two languages diverged in the phrase, he thought: *Gariba Sotalara* meant "Makers of the Earth." The makers were neutral. But *Sterkar afi Dhkem* meant both "powers" and "good things" of the world. To the Badakhar, what was strong was good; the word *mela* meant both weak and evil. No wonder they despised their slaves and respected their foes.

The beer was cool and rich, with a thick head on it. He drank deep and called for another.

This was much like focusing, he thought: a way of sealing off whatever was around you, so that you could concentrate on what mattered. What mattered now was getting pleasantly drunk and then going home to a good night's sleep.

The beer hall was full now, with a burning candle at every table and most tables crowded with men. He recognized many of them, including Blaidakh and a few others from the squadron. They were dicing for drinks with much laughter and swearing.

The hallmaster called for silence and introduced a *seribi*, a small sorcerer, as the evening's entertainment. The magician was a sallow boy, his face deeply pockmarked within a halo of tangled blond hair. He wore the gray-striped robe of his order, and seemed scarcely to notice his surroundings. Dheribi was surprised: not many magicians ever performed except at the command of their mentors or their masters. He wondered what had brought this young fellow to entertain a mob of warriors.

As the crowd quieted a little, the magician drew a vertical circle of glowing red with one hand. The circle became a sphere, hanging in midair. Within it, a fish seemed to swim in a sun-dappled lake.

The drinkers applauded by pounding their tankards. The young man ignored them, turning the lake into a mountain eyrie within which an eagle stood proudly. Next came darkness, and within it two glowing yellow sparks, and then a full-grown dragon, half again as large as a man, appeared to lean out of the sphere with grasping claws reaching out for the nearest men.

A moment ago they had been laughing and cheering; now they shouted and stumbled backward out of their seats. The dragon's jaws snapped shut and an instant later it vanished.

The beer hall erupted in cheers and oaths and guffaws. Dheribi found himself standing, one hand on his sword, and relaxed with a snort and a chuckle. By Mekhpur, this illusionist might be just a small sorcerer, but he knew a trick or two! He hadn't seen an illusion as good as the dragon since he'd been a little boy at his grandfather's anniversary feast.

"More, more!" Blaidakh yelled, but the magician only shook his head and grinned foolishly. Sweat poured down his pocked cheeks, and his eyes rolled in his head. Dheribi wondered how long it would take for the illusionist to regain his powers. Probably not until tomorrow. And until he did, he'd seem little more than half-witted.

A hard life magicians must have, he reflected as he called for a third tankard. Entrancing themselves until they scarcely knew where they were or who they were, doing their tricks for whoever would give them a meal and a place to sleep. And all they seemed to care about was learning more magic, mastering the Powers until at last they came to look upon the face of Mekhpur himself.

He shuddered as if a cold wind had blown through his cloak. Magicians had their joys, no doubt, but they paid too high a price for them.

Blaidakh was still unsatisfied. "More tricks, *Seribi*! Show us that dragon again."

"Master—" the illusionist's voice was hoarse. "I cannot."

"Bloody trickster." Blaidakh shoved the youth hard, toppling him backward onto the hearth. Dheribi, some distance away, could not see what happened next. But he heard the magician scream terribly, and Blaidakh laugh. The other carousers laughed and cheered as well, pounding fists on tables.

Dheribi caught a whiff of burned hair and seared flesh. A moment later Blaidakh hoisted the magician upright.

"How's this for an illusion?" the young warrior bellowed cheerfully. "Isn't this the very image of a roast pig?"

The illusionist's head must have fallen into the fire: his hair was gone, and the skin of his scalp and face was blackened and puffing into obscene blisters. His mouth was a black hole that opened and shut convulsively; his eyelids were gone, but he was not blind.

Dheribi felt his stomach tighten. Young warriors would have their fun with slaves and freemen, but sometimes they went too far. The sight of the magician's destroyed face had taken all the pleasure out of being drunk. Dheribi rose with a little sway and made his way through the crowd to the privy behind the beer hall.

Emptying his bladder, he felt a wave of nausea. What a wretched life this was: a life of pain endured and pain inflicted, where the only happiness seemed to lie in causing other people misery. The vision of the magician's burned face loomed before him again, as real as the dragon, and Dheribi bent over to vomit into the stinking darkness. His mouth and nostrils burned as he wiped his running nose and lurched out of the privy.

Slowly he followed a pathway that led around the building and back out to the street. In the darkness he heard someone whimpering: a girl, most likely. Then a blow, and a gasp. Yes, it was a girl, being soundly beaten. A man growled and footsteps scuffled irregularly. Dheribi saw two figures lurch into the light of a torch outside the front doors of the beer hall.

One was a tall young woman, dressed in shirt and trousers of gray homespun—doubtless a slave. In the torchlight, blood streaked down her face. The man holding her was a cavalryman, in high boots and a tight leather jacket: Blaidakh again, already in search of new amusement. He swung one hand in a casual sweep that knocked the girl back toward the dark path.

"Come on, pretty one," Blaidakh said. "Pull 'em down and let's have no more of this false modesty."

Dheribi hesitated for a moment, tempted to turn back, go into the hall once more and leave Blaidakh to his pleasure. But why should Blaidakh gain any more pleasure tonight from the pain of others?

"Is she yours, Blaidakh?" he called.

The young upermanna squinted into the darkness. "Who's that? Dheribi? What d'you want?"

Dheribi walked forward. The girl, sobbing, cringed back against the rough brick wall between the two men.

"If she's yours," Dheribi said softly, "take her home and do it in comfort. But if she's not, you have no business with her. You know that."

"And you have no business with me."

Dheribi moved past the girl and into the dim light of the torch. "I'm speaking to you as a comrade, Blaidakh. You know you could be scourged for taking another man's property."

"Scourged? *Scourged?*" Blaidakh cackled with incredulous laughter. "Be off with you, half-breed. I don't need advice from the likes of—"

The sword was in Dheribi's hand, its point within a handsbreadth of Blaidakh's sneering face. Someone lurched out of the beer hall door, saw the two men, and shouted back inside. Blaidakh did not move. Men came pouring out of the hall, forming a circle around the two. After what seemed like a long time, Blaidakh smiled.

"Is this a challenge, half-breed?"

"It is," he heard himself saying.

"Over a stray slave? Did you fancy her yourself?"

"Over a matter of respect."

"Respect? What respect could a half-breed want?"

"The respect due his father. Draw your sword or I'll cut your throat and toss you in the privy."

Blaidakh drew a breath, shook his head, shifted his weight, and seemed to relax. An instant later his sword was out and swinging down in a murderous arc.

On a stranger the ruse might have worked, as it already had on Dheribi that afternoon. He parried, stepped back, and focused.

The crowd vanished. The slave girl vanished. The beer hall and the muddy street were gone. Only Blaidakh remained, moving with the slowness of a wading man. He was recovering his balance, bringing his saber up again for a thrust. Dheribi watched the sword, saw how the *Pursterkar*, the Powers of Fire, had moved within it to make it strong in some places and weak in others. He looked into Blaidakh's eyes, and saw them focus on the spot where the blade would go next. As the sword's point sought his ribs, Dheribi flicked it aside.

In the next moment he sensed someone else watching him, and glanced away from Blaidakh. There in the dimness where the crowd had been, a man stood: tall, bald and grizzle-bearded, wearing a dark cloak with a high collar. His eyes were pale and intelligent, fixed on Dheribi yet seeming to look beyond. The man was Pelshadan. He was titled Skalkaz afi Mekhpur, Servant of the Firelord; he was the greatest of the Aryo's magicians and one of the Veikar.

How could he be inside the focus? He must be a mighty magician indeed. Yet why did he look so surprised, so intent?

Focus. Dheribi turned back to his opponent and the magician faded into the dimness. Blaidakh's sword was a thin band of reflected fire, shimmering in the dark and moving with deadly slowness. Dheribi saw the weak point in the blade, where the Sterkar had not been properly invoked. He struck it cleanly and saw the sword snap.

That should have ended the duel, but instead Dheribi kicked out with his right foot in a lunge that brought him close enough to Blaidakh for a slash.

Blood followed the blade like a ragged banner. Blaidakh convulsed, jerking back and letting fall his broken sword. He crashed backward into the mud, his belly a red fountain. For a moment he looked up at Dheribi with wide and startled eyes, and then those eyes went blind.

Dheribi recovered from his lunge and pivoted, sword up and ready for a second attack from Blaidakh's companions. No one came out of the dimness, and he let the focus blur.

Now he was back on the street under the torchlight, encircled by silent warriors and hangers-on while Blaidakh grunted and vomited his life away in a puddle of blood and beer. The slave girl was sobbing almost silently. Pelshadan stepped forward and took her arm.

"Come, Bherasha. We must get the boy home." She went to him obediently, still shuddering. Pelshadan's pale eyes, still intent and surprised, met Dheribi's. "I am indebted to you, sir, for protecting my property." He pulled the girl away through the crowd. Dheribi saw a figure in a gray-striped robe join them, tottering, and saw Pelshadan's arm go around him: the burned magician.

Dheribi lowered his sword, and a rivulet of blood reversed itself down the blade. He drew a slow breath.

"Call the night watch," he said. "My comrade has fallen."

Two

The dragon's wind had blown all night, and at sunrise was blowing still. The banners of Arekaryo Kes snapped in the wind as Albohar stepped out onto the broad balcony adjoining his private quarters, and the wind tugged at his yellow wool robe. He squinted east at the sun's yellow glare, then turned to look south down the hill and across the river.

Damn the boy! Give him every opportunity, encourage him in the profession of arms, ensure that he be treated exactly like any other officer in training—and he kills one of his fellows. Worse yet, he does it in a street brawl, and his victim is none other than old Aghwesi's son—virtually a nephew to the Aryo.

He could well imagine what Ghelasha would say, and he would have no answer for her. His half-breed son had caused a major political embarrassment, an offense to one of the greatest upermannar, and right on the eve of the Trame Mod, the Spring Gathering. All the upermannar, the landowners of the kingdom, would be there to renew their oaths and bring their grievances to him for settlement. This would be a grievance he must settle fairly yet firmly. He needed the upermannar's support for the war he planned against Ner Kes, and he would get it, but they would charge him a high price.

He leaned against the stone railing, consoling himself with the view across the great plain. All that he could see was his, and far beyond. In the scattered villages, in the garrisons, in the chapels of the upermannar estates, they would be praying to Mekhpur for their Aryo's continued health and might. He could see the smoke from the sacrifices made in the garrison across the bridge, and knew that scores of lambs, hundreds of chickens, had given their blood at sunrise to ensure Mekhpur's blessing.

I'll need it, he thought. The war against Ner Kes would not be long: a few skirmishes, a short siege, and a negotiated peace. But it would harden his army and enrich his treasury for the next one—the one against Halamor that would make it a mere province of Aishadan, and cut off Ghrirei from Ner Kes. Then, using his marriage to Ghelasha, he would claim the throne of Ghrirei as well, and invite Ner Kes and Kormannalendh to submit themselves.

No one had ever united all the kingdoms of the Badakhar. Many had imagined they held Mekhpur's favor, and had warred against their rivals only to be overthrown.

But I can do it. The others didn't understand how to do it, how to prepare. And now this foolish boy blunders into my path.

He prowled down to the east end of the terrace, squinting into the sun. The city looked proud and powerful this morning, its dark slate roofs glaring with the sun's reflected light. He heard Aishadan rumble: carts rolled through its streets, hammers clanged in its smithies, work crews chanted as they dug and carried and hauled. In the market squares he could see long-skirted women crowding the booths and shops.

Yes, he could just make out the roof of the damned beer hall. Albohar smiled grimly. He'd gotten drunk himself in that hall many a time, back in his youth, and done his share of brawling. The boy was taking after his father after all, perhaps, but he'd chosen a bad time and a bad opponent.

Well, he would talk to Ghelasha, and to Pelkhven, and then to Dheribi himself. Aghwesi was still out at his manor, Vidhumen; a courier was on his way with the bad news, but the old man wouldn't be here until tomorrow at the earliest. Time enough to settle the matter.

He turned and strode back into his wide, low-ceilinged apartment, setting his servants in a flutter. In their yellow tunics they stood out vividly against the coarsely mortared red-brick walls and the bare gray boards of the floor. Albohar glared at a servant. "Send word to the Aryasha that I wish her to attend on me here after she breakfasts."

"At once, my lord."

He broke his own fast on hard bread and honey and a cup of hot water, consumed while he sat on the edge of his hard bed. Ghelasha arrived before he had finished.

"Good morning, my lord."

"My lady."

She was dressed in a lambswool gown and a cloak of wolf-skins. Her yellow hair tumbled down over her shoulders, a golden frame for her pale and perfect face. Ghelasha's slightly slanted blue eyes, bright with the cold fire of her intelligence, met his and did not look away.

"Please come and sit beside me. I need your advice."

"This is about the killing last night."

He enjoyed the perfume of her body as she settled gracefully beside him. "Yes. Dheribi behaved like a fool."

"I'm very disappointed in him. He seemed to be coming along well. It's his Menmannar blood coming out."

Albohar grunted and slurped hot water. "It was Blaidakh's blood that came out, more's the pity. I'll have to punish Dheribi, of course, and I want your suggestions."

"Exile. Banishment from Aishadan for—oh, five years. Put him in some forsaken little garrison and let him practice his swordcraft on bears and peasants."

He nodded. It was a quick answer; it always was, and always well thought out. "We have plenty of similar precedents. I will consider it seriously. How is Eskel taking the news?"

"He's furious. He always idolized Blaidakh. Now he's saying he'll challenge the half- "

"My lady, curb your tongue. And tell our son to curb his." Albohar's voice was quiet, but she saw the wrath in his eyes. "I will not have the Aryo's sons brawling with one another and pretending to be duelists."

"As you command, my lord. Eskel, at least, will not dishonor you. That I promise."

"I'm grateful for your advice. Will you join me at dinner tonight?"

"Most gladly."

"Until then."

She rose, bowed, and glided out. Albohar smiled faintly. None of the wolves whose skins she wore had ever been as dangerous as she. His father had chosen her well.

He summoned Pelkhven next. She did not stride into the apartment; she went to her knees like any slave, and for once he did not give her his hand to help her up. But she walked to her accustomed chair with the grace and confidence he still remembered from the meadow where he had first seen her.

"Your son has humiliated and embarrassed me, Pelkhven. Have I wasted my generosity on him?"

"I hope not, master." Her eyes did not meet his; they rarely did, and he was glad of it. Ghelasha's intelligence was there for all to see in her eyes, but Pelkhven's was hidden, unknowable even after all these years.

"I had some hopes for him, you know. And suffered some gossip for his sake. Worse than gossip. Some people around here think I should have sold him like any other half-breed slave, and sold you too. Maybe I should have. Poor Blaidakh would still be alive if I had."

She said nothing; she spoke only to direct questions, as a slave should in such an interview.

"I have it in mind to send him off to one of the frontier posts along the border with Ner Kes. Let him learn the profession of arms where he's more likely to kill an enemy than a comrade. What would you say to that?"

"I would say you have the power of life and death over him, as you always have."

"You know that's not what I asked, Pelkhven. Speak plainly. Would you consider it a just decision?"

"What the Aryo decrees is just, master."

He struggled to keep his temper, and won. "What would you do about him?"

"I would find him a way to atone for his crime, and to serve you. It would not be as a warrior. Perhaps as a spy against Ner Kes."

Albohar's eyes widened. "A spy—"

It made sense. Dress him in homespun and the boy would look like any slave. Slip him across the border in a batch of slaves, sell him at a bargain price to some Ner Kes upermanna, let him learn all he could and then make his way home before the war began in the summer. The stratagem had been tried before, but not with a trained, educated warrior who knew what to look for.

"Too dangerous," he said. "Don't you think so?"

"He has taken a warrior's life. He must risk his own."

"Let Mekhpur hear me, you sound more like a Badakh woman than the real ones do!" He rubbed his beard. "Well, I'll consider it."

She sat silently, eyes downcast. Albohar sucked his teeth and then dismissed her.

The idea was a good one. Ghelasha would approve, if only because it put Dheribi at more risk than he would be under her own proposal. The boy might well bring back useful intelligence; even if he came back empty-handed, his time in the enemy camp would help to purge his offense. And if he did not come back at all—

Albohar felt a pang of dread. The boy was a half-breed, all right, but still he was his firstborn son. When he thought of the happy moments in his life, Dheribi and his mother always seemed to figure in them: the great moment of his conception far up the river, while the Menmannar hunted them; the boy's first toddling steps in the garden; the look of dazzled joy when his line hooked his first fish; the serenity of his sleeping face under candlelight.

He cursed himself for a weakling. Surely the old Aryo had never felt such tender affection for *him*, never fretted about the foray up the river to Pelkhven's village. Dheribi would have to take his chances.

The official day was beginning. He changed from his robe into working clothes: leather trousers, soft boots, a finely woven wool tunic and an ornately embroidered buckskin vest. With his apartment servants going ahead to announce him, he strode quickly across a small garden to the Hearing Hall. At his approach, the guards at the doorway drummed the iron-shod butts of their spears against the flagstones. The twenty supplicants inside the hall promptly knelt.

Albohar walked in under the tattered banners of his forefathers, hanging between the narrow, lead-glazed windows. Under the blackened beams, the air was still and thick. Many a feud and war had begun here, and ended here as well. Upermannar had entered here in their proud finery and left as condemned men, chains their only garment and beheading their only prospect. Freemen had sometimes left this room as upermannar, awkward and exultant in their new green cloaks and swords of best Staldhuno steel. If the Aryo was king over Aishadan, Albohar reflected, in this room he was god.

Or not quite: as ritual demanded, he bowed to the small altar set in the wall beside his throne. It was a shelf mounted within a niche, and on the shelf rested a small sphere of gold set on a base of green-and-red bloodstone. This was the altar of Mekhpur; from it the Firelord oversaw all that the Aryo said and did. In the early days of the kingdom, when Aishadan had been hard-pressed by its foes, slaves had been given to Mekhpur before the altar. But that had been long ago; the custom had long since lapsed.

The morning passed quickly enough in administrative chores: granting a small pension to a favored old blacksmith, judging a boundary dispute, appointing a promising youth to a job as a tax-gatherer: Albohar liked the hard set of the boy's mouth. But he thought more about Dheribi than about the cases before him.

The hall was almost empty, and Albohar was thinking about a quick ride down to the river and back before the noon meal, when Pelshadan slipped quietly in. He knelt and remained on his knees until the Aryo nodded.

"Do you have business with me, Skalkaz?"

"A trifle, my lord. It will wait until you have disposed of these worthy subjects."

The three men remaining in the hall glanced gratefully at the magician; their cases might well have been dismissed without a hearing if one of the Veikar—the Skalkaz afi Mekhpur himself—chose to assert his rank.

Albohar completed the morning's work and beckoned Pelshadan to stand before him.

"What is it, my friend?"

Pelshadan's pale eyes stared into some unknown distance while with two fingers he rapidly curled and uncurled a strand of gray hair. "It has to do with the disturbance at the beer hall, my lord."

"Since when are you concerning yourself with warriors' brawls?"

Pelshadan smiled; his fingers turned yet another strand into ringlets. "I concern myself with little else, my lord."

Albohar laughed shortly. "Fair enough. But what about last night?"

"My apprentice Minukhi and my slave Bherasha were both involved. Minukhi slipped out of his quarters to try to earn some money displaying illusions. Bherasha went looking for him—she knew he was forbidden to leave his room, and she hoped to bring him back before I learned of it. Blaidakh threw the boy into the fire, and then encountered Bherasha outside. He attempted to rape her. I was following close behind, but I arrived too late to end matters. Blaidakh had called Dheribi a half-breed, and Dheribi challenged him in defense of your name."

"Did he indeed? This is part of the story no one has told me."

"It is perhaps of interest to you, but not to me. I watched the duel, my lord. Your son fought ensorcelled."

"Pelshadan." The Aryo's voice was very quiet in the empty hall. "You aided him?"

"No, my lord." Pelshadan sounded scandalized. "He did it

himself, but I do not think he knew what he was doing. He merely displayed the untutored talent. It enabled him to see a weak point in his opponent's blade, and to strike with unusual speed and force."

"That they told me, all right. Almost cut the lad in two, I understand."

"No, my lord, merely a very deep disembowelment. Any of your veterans could do as well. But it was impossible for a novice warrior, especially one who had drunk three flagons of beer in little more than an hour."

"So he has the talent."

"Without doubt. I realize that you must deal with him as justly as you would any other warrior, my lord. But I sense in him a power that could serve you better than a squadron of Blaidakhs. When he has repaid his debt, I ask that you put him in my tutelage. He belongs with the Veikar."

Albohar hesitated. He rubbed his lip uncertainly. "It's too late, isn't it? Magicians must start as boys."

"Ordinary magicians, yes. And most get no further than the sorry illusions that Minukhi was so proud of. But—your son, my lord, accomplished last night what most magicians can only dream of attaining. I think—I must force myself to say it—I think he has been sent by Mekhpur to aid you."

"And what would you make of him, Skalkaz?"

"A Master Veik, to defend you and yours against the most baleful magic. A Master Veik to keep you on the throne of the five kingdoms." Pelshadan smacked his lips loudly, another of his mannerisms.

Albohar stood and tried to look into the Veik's eyes. He failed: no magician would meet an ordinary man's gaze. "You are no flatterer, and you have never dabbled in intrigue, have you?"

Pelshadan's smile was cool. "Only against my colleagues, my lord."

"I have granted you great freedom in recruiting the best talent you could find. You have assured me that with enough good magicians, we could withstand any spell our enemies might send against us." He ignored Pelshadan's slight nod. "Now you ask to recruit my son. Suppose you trained him in all your lore. Suppose he was as great as you suppose. What would keep him from slaying his half-brother, the heir, and taking the throne himself?"

From any other man, the magician's smile would have been

an insulting smirk. His voice took on a familiar half-crazed whine.

"My lord, you know as well as I, as well as I, that we magicians have no interest in power over this world. This is a place of dim and transient shadows compared to the world we see through the eyes of Mekhpur. The lords of this earth give us food and shelter, yes, and time to master our lore; to grant you power and protection is a small enough price to pay. But what would we want with your throne? We could not sit in judgment, as you have done this morning. We could not plan wars, no, though we help you fight them. We would turn instead to our books and dreams, while our kingdoms dwindled to nothing— or someone slew us, more likely. If Dheribi is what I think him, he will serve his half-brother as loyally as I have served you."

Albohar frowned. "I will ponder your words, Skalkaz. Return to your books. I will call you when I wish to speak further about this."

The magician knelt. "I await your call, my lord."

The Aryo waved impatiently to one of the servants standing by the door. "Get me a horse." He strode off, ignoring the bearded magician who still knelt, trembling slightly, on the cold tiles. Dheribi sat up in bed. The night before seemed more real than the late-morning light streaming through his apartment windows. When he stood, his head ached; he felt weary, but not as he had at the end of yesterday's training. This was a tiredness in the soul, a sadness he had never felt before. Was this what it felt like after killing a man? If it was, who would kill twice?

He called for a slave but no one answered. Getting out of bed, he pulled on the robe he had worn last night, and almost gagged at the smell of smoke and beer that clung to it. He went to the door and pulled it open.

Three Badakh guards stood on his doorstep, looking warily at him. He recognized them all: members of his father's bodyguard, trusted veterans and skilled warriors. The oldest of them cleared his throat.

"Good morning, lad. We're under orders to see you stay in your quarters until the Aryo calls for you. You're to have no servants or weapons with you. Should you want food or drink, ask and we'll see you get it."

Dheribi thought for a moment. The idea of food nauseated him. "Only water, please."

"Very good. We'll knock when it's here." The guard reached out and pulled the door shut again, but not before Dheribi glimpsed his mother, watching from across the garden.

He sat on the edge of his bed, head in his hands as he recalled every movement of the fight. He had seen the weak point in the blade, struck it cleanly; why had he not stepped back and let Blaidakh step back also? Why had he lunged and slashed at a foe who could no longer defend himself?

Because he deserved it. The thought persisted. Blaidakh had mutilated a harmless small sorcerer, and then gone in search of the nearest girl. Even if Blaidakh had been bested this time, and allowed to live, he would have slain or raped others. His every joy would have been some poor slave's misery.

And what made Blaidakh different from all his comrades? he asked himself. Why kill him, when most of the men in the beer hall would have done the same, given a little more courage or a little more beer? Rape and murder were the privileges of any Badakh warrior. Dheribi imagined himself in the Hearing Hall, standing before his father and bleating, "He deserved it." And then going to the headsman's block with every warrior in the fortress laughing, "You deserve it!"

Dheribi himself laughed, softly and to himself. Under the sadness, the weariness, he felt a kind of liberation. Perhaps they would kill him, or bury him alive in one of the dungeons deep under Arekaryo Kes. At least he would not have to be a warrior, to keep up the pretense of being just another Blaidakh with a brown and beardless face.

The guards brought him boiled water, and he drank it gladly. Then he dressed simply in leather breeches and a wool shirt, sat upon his bed, and focused.

A shaft of sunlight, falling through a small window, gave him an object: a trapezoid of light upon the wooden floor. It brightened under focus until the dust particles around it seemed like a night sky full of stars. He watched the particles move here and there as the Powers of Air chose; after a time he joined their game and moved the dust into slow vortices with a whispered word or two. It was a gentle enough amusement, one he had taught himself as a boy.

The exercise cleared his head, and after a few minutes he felt better. His mother had taught him the Cantarean discipline of focusing years ago, as she had taught him her language and tales of the mountains. It was one of the many secrets they kept from others, even from the Cantarean slaves around them. Sometimes, though, Dheribi suspected she kept some secrets from him as well—as he had always kept from her the secret of the dust-mote game.

He read for a time, a hand-copied tale of old Ekvush's time when this had all been empty wilderness, deserted even by the Cantareans. Tiring of the tale's predictable rhymes and images, he tossed the scroll aside and exercised. It was odd to go through the motions of swordplay without a sword, especially after reading of great battles and duels, but it passed the time.

At noon the door opened and his mother entered, bearing a plain wooden tray covered with a cloth. She was plainly dressed in dark-blue homespun, and she smiled at Dheribi as she came into the apartment.

"I've brought you something to eat," she said calmly. It was a substantial meal of lamb stew, with good coarse bread and dried fruit for dessert. Dheribi found himself hungry, and sat down to eat.

"I'm sorry to bring this trouble on you," he said.

"It had to come, one way or another. I'm sorry a young man had to die, but I knew you wouldn't last as a warrior. Still, I'm glad you've trained as one."

He frowned at the remark, but let it pass. "Have you spoken to my father?"

Tilcalli's voice dropped to a murmur; she spoke in Cantarean now. "Briefly. Ghelasha wants to send you off to some border post, where it would be easier to kill you. I suggested you go instead to Ner Kes as a spy."

He gaped at her, his spoon halfway to his mouth.

"You would be safer as a slave there than as a soldier on the frontier. Ghelasha would only pay someone to stab you in the back."

"But—"

"Besides, your education is not complete. You've hated training as a warrior, even though you're skilled at it. That's because you have no reason to fight. Spend some time as a slave and you'll have reason enough."

He sat back, baffled. "Are you saying I'll fight the Nerkesar more gladly once they've laid their whips into my back?"

"Quietly, Dheribi. The Nerkesar mean nothing. Their slaves, and all the slaves of the Badakhar, are your people. They are the ones you should be fighting for."

He turned back to his stew, shaking his head. "You're making no sense."

"Look at me, my son." Her eyes met his, with a force that made him wince. "You are a Cantarean. Your mother is a Cantarean, and so is your father."

"My father is—"

"A man of the Coldspring clan, the Siragi Aibela, like myself. His name is Dragasa, and you look so much like him I—" She paused. "He and I conceived you not long before Albohar and his companions came to raid our village. Albohar thinks he sired you, and I never told him otherwise."

Dheribi felt dizzy. He pushed away his meal, looked across the room for a moment, and then looked back at Tilcalli. "Badakh men sire children on their slaves all the time," he whispered hoarsely. "And the children are slaves also. Why has Albohar favored me, when he couldn't even be sure he was my father?"

A faint and frightening smile curved Tilcalli's lips.

"You know the answer or you would never think to ask. The Coldspring clan are the magicians of the Cantareans, Dheribi. I enchanted him."

Though she spoke in Cantarean, and so softly that the guards could not have heard, Dheribi glanced at the door. "So I guessed right—the thought has worried me for years. If they know you're a *shandataringol*, a witch, they'll kill you. Especially if they know you have the power to enchant a man's soul."

"I know that better than you, dear one. They despise our people, but they dread our magic. Some have suspected me, like Ghelasha, but most simply think him a loving fool who spoils his slave mistress and his half-breed son. They're not far wrong—he's a good enough man in his way. But he's a man of his people, and that makes him an enemy of ours."

"He's still my father. I know no other. How can I think him an enemy?"

Tilcalli's dark eyes turned cold and hard. "How many slaves have you seen with scarred backs and gouged eyes? How many slaves' heads have you seen on pikes in the marketplaces? How many Blaidakhs have you seen, killing and crippling others for their sport? The Aryo permits it all, Dheribi. The Aryo makes it all possible. The Badakhar give their Aryos power over them, and in return the Aryos give the Badakhar the same power over their slaves. No, Albohar is not a very evil man, but he is lord of an evil people."

"Wait. Wait." He shoved his half-eaten meal to one side, and reached out to grip her wrists. "You say you enchanted him.

Why did you not enchant him into freeing you, into letting you go back up the river? Why did you stay here?"

"My spells can soften him toward me, and toward you. But they cannot change him or his people. Their magic is great, and their knowledge is endless. They came into Cantarea as a few tribes of herders, when the prairie was ours and our villages were everywhere. Now they rule, now their villages stand everywhere, and we have been enslaved or driven into the mountains. Soon they will drive us even from there, and push us west into the lands of the dragons. Mekhpur has taught the Badakhar how to conquer. Now we must learn from them. *You* must learn from them."

He released her. "I? Learn what?"

"Their warlore, for one. And you have made a good start there. Their sorcery, for another. I will train you in ours, but it is their magic you must learn and wield."

Dheribi shook his head slowly. "This is impossible. I have no talent for magic. I'm too old to apprentice. That small sorcerer in the beer hall—he must have trained since boyhood just to create those illusions."

"You have apprenticed with me already. You can focus, Dheribi, and that is the most important thing: to see things as they really are, and to understand them. The spells and enchantments are empty without that power. And you have the talent. I told you your father and I are Coldsprings—and we were the best magicians of our generation. I conceived you under a spell, and I have reared you under spells to keep your talent strong yet hidden. Once you became a warrior, I planned to reveal all this to you, and to find a pretext to apprentice you to Pelshadan. Now you've rushed matters, and I must change my plans. But you will go to Ner Kes as a powerful *shandatarindor*, and when you return we will find a way to make Pelshadan notice you."

"He already has. When I fought Blaidakh, the Skalkaz was there. He broke into my focus for a moment, and met my eyes."

Tilcalli smiled, as brightly and gaily as a young girl. "I had heard he was there, but not that he broke into your focus. What good news! Here, finish your lunch—I don't want you going to Albohar on an empty stomach, and this may be the last good meal you have for a long time."

"Wait, wait, Mother. You have everything all planned, but you haven't asked me if I *want* to do all these things—to spy against Ner Kes, to learn Badakh sorcery. Don't my wishes mean anything?"

She looked calmly at him, her smile gone but some glint of it still in her dark eyes. "You sound like some upermanna's brat. Remember, my son, that you killed a man last night. Remember that you will keep your head on your shoulders only by the mercy of the Aryo. You will go to Ner Kes as he commands."

"And what if I come back? Suppose I choose not to avenge the Cantareans?"

Tilcalli paused, and took his hands gently in hers. "What a Badakh idea," she said. "Vengeance is the consolation of fools, Dheribi. That's why the Badakhar seek it so often. Your task will not be to avenge anyone. You must make Callia strong again, and her people strong through her, so that the Badakhar can no longer oppress us. That is all."

"To make Callia strong?" he echoed. "To make Beauty so strong that she can overpower the five kingdoms, and even Mekhpur himself?"

"And make them walk with her. You understand me perfectly," his mother said, smiling again.

Three

No wonder the Cantareans had been driven out of their land, Dheribi thought as he walked under guard to the Hearing Hall. The Badakhar had proper gods, gods of power and will, and Mekhpur over all—a god with an abode here on earth, a place where Veikar like Pelshadan could commune with the Firelord and return to express his wishes.

But the Cantareans had Callia—a goddess whose only strength was her people's thoughts and words and deeds. To strike a child, to beat a horse, to curse a neighbor would weaken her. To kill someone would weaken her more, though Menmannar warriors had slain many Badakhar in the days of the Slave Wars. To plant a seed, to make love, to sing about the ancestors would make her grow and smile. Yet she had no place, no voice, no visage; she existed in thoughts and words and deeds, and in the shape and life men gave to the land. How could she protect her people against the iron and fire of the Badakhar?

And how could his mother have let him be trained in the arts of war? His slaying of Blaidakh must be close to blasphemy against Callia, yet Tilcalli had not seemed greatly disturbed.

Well, his mother was more than she seemed; perhaps Callia was more also. In any case, neither would be able to serve him in the moments to come.

The halls and rooms of the fortress seemed almost deserted. Dheribi saw only a few people, court officials and guards, and none looked at him as he passed. The only sounds were the ringing echoes of boot heels on the stone floors.

The Hearing Hall was empty except for Albohar and four silent guards. Late afternoon sun fell through the narrow windows and splashed across the walls, turning their whitewash to gold. Dheribi entered behind his two guards and knelt as they did. The Aryo dismissed the escort and sat upon a bench by the windows. A sunbeam struck his hair and left his eyes in shadow.

"Come and attend me," he said. Dheribi strode quickly across the floor and stopped a respectful five paces away.

"You are a fool." The Aryo's voice was cold and hoarse.

"Yes, my lord."

"Brawling over some slave bitch, killing a comrade who might have saved your life in a real fight."

"Yes, my lord."

"Fighting ensorcelled."

Dheribi stared at the countless dust motes gleaming in the sunbeam, feeling a terrible dread: Did the Aryo know about Tilcalli? Was he closing some slow and malevolent trap upon her?

"You need not deny it. Pelshadan himself saw you. He says you fought in a state of magic. You saw the weakness in Blaidakh's sword, and broke it. And you did as good a job of gutting Blaidakh as I might have."

"I do not deny it, my lord."

"A remarkable talent, but ill-used. Pelshadan also tells me you fought for my respect."

"Yes, my lord."

"Him alone would I trust to give me truth in this. Only the Veikar never flatter their lords. Had he not spoken for you, your head would be on a pike at the Gathering next week."

Dheribi said nothing, but watched the dust motes drift to the edge of the sunbeam and vanish into nothingness.

"This is my judgment on you. You are to be flogged before your squadron tomorrow and imprisoned until the Trame Mod. There you will be flogged again and sold into slavery."

The Aryo looked up, and the sinking sun made his face a mask of gold. "All will be told that you are going to the gold mines in the south. They will see you leave. But in the slave camp in Staldhuno you will be sold again, to a merchant from Kormannalendh. He will know you only as a slave, and not a very fit one after your floggings, and he will take you to the market in Ner Kes. He will sell you to the stewards there, to toil on the new wall they're building. And you will help them build it, Dheribi, while you spy out all their strengths and weaknesses."

His mouth was dry. "As my lord wills it."

"In midsummer you will hear that the army of Aishadan is on the march against Ner Kes. You will slip away and meet us, and give me a good account of the defenses. After that, you will become the apprentice of Pelshadan.''

Dheribi felt himself shuddering. His mother must be a very great magician, to make all this to come to pass, but he doubted that her powers would reach to protect him as far as Ner Kes.

"As my lord wills it,'' he repeated. Looking down at the floor, Dheribi focused. The Hearing Hall became just himself and Albohar and streams of golden dust. He looked up at the Aryo, and thought for the first time: *He is not my father. But he is the only father I know.*

Then he shivered. The Aryo no longer seemed powerful and arrogant, a compact mass of muscle and will; he was just another man, surrounded by dangers he scarcely sensed. The empty chamber seemed suddenly full of murmurous spirits, their whispers loud in Dheribi's ears yet unheard by Albohar.

Dheribi shivered again: something evil was astir in the fortress. He had sometimes felt it before, beyond the edges of the focus, but now it was close and strong. It was a presence, and he sensed it hated him, but it was no guardian of the Aryo.

"What's the matter, boy?''

"Nothing, my lord. I am grateful for your mercy.''

Albohar turned, and his eyes met Dheribi's for an instant. Dheribi saw love in them—the helpless, angry love of a father for a failed son.

But Dheribi could no longer feel any love for the Aryo, nor even any sadness at the loss.

A week later, winter returned. Snow fell all night before the Spring Gathering. Albohar woke early, roused by the silence and the gray light in the windows. Ghelasha stirred beside him, sighed, and pressed herself closer against him under the bearskin blanket. On any other day he would have rolled onto her, but this morning he could think only of what would happen in a few hours at the Gathering.

For a time he lay still, looking at the blue-gray light in the frosted windows. Ghelasha's warmth was some comfort, but he would not be able to lie beside her when he passed judgment on Dheribi. Well, he reassured himself, it would pass quickly; then the boy would be gone, and if he came back it would be with new honor. If he did not—

If he did not, then Pelshadan would be called upon to summon Dheribi's soul, and put it to rest in the Crypt of the Kings.

Grunting, he got out of bed and pulled on trousers and undershirt and tunic. A servant in the hall heard him pissing loudly into a chamberpot, bowed himself into the room to revive the fire, and bowed himself out again. Ghelasha groaned and burrowed deeper under the blanket.

"Come on, girl," Albohar said with forced cheer, "the fire's burning nicely and the snow is beautiful."

"It's freezing," she mumbled.

"Nonsense. A bowl of oatmeal and a flagon of medh will warm you properly. Up, now. They'll be expecting us across the river soon."

Ghelasha sighed, sat up, and stepped naked from the bed. That was like her, Albohar thought: when something unpleasant must be done, she would do it with no more complaint. He enjoyed watching her stride to the wall where her robe hung on a peg. She dressed in a single graceful gesture, then sat by the fire.

"The Field will be a mess. Serve the upermannar right to wait for us," she said with a faint smile. "Shivering in their tents and wishing they were home by their firesides. Perhaps they'll remember who's Aryo in Aishadan."

"Have you ever let them forget?" He chuckled.

After breakfast Ghelasha went to her own apartment to dress for the Gathering. Albohar summoned Eskel to attend him. The boy came promptly, already dressed in embroidered buckskin and a long leather cavalry coat lined with wool.

"You called me, my lord."

Albohar studied the prince for a moment: he was fair-skinned, with curly blond-brown hair and something of his mother's eyes. But he was as barrel-chested and broad-shouldered as Albohar himself, and already as tall as the Aryo. He had begun to sprout a moustache that did little to conceal a mouth as soft-lipped as a girl's.

"We are almost ready to attend the Gathering. You will ride beside our sleigh."

He smiled at the honor. "I will be glad to, my lord."

Another reminder of his position, Albohar thought. Eskel was too eager to play the prince, to assert his role. He was still only seventeen, unblooded in combat, yet he loved the panoply of warfare and the tales of the old campaigns. Well, let him enjoy the softness of fortress life while he still could: this summer the boy would be riding to Ner Kes with everyone else. A taste of real war would temper him, turn him from an overgrown boy into a man.

A thought crossed his mind: after the war, it would be time for Eskel to lead his own raid up the river. For some reason the custom had died out in recent years, but the boy could revive it. It would do him good to test himself against the mountaineers. Perhaps he could bring home his own slaves.

"My lord?"

Eskel was looking at him curiously, and Albohar realized he was smiling at the thought of his son capturing a mountaineer concubine like Pelkhven.

"Nothing—I was just thinking about what must be done today. Go and see to your mount. Your mother and I will be in the courtyard presently."

They rode out of Arekaryo Kes in a fine sleigh, down the winding streets from the fortress through the walled town to the freemen's town where the smiths and armorers lived. Around them rode the Aryo's bodyguard, looking proud in their winter furs; they kept swords in their hands and looked suspiciously even at the onlookers who stood in the gutters to cheer their lord. Others watched the procession from their windows and doorways, kneeling as the sleigh passed. The slaves knelt too, but kept their eyes downcast.

Among the crowds moved the arekakhar, the city guardians—Cantarean slaves themselves, their faces scarred and tattooed with swastikas so no one could mistake them, with heavy truncheons in their fists. Their officers were young Badakhar, those judged unfit for cavalry service but good enough to police the city. The arekakhar and the ordinary slaves seemed never to notice one another, but no arekakh ever had to pause for a slave to get out of his way.

Sitting in the back of the sleigh with Ghelasha, Albohar answered the onlookers' cheers with casual waves. The arekakhar and their officers ignored him, as they should; their job was to keep their eyes on the crowds. Albohar observed them with mixed respect and distaste: they were necessary evils, like the vicious dogs that patrolled the fortress at night.

He thought of the others already on their way across the bridge to the Gathering site: the supplicants, the convicts, and Dheribi. More necessary evils: why should so many evils be necessary?

The snow was beginning to taper off as the procession reached the crowded tents on the south bank of the river. Slaves of the upermannar were sweeping snow from the roofs of the tents with long-handled brooms, or tending the fires that burned before the awnings where each upermanna sat with his family and retainers. The lanes between tents were muddy quagmires; in Trame Modatun, Gathering Field, young horsemen raced as their elders gambled slaves and furs on the outcomes. Half the people seemed already thoroughly drunk on medh or beer.

Still smiling, Albohar stood in his sleigh to acknowledge the salutes of the upermannar. The chilly air was loud with the shrill cries of the women, the deep roars of the men and the drumming of swords and spears on shields. Horses reared as their riders saluted with extended sabers, and the Aryo's red and gold banners waved from a hundred lances.

He ignored them all. Instead he looked at the tents: they were patched and stained, their once-bright colors faded. Most of the horses looked gaunt, and the slaves even more so. If the upermannar and their families were dressed as gaudily as ever, in fine wools and furs, their slaves wore little more than rags.

He had seen it coming in the last few years, and heard it in every protest against new taxes, but never had the upermannar looked so poor as now. In his father's time each landowner had vied with the others to make the finest show, to dress even his lowest slaves in good clothes and solid boots; now the slaves stumbled barefoot through the slush and mud, skinny arms wrapped round themselves. Their masters' lands could no longer sustain all in comfort and plenty.

The Veikar, he recalled, said it was the cycle of life: break new land, cultivate it until it died, and move on. That was how Aishadan had come to be founded a century ago, by upermannar from the exhausted lands far to the east. But now Aishadan would break the cycle itself.

They'll look their old selves a year from now, he thought as he stepped from the sleigh to the tent his retainers had set up for him on the north side of the field. They would have all the plunder of Ner Kes, all the horses and slaves and grain, and the strength to go against the other kingdoms—and Pelshadan would go to Mekhpur. When the Firelord saw the sorcerer's gifts, he would surely grant what all the Badakhar had dreamed of: the blessing of ever-fertile land.

A low fire crackled before the awning, but Albohar ignored it as he stood before the tent with gloved hands upraised. The upermannar returned the salute and fell silent. Behind him, Albohar was aware of Ghelasha and Eskel. Before him, he saw old Aghwesi dressed in mourning gray, with a fresh scab across his wrinkled forehead. The old man had drowned his sight in blood on the news of his son's death, but now his eyes were clear and hard.

"Let Mekhpur hear me! I declare this Gathering called!" Albohar shouted. "Let the Veik purify this field and all who stand upon it."

From a nearby tent, Pelshadan emerged in robes of white felt trimmed with ermine. Behind him came several young apprentices, and as many full magicians. Last came a strange couple: a beautiful young slave girl, swinging a censer, and a youth with a terribly scarred face. He seemed to stare with unnatural fixity; Albohar realized at last that the youth's eyelids were gone. This must be Minukhi, the small sorcerer mutilated by Blaidakh.

The procession of magicians walked slowly around the edge of the field, while Pelshadan at their head muttered unheard spells. The watching upermannar and warriors stood silent, or sat in stillness upon their horses. Jeer at magicians when they're away, Albohar thought, but don't cross one when he's casting a spell.

As Pelshadan circled the field he seemed to become agitated, and by the time he had passed behind the Aryo's tent Albohar could hear the Veik's labored breathing. The procession went on until it returned to Pelshadan's tent. There he stood, swaying, for a long moment before collapsing into the waiting arms of one of his assistants. They and the beautiful slave carried him inside.

The grotesque, glaring face of Minukhi swept the field.

"My lord, the field is purified," he called out.

"I thank Pelshadan and through him our lord Mekhpur. This Gathering is well begun!" The upermannar and their retinues cheered again, brandishing their swords. "And now I again invoke the Firelord, that I may do justice in his honored name. Bring forward the convicts for judgment."

He had ordered Dheribi to be brought in neither first nor last, to be handled like just another criminal. As he passed judgment on the first convict, Albohar saw the upermannar families shifting restlessly, murmuring to one another in anticipation. They paid no attention to the wails of the convicts, to the gouts of blood sprayed across the snow with each beheading or flogging. Instead they watched Aghwesi, or the Aryo himself.

The wind picked up, throwing sparks across the field from every fire. Albohar felt a chill but refused to pull his cloak closer about him. He counted the eight headless bodies piled on the edge of the field, added the six who had been flogged and dragged off, and waited for Dheribi.

Focus: He shut out the world, the cold wind and the sting of his half-healed scars. The wagon where he had lain in chains all night with the other convicts already seemed long ago and far away, though it was no more than a few steps behind him. From the wagon they had dragged him blindfolded, then pulled the rag from his eyes. Blinking, his eyes watering in the wind, he stood in bloodsoaked snow. Apart from his chains he wore only a slave's ragged loincloth. *Focus.*

Before him at a little distance stood the Aryo, looking pink-cheeked above his beard. Not far beyond, just at the edge of the focus, Ghelasha and Eskel watched over the Aryo's shoulders. Ghelasha's lips were upturned in a faint smile; her son's rosebud mouth was open, his eyes intently fixed on Dheribi.

Tilcalli was not there; she never attended the Gatherings. Dheribi wondered if he would ever see her again.

"—to be flogged with twenty strokes and then to be sold into slavery," Albohar was saying. Dheribi kept his eyes down, but heard a commotion to his right and risked a quick sideways glance. On the edge of the watching crowd an old upermanna in gray was shouting, shaking his fist.

"Justice, Aryo! I demand justice for my son!"

Focus. So Blaidakh's father wanted more blood than twenty strokes would yield. But the others around him looked uneasy and did not take up his cry.

Guards marched forward and Dheribi recognized them as his fellow-trainees. Some of them had witnessed the scarring of Minukhi and the death of Blaidakh; all had witnessed his own flogging a week before. They gripped him by his arms and dragged him to a flogging post still steaming from the blood of the last convict. A few paces away stood an arekakh, his face a mask of tattoos and scars and a rawhide whip curled in one hand.

Would this be worse than the first flogging? The healing flesh would tear easily—The arekakh smiled through his scars and uncoiled his whip. Dheribi looked at his wrists, pimpled with cold and lashed to the post. The stinks of blood and vomit and excrement rose up around him. The whip whispered through the air.

Focus.

* * *

Albohar watched impassively. With the fourth stroke blood spurted from Dheribi's back, while Aghwesi kept up his hoarse cries for justice. The Aryo beckoned to Eskel.

"Go over to Aghwesi and tell him I am not pleased with his rantings. If he doesn't shut his mouth I'll give him the same justice that slave is getting."

"Yes, my lord father!" Eskel, looking very pleased, hurried from the Aryo's tent, keeping his eyes on the flogging post. The old upermanna bowed perfunctorily to Eskel, who stood with fists on hips before him.

Albohar saw Aghwesi bow again, more sincerely, and wrap himself more tightly in his gray robe. The old man's retainers closed in around him, as if fearing an assault, but they too bowed as Eskel pivoted and strode back through the mud and snow.

"He did that well, my lord," Ghelasha said behind him. "Thank you for giving him the opportunity to speak for you."

The Aryo said nothing as his son resumed his place under the awning. It had not been the chance to bully an upermanna that had cheered Eskel; Albohar knew it had been his calling Dheribi a slave.

The arekakh was just finishing his job, and two other slaves cut Dheribi from the flogging post. Experienced in their job, they gripped his wrists and ankles before he could collapse. Carrying him like a trussed calf, they hauled him back to the wagon where the other flogged convicts lay groaning.

"This one dead?" one slave asked the other. "He's not making any noise."

"Don't know." The second slave looked at Dheribi's face. The eyes were open but seemed blind. His chest rose and fell with slow breaths.

"He's all right. Funny, though—they usually yell."

From Pelshadan's tent came a cry that turned to a shriek and suddenly ended. The two slaves glanced that way, then shivered and trotted back to wait for the next convict.

Tilcalli lay in bed in her apartment while she sought the Open Dream. It seemed hard to find; she realized how many years it had been since last she had sought counsel with her great-grandmother and the other ancestors.

At last she stood under the endless noon by the Silent River that ran from past to future. Her great-grandmother Calihalingol was standing beside her, looking at her. Across the river, a great stag lifted his proud antlers, looked at them, and then vanished into the trees.

Have I done what I should have? Tilcalli asked.

Yes. It has been hard. I hear your heart cry out. I hear your regrets. But you chose your path and might have chosen another.

If he dies—

You gave him life only that he might die, as your mother gave life to you. Alive or dead, he will find his way to the Open Dream.

We should all die, and remain here by the river forever.

The old woman laughed. *What would become of poor Callia then, with no one to honor and strengthen her in Sotalar? And how dull it would be with no children coming to bring us news of our old fields.* She put out a wrinkled hand and stroked her great-granddaughter's face. *Sotalar is ours, as the Open Dream is ours. If we leave that world, who will care for it? The Badakhar?*

Tilcalli shivered, though the sun was warm on her face and shoulders. *I should have prepared him more. He knows almost nothing.*

We have already felt his power here. Listen.

In that silent place where voices spoke only in hearts, Tilcalli heard a faint and far away cry and recognized Dheribi's voice. A moment later a hawk appeared overhead, circling the river. It too cried out.

He is finding his own way to the Open Dream. When he draws the world into himself, he steps out of it toward this one. Soon he will stand here beside me, and learn from his ancestors, and from you. You have done well, Little Beauty.

Tilcalli felt some comfort at her great-grandmother's words. She turned away from the river, preparing to return to the cold and stench of Sotalar, when she saw a tall man standing a few paces away.

Dragasa. Dragasa!

He looked at her, his face unreadable, and then turned and walked away. Before he reached the village where the ancestors danced the past and future, he was gone.

Tilcalli looked back into the sky. The hawk was gone, the sky an empty blue. Calihalingol, smiling slightly, was looking across the Silent River at nothing in particular.

We will meet again, great-granddaughter.

Tilcalli left the Open Dream. She lay on her bed, under warm furs, and wept.

* * *

Bherasha knelt by the crude pallet where her master lay shuddering in his white felt robes. His pale blue eyes gaped sightlessly, and his mouth gaped as if with the effort to find speech. She found a small flagon of medh, tipped it into a square of linen, and moistened the magician's lips with it. Around her stood the other magicians, gasping and muttering.

A monstrous face appeared beside her: Minukhi. He squatted with elbows on knees, studying Pelshadan.

"I've never seen him like this," the small sorcerer whispered. "It tires him to cleanse the field, but he always recovers quickly."

"Sometimes I've seen him call upon a great name and then fall into a trance like this."

Minukhi's lidless eyes glared; he wiped absently at the constant tears trickling down his blistered cheeks. "But the only invocation was the Aryo's, a simple ritual of no power."

"I know. Something else must have happened. The master felt it most, but even the others are dazed."

Minukhi looked up. The other magicians looked pale and ill, their eyes focused as far away as Pelshadan's. "Perhaps I should thank my lack of talent," he said softly. "Some Sterk, some Power, was here."

"Perhaps. Look, he wakes."

Pelshadan's eyes cleared. His breathing grew less harsh. When he saw the faces looming over him, his face darkened with wrath.

"Get back, you mooing oxen!" he grated. "Give me room to stand. Girl, help me up."

She took his arm around her shoulders and pulled him upright while his retinue retreated a pace or two across the crowded tent. The Veik smiled unpleasantly at them.

"So you are at least sensitive enough to feel a great invocation. That is some comfort."

"What invocation, master?" Minukhi asked.

Pelshadan's pale eyes swept the tent; Bherasha thought he was seeing his retinue as he had never done before.

"The invocation made by a very powerful Veik," he replied. "Girl, give me that medh."

The wagon made slow progress down the rutted trail. The morning's snow had melted, and cold rain spat down out of a dark sky and leaked through the wagon's rotting canvas roof. The convicts lay together, shielding one another from the cold with their bloodstreaked bodies. With every sway and bounce of the wagon someone cried out or swore.

Dheribi lay on his stomach, feeling the rain strike his torn back like needles. The focus was still with him, but it no longer shielded him; he drew each breath in a fog of pain. To either side lay men flogged worse than he had been; one moaned endlessly, while the other drifted in and out of consciousness. They all stank of piss and vomit; Dheribi was grateful that the floor of the wagon let most of it leak out with the rain.

The rough floor of the wagon scraped at his chest and legs, but to shift or turn brought blinding pain. He lay with his head on his chained wrists, breathing shallowly and thinking of the vision.

He had been high above a broad green land, with thickly wooded dales and rolling grasslands that stretched to snowy mountains. Below him had been a river, broad and blue, and on its bank had stood a small village of skin tents. He had seen people dancing and chanting near the village, though he could hear nothing, and he could see as well two women standing by the water's edge: an old woman in fringed and beaded buckskin, and a younger one in red linen and a wool cloak. She had looked up, and he had cried out to her, for it had been Tilcalli.

Nearby he had seen a man also, tall and lean, in a simple tunic and trousers, walking toward the women. He too had looked up, and Dheribi had felt the shock of the man's gaze.

Then the vision had gone, and he had been back at the flogging post. His own blood had warmed him as it ran down his back and legs, and the whip had bitten deep; yet it had seemed less real than the broad green land and the power in the tall man's eyes.

Somehow, Dheribi thought, I must find that place again. Somehow, when I have healed.

He closed his eyes, hoping that perhaps he might see the vision in a dream, but he could not sleep.

Near sundown, the moaning man beside him fell silent. Dheribi looked at him and saw that he was dead.

Four

The slaver in Staldhuno was Sveit, a short, grizzle-bearded man. But Dheribi and his fellow-convicts were too exhausted and hungry to be amused by a man named Honey. Sveit lined up his five potential new purchases alongside his wagon and studied each in turn. When he came to Dheribi, Sveit paused and began a detailed examination: scalp, teeth, arms and groin and legs. When he was done, he gave Dheribi a cheerful slap in the face.

"What's your name, boy?" he asked in hoarse Cantarean.

"Dherhar, master."

"Dark Hair indeed. You and a million like you. Poor little houseboy." He chuckled. "Your mistress got tired of you, eh? Or did she catch you tupping one of her handmaidens? Well, indoors is for catamites and eunuchs, and you're neither. I'll find you some real man's work in Ner Kes, and you'll bless me for it. Won't you?" he added, prodding Dheribi in the belly with the weighted butt of his whip.

"Yes, master."

"Good. Get in the wagon, and don't let me hear you complaining about your back. My wives put deeper scratches in me every time I bed them."

Dheribi pulled himself into the back of the slaver's wagon. It was smaller than the one that had carried the convicts south from Aishadan to Staldhuno, with a low roof of iron-strapped planks and a rear door made of iron bars. Within it was a cramped and stinking space, cushioned with rotten straw, where the four other newly purchased slaves crouched together.

"No talking," Sveit said calmly. "Svordo, move over and make room."

Svordo was a short young man with black hair and sundarkened skin; he obeyed his new master, giving Dheribi a narrow space beside the barred door. No one spoke, or even took notice of anyone else; the slaves seemed lost in a trance, unaware of their surroundings and deaf to the dealings of the slavers beside the wagon.

Dheribi envied the slaves. In the three days since the flogging, he had been permanently focused. Whatever he looked at, whatever he heard, revealed its inner strengths and weaknesses. Sveit, in his eyes, his voice, even the weight of his hand against Dheribi's face, had exposed the cancer growing in his stomach that would soon kill him in agony.

This new focus seemed to have no boundaries. Above the smithies of Staldhuno, Dheribi could see the Pursterkar, the Powers of Fire, appear like shimmering beams of white light as the stalmaghar—the magicians of the forges—invoked them to enter the red-hot blades.

Even in sleep, he had seen strange things: that silent sunlit land he had glimpsed during the flogging and Cantareans dancing beside a great river. Sometimes they had seemed to see him, but none had spoken to him. The old woman he had seen with Tilcalli had been there; she had looked at him, and then giggled behind her hand. Dheribi knew it had been only a dream, a memory of that vision he had experienced under the whip. Yet it had been more real than any dream he had had before.

He had heard tales of people born blind who had miraculously gained their sight; this endless focus, he thought, might be like such a transformation. It was painful and frightening, almost a waking dream, yet he suspected that to lose the focus would be more painful still.

When he glanced at the other slaves in the wagon, Dheribi saw that Svordo, though he seemed to be dozing, was in fact completely awake and watching everything. Their eyes met; Svordo winked.

"Lucky to be out of Aishadan," the little slave murmured. "I hear it's a bad place. As bad as everywhere else."

Dheribi nodded, amused. "Maybe even worse."

Though it was late in the day, Sveit seemed eager to leave the slave market and to be on the road. The wagon creaked and groaned, followed by two other wagons and a mounted guard of six warriors. Looking at them, Dheribi remembered the slave-wagon escorts who had ridden so proudly past Demazakh's squadron of trainees, long weeks ago. The escorts looked less dashing here: tired, dirty men with no one to impress but slaves and traders.

The little caravan rolled slowly out of the Staldhuno slave market, on the northern edge of town, and through narrow lanes of mud. This must be the freemen's town, Dheribi thought, yet it was as dirty and neglected as the slaves' quarters in Aishadan. Idlers stood on every corner, gaming with one another and joking about the slaves in the passing caravan.

Soon they were on the Ner Kes road, rolling past spike-topped walls of brick that guarded the houses of the town's armorers and stalmaghar. In the distance Dheribi heard the ring of hammers on anvils in Staldhuno's great smithies; the sword that had slain Blaidakh had come from here. He wondered if the Stalmagh who had misinvoked Blaidakh's own sword to weaken its blade was still at work.

Patches of snow lingered along the road, but sunlight fell warmly enough through the bars of the gate. Dheribi peered out, watching as the wagons left the town walls behind and rolled slowly out into the countryside.

The road was rutted and muddy, ill-maintained compared to the roads around the capital. Slave villages stood here and there on the bleak prairie, their mud walls pitted and eroded. The slaves themselves moved slowly about the fields, while overseers on bony nags rode among them. Some slaves pulled plows, breaking up the still-cold soil; others dug halfheartedly to clear the irrigation ditches of the winter's debris.

The land looked much like that around Aishadan, Dheribi thought, only more heavily used. The smell of night soil was thick on the breeze. Every field had its stone wall and every creek its dam. Yet in many places the dams had broken, and the creeks had cut deeply into their beds. The slopes above them were spotted with stumps, but few large trees grew anywhere but near the upermannar castles. The Sterkar of the earth seemed weak and thin in Dheribi's vision, though the Powers of Air, Water and Fire were strong.

Twice the caravan stopped and Sveit paid a toll to the local upermanna's guards. The second time, the caravan pulled off the road into a walled field. Darkness was falling. Fires burned on stone hearths scattered across the field, tended by travelers who, like Sveit, had paid for the relative safety here rather than sleep out on the prairie. He and his freemen, including the armed escort, soon had a coal fire glowing on one of the hearths. They huddled around it while the slaves remained in the wagons.

Sveit's cook boiled a kettle full of porridge, and served it out to the slaves. They devoured it silently. The guards let the slaves out to make water and move their bowels at a stinking ditch latrine, and then locked them in again.

After that the Badakhar settled comfortably around their fire and sang or gamed or slept. The slaves huddled together in their ragged blanket-ponchos and tried to keep warm.

"I wonder where we're going," Svordo murmured to Dheribi.

"Ner Kes. He's going to sell us to the Nerkesar stewards to help build their city walls."

"Who told you?" Svordo sounded genuinely surprised. Dheribi shrugged. "How far is Ner Kes?" the little slave went on.

"Several days, at this rate. We'd get there faster if they made us walk."

"I'm in no hurry." Svordo laughed softly. "We may never ride in a wagon again. Tell me, Dherhar, were you a house slave as Sveit said?"

"Yes." It seemed as good a lie as any, Dheribi thought, and closer to the truth than he liked to think.

"And you slept in a proper bed, in a house and all?"

"Yes."

"Ah, that must be fine, a proper bed. When I was little I slept in a barn all one winter, with the hay piled up all warm and soft. A proper bed must be as good as that."

"It is."

"You must miss it, then."

Dheribi paused before he spoke. "No, not much. Not as much as I thought I would." His fingers brushed the inside of his earthenware bowl, searching for any last grains of porridge. Sometime between the flogging and Staldhuno, he realized, he had simply come to accept what had happened to him. It was not all that different from being a warrior: take orders, carry them out, endure discomfort and fear and boredom, enjoy whatever was enjoyable. "This won't go on forever."

Again Svordo laughed, no louder than a whisper. "And neither will we." He looked at Dheribi with a glint in his eye. "Maybe, before we get to Ner Kes, we'll find a Burrower hole. They say a lot of Burrowers live around here."

"They say that everywhere. But I've never seen a Burrower or his hole."

"Of course not—you're a house slave. But I've seen one. It

was a year or two ago, when I was toiling in a mine down south. One morning, early, I was hauling water up to a mineshaft for the men, and a Burrower came out from behind a great boulder and asked me for a drink.''

"How did you know it was a Burrower, and not just another slave?''

Svordo's grin glinted in the light from the nearby fire. "Pale he was, pale as a Badakh's ass, but with a Cantarean face and as tall as you. And he wore a strange cloak, magic I'd say, because it blended in with the soil and stone so you could hardly see him. And he talked strange too, like one of the old songs, only he was talking and not singing. I gave him a cup of water, and he drank it and thanked me, and then went back around his rock. I followed him, I did, just like they do in the stories, and saw him step right into a doorway in the boulder, and the doorway disappear a moment later. Like stepping into one of the old mothers' tales, it was, except I didn't get to go underground with him to be rich and free.''

Dheribi heard only truth in the slave's soft words. It was indeed like one of the old mothers' tales that children first learned at the breast. Burrowers were said to be Cantareans who had fled underground, into caves and man-made tunnels, rather than be enslaved or driven into the mountains. The Badakhar used the threat of them to frighten their own children into behaving, and some thought fear of Burrowers was why the Badakhar rarely went into the mines themselves.

Tilcalli had talked of them sometimes, but never as more than legends; Dheribi remembered her wondering, half-seriously, if Burrowers would know the magic to control the Sterkar of the air, water and fire, as the Badakhar did. He suspected they must, if they could live beneath the surface of the Badakhar's lands. And wouldn't that be a present to take back to his mother: a Cantarean magic she knew nothing about.

Svordo and the other slaves in the wagon dropped off to sleep, but Dheribi stayed wakeful. He listened to Sveit and the others gossiping by the fire, trading rumors.

"Would that I could buy a thousand slaves, not just these two-and-twenty,'' Sveit lamented. "The Nerkesar are paying gold for anything on two legs.''

"I hear they might even make their freemen toil alongside slaves.'' Someone else laughed.

"If not, they'll all be slaves soon enough,'' said another. "The Aryo of Aishadan is building a great army. Unless the

Veikar of Ner Kes can shape a spell against him, he'll make himself master of all the north. And then what of Ghrirei and Kormannalendh?''

"Here, now," growled Sveit, "I'm Kormannalendhi myself. We're no weaklings, you know, and our Veikar are mighty enchanters. Let Aishadan come south to us, and we'll show them why we're called Brave Men's Land."

The slaver wasn't just boasting, Dheribi thought. Each kingdom's Veikar with their subordinate magicians could send deadly spells against their counterparts. That was why no single kingdom had ever dominated the others. If Albohar did conquer Ner Kes, the Veikar of the other kingdoms would soon ally themselves against Pelshadan, destroy him or at least weaken his powers—and perhaps even break through the deadly web of counterspells that protected Albohar.

Tilcalli had not seemed to worry about such an attack, or she would not have planned for Dheribi to apprentice himself to the Veik. But it was not a pleasant thought, to imagine oneself assailed by some terrible spell, a deadly illusion or even a jenji.

Looking out through the bars at the glowing red eyes of the coal fires, Dheribi shuddered. No matter that the not-people, the jenji, were old legends too. Cantarean mothers whispered about them to quiet their children as the Badakhar mothers used the Burrowers. Svordo had seen a Burrower; a magician might well see a jenji. But he would not likely see anything else.

That night he slept without dreaming of the silent land, and woke when Sveit rousted them out to help harness the horses. Dawn was not far away; the eastern sky was a blaze of reds and pinks. After another meal of porridge the party got under way again, with the slaves loosely chained to their wagons and walking alongside them.

"Can't have them fat and soft when we get 'em to market," Sveit muttered cheerfully to one of the teamsters. "Besides, the road climbs a bit all the way to the border. Got to be easy on the horses."

The sun rose over the eroded prairie. The land had turned almost to desert here, a wasteland of clumpgrass and sagebrush. The slave villages were no more; Dheribi saw only an occasional herder's hut, and off in the distance a herd of cattle tended by slave boys. No birds sang, though hawks wheeled slowly overhead. The road was a rutted track, already half-destroyed by the scant rains of early spring. As Sveit had predicted, the road gradually rose toward a line of low hills in the east; several times the wagons bogged down and the slaves had to push and pull to help the horses free them from a mudhole.

Near noon, however, the lead wagon sank to its hubs and would not move. Sveit looked around alertly: they were in a narrow canyon, not a bad place for an ambush if some upermanna was in the mood to acquire slaves without paying for them. He ordered the other horse teams brought up and hitched to the first wagon. The escorts stayed on their horses, scanning the canyon slopes for any hint of attack.

With the help of the slaves and extra horses, the lead wagon was pulled out of the mud. Sveit looked worried about the other two wagons. They were much larger, built to hold more slaves. They would sink still deeper into the mire.

And so it happened, though Sveit's best teamster ran the horses at a gallop to give the wagon some momentum. Sveit, standing on the edge of the mud, swore and spat.

"All right, put all those slaves behind a wheel and get some work out of them!"

Dheribi and Svordo waded back into the mud; it was cold and deep, gripping their legs up to the knees. Each step was harder than walking in deep snow. Dheribi could sense the Sterkar in the mire, Powers of Earth and Water, playing with the sunken wheels.

"Push!" Sveit roared. "Put your backs into it!"

Gripping the crusted spoke of a rear wheel, Dheribi shoved while his feet tried to find some purchase. Beside him, Svordo slipped and fell; he rose giggling and filthy, and resumed his post.

"Move, damn you," Svordo muttered. "Move."

Dheribi suppressed bitter laughter. They were all straining to free a slaver's wagon, the better to continue their own slavery. If they succeeded, they would go on to toil and suffer in building walls that would not stand against the assault of Albohar, and those slaves who survived would face only more toil under different masters. Why didn't they just refuse, and dare Sveit to throw away his investment by slaying them? Better yet, why not seize an escort's sword or spear, and see how many Badakhar they could take with them?

The Sterkar were amusedly gripping his legs as well as the wagons. Anger flared in Dheribi.

"Begone!" He growled. "Leave us in peace!"

The wagon lurched forward, its wheels rolling freely and

spraying mud over the slaves beside it. Sveit howled encouragement. In moments the wagon was on solid ground; the slaves followed through mud that had grown thin and liquid.

"Well done, boys! Unhitch the horses and get the last wagon through. With luck we'll reach Ner Kes country by sundown, and be out of these damned gullies."

The last wagon rolled through with no trouble, and the muddy slaves trudged on up the trail. Occasionally one stumbled or simply sat to rest, but the escorts were quick to hurry them along with whips and lances.

At last they reached the end of the canyon, and emerged back onto open prairie. The caravan rolled past a ruined village at the foot of a fire-gutted castle. Dheribi guessed they were near the edge of Aishadan's power, and in frontier country not many settlements survived.

Sveit called a short break to rest the horses, and the slaves collapsed wearily on the sunward side of the wagons. The mud had dried on their ponchos and trousers, making them look to Dheribi like crude clay figures. Svordo especially was brown from head to foot save where his sweat had left clean streaks down his face.

"What happened back there?" Svordo asked in a murmur.

"Hm?"

"You said something, and we got out of the mud. Do you know some kind of spell?"

Dheribi would have laughed, but did not want to attract the guards' attention. "We were all swearing and cursing," he answered. "Maybe the gods can hear even Cantarean prayers."

Svordo looked unpersuaded. "Better if they heard Cantarean curses."

Dheribi closed his eyes, basking in the late-afternoon warmth of the sun. A breeze off the prairie brought scents of sagebrush and new grass.

—To know no spell, and yet to command the Sterkar of earth and water! How had he done it? Why had they obeyed him? Was it just the growing power of his inheritance, the magic of his mother and his unknown father?

And even if it was, why was he not exhausted and half-crazed, as any Badakh magician would be after such an exertion?

Giddy with physical fatigue and mental excitement, he was tempted to command the Sterkar again—perhaps to create another quagmire beneath Sveit where he stood swilling beer with the head of the guards. No—let him call out a spell and it might not work this time. Even if it did, some guard might put a lance through him in the next moment.

The forces within him had offered a glimpse of themselves. He would have to learn much more about them before he presumed to use them at will.

Sveit drained the last of his mug. "All right, up we get! We've got three hours to reach Aryomen, and then we'll all sleep under a proper roof tonight. Tomorrow it's Ner Kes and plenty of good food. Up, up!"

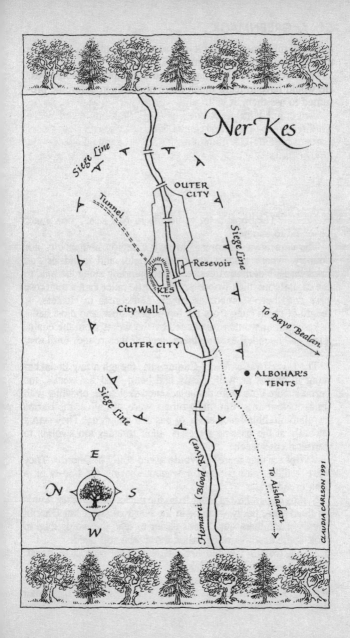

Five

"They post a lot of people in Ner Kes," one guard observed to another.

The caravan was moving through a region neither city nor country, where villages stood amid fields and foundries and brickyards. Not many trees remained standing along the road to the capital, but thick wooden posts a little taller than a man rose here and there—sometimes singly, sometimes in clusters. A length of chain hung from the top of each post, and most had a naked man or woman suspended by the wrists from the chain. They had been left to hang there, feet off the ground, until they died.

The posted were mostly Cantareans, though a few Badakhar hung in chains as well. Many had been dead for weeks; the corpses were little more than blackened skeletons, crawling with maggots and ants. But many others were still alive, their arms swollen into blue-black sacks of pus and gangrene. They stared vacantly at the passing travelers, their tongues too swollen to permit them speech.

"Why are they there?" Svordo asked softly of Dheribi. They were walking alongside their wagon, sparing the horses on a long uphill grade.

Scraps of parchment hung from the necks of some; the words on them were oddly written, in the Ner Kes style, but Dheribi could puzzle them out. It was easier to read the words than to look at the death working inside those who still lived.

"That woman insulted her mistress. That man stole bread. The man next to him was lazy."

Svordo grunted, the corner of his mouth quirking in a half-smile. "Better in Ghrirei. They chop off your head right after they cut off your balls."

56

Dheribi looked at one man, who must have been castrated after being posted; he had sprayed blood and excrement all over the ground, and was still alive. His parchment said he had spoken insolently to his master's son.

Brutal fools, he thought. Why list the slaves' offenses, when other slaves could not read them to be deterred? And why squander valuable slaves for trivial reasons? The Nerkesar deserved to be conquered: they were too stupid to rule themselves.

Or was that thought stupid also? The coming war would not strengthen Callia, or make Aishadan a better place. To the Cantareans of Ner Kes, it would mean only a change of masters, and perhaps a chance to see some of their former masters hanging gangrenously from these posts.

Dheribi rubbed his eyes. The focus seemed permanent now, yet he could sometimes distract himself from what it showed him. Murmured conversations with Svordo helped. Most of the Cantarean slaves in the caravan were dull and sullen, fearful of expressing themselves even in a glance, but Svordo's cheerfulness and curiosity were infectious. He took beatings and bad food as stoically as he took the weather.

"Look," Svordo whispered. "Look how the wild roses bloom around the posts."

Dheribi coughed in surprise, and again in self-rebuke. He might see Sterkar, or death working in a man's guts, but he, who had always loved flowers and the look of the land, had not seen the roses that fluttered like pink flames almost at his feet.

Tilcalli lay in her bed and ignored the drum of rain on the rooftiles. She put herself into trance and sought the Open Dream; its sunlight was cheering, and the Silent River glinted in countless shades of blue.

Her great-grandmother Calihalingol was cutting reeds by the bank. The old woman looked up and smiled.

He is very strong, your son. I hope he finds his way again to the Open Dream.

Tilcalli turned away, looking across the fields and woods to the mountains that some sought to cross, and from which no one ever returned. *I should have taught him sooner. All I could think of was to protect him, to hide his powers from himself and others. I thought I would have more time.*

The old woman laughed. *Tilcalli, you did not believe he would be as strong as this, did you?*

Tilcalli shook her head.

But we talked about it so many times, great-granddaughter. We saw what you would give such a child, and what Dragasa would give as his father. We knew he would be the greatest magician the Coldspring clan ever knew.

Tilcalli nodded but did not speak. Calihalingol in any case knew what she was thinking: that she had been lulled by the long years in Aishadan, that like many mothers she still thought her son a little child. She could still feel the weight of him on her hip, feel his mouth at her breast, and the memories had overpowered her reason.

You are like a poet who will not quit polishing her verses, Tilcalli. Now you must begin his schooling in earnest.

How, great-grandmother? He's so far away.

He will find the way here again, and next time I will hold him, and teach him what I can until you come.

You are right. But do not hold him too hard. If he comes because he is hurt again, he may die and be trapped in the Dream forever.

Her great-grandmother nodded and smiled. *Go back to the world, Tilcalli.*

She awoke from her trance, hearing the rain and the splashing of guards' boots as they tramped down a nearby lane. The windows showed a little light. The lengthening days gave her small comfort: soon it would be summer, season of war.

The next day the caravan came to the capital. Ner Kes stood on a low hill above the deep, slow river Hemarei. The fortress overlooked a town of log cabins, many of great size; the northern forests were still close here, and the Nerkesar used wood as generously as the people of Aishadan used brick.

In the old chants, the founders of the kingdom had vowed that they would never build a wall around their fortress: *"Water and warriors are wall enough,"* the Aryo Parsur Onush had boasted. But that had been in days when Ner Kes was small, and the larger kingdoms were too embroiled in the Slave Wars to covet a remote outpost.

Now the city was larger than Aishadan, sprawled across both sides of the river. The Aryo was Parsur Seggas, sixth of that name; Dheribi had heard little of him save that he was new to the throne and eager to keep it. So a wall of stone was going up, leaving the outer fringes of the city exposed but enclosing most of it on both banks.

The road led up the right bank of the river, through villages that merged into one another and at last into the city itself. Walking beside the wagon, Dheribi could see the wall rising ahead, linking to a bridge. The Hemarei was much narrower than the Vesparushrei, and a single stone span carried the bridge from one bank to the other. Even here, slave teams were at work fixing long tree trunks at an angle between the upriver side of the bridge and the river's floor: anyone seeking to assault the city by water would find himself trapped against the barrier, in easy bowshot of the bridge walls.

Sveit's caravan was arriving near noon on a sunny day. The wagons were just a part of the busy traffic on the road, along with lines of cavalry, peasants' carts, and construction wagons creaking under the weight of stone and lumber. Slaves on foot shuffled past, bearing burdens of every kind: baskets of food, bales of wool, cowhides, shrieking pigs slung live under carrying poles. Bawling cattle blocked the road for a long time as their drovers cursed and whipped them to the shambles on the south side of the city.

The slave market, a muddy field, was next to the shambles and downwind; the fetor made slaves and guards gag and spit. They stood about the field in scattered clusters while buyers moved from one group to the next. But the actual purchases, Dheribi saw, were made only at the platform in the center of the field.

The sun was warm, the stinking air full of flies and mosquitos. Sveit patiently waited his turn to speak with the market master, a narrow-faced man with a red beard half-concealing a weak chin. Dheribi, standing not far away with Svordo, saw a small pouch move quickly from Sveit's hand to the red-bearded man's; then they clapped each other's shoulder, grinned, and walked away.

"All right, lads, over by the platform. We're next."

On the platform stood a small crowd of middle-aged men in dirty blue cloaks—stewards of the Aryo, Dheribi guessed, with first pick of whatever slaves were available. They laughed and joked together, but when the first slave stumbled up the steps to the platform they turned at once to business. The slave stood motionless while the men prodded and stroked him, seeking some weakness or ailment.

"These are the culls of the death houses," one of the stewards complained to Sveit.

"Or the whorehouses." Another laughed. "I hear the Ghrireiar like a soft boy."

"Masters, you bargain most unkindly," Sveit protested, pawing his beard and grinning. "These are tough young bucks, not a bit of fat on them, and the march here has put them in prime condition. You should have seen them push that wagon out of the mud just the other day. Any two of these boys will serve like five or six of what you've got."

The haggling began in earnest, and at last Sveit sold them all. Dheribi and Svordo, together with three others, went with a buyer who marched them quickly back to the city wall. An overseer received them in a dusty tent. He did not look pleased at what he saw.

"Lucky to get a month's toil out of them," he muttered to the buyer, who only shrugged and left. The overseer shook his head and escorted them through the construction site to the river's edge.

"This is Kamba," he said, gesturing to a stocky man in a black leather tunic and knee-length wool trousers. "You work for him now. Get to it."

The overseer left and Kamba inspected his five new workers. He was a Cantarean, doubtless with Badakh blood as well to judge by his build and pale skin. With dangerous gentleness he tapped three of the slaves on the shoulder.

"You'll carry stone. Join that team. You two—" He touched Dheribi and Svordo—"You'll mix and carry mortar. Get on with it. You've got plenty of time before sundown." He stared irritably at Dheribi. "You awake, boy?" Kamba snarled. "Did you hear me?"

"Yes, master."

Dheribi forced himself to concentrate. This endless focus made it too easy to be distracted, to watch the Sterkar shift and flow around him in flesh and fire and water. It was a tolerable eccentricity in a magician, perhaps, but not in a slave.

For the rest of the afternoon, he hauled water from the river in yoked leather buckets, and helped Svordo and four others to mix mortar in a great pit beside the wall. Others carried away the mortar up into the scaffolding along the wall, while still others hoisted rough-shaped blocks of stone into place. After each stone was set, a magician said a spell of resistance to keep it in its place.

Watching from below, Dheribi saw few signs of Dhkemsterkar—the Powers inherent in earth and stone. The Badakh simply did not know enough about them, however they might boast of their control of air, water and fire. Their spells were weak; the chants were little more than superstition.

And if the walls of Ner Kes stood ill-enchanted, Dheribi reflected, Pelshadan could bring them down in ruins.

All that afternoon he mixed mortar and hauled water, until his shoulders were scraped raw and his legs trembled. He and Svordo said nothing, after they saw Kamba lay his whip across another slave's back for breaking silence with a simple oath. The pace of work was steady but slow: hungry men, Dheribi thought, could not be quick.

At last sundown came, and guards marched them away to the feeding pens and slave barns. With his meal of porridge swiftly eaten, Dheribi pushed into one of the barns with Svordo at his side, looking for a sleeping spot that was warm, dry, and defensible. Others had found those places already, and held them.

"Shall we fight someone?" Svordo asked.

Dheribi looked at the clusters of men huddled in piles of straw and rags. They were gaunt and tired, but they met a challenging gaze and did not look away. He supposed he could drive some group out of its sleeping spot, but he might not wake up in the morning.

"No. Come on."

They settled into a dank corner near the latrines, sat against a crudely planked wall, and pulled up their legs under their ponchos. In the darkness nearby, someone giggled and scuffled for a moment before a rat squealed in death. Dheribi listened with envy. The man who trapped it would have meat to eat, if he chose not to trade it to someone else.

Darkness fell. The barn never became fully silent: someone was always snoring, moaning, arguing, laughing, gasping in the arms of a lover. The stink from the latrines kept most of the slaves at a distance, allowing Dheribi and Svordo to stretch out. Svordo was soon asleep; Dheribi lay awake, thinking about the vision he had seen at the Trame Modatum while the lash bit into his back. The river below him, and Tilcalli standing beside an old woman, and the man looking up and turning away: it had been real, yet not like the world of Sotalar.

He tried to recall how he had felt at the whipping post before that glimpse of the silent world. He tried to concentrate into a focus, as he used to before the focus became permanent. Nothing happened. He still lay in stinking darkness, shivering under his ragged wool poncho. At last he fell into an exhausted sleep, hoping that a dream of the silent world might come.

But he woke only to the blue gloom before dawn, as the overseers walked about the barn rousing everyone with kicks and shouts to begin another day of toil.

The house of Pelshadan lay at the end of a crooked lane, not far below the Arekaryo Kes. It offered a blank face to the street, pierced high up by two narrow, barred windows. The doorway was narrow also, and the door itself was a double slab of iron.

Bherasha returned from her morning's shopping to see Minukhi scraping rust from the door. He crouched in the doorway, a chisel in one hand; with the other he wiped at the tears trickling down his scarred cheeks.

"He's better today," the small sorcerer murmured. "He drank his tea and ate some of your honey cake when he woke."

"Good. I'll see to his lunch."

She slipped past him into the house. It was a dark place, with small rooms linked by narrow corridors and steep stairs. Bherasha, Minukhi, and some of the other young magicians slept on the first floor; the master lived on the second. What the third floor was used for, Bherasha did not know; no one knew even where the entryway was for it.

Going down the main hall, Bherasha entered the kitchen and put down her sack. It did not hold much; this was the worst time of the year, late spring, when the first garden vegetables were not yet ready and last year's apples and cabbages were half-rotten. Still, she had found some eggs, an excellent blueberry preserve and some dried beef. With vegetables from the root cellar she could make a passable soup, and then a dessert of cakes with preserve.

The oven fire was still glowing; she scooped more coal onto it and then went to the rain barrel for a pot of water. Perhaps he would like some porridge for his lunch. While the water heated, she busied herself with chores.

She was still amazed at her luck. An ordinary master would have had her flogged and sold into the brothels after her involvement with Blaidakh and Dheribi. Yet he had done nothing, not even slapped her, and when the old cook had died Pelshadan had appointed Bherasha in her place.

And Minukhi deserved flogging or worse for his slipping out to the beer hall; he had returned to the household without a word of criticism. Perhaps Pelshadan thought the small sorcerer had suffered enough, she thought.

Well, who could fathom a magician's thoughts? It was enough

to be warm, dry and fed, to be trusted with the household money, and unmolested. Another good thing about service in a magician's house: they had no interest in bedmates. Someday all this would end, but for now she was content to enjoy it.

When the porridge had cooked she poured it into a bowl, adorned it with a lump of butter and a generous spoon of honey, and carried it upstairs on a tray with a cup of medh.

Pelshadan's apartment was a wide, dark room with a small window overlooking the yard and privy. Shelves held books and scrolls and tightly sealed jars. Other than a bed, a small table and a couple of chairs and chests, the room was bare. In one corner a staff rested. It was made of some dark wood, with an unadorned cap of hammered gold. Bherasha had never seen Pelshadan touch it, and she avoided it also.

The Veik lay upon his bed in the farthest corner, sitting up and reading by the light from the window. As usual, one finger twisted strands of his hair into curls. He glanced at her, and almost smiled.

"Master. I thought you would like some porridge."

"Put it by me."

"Please tell me if I can be of any other service, master."

He looked up from his book without meeting her eyes. "Go into my closet and bring me another blanket. It's chilly in here."

She knelt and turned to obey. He sounded much better, she thought, his voice stronger. His collapse at the Trame Mod had alarmed everyone in the house and all the magicians under his tutelage—even the senior ones in the Kes, who now sought to protect the Aryo with their own spells. To see him on the mend made her feel good.

Just as she entered the large, deep closet, she heard a clatter of boots on the stairs, then the thump of the door shoved aside.

"Good day to you, Skalkaz!" a deep voice rang out. Bherasha turned, the blanket in her hands, and froze. Striding into the room was the Aryo Albohar himself.

"My lord. This is a—a welcome surprise." She saw the Veik try to get up. The Aryo pushed him gently back against the pillow.

"Never mind the courtesies. How are you? You're looking rested."

"I am, my lord. I feel much better. Your concern is most touching."

The Aryo pulled up a chair beside the bed, saw the meal on the table, and helped himself to the medh. "Mm. Dreadful stuff.

I'll have my cellarmaster send you a keg or two of better drink than this. Porridge isn't bad at all. Excellent, in fact. Well, Master Veik, I have a request to make of you, if you feel you're up to it.''

"If I can, my lord.''

The Aryo's voice dropped, but Bherasha could hear him perfectly. "I want you to send a deivushibi to Ner Kes. As soon as possible."

"That—that is a serious undertaking, my lord. I had assumed I would perform no great sorcery until the war this summer. If I summon a deivushibi, I shall need a month to recover—perhaps more.''

"If the deivushibi succeeds, I shall have little need for your talents in the war.''

"Of course I shall do your bidding, my lord. Against whom is the deivushibi to be sent?''

The Aryo paused, then chuckled. "Against their Veik.''

Bherasha could see the two men only as dark outlines against the light from the window, but the slump of Pelshadan's shoulders told her as much as his expression would have.

"This is a very dangerous business you propose, my lord. If it fails, the magicians of Ner Kes will surely counterattack. And if it succeeds, the Veikar of the other kingdoms will soon band together to strike at me.''

"Not if they don't suspect a deivushibi at all,'' Albohar murmured. "Not if the deivushibi possesses the Aryo of Ner Kes.''

For a long moment the Veik said nothing. Then he spoke in a whisper so low Bherasha could scarcely hear him: "My lord, it is a brilliant scheme. But think where it may lead.''

"It may lead to an empire of the five kingdoms, Skalkaz. I won't keep you longer. Rest well. I will need this deed done within a month.''

"It requires a sacrifice, my lord. A young woman, preferably, in good health.''

"I'll see that you get one. A virgin?''

"That will not be necessary, my lord.''

"You make my job easier. We shall speak again soon.''

As quickly as he had arrived, the Aryo was gone. When the front door had boomed shut, Pelshadan sat up in bed.

"Bherasha, bring that blanket now.''

She obeyed. As she was about to leave, his hand gripped her wrist, startlingly strong.

"Not a word about this, girl. You were not in the room. You

know nothing about this, or you will go down into the Pit of the Firelord."

Her throat constricted. She could only nod, kneel, and leave the room.

Her head felt light, as if she and not the Aryo had been drinking medh. Deivushibi: small god. What the Badakhar also called Wanderers, spirits given access to human bodies and so great power to do ill. They were a rare and terrible threat, monsters that could turn upon their invokers. The Cantareans had another name for them. They were the not-people. *Jenji*. To bring one from the Black World to Sotalar, the Veik must sacrifice a human life.

She realized without gratitude that Pelshadan evidently did not intend to use her. But he would use someone.

Weeks passed, and the wall around Ner Kes slowly grew higher and thicker. Dheribi and Svordo learned their jobs quickly and did them well; their overseers and the stewards were pleased and put them to other tasks, supervising teams of slaves. One job was the digging and bricking of an escape tunnel under the wall; the Aryo and his upermannar planned for all events. Dheribi saw the job done in less time than the stewards had planned.

They went on to build a reservoir on the south bank of the river, just within the wall. The task gave Dheribi a chance to watch the Nerkesar warriors at practice on a field below the wall. As horsemen they were good, but he considered them indifferent with lances and clumsy with swords. Ner Kes had been too long at peace, he thought. The veterans were old, and remembered the tactics and weapons of an earlier generation. The young warriors recognized their trainers' weaknesses, but could not train themselves. A squadron of Aishadanar cavalry—even trainees such as Dheribi had been—would blow through these youths like the wind.

Still, Ner Kes was populous; its Aryo could throw far more men into battle than Albohar. If Aishadan could not score a quick victory, or at worst achieve a firm siege, the Nerkesar could well outlast the invaders.

On a muggy and overcast day, not long before the summer solstice, Kamba the overseer came to the reservoir site. He was not running—he never ran—but Dheribi had never seen him walk so fast.

"The Aryo is coming," he barked. "He wants to see everything. And he's bringing the Veik Tenglekur with him."

"Everything is in good order, master."

And it was. The curving walls of the reservoir, four times the height of a man, were smoothly mortared; most of the scaffolding was down, and the sealing of the reservoir floor was nearly done. Yet Dheribi felt a tremor of anxiety. If the Aryo or the Veik found fault with anything, the slaves as well as the engineers would suffer.

Parsur announced his arrival with a squad of drummers, each carrying a long wooden tambour on a leather shoulder strap. Behind them came a score of pikemen, then the Aryo and his personal retinue; another score of pikemen brought up the rear.

Parsur Seggas was a young man, narrow-faced and lean, who wore a cloak of red-dyed leather over a fine linen tunic and trousers. He seemed unaffected by the humidity that kept everyone else sweating, and walked with an easy grace. Beside him walked the Veik Tenglekur, a man in his old age with thin white hair and a close-cropped white beard. He kept up with his monarch, using a gnarled staff.

It was no ordinary walking stick, Dheribi saw. Great Sterkar were imprisoned within it, filling the space around the Veik and Aryo with energy. Tenglekur's eyes had the same distant focus Dheribi had seen in Pelshadan's: they saw no beauty in the world to compare with that of the Sterkar. And perhaps, thought Dheribi, they were right. He drew his eyes with an effort from the glowing forces within the Veik's staff.

"When can we begin to fill it?" the Aryo asked the chief engineer. This was a man of middle age, with a bulging belly and deep-set eyes. He was a Veik as well, though of a far lesser degree than Tenglekur. Nervously, the engineer rubbed his knuckles against his beard.

"Three days, my lord. No more than that. And it will take no more than six days to fill it. To fill it. Six days. Days to fill it."

Parsur glanced sharply at the engineer. "Are you well?"

Dheribi felt a chill in the air despite the sun, and the hair rose on his nape. Something was nearby, something as powerful as a Sterk yet utterly different. He remembered the sense of present evil in the Arekaryo Kes; this was far stronger.

Yet all about him were slaves and stewards and warriors, tending to their business as if nothing were wrong. Only the engineer and Dheribi seemed to sense something amiss: the engineer was staring at the Aryo now, unable to speak. Parsur frowned and turned to go.

The Sterkar in Tenglekur's staff suddenly flared into a terrible intensity, and the web of energy around the Veik and the Aryo vanished. Dheribi stepped back without willing it, one hand raised as if to ward off a blow.

In that moment Parsur's eyes changed. He was no longer looking over his property as a master; he was glancing about him, as if seeing this place for the first time. A faint smile appeared on his lips, and turned into a madman's grin. A cry of dreadful joy came from him; he snatched Tenglekur's staff with both hands and raised it high.

"I welcome you to the Black World, O Veik!" he roared and swung the staff.

It struck Tenglekur across the neck. The Veik gasped and fell to his knees. Before anyone could move, Parsur threw the staff aside. He gripped the magician by the throat, lifted him back to his feet, and flung him lightly away.

The Veik fell backward into the reservoir and struck the bottom; Dheribi could hear bones snap and the heavy gasp of air driven from the old man's lungs for the last time. The slaves working on the reservoir floor stared in horror at the body lying within a few paces of them.

The Aryo glanced down for only an instant, and then bolted along the walkway at the reservoir's rim. The engineer, still mute, recoiled out of Parsur's path. Dheribi, close by, met the Aryo's eyes for a long instant and looked quickly away.

They were like the eyes of the dead slaves hanging on their posts, yet this was a living emptiness, a kind of unbeing that somehow knew itself. He too fell back, skin prickling with cold.

"Treason!" Parsur screamed in a shrill, hoarse voice not his own. "The Veik has tried to betray us! I've executed him!"

The soldiers and slaves crowded to the rim of the reservoir, while Dheribi pushed through them. He slipped along the walkway, past the dead warrior, and snatched up the gnarled staff. Its Sterkar were quiescent now, as if drained of their life.

"Svordo!"

"Here!"

Svordo came toward him, his face a mask of shock. Dheribi caught him by the arm.

"We're getting out of here. Now."

"But—we must wait for orders."

"We'll die if we stay. Come on."

Svordo laughed, a hollow and uncertain laugh, but he followed quickly at Dheribi's heels as they hastened against the growing throngs.

Their ponchos were rolled on their backs; they owned nothing else. If they could get out of Ner Kes in the confusion, it would be hours before anyone would notice their absence, and longer still before anyone acted on it. If he could find a sword, a freeman's cloak, and a horse, they would be safely away.

"Dherhar, what happened?" Svordo panted as they skipped down a flight of steps toward the wall.

Dheribi did not answer; he could not trust his voice. The emptiness in the Aryo's eyes had seen him, measured him, and dismissed him in contempt. Had it chosen, it might have slain him as easily as the old Veik.

I have seen a jenji, he thought. *And a jenji has seen me.*

Six

They walked slowly through the crowded streets toward a gate in the new wall. The air was thick and humid, and the overcast had darkened to a portent of storm. Dheribi gripped the Veik's staff, feeling the reviving turmoil of the Sterkar within it. They were like fish in a pool disturbed by a great stone, he thought. Some sudden force had overwhelmed them, destroyed the protective shield they had wrapped around their master and his Aryo.

Behind them the tumult around the reservoir was fading. Dheribi wondered what had happened. If the jenji still possessed Parsur, it might kill others, or simply destroy its host. Some old legends claimed that jenji could live in human bodies for years, unless slain in the first moments of their invasion. But some had been said to destroy themselves quickly, returning to whatever world they dwelt in.

No one would be likely to slay the Aryo, no matter how strangely he behaved; most would not even notice the emptiness that Dheribi had seen in Parsur's eyes. The jenji might do as it pleased for days or weeks, perhaps longer—

—Until the Aishadanar came.

Dheribi stopped suddenly; Svordo gave him a puzzled look.

"What's the matter?"

"Nothing," Dheribi muttered. "Come on."

Pelshadan must have sent it. Pelshadan must have invoked it through some dreadful spell, hurled it here, and in the same moment battered down Tenglekur's defenses.

They were nearing the gate, merging with a line of slaves and freemen passing the guards, but Dheribi scarcely noticed. *And I must go back to apprentice under him. Under a man who invokes jenji.*

The idea chilled him, and thoughts of escape whirled in his head like the Sterkar in the staff. Where else might he go? To Ghrirei, to Kormannalendh or Halamor? Could he leave false traces of his own death, and vanish into the western mountains?

His fear grew. Others would guess the invoker's identity as easily as he: the Veikar would know very soon, and would surely prepare reprisals. The Aryos would give their magicians every resource, and as well send assassins into Aishadan. In the past, Veikar of great power and courage had sent jenji against enemy generals, or to spread panic among the people of a city. To send one to possess an Aryo, and to use it to slay a Veik, was to make mortal enemies of all others.

They passed through the gate with little more than a bored glance from the guards. Ahead were the stables and forges of the suburbs, offering reasonable chance of acquiring a horse and cloak and sword. Numbly, Dheribi steered Svordo down a muddy lane echoing with the clang of hammer on hot steel. What did it matter if they escaped from Ner Kes only to be destroyed in Aishadan by spells or poison or an assassin's dagger?

And Pelshadan would be almost defenseless for a long time to come. Invoking the jenji would have exhausted him; only his subordinates could save him from a concerted attack. More likely they themselves would be overwhelmed—perhaps by other jenji.

Perhaps I will be the jenji's host.

Think about it later. For now they must simply get away. Perhaps an answer would come when they had won rest and freedom.

He led Svordo into a smithy. It was a small place, with one man acting as smith and stalmagh alike. Three slaves fed the furnace, while the smith hammered and chanted. Lost in his spell, the smith did not look up though his slaves glanced curiously at the two Cantareans.

Dheribi scanned the smithy and saw no freeman's cloak. No matter; a weapon was more important. Sheathed swords lay on pegs against the far wall, beyond the smith's anvil. Any thief would have the smith to deal with first, and he was a powerful man. He might be caught up in his spell, but a stranger walking past him would rouse him soon enough.

Quickly, without thought—Dheribi walked forward, came around the side of the anvil, and swung Tenglekur's staff with all his strength into the smith's face.

The man staggered back and fell to the hard dirt floor, blood gouting from his broken nose and torn cheek. He was not quite unconscious, but stunned enough to be no threat. Dheribi turned to the rack of swords, chose one and drew one from its sheath. The Sterkar pulsed and shimmered in it; the smith had cast his spells well.

"Let's go," Dheribi said. Svordo stared at him, horrified. "Quickly, Svordo!"

While the slaves hurried to the aid of their master, Dheribi pulled Svordo out of the smithy and down the lane. They would have a little time before the slaves raised an alarm, and perhaps—as the confusion over the Veik's death spread across the city—the mysterious assault and robbery of a smith would go unnoticed.

The thought made him smile in self-derision: they were already drawing curious glances from other slaves as they jogged down the lane. And who would not look at a Cantarean slave who carried a strangely gnarled staff and a sword slung from one shoulder?

Coming out of the lane, they headed south down a wider street. Rough shacks and kitchen gardens lined it, and naked children played in the mud alongside grunting pigs. This was a freemen's quarter, and not a rich one, but someone must have a horse. Up ahead, he saw, the road dwindled to a track across a cattle pasture.

"Hey! You two! Come back here."

Cantering up behind them was a warrior on a tough-looking gray mare. Dheribi looked, then turned and obeyed.

"We're going to be killed now," Svordo said quietly. "They'll post us for sure. And all I've done is follow you."

"Then do something now to earn your punishment," Dheribi answered without taking his eyes off the warrior.

The horseman was a boy, his beard still soft and short. He wore a stiffened leather cuirass over his tunic; his clothes looked new, and he was clearly not long out of a training squadron.

"Master." Dheribi stopped and bowed, within reach of the warrior as custom demanded. If an order must be backed up with a blow, the Badakhar did not like to be inconvenienced.

"What's that sword? Whose is it?"

"My master's, master. He sent me to fetch it from the smith."

"Who's your master? Don't tell me he lives out here."

Svordo, following close behind Dheribi, stumbled and fell to one knee. As he regained his feet, he flung a handful of mud up into the boy-warrior's face. An instant later he gripped the boy's belt and pulled, toppling him from his saddle. The boy hit the ground hard; before he could scramble to his feet, Dheribi's sword was at his throat and Svordo held the mare's reins.

"Don't move," Dheribi commanded. The boy stared up at him, incredulous, and obeyed. Dheribi drew the boy's sword and tossed it across the road. Children and slaves watched from a safe distance; no one raised an alarm. Stepping back, Dheribi took the mare's reins from Svordo, pulled himself into the saddle, and then pulled Svordo up behind him. The boy sat up, his face pale beneath the dust.

"I'll post you myself, you dogs! I'll cut your livers out and feed them to you."

Dheribi laughed and turned the mare. The stirrups were too short, but he had no time to adjust them. A few drops of rain were beginning to spatter in the dust, and a breeze sprang up. Thunder rumbled far away.

The boy's curses followed them down the road. Dheribi glanced over his shoulder at Svordo.

"Have you ever ridden a horse before?"

"I'm learning quickly. Did I do the right thing, pulling him over like that?"

"You heard him. You did it well enough to deserve posting."

The rain came down in a rush, so heavy that the city and prairie disappeared. Svordo laughed. "So this is what it's like to be free! Sitting on a horse's ass, getting soaking wet. I like it."

Dheribi thought of the jenji behind them, and the road ahead, and shook his head. Then he saw a patch of pink wild roses, nodding in the rain, and his heart caught some of Svordo's joy.

All through the spring, the sons of the upermannar had been riding into Aishadan. The richer ones lived in their families' town homes; the rest camped cheerfully enough on the open plain north of the city. As the spring planting ended, the upermannar themselves came, along with slaves and freemen who could be spared. The arekakhar, with their swastika-scarred faces and heavy truncheons, were busy every night keeping the peace in the streets and beer halls.

When Tilcalli went walking around Arekaryo Kes, she could see the encampments from the northern walls. They grew bigger every day, though less colorfully than in the old days. Then, each upermanna had set up tents of his own household's colors— orange, red, yellow, green, or blue. Now those tents looked stained and colorless. The upermannar no longer spent money as recklessly as they once had.

But she did not go walking often. Not long after the Trame Mod, when the upermannar had dispersed to their estates, she had ventured into a favorite garden and by chance encountered Ghelasha and her son Eskel. They were sitting together on a stone bench beside a fountain, without attendants. Ghelasha had looked up and met Tilcalli's eyes for a moment, before Tilcalli had bowed and turned away. She had seen the menace in the Aryasha's gaze.

Now as summer approached she kept within her apartment, fighting the urge to go into the Open Dream every day. Dheribi had not returned to it; that meant at least that he still lived, but had not found the way again.

Today she had gone into trance, lonely for her great-grandmother Calihalingol as well as for Dheribi. But before she could reach the Open Dream, something had disturbed her concentration: like thunder in the mountains, or a distant cry in the dark. She had roused herself, frightened, and spent the rest of the afternoon pacing restlessly about her rooms.

Then Albohar had summoned her to visit him tonight. Such invitations were rare these days. He was busy with plans for his war, and when he wished to relax he usually preferred a keg of medh and conversation with a couple of old friends from his raiding days.

In the hour after sundown she went to him. The apartment was full of warriors; she recognized Snegh, who had been just another pimply boy on that raid up the river. Then he had been Sneghibi, Little Snake. Now he was an upermanna of great estates. He and the other warriors glanced at her with meaningless half-smiles, wanting neither to recognize a slave nor annoy her master. She found her usual corner and settled into it, her legs crossed. The warriors knew as well as she that her arrival meant the meeting soon must end.

"—ready to march in two weeks," Albohar was saying. "We should have five thousand warriors and another three thousand foot soldiers, most of them freemen. I'll go with the foot soldiers four days before the bulk of the cavalry, and you'll overtake us a day's march out of Ner Kes."

"I don't like the idea of a siege," Snegh said. "The Nerkesar know we're coming. They'll burn every hayfield they haven't harvested yet, and there we'll be with thousands of hungry horses. Not to mention the hungry men."

"Don't worry," Albohar said. He was standing at a table, looking down at a map of Ner Kes. The ceiling lamp threw a rich yellow light over everything, and made the Aryo's hair glow. Tilcalli thought he looked beautiful, a fighting man utterly concentrated on his task.

"We will be inside their new wall almost without breaking stride," Albohar went on. He grinned at his old friend. "Get out of your saddle long enough to take a piss, and you'll miss the assault."

"When did Snegh ever bother to get out of the saddle for that?" another man guffawed, and Tilcalli recognized Vulkvo. He had run to fat in the years since the raid, and she saw he had the questioning look many Badakh men got after a certain age— a vague disappointment, as if life had promised them more than it had given.

Albohar ignored the joke. "Today we sent the Nerkesar a gift," he said quietly. "Their Veik, Tenglekur, is slain. Their Aryo is—not himself. And we have spies in Ner Kes who will tell us where the weak places are in the defenses. It will be the easiest conquest since the Slave Wars."

Tilcalli forced herself to be calm without drawing a deep breath. *That* had been the cry in the dark, the distant thunder! Pelshadan had made a great invocation, and had sent a jenji to possess the soul of the Aryo Parsur Seggas. Though her magic was far different from Pelshadan's, yet she had felt the power of that spell.

Strong emotions warred within her: awe at the courage and skill of Pelshadan, fear at their consequences, anger and contempt for Albohar's recklessness. He chattered about sieges and easy victories, like a little boy planning to kick open an ant hill while a lion crouched in the bushes behind him.

Every Veik in the other Badakh kingdoms would soon invisibly besiege this citadel. No one here would be safe. The most secret and powerful Badakh spells would assail Aishadan, and she would be near-powerless to turn them away.

Like a good slave, she had kept her eyes downcast and could not see the faces of the men in the council. But she could sense their surprise and growing alarm. Even Badakh warriors could think ahead.

"Aryo—" It was Vulkvo. "So great a spell must have greatly weakened Pelshadan."

"He'll recover."

"But in the meantime you are exposed to reprisals."

Albohar chuckled. "Pelshadan cast spells of protection about me and my family, before he set about his task. And we will be on the move before any enemy Veikar can respond. They will be swearing fealty to Aishadan before they can gather up their oils and blood and incense."

And Parsur was safe within his own Veik's spells, Tilcalli thought. Yet a thought had occurred to her. She tested it, turning it this way and that in her mind: a dangerous thought, but also perhaps an escape from danger.

The council ended with loud promises of feats to be accomplished and glory won. When the upermannar had left, Albohar swaggered to a table and poured himself a flagon of medh.

"Come and join me," he commanded, sitting on the edge of his bed. She stood at once and walked gracefully across the room. He put his arm around her shoulders, and out of old habit she leaned against him, took in his familiar male scent.

"I've neglected you, Pelkhven. But these are great days. Soon we'll have our boy back."

"Have you heard news of him, master?"

"No, but I'm sure he's well. Perhaps on his way home by now. Though he might be more use to us if he stayed inside Ner Kes. In any case, he'll be home safe by the end of summer, and under Pelshadan's hand."

"I will be always grateful, master."

"I hope I have reason to be grateful to him. He caused me grief enough before the Gathering."

"Master, will Pelshadan be well enough to take Dheribi as an apprentice? If he's done a great magic, he will be unwell. I recall how he fell ill at the Gathering."

"Mm, yes. He never explained that. Well, I expect he'll be all right."

"Master—I have done little to serve you all this spring. May I serve you now by caring for Pelshadan?"

"You?"

"I hear he has only a simple slave girl to serve him, and a crew of magicians."

Albohar chuckled. "As well be served by drunken blockheads as a magician's apprentices," he said, nodding. "But he lives as he does by choice. I won't have him sulking because I've sent him help he doesn't want."

"Perhaps you could ask him, master. I would not want him to see me forced upon him."

"Of course not. Still, it's not a bad idea. You're a good housekeeper. And you could keep track of what goes on in that house.'' Albohar took a mouthful of medh. ''Yes, a good idea. A pair of sharp eyes would serve me well there.''

She said nothing, but knew what he meant: if reprisals did come, they would not all be spells. Absentminded magicians would make poor bodyguards for a sorcerer. A sharp knife in the darkness could work as well as sorcery, and Albohar needed his Veik kept alive.

I am walking into that meadow again, she thought, remembering how she had gone to meet Albohar and his raiders in the summer twilight long ago. Somehow, the safest place for her was always in a place of great peril.

''Well, I'll ask him tomorrow. Now come and keep me warm.''

And as he grunted and sighed above her, she thought of sharp knives and dark corners here in Arekaryo Kes.

The rain lasted the rest of the day. Dheribi and Svordo rode south until twilight darkened. A shepherd's hut gave them cold shelter for the night, and in the morning they turned west. Ner Kes was almost due east of Aishadan, Dheribi knew. If they could move west parallel to the road between the cities, they could evade detection; if Albohar's army was already on the way, they could intercept it.

Late in the morning they came to another shepherd's camp, this one occupied by Cantarean slaves. The shepherds gave them porridge and mutton, and a leather water bottle. Their fear smelled as sharp as sheep dung.

''Now we must hurry,'' Svordo said as the gray mare carried them out of the camp and up a hillside. ''They'll warn their masters as soon as they can.''

''Do you think so?''

''I know it. Couldn't you tell?'' Perched on the mare's rump, he turned to look back down at the camp. One of the shepherds was trotting down a streambed. Svordo grunted, his suspicions confirmed. ''We could always go back and kill them.''

''Kill fellow-slaves?''

''We're not slaves anymore, are we? And you've not been one long.''

Surprised, Dheribi blurted: ''What makes you say so?''

''I could tell as soon as Sveit bought you. Those scars were too fresh. You talk Cantarean almost like a Badakh. You look about you too much, and you don't notice what slaves are thinking.''

"Like the shepherds.''

"And like me. Here you've dragged me off into some adventure, without a reason, and I've come along because I've no more choice than when I was mixing mortar.''

"I—'' An outright apology stuck in his throat. "I knew something dangerous was happening up at the reservoir. I thought you might be safer with me than in the city.''

"And what would be a danger to me? Would the Aryo have come hunting *me*, once he knew his Veik was dead?''

"Someone might have come hunting you, once they knew I was gone. They know we're friends.''

Svordo laughed, without malice. "Slaves don't have friends. Now tell me what this is about.''

Dheribi reined in the mare and slid from the saddle. He helped Svordo down. They sat side by side on a rock outcropping, looking back down the hill at the shepherds' camp. The trotting shepherd was already out of sight, and over the next ridge Dheribi could see a smudge of smoke: the sign of the local upermanna's manor. He would not have much time.

"All right. Maybe slaves don't have friends, but free men do, and you're a free man now. I'll tell you what I have to tell you, and then you can choose to stay with me or go your own way.''

The story took little time to tell. Svordo listened impassively, arms folded under his poncho. Wind blew his black hair about his face. When Dheribi was done, Svordo said nothing for a moment.

"Well, and here I was boasting about meeting a Burrower to a son of the Coldspring clan. Your mother sounds like a great lady. I would be honored to meet her some day, but until then I will serve her through her son.''

"You don't have to serve me, Svordo—''

"I said I would serve her. Through you. Now, let's get out of here before that cursed shepherd brings his master after us.''

Seven

The pursuers came in sight not long after noon.

Looking over his shoulder at a ridge behind them, Dheribi saw the sun glance off a helmet or lance. A moment later, a puff of dust rose from the same place into the pale blue sky.

How many? Five, six, ten? Too far to tell. But they would be good horsemen, and they would know this country as well as they knew their own horse corrals.

The gray mare trotted down a hillside and onto a broad prairie already turning yellow in the heat of summer. It stretched to the horizon, flat and bare.

"I don't like this," Dheribi muttered. "We're too exposed."

"Where else could we go?" Svordo asked.

Dheribi guided the mare a little to the northwest, following the path of the summer sun. In that direction lay the road to Aishadan. It was no doubt crowded with Nerkesar soldiers, but it also meant the army of Albohar. Surely, surely they must be on their way by now—

The afternoon wore on as they and their pursuers plodded steadily across a plain of bunchgrass and sagebrush. The sun was sweeping gradually around to the northwest. Dheribi felt a little encouraged: the riders might find it harder to see them against the glare of late afternoon. He kept the mare at an easy walk, not wanting to tire her. Wait until they could get into broken terrain, out of sight of the horsemen, and then he would goad her into a gallop.

But the terrain did not change. The pursuers neither fell behind nor advanced. They were resting their own mounts, Dheribi knew, and would be ready for a sudden burst of speed if they needed it. Their horses would be lighter, quicker.

With the sun in his eyes, Dheribi felt another kind of illumination: "They're not following us," he said. "They're driving us, like horses into a pen. Something ahead will block our way, and then they'll close with us."

Svordo, riding behind, twisted to look again at the Nerkesar horsemen. "Then what should we do?"

"I don't know."

Reining in the mare, Dheribi slid from the saddle. Svordo gratefully dismounted as well. He took a mouthful from the water bag and passed the bag on to Dheribi. Lifting it thirstily to his lips, Dheribi paused to give thanks to the Powers of Earth.

The Powers—

His focus had not left him, but he had been paying attention to the pursuers and to the chances of escape to the northwest. Now he sensed again the Sterkar of air, of earth, and of water.

Taking a step or two, he sensed small shifts in the balance of the Sterkar. Those of water were nearby, yet below the surface. An underground stream was flowing beneath his feet, flowing from the northwestern hills beyond the horizon. But now he sensed the Sterkar of air as well; the underground stream did not entirely fill its channel. And while the water flowed southeast, the air flowed in the opposite direction.

Dheribi laughed, ignoring Svordo's wary look. "Somewhere to the south, Svordo—that's where we must go. There must be a cave or pit of some kind, and it leads to an underground river. The Nerkesar won't follow us there."

Svordo looked east, where the riders' dust hung in the still, hot air. Insects buzzed and chirped in the sagebrush. "They'll cut us off," he said quietly.

"If we go on as we have, they'll surely trap us."

Svordo sighed. "Dherhar or Dheribi, whatever your name is—you're a son of the Siragi Aibela, the Coldspring clan, so if you say there's an underground river I believe you. Do as you will. But before we die, let's at least finish the mutton."

"Why not?"

They stood under the glare of the sun, listening to the insects and chewing on the leathery lumps of meat. After each had taken another gulp of water from the water pouch, Dheribi opened it so the mare could drink. When the pouch was dry, Dheribi climbed back up into the saddle and pulled Svordo up behind him.

"Hang on tight. We're going to show them how we ride in Aishadan."

He drew his sword and smacked the flat of its blade against

the mare's flank. She snorted and broke into a run. Dheribi lifted his face to the sky and wailed a cavalryman's war cry: let them know that they pursued a warrior!

Now the riders were on their left flank, and could indeed intercept them before long. While Svordo bounced and grunted and swore behind him, Dheribi tried to plan. If they could find and enter the cave leading to the underground river, the Nerkesar would not likely follow. All the Badakhar had a notorious horror of going underground: they feared the Burrowers, and the Powers of Earth that they could not control.

Perhaps the pursuers might encamp at the mouth of the cave and try to starve them out, but Dheribi suspected they had come away expecting a short pursuit and a meal tonight under a roof. They would not enjoy a long and hungry wait simply to recapture someone else's slaves.

But if the Nerkesar intercepted them before they could reach the cave, it would be all over; they would swarm around the mare like wolves around a deer. His sword would be useless against their lances. He remembered an old tactic Demazakh had taught: lance the horse, make it stumble or rear and throw its rider, and then spit him where he lay in the dust. The Nerkesar would know it well.

Focusing, he could sense the course of the river below. It was like traveling a road in dense mist—clear enough beneath him, but vague and uncertain at a distance. It curved farther east; he would have to follow it, or lose it altogether.

But it meant giving up much of the distance between them and their pursuers. The Nerkesar were quickening their pace now, as if suspecting a trap yet reluctant to throw away a chance for a quick finish. They were close enough now to be counted: eight of them, all well armed, with one carrying an upermanna's banner fluttering from a shoulder rod. The colors were yellow and black, much like those of Blaidakh's family.

Gradually the land began to sink and to ripple into shallow gullies. They trended southeast, following the course of the underground river, and eventually deepened enough to conceal the mare and her riders from their pursuers. But the clatter of hooves on rock and gravel was loud.

The mare was failing. She had borne a double load, and Dheribi did not expect her to bear it much longer. The river was close below now, yet he could see no sign of a cave or pit—only the steepening sides of the gully.

He could not bring himself to goad the mare again, though

she had slowed to a shuddering trot. Let her get just a little farther down this gully, he thought, and perhaps we can leave her, scramble up the slope and over the ridge before the Nerkesar reach us—

Then a man was standing almost before them, by the left side of the gully. His face was hairless but pale, his eyes shadowed by a hood. A simple wool tunic hung to his knees. He raised a hand, and Dheribi reined in. The mare halted, panting.

"Come with me," the man said in strangely accented Cantarean. "Let the horse go."

"We've got to find the cave," Dheribi said. "They're close behind us."

"The cave is here." A long, pale hand gestured toward the steep side of the gully. Dheribi's gaze followed, and the gravel and sand disappeared like the poor illusion of a small sorcerer. Now an opening led down into darkness and the noise of rushing water.

They dismounted quickly. Dheribi gave the mare a grateful slap and sent her off down the trail. The hoofbeats of the pursuers were growing louder. He turned to look at the pale man.

"And you are a Burrower?"

The man looked back at him, eyes still shaded and unseen.

"Just as you are a magician," he said quietly.

Yesterday the city had been in turmoil as the foot soldiers marched out onto the Ner Kes road, accompanied by Albohar and a few squadrons of cavalry. Today it seemed oddly hushed, and the arekakh patrols seemingly had nothing to do but to swing their truncheons and growl at one another in the empty streets.

They had not growled at Tilcalli and her manservant Andho: both wore the red and yellow sash of the Aryo's household, and the Aryo's seal was upon the wheeled wicker carts they dragged behind them. Protection enough, she thought, against the patrols—but no sash could ward off the malice of Ghelasha. With Albohar out of the city, Tilcalli had wasted no time in moving out of the Arekaryo Kes.

They walked through street after winding street in the unusual midmorning quiet. Even after all these years, she still marveled at how the Badakhar could cram themselves into these dark and smelly warrens when the whole prairie beckoned to them. Why conquer so much land, only to leave it to the herds of the upermannar?

Andho thumped on the door of the dark house at the end of

the alley. After some time, it swung noisily open and a scarred face peered out. Tilcalli knew it must be Minukhi.

"We have a good deal of baggage," Andho said pompously, as befitted one of the Aryo's senior slaves. "Call out the servants to help us."

Minukhi's face crumpled into a terrible parody of a smile. "Magicians are not servants of slaves," he said in a sweet and musical voice. "I'll call Bherasha."

While Andho fumed and dragged the wicker baskets through the door, Tilcalli stepped inside. The antechamber was dark, though sunlight gleamed at the end of the hallway. The ceiling was low, blackened by years of candles and torches. A flight of wooden steps led to the upper floors.

She felt a chill creep slowly over her skin. This place stank of Badakh magic, of dangerous spells. The Powers of Air, Fire and Water had knotted themselves into the very fabric of the house, yet those of Earth were almost undetectable. How had the Badakhar learned to rule the three lesser Powers when they knew so little about the great one?

Light feet stuttered down the steps, and a Cantarean girl in a sleeveless smock bowed before her.

"My lady Pelkhven, we are honored."

"You are Bherasha? I'm pleased to meet you. Will you help my servant bring these baskets to my rooms?"

"Gladly, my lady."

Tilcalli liked the quick intelligence in the girl's eyes, and the grace and strength with which she took up a burden. Bherasha seemed more like a mountaineer than a city-bred slave. This girl would be an ally.

Bherasha led the way down a narrow hall to a suite of two small rooms overlooking a walled yard.

"It's a poor shelter, my lady, but we will try to make it comfortable for you."

"My comfort is not important." But she was grateful when Bherasha opened the shutters and let a breath of air into the stifling room.

"Three of the magicians have left to attend to the Aryo, my lady. These were their rooms. The remaining apprentices sleep in other rooms on this floor. My lord Pelshadan has told them to make themselves useful to you, my lady, and not to trouble you."

"Thank you. Leave the luggage for now. Please go and tell the Veik that I will be glad to wait upon him at his pleasure."

"Of course, my lady." She bowed again and was gone.

And this was the girl for whom Dheribi had killed Blaidakh. Well, better men had died for worse women, Tilcalli reflected.

Bherasha returned soon with the Veik's invitation to visit him at once. Tilcalli climbed to the second floor, and felt still more intensely the fields of enchantment that armored the house. It was like walking across an empty field in the moments before a thunderstorm, when a lightning bolt might smash down at any instant from the clouds overhead. But overhead was only the ceiling, and a space above that which, she sensed, was a focus of dangerous energies.

Pelshadan lay in his bed, propped up with pillows and with a blanket drawn to his armpits despite the warmth of the summer day. Tilcalli kept her face calm, though the Veik's appearance shocked her. His face was chalky gray, his eyes deep sunk, his hands wasted into claws.

He ignored her bow and murmured greeting, and gestured vaguely for her to approach. She took the stool he glanced at, and waited.

"I am grateful," he rasped, "for the Aryo's kindness in sending you."

"It is no more than our lord's gratitude for your service, master Veik. I am here to carry out his will and help restore you to health. He says he hopes you will soon be well enough to accompany him to Ner Kes."

His eyes seemed to focus on her for the first time, and a faint smile twitched at the corners of his thin-lipped mouth. Tilcalli looked down, grateful not to have to meet that gaze. Whatever price he had paid to send a jenji to possess the Aryo of Ner Kes, Pelshadan had lost none of his intelligence and perception.

"He will have little need of me at Ner Kes," the Veik said hoarsely. "Now to business. I grant you the freedom of all this house, save the topmost floor. Order everything to suit yourself. Only leave the magicians to practice their disciplines, and do not beat Bherasha. She's a good girl."

"I obey you, master Veik."

"Good. You may leave now."

She had often heard that the invocation of a jenji, like many other great Badakh enchantments, required a human sacrifice. Now she understood why this house seemed clenched by powerful spells. Someone had come here and had died to bring an evil being into Sotalar.

"Callia give you peace and beauty," Tilcalli murmured to the lost soul of the sacrifice. "And may you be the last to have suffered."

The rest of the day was a flurry of housekeeping: inventory in the kitchen and storerooms, hauling of water from the fountain at the end of the alley, hurried trips to the nearest market, and the cooking of a great kettle of rabbit stew. The magicians, four young men including Minukhi, seemed more surprised than grateful to be invited to share in the meal. They carried away bowls of stew to eat in their rooms, and returned for second helpings.

The long summer twilight gave Tilcalli time to finish unpacking, and to rest for a while in her room. In the hallway outside, Andho had spread his pallet on the floor and was humming contentedly while he repaired Tilcalli's sandals. Nearby, Bherasha was cheerfully clattering away in the kitchen, scouring the kettle and bowls. Tilcalli thought she might almost close her eyes and imagine herself back in the Arekaryo Kes, if not for the tension of the spells that vibrated like plucked strings around her.

She thought of going into trance and seeking the Open Dream, and then scorned herself for such a foolish impulse. Pelshadan and his apprentices would sense at once if she exerted any magical force in this house. She would have to be well away from here if she wished to take counsel with her great-grandmother.

And why had Dheribi not returned to the Open Dream? He had the strength; he had found the way when they flogged him at the Gathering.

She put the thought away. Time enough to find out when he returned from Ner Kes, and joined her here as Pelshadan's newest apprentice. Then, when he had mastered Badakh spells and Cantarean magic as well, he might win back the prairies for his people and for Callia.

Lying on her bed and looking out the narrow window at the still-bright northwestern sky, she fell into a doze. The chants of the magicians came muffled through the walls; Andho's humming and Bherasha's busy noise seemed to fade.

She shivered. The air seemed to thicken, and she could hear her own blood drumming in her ears. Beyond that sound she could hear nothing, as if Andho and the apprentices and Bherasha had all fallen dead in the same instant. Tilcalli tried to sit up, and failed. The sky was dark now, and the stars were few and faint.

In a whisper so faint she could not hear herself, she invoked spells of protection around the house. Something was coming, something powerful and evil, fed on blood and magic. She could sense its might and hunger, its bright malevolence; it was coming through the night air, winged yet not a bird.

With every beat of its pinions she could sense it more clearly; fear held her throat clenched. Her spells of protection were weak in the face of its power. It would smash through walls and spells alike, seeking Pelshadan's soul and hungry enough to feed on others' as well.

Her whispers turned to moans as she cast new spells upon herself and her paralyzed limbs. At last they responded, lifting her awkwardly from her bed and propelling her to the window. The roar of her own blood sounded like the great waterfalls in the mountains, and she thought of home. The image gladdened her soul and strengthened her focus. Hands raised, palms outward, she invoked the Sending.

Thunder crashed out of the clear sky, and some of the stars vanished as a vast black wing obscured them. The being was overhead, hovering above the roof. She could not see it but she could sense it, hanging above her in cold wrath. The spells of protection had worked better than she had thought, and the being's passage had slowed. Now it knew she was there, and she forced herself to stand against its hatred and contempt.

Now begone, back to the Black World that spawned you. Begone. Begone.

She felt the Sending burst through her, out into the darkness, and felt the being recoil in shock. Thunder cracked again, sending a shudder through the house, and then the night was once more calm.

Too weak to stand, Tilcalli staggered back and collapsed onto the bed. Andho had stopped his humming. The apprentices were calling out in alarm, and one of them was already on the stairs up to his master's room. With all her strength she pulled her legs up onto the bed and lay panting. A cool breeze from the window chilled her.

"Pelkhven!"

It was Minukhi at the doorway, his face a nightmare in the light of a fluttering candle.

"What is it?" she mumbled.

"Our lord summons you to his chamber at once."

"Tell him I am ill."

"I dare not. Come on, I'll help you."

He crossed the little room to her bed and lifted her upright.

She was surprised at how strong he was, and how gentle. Gratefully she leaned against him as he guided her out the door, past worried Andho.

They lurched up the stairs and into Pelshadan's room. He lay as she had seen him earlier, though now a lamp beside his bed threw a yellow light across his bearded face. The Veik's eyes glinted in the lamplight as Tilcalli made her way across the room with Minukhi's strong arm around her.

"I beg your pardon, master Veik. I fear I am not well. Something I ate tonight—"

"Pelkhven, this house has just been attacked."

"By whom, my lord?"

"By a demonic creature. A gheishauka. All my spells were not enough to ward it off, yet it turned away. I had called on Mekhpur to receive my soul. Yet the creature turned away. I felt a greater magic assail it."

"Master Veik, you frighten me." It was no effort to let fear widen her eyes. "I know nothing of these things. But if I can make you more at ease, I will do what I can."

His blue eyes glinted. "Never mind, Pelkhven. I should not have disturbed you. Return to your room. Rest. We do not want you to fall seriously ill."

"You are most kind, master Veik."

She let Minukhi escort her back down again, and closed the door with a trembling hand.

Pelshadan *knew*. He must know. A Cantarean witch was under his roof, insolently casting spells so strong even the apprentices could sense them. And no Badakh magician would suffer a Cantarean witch to live.

Eight

The Burrower led them into a narrow cave, its brown walls smoothed by chisels and engraved in strange curving designs. Light fell onto the sandy floor of the cave, and a breeze blew into it; Dheribi smelled sagebrush.

"Wait here, and say nothing," the Burrower said.

The rumble of the pursuers' hoofbeats grew louder. Suddenly they were right outside, riding hard and close enough to reach out and touch. Dheribi and Svordo shrank back against the cave wall, blinking at the dust that stung their eyes.

Dheribi felt a strange heat from the wall—no, not heat but an aura. The carvings must themselves be a form of ensorcellment, part of the spell that hid the entrance. The thought was unsettling: all the magic he knew was that of the spoken word uttered in focus. He felt the Sterkar in the staff stir and turn, like dogs catching a strange scent on the wind.

The horsemen were gone, and sunlight glowed through the dust hanging in the cave. Dheribi muffled a cough and turned to the Burrower.

"We owe you our lives. I thank you."

The Burrower's face, still shadowed by his hood, was unreadable. "We took a great gamble," he said. "If the Badakhar had been a little closer behind you, I would have had to let you ride by. This is one of the last of our doorways."

"Then we owe you even greater thanks. I am Dheribi; this is Svordo."

"Those are Badakh names. What are your true names?"

Dheribi hesitated. "I have no other. My mother is a slave of the Aryo of Aishadan; he named me. Svordo has been a slave all his life, and knows no other name."

"I am Silisihan. I welcome you to Bayo Bealar, the Underland. Come with me; you must rest and eat, and speak with Renjosudaldor.''

He turned and walked quickly into the cave, away from the sunlight. Dheribi and Svordo looked at one another.

"Well, you have your wish," Dheribi said. "You've been invited into the Burrowers' land."

"Now I'm not so sure I want to go."

Dheribi smiled faintly. "The Nerkesar will be back soon. Would you like to take your chances outside?''

Svordo shrugged and set off after Silisihan. Dheribi followed close behind, one hand gripping both the staff and his sheathed sword.

Within a few paces the carved walls gave way to water-worn limestone, though the floor was smooth sand and rock precisely carved into stairways. The low ceiling glowed faintly, just enough to let them see the way. As Silisihan walked ahead, the glow kept pace with him; behind Dheribi, darkness returned.

This was a spell worth knowing, Dheribi thought. The Veikar were rumored to be able to create coldfire light, but at great cost. Here it seemed no more than a convenience.

The cave widened into a series of great chambers, some so large that the walls were lost in darkness. Where coldfire glowed, the colors were many and subtle: white, pink, pale yellow, streaked green and red. Dheribi saw pillars like a forest of stone, and sometimes the coldfire glinted in still pools beside the path. The sand muffled their footfalls, but when Svordo cleared his throat the echoes were loud and frightening.

The caverns of Bayo Bealar were beautiful, Dheribi thought, yet somehow desolate. Great men and women had wielded great Powers here, shaping stone and guiding water with skill and art. He could both sense and see their work, and wondered at its beauty. Stone and water remained, and the spells carved into rock, but the people did not.

Now they came to a narrow aperture that plunged steeply. Silisihan turned to face them, and stepped lightly onto a ladder of finely carved wood. He disappeared into the darkness below.

Svordo paused. The only sounds were the scuff of the Burrower's feet on the rungs, and a distant chuckling flow of water. The coldfire around the aperture began to fade.

"Go on, Svordo. These people mean us no harm."

Svordo drew a deep breath and stepped onto the ladder. A moment later Dheribi followed, as the coldfire dimmed and died. They descended slowly in darkness, one rung at a time, while a breeze still smelling of sagebrush blew past them. The noise of moving water grew louder.

"We are at the bottom," Silisihan said. His voice echoed in an immense blackness. Then coldfire sprang up again, this time from the worn stone beneath their feet. Dheribi saw they had climbed down an almost vertical cliff, and now stood on a narrow shelf of limestone beside an ink-black pool. The remains of a fire lay within a circle of stones near the foot of the ladder, and blankets lay neatly folded beside it. Just within the glow of the coldfire, Dheribi glimpsed a pile of firewood and two small chests. Clearly this was a camp or station of some kind, a place where Burrowers could pause to rest. An odd glint caught his eye; he looked up to see a small colony of bats hanging from the roof, their glossy wings folded smoothly around them.

The Burrower walked to the edge of the pool and grasped a rope. With it he drew a strange craft partly out of the water and into the light. Dheribi thought of the Menmannar canoes that sometimes drifted down the river to Aishadan: this was something like them, though its sides were lower and its ends rose higher. It was made of wood, beautifully carved and inlaid with polished agates and hammered copper.

"Step into the boat," Silisihan murmured. Dheribi obeyed, balancing himself carefully, and was surprised to find the boat did not move under his feet; he might have stepped onto solid rock. He sensed Powers of Water poised all around the craft, holding it in place.

Svordo followed, and looked equally surprised at the firm footing. They stood uncertainly in the middle of the boat, wondering whether they should try to sit.

The Burrower stepped aboard and squatted comfortably near the stern, which was drawn up on the shelf. Svordo and Dheribi squatted also, as Silisihan murmured something. His words evidently made a spell, for the boat slid smoothly off the limestone and into the black water. The tip of the stern began to glow with coldfire now, throwing its light around them. Stalactites, hanging from the roof of the cave, gleamed in the coldfire and seemed to sway as the boat glided by beneath.

At the far end of the pool the boat slipped through a narrow cleft and the noise of water grew to a roar. This was the true bed of the underground river, running through a cavern whose roof was too high to reflect the glow of the coldfire on the boat. Dheribi felt the Powers of Water running deep beneath him, cold and powerful and exulting in their blind plunge. The air was chill and humid.

The boat pushed out into the stream, but did not obey the current; instead, it swung left and began to move upstream. The river occasionally splashed a little white foam where the boat met the black surface, but it offered no real resistance.

"This is a great spell," Dheribi said.

"No, it is a simple one that some of us can invoke," said Silisihan. "Without it we would be trapped within a few caves."

"Your people are mighty magicians. The deeds of the Burrowers are legends all over Cantarea."

Silisihan, his head outlined by the glowing coldfire behind him, seemed to nod; but Dheribi could not see his face.

They glided almost silently up the river, faster than a man could run. At times the walls were close around them, glittering in coldfire; then new caves opened, their walls remote and invisible. In some of the caves true fires burned, and the damp air held the scent of smoke. Dheribi saw people moving through the firelight, or standing beside the river to raise a hand in greeting.

"How many live in these caves?" he asked Silisihan.

"Six hundred."

Svordo grunted in surprise. "I'd always heard that the Underland held thousands."

"So it once did."

"Have you suffered some misfortune?" Dheribi asked.

"Renjosudaldor will tell you."

Dheribi turned the name over in his mind: it meant Protector. Did the Burrowers have an Aryo, like the Badakhar? They were clearly unlike ordinary Cantareans, however similar their appearance and language.

He let his focus widen until he could sense again the Powers on the surface far above. The boat, he could tell, was moving northwest; they were returning toward the hills between Aishadan and Ner Kes. Up on the prairie, the sun was sinking into the northwest. He wondered what the Nerkesar horsemen were doing—returning home, or still searching the gullies for a trace of their quarry.

A light glowed up ahead, and the boat slipped out into the largest cavern yet. Here the whole roof blazed with coldfire, making Dheribi think for a moment that they had emerged onto the surface under a thin overcast. The great chamber's floor was green with grass, on which sheep and cattle grazed; even trees

grew here and there, and Dheribi heard the unmistakable tr.
a red-winged blackbird. When his eyes had adjusted to the light,
he estimated the chamber must extend a good thousand strides
from side to side, and its roof must be ten times a man's height
above the floor.

In some places small houses stood, built of stone and roofed
with wooden shingles. The air held the tang of smoke. More
Burrowers stood along the shore or tended their herds. If all
these caves held six hundred people, Dheribi thought, then this
cave alone must hold most of them.

The boat angled against the current and slid easily up onto a
gravel shelf. Dheribi and Svordo stepped ashore; Silisihan followed, murmuring a few words to secure the boat. A dozen
Burrowers stood nearby, men and women, looking calmly at the
newcomers. They wore simple wool tunics, though the women's
were embroidered in strange patterns of brown and red. Their
faces were more than pale, Dheribi thought: they were drawn
and weary, as if beset by a sorrow known so long they scarcely
noticed it anymore. Svordo bowed awkwardly to them in greeting, but they made no reply.

"Renjosudaldor lives not far from here," Silisihan said.
"Come with me."

They set out along a footpath worn deep into the limestone
and bounded on either side by beds of pale mushrooms. The
path led away from the river, past stone corrals and a few huts,
until it came to a kind of plaza. Here low buildings of rough-
cut stone faced one another across a little square of slate flagstones. This was clearly the Gathering Field of the Burrowers,
Dheribi decided.

The only people in the plaza were those with business of some
kind in one of the buildings; no one gathered simply to gawk at
the newcomers. Those who spoke with one another were quiet;
the loudest sounds were the rush of the river and the occasional
bellow of a cow.

Silisihan led them to a low-roofed building whose windows
overlooked both the plaza and the river. He knocked on the
door, which was made of finely carved planks of cedar.

"Come in," a deep voice answered. Silisihan pushed the door
open and gestured to Dheribi and Svordo to enter first.

The interior was a single room, sparely furnished and with a
fireplace in one wall. Apart from a small fire, the only light
came through the windows from the cavern roof. A man rose
from a stool by the fire. He was taller than Dheribi, pale and

white-haired. Though his face was seamed with age, he seemed strong and lean beneath his plain wool robe. His eyes, deep-set under white brows, revealed both pain and power.

"I greet you," he said with a smile full of sadness. "I am Renjosudaldor, Protector of the Gulyaji. We have need of you."

For two days Tilcalli lay ill in her room, uncaring whether rain fell or the sun shone. Bherasha tended her, and Minukhi, while Andho hurried to the markets for herbs and medicines. The other magicians seemed ill as well, as if they had felt some echo of the spells that had lashed around the house.

On the third day, Tilcalli woke in midmorning. The day was already hot, and the air smelled of foundries' smoke. Beside the bed, Bherasha had left a half-loaf of bread and a pot of honey. They tasted wonderful, and revived her.

She dressed and groomed herself, and went into the kitchen.

"Are you well, my lady?" Bherasha asked, turning away from the fire where a pot of soup bubbled.

"Well enough. Thank you for your service. How is the Veik?"

"Much better also, my lady. He is reading in his apartment; he said he wished to see you as soon as you were recovered."

"Very good. Is everything in order in the house?"

"Yes, my lady."

Tilcalli went upstairs to Pelshadan's room. She wondered if she had fully recovered: if he wished to, the Veik could kill her perhaps more easily than the flying demon could have, yet she felt no fear. She knocked softly on the carved wooden door, and entered at his calm command.

The magician was sitting by the window, dressed in a loose linen robe. One of his books lay open on his lap—a large volume of thick parchment pages with covers of etched copper.

"Come and sit beside me, Pelkhven," he said, gesturing to a three-legged stool near him. Tilcalli obeyed. The Veik was indeed recovered, she saw. Though their gazes did not meet, she glimpsed restored power and perception in his cold blue eyes.

"You have done me a great service," he said. "Greater than I would have thought you capable of."

She said nothing. Even if he denounced her and had her tortured, it would be a better fate than to have fallen into the talons of the winged horror.

"Pelkhven, you are a Menmanna witch. Do you deny it?" His voice was mild.

She lifted her gaze from the floor and met his eyes. Let him see that she was as powerful in her way as he in his. The Veik stared long into her face, and then looked away.

"A woman Veik," he murmured. "Many magicians would think that an obscenity. But do you know the first Veikar were Badakh women? We learned from them, and then overthrew them, long ago. They still practice healing and warding, in secret, but they have lost all the great spells. But not your people—your men and women alike can practice magic, can they not?"

"Some of us, Veik."

"And very well indeed. In all these generations we have learned nothing of your magic. Your witches kill themselves before we can win their secrets. Are you going to kill yourself, Pelkhven?"

She could feel herself trembling now, and hoped he could not see. It was not fear, but he might think it so. "If I must."

"I hope you will not feel the need. You present me with a dilemma. Three nights ago you warded off a great spell, perhaps the greatest ever sent against me. My soul would be screaming in the Black World now, if not for you. So I owe you something."

"Masters owe their slaves nothing, Veik."

"Magicians owe their Aryos a great deal. You have enchanted Albohar, have you not? Bound him to you?"

"Only lightly, to give him joy in me and Dheribi. I have not bound Ghelasha or Eskel, or anyone else."

"No. You have done only what you must, and escaped attention. May I ask you why?"

Better silence than a lie. She said nothing. Pelshadan's lips twitched in a half-smile.

"I will not threaten you, Pelkhven. I do not think you enchanted Albohar out of love for him, and a Menmanna witch cannot love the Badakhar. You are an enemy within our gates."

"So is every slave."

"Yet we tolerate our slaves' hatred for the sake of the service they do us, as they tolerate our rule for the sake of their lives. If you wish to die, Pelkhven, I cannot stop you. And I will soon join you in death, I suspect. My fellow Veikar will not soon forgive me for what I have done to Tenglekur, and I am not yet recovered from my efforts. But if you wish to live, I shall not denounce you."

"What is your price, Veik?"

His blue eyes met hers again. His hands left the book and

twirled strands of white hair while he grinned, snuffling with amusement. "You want me to teach your son, who is a magician of great power. I have agreed to it. But now I wish you to teach me also."

Silisihan soon left the hut. With his hood down, he revealed to Dheribi the typical exhaustion of a magician who has invoked too many spells in too short a time. The Protector sent him to rest with a smile and murmured thanks.

Renjosudaldor served them porridge and cheese. Only when he had half-finished his meal did Dheribi realize the bowls were polished hemispheres of agate, streaked with yellow, white and glowing orange. He wondered how many slaves Albohar might trade for even a single bowl.

"We sensed your presence above us," the Protector said as the two men ate. "Your focus was so strong it disturbed the Gariba." Dheribi did not recognize the word in the Burrower's strange pronunciation; then he realized it was the Cantarean word for the Sterkar.

"When we realized you were fleeing from the Badakhar," the Protector went on, "we sent a bat downstream with a message to Silisihan. He is the guardian of the southern door." He paused. "I did not truly expect we would be able to rescue you. But we did, and Callia is stronger now."

"We are in your debt," Dheribi said, gently putting down the bowl. Svordo, licking his clean, dropped it casually on the table.

"Debt." Renjosudaldor smiled sadly again. "A Badakh idea. I think it means that we have given you something freely, yet you feel you must give us something back."

"Something like that," Dheribi answered, feeling unsure of himself.

"We give for the joy of the giving, and for the beauty of Callia. But we have need of what you might give us."

"We have only what you see, Protector. But whatever it may be, we shall give it gladly."

Renjosudaldor looked out his doorway at the great cave. A few Burrowers sat at some distance, on a row of carved benches. Their faces were pale in the coldfire light from the cavern roof. Dheribi felt their weariness, their sorrow, and remembered the slave pens of Ner Kes.

"We want the sun again."

"Excuse me, Protector. I do not understand."

"Let me explain, Dheribi. Do your people talk about the wars we Cantareans once fought against the Badakhar?"

"The Slave Wars. Yes. My mother told me about them. The Badakhar came into our land and lived in peace with us, until their numbers were too great. Then they began to build their cities, and to raid our villages for slaves."

"And some of us accepted slavery," the Protector said, "while others left the prairie and fled into the mountains, and others still descended into the Bayo Bealar. We Gulyaji are the descendants of those who sought refuge in the caves."

"The Badakhar fear you more than any others," Svordo said, grinning. "They dare not even go down into their own mines."

"They have long memories," the Protector said. "Once we ruled everything under the grass, and they had reason to fear us. But no more."

Dheribi said nothing, but Svordo naively asked: "Why not?"

"We grow weaker with every generation. We have survived here, but we are dying."

"I—I do not quarrel with you, Protector," Dheribi said slowly. "But I do not understand. You have herds, you have light and water. Your boats move against the current. Your bowls are of precious stone, and your spoons—" He picked up the one he had eaten with, and hefted it again. "Your spoons are gold."

Renjosudaldor nodded absently. "Some of us still know how to make things of beauty that will please Callia. But we are dying. Our wives rarely conceive, and too often die in childbirth. Our children are stillborn, or die young. No child has grown up in these caves since I myself was a boy."

Dheribi frowned. "But surely you have spells for fertility, for easy births, for warding off disease."

"They have lost their power. Or better said, we have lost the power to invoke them. Magic is a talent, like a skill with stone or music. Many of us once had it, but it has weakened. We know the spells, yet they do not work as they should."

He paused and looked long at Dheribi. "Another thing I must tell you. Our weakness is known. When we pray to Callia, an echo comes back out of the caverns, like a—" He fell silent. After some time he spoke again: "Something has come into the Bayo Bealar, a being that seeks to destroy us. It despises us, hates us, and mocks our hopes. We have spells to keep it at a distance, but they too grow weaker. Every year it comes closer; we hear it howling in the far caves, and sometimes it comes into our dreams."

"And you dare not return to the surface."

"The Badakhar are stronger, in arms and magic alike. We are only six hundred now. We have lost touch with the other Gulyaji tribes. The nearest, our cousins, are dead."

"Not all your magic is lost," Dheribi said. "You still conceal your doorways, you still have coldfire and boats that go against the current."

"Almost all the doorways are gone. We can summon only enough coldfire for urgent needs, and the boat that brought you here is among the last three we possess."

Dheribi and Svordo said nothing. The Protector stirred restlessly. "Come with me."

They followed him out of the hut, and down a well-worn path. Dheribi saw how the hands and craft of the Burrowers had shaped almost everything around them: every boulder, every stalagmite and stalactite, every wall was carved and decorated. Where grass grew, the soil was rich and black beneath it—a soil, Dheribi suspected, created as much out of dust and toil as out of magic.

"We love this place," the Protector said. "But once this tribe alone lived in ten other caves as well, all of them greater and more beautiful than this. Soon we shall be gone from the Bayo Bealar. Either the being that lurks in the far caves will come to destroy us, or we shall go back to the upper world and face the swords of the Badakhar."

"You said you had need of me."

The Protector sat on a bench cut from the stone and inlaid with hammered gold. Dheribi and Svordo sat beside him. The Burrower smiled at them.

"You are a Cantarean with great talent, reared among Badakhar. Is that an accident?"

"I once thought so. But my mother conceived me in the mountains; she and my father are both of the Siragi Aibela, the Coldspring clan."

Renjosudaldor's dark eyes widened in surprise. "Great magicians in the ancient times."

"And she went into slavery so that I might eventually learn Badakh magic as well as our own. She wishes me to break the hold of the Badakhar and to restore Cantarea to its people."

"Yet you have not learned, or you would not have fled the Badakhar."

"I have learned a little, but only a little." He explained how he had been sent to Ner Kes, and what had happened there. "When I return to Aishadan I am to apprentice under the Veik."

"And under your mother as well."

"Yes."

"First I would have you apprentice under me."

For a time the only sound was the echoing rush of water in the river nearby. Dheribi looked at the older man, looked into him, and saw life hanging within him like a tendril of white smoke. A breeze might blow it away—or, falling on the coals that sent the tendril out, turn it back into a flame.

"How long would you keep us with you?"

"Not long," the Protector whispered. "Perhaps fifteen or twenty sleeps. I need only pass on to you the great spells; if you fail with them, it will not matter that the lesser spells go down into the darkness with you and us."

"Svordo, will you stay while he teaches me?"

"I will, and gladly."

"Then I agree."

The Protector's life brightened within him. "You honor us, Dheribi. Come with me; we have a shelter for you, and many books. If you are to know our great spells in fifteen sleeps, we should begin at once."

"And what do you wish of me in return?" Dheribi asked.

"You speak like a Badakh again. We wish nothing in return. But we hope that when you have mastered the spells, you will send the being away from these caves. And we hope that when you have done so, you will go back into the upper world and make it safe for us to stand beneath the sun once more."

Nine

The battlefield was a narrow strip of marsh, thick with mosquitos and blackflies that maddened horses and men alike. There, almost within sight of Ner Kes, a ragged army of freemen infantry and upermannar cavalry had finally met the Aishadanar columns.

Albohar and Eskel watched the fight from a low ridge west of the marsh. Flanking them were other riders: messengers, servants, and two of Pelshadan's senior magicians. The older of them, Potiari, was a round-faced man of Albohar's age; the younger, Dvoi, was in his twenties. Both seemed oblivious of the battle going on just a few hundred strides away.

"They picked their site well," Albohar said to his son. "If we leave the trails through the marsh, we bog down and their pikemen can get at us. If we stay on the trails and fight through to that meadow, their squadrons will be waiting." He watched the turmoil impassively for a time. "This is where training and discipline mean victory."

The Aishadanar cavalry moved steadily east through the marsh, enduring slingstones and arrows. Nerkesar pikemen skirmished with the Aishadanar infantry, who had waded out on the cavalry's flanks, but the main forces on each side remained unengaged. The late-morning sun glared down out of a cloudless sky.

"Ha! The fools haven't even set traps in the marsh." Albohar chuckled. "They could have taken some of our lads quite nicely if they'd thought ahead. Are you listening, boy?"

"Yes, Aryo," Eskel said. Under the brim of his helmet, his eyes were cold and intelligent. He ignored the mosquitos whining about his face.

"What's going to happen when our men get into the meadow?"

"The Nerkesar cavalry will wait until a good number of us get through, and then charge. They'll try to drive us back into the marsh and their pikemen."

"Good. And why won't they succeed?"

"We won't retreat."

"Ah, and why won't we retreat?"

"Because we would die."

Albohar grinned. "And you think our men will remember that when the Nerkesar are charging them, lances down?"

"Yes, Aryo, because our men have been trained to remember it."

The Aryo roared with laughter and slapped his son's back. "We'll see how good our boys' memories really are."

The first squadrons reached the meadow; instead of pausing to wait for others to reach them, they moved out smartly in open formation. Even at this distance, the men on the ridge could see the riders' lance pennons of red and gold.

Beyond the meadow stood a forest of willow and scrub pine, and out of it came three columns of Nerkesar cavalry. They were moving at an easy trot, in good formation. Albohar watched them slow as they saw the Aishadanar riders, heavily outnumbered, galloping toward them.

"They can't believe their eyes," Albohar said. "See, they have ten squadrons to our two. They'll be thinking we've set a trap for them, or cast a spell. So they'll slow, and break formation, and let themselves be distracted while the rest of our men get out of the marsh and form up. Then the numbers will favor us."

The Nerkesar reacted as Albohar foretold. What should have been an overwhelming charge turned into disorganized clumps of riders; they duelled with sword or lance, pursued one another, or even retreated into the forest. Meanwhile the rest of the columns moved up out of the marsh, their flanks secured by the Aishadanar infantry.

Wherever the Nerkesar general might be, he could foresee Albohar's next move and declined to meet it; the defenders soon broke off their skirmishes and retreated into the woods.

"Too bad," Albohar said with a grin as he spurred his horse down the ridge. The others followed. "If they'd stayed and fought we could have slaughtered two or three hundred. Now they'll fall back inside the city walls and we'll have to starve them out."

Eskel glanced over his shoulder at the retinue. "Aryo, do we need to besiege them? Can't these magicians earn their keep?"

Albohar said nothing for a moment. Then he muttered: "Listen well, boy. At my command Pelshadan sent a deivushibi against Ner Kes, and slew their Veik. I reckoned that would weaken them past the point where I would need more magic, so it would be worth it to exhaust my own Veik. Now it looks as if the Nerkesar haven't given up, so I must keep these two magicians in reserve for emergencies. They're good men, and I can't squander them. So we will besiege the city and choke the Nerkesar to death, whatever the time it takes."

His son nodded. "What about our food and fodder? They've burned their land down to the rocks."

"We'll manage."

A messenger rode up the ridge with news that the marsh had been cleared. Without a word, Albohar spurred his horse eastward; the others followed. He kept his face without expression, but inwardly he felt the faint scratchings of worry. They were already running short of fodder for the horses, and the Nerkesar were sure to harass the invaders right up to the city walls. He could not sustain the siege more than a few days if the Nerkesar actually defended their city.

Impossible. Albohar put the thought out of his mind. No one had ever heard of a deivushibi possessing its host for long. When it returned to the Black World and Parsur died, the Nerkesar would despair. The siege would succeed, and then he could turn to thoughts of the next war, the real war.

Renjosudaldor took them into his home. While Svordo swept out an unused room and learned his way about the Protector's small kitchen, Dheribi and the old man sat together before a thick book of parchment pages bound in bronze covers.

"These are the *Shandatarava Goribisalo*: the Magic Writings. They come to us from the ancient days, and they alone have enabled us to live in the Underland."

Dheribi studied the first page, surprised to be able to read most of the text. Tilcalli had secretly taught him Cantarean writing, an art long lost except among the mountaineers. These small, angular letters were almost the same, and the words sang in his mind with Tilcalli's voice.

"We know the four Gariba, the Powers of Earth, Air, Water and Fire," Renjosudaldor said. "Of these, the Gariba of Earth are greatest and source of the others. They seek only harmony and balance; the lesser Gariba rejoice in distubance, but Earth restores them to calm.

"Cantarean magic has always sought understanding of Earth, much more than of the lesser Gariba. The Badakhar know almost nothing of Earth, but their mastery of Air, Water and Fire is very great."

He looked at the staff of Tenglekur, which leaned against the wall beside Dheribi. "I see the power in your staff, but I do not understand it well."

"No more do I, Protector. I seized it when a jenji slew the Veik of Ner Kes. Some day I will know how to use the staff."

Renjosudaldor paused, and seemed to shiver slightly. Then he continued: "Theirs is a magic of war and death, ours of peace and life."

"But war and death are part of life."

"Death, yes, when it serves life. Their magic serves only their own fear and hatred: fear of their dark gods and hatred of themselves. They can scarcely draw breath without weakening Callia."

"When I master your spells, Protector, and those of the Badakhar, I will destroy their magic forever."

Renjosudaldor smiled. "As soon destroy the wind, or the flame, or a raindrop. Come, I must teach you the Great Callings and the Great Sendings."

Much of that first lesson was familiar: though Tilcalli had not trained him formally in magic, she had told him many of the simpler facts. And the principles of most spells were the same for Badakh magic as well, and at least vaguely known to ordinary people.

So he learned again that the Powers, whether called Sterkar or Gariba, were beings aware of the world yet unaware of themselves. They could know fear and joy and wrath; sometimes they warred upon one another, or upon humans. Invoked properly, they could do great good. Invoked with evil intent, or ineptly, they could spread havoc. Themselves neither good nor evil, they enjoyed the sheer exercise of their own powers.

Most people, the Protector told Dheribi, could not sway the Powers even if they knew the spells. But a few, with the talent and the will, could direct the Powers like a rider guiding a horse.

"All our people once had some talent," he said. "When our ancestors chose to go into the Bayo Bealar, they asked only magicians; they knew they would need magic to survive here. But the talent has slipped from us; only twenty or thirty can still invoke even the simplest spells, like that for the river boats. Even fewer can sustain the illusions that guard our doorways; Silisihan is one of them.''

''Will I learn such illusions, and the spell for coldfire?''

''Among many others. Some I can teach you, but I cannot cast the spells myself. First you must learn the *culim shandala*, the deep names of the Gariba. Then you must learn their invocations, and the ways to please them into doing what you seek.''

On the third page of the Magic Writings, the deep names of the Powers began. They went on for page after page; Dheribi read them all, murmuring each to himself and sometimes turning to Renjosudaldor for help in speaking the name properly.

At length the glow of the coldfire began to fade from the roof of the cavern, and herders led the sheep and cattle back to their pens. Night was falling in the Underland, and Dheribi felt an aching weariness.

''You have done well,'' the Protector said. ''Enough for now. Go and sleep; in the morning we will resume.''

Nodding, Dheribi rose from the book, took up the staff of Tenglekur and shuffled into the room Svordo had prepared for them. Two simple straw pallets lay against opposing walls, almost invisible in the deepening gloom. Svordo lay upon one, his cloak pulled tight around him.

''Are you learning great spells?'' he asked in a whisper.

''Only beginning.'' Dheribi slumped onto the pallet. Despite his weariness he felt the kind of elation he had known on first riding a horse in the Arekaryo Kes long ago. Lying down, he held the staff beside him in one hand. The Powers in it moved and gleamed as they always had. But now he knew their names.

''Explain to me,'' Pelshadan said quietly, ''the principles of your magic.''

The summer afternoon was warm and humid; the window of the Veik's chamber admitted no breeze, and the sky was darkening for a thunderstorm.

''Sotalar, the Earth, is the source of all life and power,'' Tilcalli answered. The words, like a betrayal, came hesitantly to her lips. ''Our histories say that for a long time Sotalar and its creatures lived in harmony. And that harmony created the goddess Callia.''

''I have heard of Callia.''

''She is aware, as Sotalar and its Powers are not, and she lets them see and know themselves. After a long time, people first came here. They didn't know anything about Sotalar, and many of them died. Then Callia gave people a little of her own awareness." The words flowed more easily now. "We could see Sotalar for ourselves, and Callia, but we could also see into our own minds and hearts. Sometimes our imaginings led us away from Callia, and into worlds of our own. At last we realized that we were hurting Callia, weakening her, and we returned to her."

"How could you hurt a divine being?"

"By fighting among ourselves, by fouling her streams, by cutting the soil that is her flesh." She hesitated. "By trying to be her master, not her lover."

The Veik's eyes reflected his restlessness. "These are mothers' tales, not principles of sorcery."

"I'm sorry—I am telling you as I was told. I know no other way."

"All right, go on."

She did as he asked, but could see his attention fade. Still she pressed on, trying to explain how Cantarean magic tried only to help the world become what it wished to be, to speed up or slow down the processes of life. Pelshadan's expressionless face at last revealed a smile.

"Pelkhven, Pelkhven! I feel I have been eavesdropping on chatter in a slave barracks, not learning from a great magician. Come, enough of the world's wishes. Explain just this to me: My enemies sent a gheishauka from the Black World. I sensed it coming, and could do nothing to stop it. Even with my full powers I could not have stopped it. Yet you commanded it and drove it away. How could your Callia-magic do such a thing?"

"The spell is called a Sending, Veik. It is very powerful, but it too obeys the wishes of the world. The demon did not wish to be here, did not belong here. Sotalar itself did not want it. A great Badakh spell dragged it here and set it upon you, but the demon yearned for its own world. The Sending did not command the demon—it freed the demon."

"This is madness." The magician's pale blue eyes cooled to ice. "All the magic I have ever learned has but one purpose—to make the world obey the magician's will. Magic is power, and power is nothing if it does not serve the magician. Your magic enslaves your magicians, makes them servants of your Callia. You do her will, not your own."

"One of your titles is Skalkaz afi Mekhpur, Servant of the Firelord."

"Do not taunt me with blasphemy, woman. To serve the Firelord is to rule the world."

"Our world rules itself, Veik, and us as well. When we understand what it wishes, and help it, we know joy. When we stand in the way, we know—"

"Power!" Pelshadan declared. "And the true joy that only power and knowledge can bring. Pelkhven, look at me. Look at yourself. Once we were young, and now we age and soon we shall die. The world does not love us. It is a vast stupid stone, on which we live like ants. We survive only by learning how to trick the world, how to force it to do as we wish, or it will crush us."

"I cannot argue, Veik. Your magic defeated ours. I have only tried to explain what ours is like."

Pelshadan smiled again, grimly. "Defeated you indeed. Well, you have cheered me up, Pelkhven. Cantarean magic has always worried us because we know so little about it, and now I am relieved to know that it is based on nonsense. Doubtless your people have learned some good spells by chance, and I will be grateful to master them—I'll put them to better use than you could, I'm sure. You must certainly teach me that Sending. And I'm doubly grateful that you have sought to put your son in my care. He is going to be a great magician indeed, and he would have been utterly wasted among your people."

Tilcalli bowed her head. "As the Veik says."

Her surrender seemed to put him in a better mood. "Tell me this: Why do your magicians always die when captured?"

"To spare themselves torture and slavery, Vcik."

"But most Cantareans endure torture and slavery all their lives. Only your magicians choose death."

"I have not."

"No. You live so that your son may live and master my magic." The old man, sitting by the window in a wooden armchair, studied her pensively. "You are hard to understand, Pelkhven. Every magician wants to learn more magic; that is what binds my apprentices to me. So I can understand that Dheribi will want to learn all he can, both from me and from you. But you yourself seem to have no interest in my knowledge, and that I find strange when we agree that Badakh magic is far greater than Cantarean."

"I grew up among my own people, Veik. Our ways of thinking are very different, as you have said. I could not learn your magic even if I wanted to. But my son has grown up here, he thinks like a Badakh, and he will learn where I cannot."

Pelshadan nodded, his fingertips steepled under his chin. "Yet I can learn your people's magic."

"You are a very great magician, greater than I."

"But not greater than Dheribi will someday be. I felt his power at the Gathering. Even my own master could not invoke such might. I felt like a twig fallen into white water."

She felt pride in her son, and then suppressed it: this was a dangerous conversation, and she must not let him manipulate her. He had been right when he said all Badakh magicians cared only for learning more; he might use magic at his Aryo's bidding, but that was just the price one paid for gaining knowledge. Pelshadan talked about the magician's will and power, but Tilcalli heard only a slave's boasting of the strength he could give his master. The Veik had not yet grasped the thought that a magician might act on his own, exercise his power for the good of his people rather than the whim of his lord. If he did, and he realized that Dheribi would use his magic to overthrow the Badakhar, he would surely slay both herself and her son.

"He is half-Badakh," she lied. "There, I suspect, is the source of his power."

Pelshadan nodded and then dismissed the subject. "Enough. Let us get down to practical matters. Teach me your names for the Vedarsterkar, the Powers of Water."

Dheribi had lost track of the times the coldfire had dimmed and brightened again. Sometimes, before he fell exhausted into sleep, he thought that this confusion in his mind was what made Badakh magicians so foolish. Yet Renjosudaldor, who knew all the spells of his people, sat undistracted.

"The confusion will pass," the Protector said. "It is far worse for most of us. You have learned more in days than most of us learn in years."

"I feel I have learned little, Protector."

The old man smiled. "Dheribi, have you not noticed? You do not tire. Three of us must alternate invoking the coldfire to illuminate this cavern; one could not do it day after day. But you called up the coldfire and went on to cast four more spells that same day. You woke next morning as strong as any young man."

Dheribi nodded. It was true, yet he had not really noticed. Practicing magic was no more tiring than standing knee-deep in a fast-moving stream: he could feel the Powers moving around him and through him, and as long as he kept his balance he had nothing to fear.

But Renjosudaldor's lessons had also given him sharper sensibilities. His constant focus was now filled with unexpected details, ripples of energy, and emptinesses.

Especially emptinesses. Even when he had first entered the Underland Dheribi had sensed the men and women who had dwelt there before, and now were gone. With his new awareness he was more sharply aware of their absence. The great caverns were like an abandoned palace.

"Sometimes I can sense more than that," Dheribi said to Renjosudaldor one morning as they sat eating porridge and dried beef. "Tunnels and deep shafts where even the Gulyaji have never gone."

"There is where you must go to face the being that stalks us," the Protector said.

"Into the far caves? How could I? I know nothing of climbing rocks or swimming streams like this one." He gestured toward the window and the never-silent stream beyond.

"You will not walk there, or swim there. The being in those caves has never come close to us, yet it moves among us through its focus. You will send your focus out to meet it."

Dheribi glanced at Svordo, who looked worried. "I have thought about this for a long time, Protector. You have taught me how to invoke coldfire, and to create the illusions of stone, and to guide a river boat. I can call the green into grass, and the poison from a wound. But what could I use against this being?"

"All I can give you are the spells of Sending and Binding we have always used against it. They have not worked well for me, or for those who taught me. But we know our strength has faded, and the strength of that which sent the being has grown."

"Which sent—" Dheribi put down his agate bowl. "Then this being is not just a sick Power."

"It is like a jenji without a host. It comes from Bur Magundor, the Great Evil One."

"Mekhpur!" Dheribi whispered.

"I do not know that name."

"The Firelord, the great god of the Badakhar. He grants power to the Veikar; he is the source of all their magic."

The Protector nodded. "Yes, he who overthrew Callia and her people. We escaped his notice for a long time, but now he means to destroy us. But we are nothing serious to him, only an amusement."

"Protector—not long ago I looked into the eyes of a jenji in Ner Kes, and it looked into mine. I want never to face such a being again."

"The choice is yours." The old man smiled. "We hope you will choose to send the being away."

* * *

His scouts had described the wall around Ner Kes, but the actual sight of it made Albohar fall silent. The army was camping on both sides of the river Hemarei, well out of bowshot of the wall. Only a fool would venture closer on horseback: the land had been gouged with ditches and mined with pits and iron spikes that could easily pierce a hoof.

Well, Little Dark One, thought Albohar, *did you have a hand in building those walls? Or did you die before you ever reached here?* Sadness stabbed him like an unexpected knife. It had been a clever idea of Pelkhven's, to send him here as penance for his crime, but perhaps he would have died more easily at the flogging post than at the hands of the Nerkesar slave masters.

The thought was unworthy, and he put it from him. No warrior would want an easy death, when glory from Mekhpur came in battle. However Dheribi had met his end, he had died in the service of his Aryo; no one needed a greater epitaph than that.

With Eskel, Snegh, and a squadron of cavalry, Albohar rode around the city. Both upstream and downstream of the walls, the Aishadanar had built rough bridges to replace those burned by the defenders. From those it was clear that the river might pass through the walls, but it was no means of entry.

"Upstream the current is strong enough to carry a boat right onto those cursed spikes," he said to Eskel as they stood on the bridge downstream of Ner Kes. "Here, you'd have to fight the current to reach the opening in the wall, and you can see the posts they've driven from the wall into the riverbed. Even if you could reach them and somehow get through the posts, the guards would cut you to pieces."

He glanced about him. The fields and villages around the city were black and still smoking; the sun, low in the morning sky, glared redly through a yellow pall.

"The fools have destroyed most of their own crops," he commented as he led the riders off the bridge and back toward his headquarters on the south side of the river. "They won't be able to hold out for long."

"No, Aryo," several of the riders agreed, almost in chorus. But Albohar saw the worry in their eyes, and in Eskel's. If the Nerkesar did not surrender, or the city could not be conquered, the invasion would fail.

"Aryo—"

"Yes, Son?"

"What if the river weren't there? Suppose our magicians could dry it up, or freeze it."

Snegh, riding close behind, chuckled. "We'd have our choice of roads into the place, wouldn't we, my lord! A quick charge down the riverbed, a little ax work on the posts under cover of shields, and we're through."

"I'll speak of it with Potiari and Dvoi," Albohar said.

He hawked and spat to keep himself from grinning. The boy had looked at a barrier and seen a highway. That kind of thinking would help Eskel keep the empire that his father was winning for him.

The Protector and Dheribi walked up a path through the great cavern to a tunnel half-hidden behind a grove of stalagmites. Dheribi filled the tunnel with coldfire and stood aside to let his teacher enter first.

"This passage leads to a series of caves that few have explored," Renjosudaldor said. "Our young magicians come here to rest and meditate. It will do for a battlefield." His eyes caught Dheribi's. The old man was smiling slightly, but he seemed worried.

"And if I lose the battle?"

The Protector walked down the narrow tunnel without speaking for a time. When he answered, his voice echoed: "You will lie deep in Sotalar's breast and there we shall join you before long."

At last they came to a small chamber where water dripped slowly from the roof into little pools, and the ashes of ancient fires lay black upon the stone.

"No one will disturb you here, except the being you seek to send away. When you have finished your task, return to us."

"I shall."

"Yes—I think you shall." Renjosudaldor stepped close to Dheribi. "I must give you one thing more. You came to us with a slave's name, and you say you know no other. I will not have you go against a creature of the Bur Magundor almost as nameless as the being itself. I give you your true name."

He extended a hand above one of the pools, and a thin strand of water rose, glittering in the coldfire like a snake of blue glass. It coiled upon itself, formed a torus; the Protector held it as easily as a ring of metal and placed it gently on Dheribi's hair. It glinted there.

"I give you your *culim shandal*, your deep name," the Protector repeated. "In the speech of your people, you are the One Who Goes Away. You are Calindor."

Ten

The torus burst and gushed down Calindor's face and neck. He closed his eyes and gasped, sagging into the old man's embrace. Renjosudaldor eased him gently down onto a narrow bench of stone.

"I leave you, Calindor, for a little while."

When the old man's echoing footsteps had faded into silence, Calindor sat up straight with his arms folded across his chest.

His new name felt strange and not entirely comfortable. It was a Cantarean name, and promised homelessness; yet he was still as much Badakh warrior as Cantarean magician, and suddenly knew himself homesick for the smoke and stink of Aishadan. For a moment he resented not only his naming but all the plans that others had made for him—his mother, the Aryo, the Burrowers. Why could they not leave him in peace to seek his own destiny?

Enough. He was in this little cave of his own free will, and the sooner he did what he had come here for, the sooner he could go back to the sunlight.

With flint and steel he sparked a small fire. The Gulyaji often went above ground at night in search of wood; their own trees were too few and precious for timber or fire. When the flames were strong, he sprinkled a couple of herbs over them and inhaled the faintly sweet fumes: a Gulyaji secret for intensifying a focus.

He closed his eyes, feeling trickles of water run down his neck, and focused.

First he sensed the Gulyaji close by, going about their tasks with quicker steps than usual; they knew what he was trying to do, and what it might mean to them. Then he reached out, through the abandoned caves where darkness covered treasures beyond counting and the silent graves of the Burrower dead. He sensed the pools where blind fish swam, the roofs where bats clung sleeping.

He moved beyond them, into caverns and tunnels no man had ever entered. Yet even here were the traces of ancient presences: ancestors of dragons had ventured here, and humbler creatures, and the Powers of Air and Water had contended here with the Powers of Earth for long millennia. Even in these empty depths, Sotalar's breath and blood still stirred.

Calindor choked and lunged back against the wall of the cave. He shivered and tried to breathe through a mouth suddenly dry, remembering his last day in the Arekaryo Kes when he had felt an evil presence in the fortress.

A similar presence sensed him and responded: it was crouched in the far caverns, and crouched as well within his mind.

It had a physical form that was almost manlike: two powerful legs, a thick torso, long arms and heavy shoulders. The head jutted forward into a kind of snout. He could feel its intelligence, strength and contempt as it prowled through the caves it had made its own. It was old, solitary and malevolent, a prisoner so long it had forgotten any other world.

You search for me. Wordless yet understandable, the being's thoughts hissed in Calindor's mind. He remembered the whip cutting the air before it sliced into his flesh.

Tell me who you are, Calindor asked, *and why you haunt the people of the Underland.*

Silent laughter answered him, laughter that cut into his soul. *I obey my lord. He wishes his realm cleansed of vermin.*

You have served him ill. The Gulyaji still live within their caves, and you can only pester them.

As my lord wills it. It amuses him to see them try to save themselves. Now you have come to save them.

I cannot save them. But I can send you back to your own realm in the Black World.

Again, unheard laughter echoed in his brain. It made him shudder and almost blurred his focus as he recalled the words of the Sending that the Protector had taught him.

What are the vermin to you? I sense your power as you sense mine, and I know your ignorance. The vermin have taught you a little, but I can teach you more. Serve my lord, and all will be yours—all the secrets under the sky. You will be greater than any vermin king.

The demon's thoughts were clear and hard and true. Calindor

hesitated. Wherever it came from, its lore must indeed be great. Yet it was a minor servant of Mekhpur, whose power inspired every Badakh magician and held sway over all Cantarea. To know Mekhpur's secrets! He could overthrow the Badakhar kingdoms with a wave of his hand. The upermannar would be cast down, the Cantareans restored with the combined might of their own magic and that of the Firelord. Surely the Firelord would accept such a bargain—

Despite the intensity of his adversary's focus, Calindor laughed. The temptation to accept Mekhpur was great, but he rejected it. The demon's intelligence and power had gained it nothing in Mekhpur's service but long years in empty solitude. Calindor could imagine himself imprisoned on some other world to exterminate some other race of vermin. Better to be Mekhpur's defeated enemy than his triumphant slave.

Quietly he spoke the first invocation: "I call on my soul and my name, Calindor, to honor Callia and the Powers I have need of."

A breeze sprang up and whirled around the little cave—a mocking message from Mekhpur's slave.

Calindor scarcely noticed. He could feel the magic gathering now, like a thunderhead building in a summer sky. The Gariba of Earth were stirring around him, disturbed by his focus, his words and the distant laughter.

He began the second invocation, speaking the Gariba's deep names he had read in the Magic Writings and then calling out: "I invoke them in stone, I invoke them in soil, I invoke them in Callia's name. Let them not hold what does not spring from them, let them free what comes enslaved to them, let them open themselves."

The breeze turned into a howling whirlwind, blowing spray from the rock pools and filling the cave with fine dust. Calindor squinted and coughed, feeling his adversary's startled fear and rage. He felt as well his own fear, and knew the demon was feeding it. The words of the third invocation tried to shape themselves in his mind, then slipped away. *Quickly,* he urged himself, *before the Powers forget*!

"I thank the Powers for their gift. I honor the Powers for their might. Let them speed the stranger home."

The Gariba of Earth poured shouting through him, knocking him over and flinging him against the far wall of the cave. The fire went out in a whirl of smoke, and then the coldfire died. Calindor lay stunned in darkness as the forces he had unleashed swept out through his focus into the far caverns. He cried out in wonder and terror, but could not hear himself over the tumult of the Powers.

The tumult lessened, and Calindor drew a shuddering breath. A high, thin cry spiked through his mind, the wail of frightened evil calling on its master. Abruptly, it ended. Calindor half-expected the Firelord to reply, but only silence filled the focus. The air within the cave grew still.

Calindor coughed dust from his throat and slowly sat up. Hoarsely, he called back the coldfire. A thin stalactite broke from the ceiling and tinkled as it struck the floor.

Getting to his feet, he shuffled toward the tunnel. He felt not tired but shaken, as if he had plunged over a waterfall and survived.

Halfway down the tunnel he met Svordo hastening to him.

"I was afraid you might be trapped after the earthquake," Svordo said. "Are you well?"

"Well enough. What earthquake?"

Svordo grinned in surprise. "Didn't you feel it? The Protector says it was you who caused it. And look at you, all dusty and muddy. Come and bathe, and then have something to eat."

Where the little tunnel opened into the great cave, what seemed to be all the Gulyaji stood waiting for them. As if with one voice, they murmured his name. Then a woman began an ancient, merry song, "The Laughter of Callia," and others joined. Beginning softly, their voices swelled until the cavern itself seemed to sing. Birds flew startled from the trees.

The song ended. Renjosudaldor stepped up onto a carved bench and raised his hands to the crowd.

"Our skill as magicians has weakened," he cried out, "but we have felt in our bones what Calindor has done. Not since our first days in the Underland, and perhaps not even then, has such a spell been cast in these caves. We thank you, and we thank Callia for sending you to us."

Calindor opened his mouth to reply, and found he could not; too many emotions held him. He raised a hand and let it fall.

"You have many more tasks before you," the Protector went on. "May what you have learned here serve you well in them. When you have regained Cantarea for Callia, we will return to the lands of the sun to do you full honor. Until then, we can at least live in peace while we honor you."

The old man embraced him as the Gulyaji sang once more. Within a river of people, Calindor and Svordo walked slowly back to the Protector's house. Renjosudaldor paused to talk with some of the others, and sent Calindor inside to rest. Svordo went with him. A rich stew was bubbling on the fire.

"Ah, these people may complain a lot, but they eat well," Svordo said, digging into his bowl with a gold spoon. "I like their beds, too, even if they're just straw and not proper beds."

Calindor smiled. "Would you rather stay here?"

"Perhaps." Svordo chewed and swallowed. "The food's good, the Protector's a kind man—not easy to talk to, but a good man. But everyone's much older than us, aren't they? And they talk funny—not just their way of speaking, but what they talk about. People you never heard of, and jokes that make no sense. Well, I think I'd soon get bored, especially once you left." He scraped out his bowl and went back to the fire for a little more.

"So if it's all right with you, I'd like to go with you. The Burrowers aren't the only ones who want to see the sun again."

"I'm glad. But you know it will be dangerous. I will have to find my father—find Albohar, I mean, and his army, and give them whatever help I can. Then we return to Aishadan and I must apprentice myself to the Veik. I will have enemies everywhere."

"Just tell them I'm a slave you captured." Svordo shrugged. "It's true enough, and no one notices one slave more or less. Besides, if we go to Aishadan perhaps I can get a proper bed to sleep in."

Dvoi had begun his apprenticeship as a vedarmagh, a water magician, so it fell to him to prepare the spells; but both he and Potiari invoked them.

Dawn was near. They sat in a small tent beside the river, well within sight of the city. The perfume of their incense was almost lost in the smoky mist that hung over the burned fields. Yet Albohar, sitting outside his tent not far away, could catch a whiff of it.

The smells of magic: incense, hot iron, a hundred spices and oils and gums. To Albohar they always seemed to evoke another scent, something familiar yet elusive. Once these smells had filled him with awe and excitement; now for some reason he felt sadness instead, as if recalling some lost joy.

He tried to put the mood aside and to concentrate on the plan they had devised. Three squadrons of cavalry stood along the riverbank. They carried shields and axes, and many wore chain mail over their heads and shoulders. The upermannar might be poor these days, Albohar reflected, but not many would sell their armor.

Magicians and cavalry were on the western, upstream side of Ner Kes. Another two squadrons waited on the far side of the city; they too would attack, and would go first, but Albohar expected them to serve as little more than a distraction.

Within the tent, the two magicians sang and chanted and struck little drums. Their voices, deep and droning, seemed to silence everything else. No horses whinnied, no birds sang, no men swore or joked.

In some spells, Albohar knew, the magician would work himself into a frenzy before the spell took effect. In this one, the invocation simply went on and on. Albohar lost interest in it and scanned the terrain in the growing light. The Nerkesar might think this a good time for a sortie, but nothing moved near the walls. In ragged lines, the besiegers' tents stretched away around the city, marked in the blue gloom by campfires.

How few we are, Albohar thought. *All our thousands are really just a handful. Yet let us win here and every Badakh will serve Aishadan. Let us win here, and we win the world.*

Eskel left his tent nearby, elegantly dressed in red trousers and gold tunic. Albohar was glad to see the boy was wearing chain mail beneath the tunic; bravery was important, but no wise prince exposed himself and his kingdom to needless dangers.

"I greet you, Aryo. This morning will be fair for us."

"If Mekhpur wills it." Albohar said nothing more. If Mekhpur did not will it, then this campaign was doomed and so was the dream of a unified empire ruled by Aishadan.

"I must join my squadron," Eskel said. "Give me your blessing, Aryo."

"I give you the blessing of a warrior: courage and joy in battle, glory in victory, praise in the songs."

They embraced briefly, and Eskel bowed before turning and mounting his horse. He cantered off to his squadron, the one that would attack as a third wave. Eskel had demanded the first place, but the Aryo's council had forbidden it. The boy had acceded calmly, and Albohar had been pleased. Let him accept reality, and he would rule long.

The chanting stopped without warning. A cold breeze suddenly blew from the river, and Albohar shivered. Turning, he saw a dull glint on the dark waters of the river. The surface paled and grew still: in the middle of summer, the river was icing over. Mist swirled up from it into a thickening fog. Through the mist, Albohar saw the mud of the riverbank rise and glisten as ice pushed up through it. A crackling noise filled the silence.

The ice extended for some distance upstream, but stopped precisely opposite the magicians' tent. Downstream of that point the river still flowed, but its level was dropping rapidly. The ice was a solid dam now, from surface to bed.

Timing would be crucial. Albohar walked closer to the bank, trying to gauge how fast the water was dropping. Wait too long, and the cavalry would ride against defenders prepared for a fight. Go too soon, and the horses would have to swim up to the barricade.

He looked east, along the siege line, and heard a faint metallic ringing that seemed to grow closer: a relayed signal of swords on shields, announcing that the diversionary force had gone into action.

"Go ahead!" Albohar shouted. "Good fighting!"

The first squadron, a hundred of the best men in the army, rumbled east along the riverbank behind red-and-gold pennants. By the time they needed to go down into the bed, Albohar calculated, the water would be too low to wet the horses' bellies. The eastern sky behind the city was brightening, with only a few wisps of pink cloud.

Albohar walked to the bank and watched the horsemen cantering easily toward Ner Kes. The wall over the river was perhaps a thousand strides away, in easy earshot of an alarm drum, but the city was silent.

Now the second squadron followed, and then the third. The first wave was nearly at the walls now, and easily visible in the morning light. In two files, the horsemen wheeled left and went down into the riverbed.

Nerkesar alarm drums were sounding, and moaning horns summoned soldiers to their posts. Faint voices cried orders from the walls, and Albohar thought he could hear the dull sound of axes chopping into the log barricade.

The sounds of strife increased; now the second squadron was in the riverbed, poising itself a little distance behind the first. How long would the first wave take to cut through and clear a path for the rest of the attackers? Would they have trouble fighting their way to the main gates and holding them long enough for reinforcements to relieve them? And what would the deivushibi do?

Eskel's squadron followed the others into the riverbed, whose exposed wet rocks now gleamed silver. Good: the boy had stationed outriders on either bank against the chance of sorties.

In the magicians' tent, Potiari's deep voice hesitated in his droning chant; Albohar heard the sound of vomiting. Dvoi cried out, and then silence fell.

Albohar frowned and turned to the tent. Before he could enter it, a deep groan turned into a thunderclap. The ground shivered a little, and men's voices called out faintly under the grinding roar. Spinning round again, Albohar saw the ice dam breaking up with eerie swiftness. Water jetted from cracks, then gushed from widening gaps, and then exploded the ice from top to bottom.

The pent-up river reclaimed its bed in a foaming charge faster than a horse could run. The Aryo watched it surge eastward, tossing great chunks of ice as if they were leaves upon the torrent. He whispered Eskel's name but could not hear himself. Spray and mist from the unbound river rose and obscured the city walls.

"My horse!" Albohar screamed. A groom was close by, holding the horse's reins. Swinging into the saddle, the Aryo spurred toward the city while a dozen guards and attendants followed in a ragged line.

Eskel's outriders had acted quickly, dismounting and going down into the riverbed to drag their comrades to safety. As Albohar reined up, he saw one young warrior extend his lance to another caught in the flood; then the rescuer was himself dragged in.

The city wall and the river barricade were here only a couple of hundred strides away, within an easy bowshot, but Albohar ignored the danger. Shouting to make himself heard over the thunder of the river, he ordered men to form human chains to help pull riders and horses out of the flood. He looked downstream, trying to judge whether the first and second squadrons could be saved.

No: the ice was already smashing against the barricade, and the water had risen to twice a man's height. The warriors in their chain mail, with shields strapped to their arms, had had no chance.

More men were coming from the siege camp to retrieve the dead and wounded. The Nerkesar launched a few arrows, but seemed as staggered as their enemies by the sudden flood. Albohar could see them gawking from the battlements, too surprised even to jeer at their dying enemies.

Eskel, on foot, staggered over the rim of the bank. His gold tunic was sodden and torn, his chain mail brown with mud, his red trousers ripped to filthy shreds. He half-carried another warrior whose face was a mask of blood.

Albohar rode up to his son. The boy looked stunned; his eyes stared, unfocused, and he was oblivious to the blood trickling down his face from abrasions across his cheek.

"Get your comrade to safety and then come back here and take charge," Albohar ordered. "I want everyone accounted for—dead, injured, or hale. Tally the horses too. The hale will get the dead and injured back into camp. When you've got them all to safety, see to the building of a pyre." He paused and glared at the foaming, heaving surface of the river. "We have sent Mekhpur many new recruits for his guards today."

"I obey, Aryo." Eskel hobbled a few steps, still supporting his wounded comrade, and then paused. In a voice like a little boy's, he asked: "My lord father, what happened? It was going so well. We were almost through the barricade. Was it the magicians?"

"I'll find out in good time. Now get on with your work!"

The Aryo wheeled his horse and galloped back to the magicians' tent. If hell-cursed Potiari and Dvoi still lived, they would soon wish themselves otherwise.

That evening, as the sun sank toward the northwestern horizon at the end of a long summer day, the siege council met in Albohar's tent. One by one, the senior upermannar gave their reports, and the mood in the tent grew blacker.

The two squadrons that had attacked from the east, downstream of the city, had succeeded for a time in diverting attention from the main attack. When the ice dam had burst, the flood had rushed through the city and drowned all but fifty-nine of the two hundred men, and only sixteen of their horses had survived. Of the fifty-nine men, thirty-seven were injured; six were not expected to live.

Out of the three hundred in the main attack, only thirty-six had escaped uninjured. Forty had various injuries serious enough to keep them from combat. All the rest were dead or presumed so; scores of bodies were still pinned against the barricade or had been retrieved by the Nerkesar. Thirty-two horses had escaped the flood in fit condition.

Albohar glared down at his meal of fresh horsemeat. "We have paid a high price for this banquet," he said quietly. "Those were our best men, our best mounts. I would have trusted my life with the worst of the men in those squadrons."

"Yes, Aryo," said Snegh. He had said little so far this evening—perhaps, Albohar thought, he did not want to seem to boast that his fears had been vindicated. "Still, the siege is unbroken. We have suffered a sad setback, but no more."

"How long can we maintain the siege?" the Aryo asked.

"If we simply sit, and consume minimum rations, we could last another fifteen or twenty days," Snegh replied. "If we send out foraging parties, and they are lucky, we might well last until autumn. But if we have not taken the city by first frost, we will not take it at all."

"We have our harvests to get in," someone muttered. "First frost is too late by thirty days."

Vulkvo had been even more silent than Snegh in the council, but now he raised one scarred hand.

"Aryo, both magicians are incapable of further spells, I understand."

"True."

"The Veik Tenglekur is dead, but the Nerkesar doubtless have other magicians. The—" he hesitated to pronounce the word "—the deivushibi may also have magical powers."

"Perhaps. We don't know."

"I would not be surprised if the ice dam failed under a counterspell," Vulkvo said. "Perhaps we may suffer other sorceries now that we cannot even defend ourselves against." He paused, gathering his thoughts. "Our magicians froze the river. Suppose the Nerkesar call down a blizzard upon us or a tornado. Suppose they attack us with endless rain. Many wars have ended that way, and few have gone home to tell about them."

Albohar nodded unhappily. Many magicians could invoke weather spells, whether through the Sterkar of air, fire or water. The Rainbow Feasts, celebrated at the summer solstice, commemorated the great floods invoked by the Veik Kharlush to protect the retreat of Kvosedakh when he led his people west to found Aishadan. Weather spells might work well, Albohar thought, but they left the land devastated, stripped of its topsoil or baked into dust and clay. If the deivushibi in Parsur's body did have magic power, it would scarcely worry about the harm a flood might to do the already ruined lands around Ner Kes.

"We may suffer sorcerous attacks," he said aloud. "Every warrior must expect them at one time or another, and bear them as he would any other violence. But every great use of magic leaves the user weak, as we know to our sorrow. The Nerkesar do not know our own magic is exhausted; they will fear reprisals. So we may assume the siege will continue as a war of men, not of magicians."

He paused and looked around the tent at the warriors seated cross-legged on the carpets.

"And the siege will continue to victory," he said.

"To victory," the upermannar chorused. But Albohar could hear the doubt in their voices, and see fear in their eyes.

Renjosudaldor and Silisihan walked down to the river with Calindor and Svordo. Around them were scores of other Burrowers, singing old songs that echoed back from the high roof of the cavern. The coldfire was unusually bright; Calindor had cast the spell for it.

"You will travel to a cave with a thick yellow pillar close to the river," Silisihan told Calindor. "The journey will take you a sleep and two wakings. A woman named Sidimon lives there; she guards the northern gate, and will guide you to the surface. Two days' walk north will bring you to the road between Ner Kes and Aishadan."

"I thank you for your help, Silisihan," said Calindor. "You saved our lives."

"You have saved ours. May we meet again, when you can guide me through your world."

At the shore, Calindor embraced Renjosudaldor. "I know you believe only in gifts and not in debts, but I cannot offer you gifts such as you have given me, Protector."

The old man smiled at him. "You will give us Cantarea, and the long grass blowing under wind and sun. That will be gift enough."

Their boat was the same one that had brought them here. Now it carried only the two of them, and two packs of food and tools. Calindor and Svordo wore new tunics, trousers and cloaks, woven of Gulyaji wool but in the style of Badakh freemen. On their feet were fine leather boots. Calindor carried his sword slung on his back, and in his left hand held the staff of Tenglekur.

They stepped aboard and Calindor spoke the words of the guiding spell. The boat slid from the shore and out into the water. The Burrowers walked along with it for a while, until the craft at last left the cave and glided into the darkness.

Calindor did not trouble with a coldfire light on the boat itself, but used a moving spell that kept them in a circle of light perhaps ten strides across. Sometimes the walls of the tunnel were close beside them, and gleamed in the light; at other times they passed through large caverns whose walls and pillars and roofs gave back only a faint gleam.

"It must have been hard to abandon caves like this," Svordo said as they passed through one. Calindor expanded the coldfire so that they could see the cavern better.

It was enormous, and along the river stood house after house. Stumps of dead trees were everywhere, some of them half-encrusted with minerals that had dripped from the roof. Splendid statues stood here and there, of men and animals and dragons; they had been inlaid with gold and jewels.

"Why didn't they bring their treasures with them when they left?" Svordo wondered.

"They did. Look beyond the houses. Where the fields would be, they left only stone. The soil and plants they took, and the trees for lumber. The gold and jewels weren't necessary."

Svordo shook his head. "The Gulyaji are good people, but very strange." Then he paused, looking over his shoulder at Calindor, and asked: "Are you strange also now?"

Calindor's laugh echoed eerily from the far corners of the cavern. "Perhaps I am, Svordo. Or perhaps I always was. A Menmanna slave, raised as a Badakh warrior, and now schooled in Burrower magic and given a new name. Sometimes I wonder who I really am. I always seem to be living someone else's life."

"What would your own life be, then, if you could choose it?"

Unbidden, an image rose in Calindor's mind: forested mountains, plunging steeply into an enormous blue lake, and strange creatures running swiftly and easily along a rocky shore. They made his heart rise up in fear and joy.

The vision passed, and for a moment Calindor said nothing. Then he drew a slow breath and said: "I would go in search of the dragons."

The boat glided on, faster than a running man but never tiring. Through cave after cave, tunnel after tunnel they moved; at last, as they grew weary, Calindor drew the boat in to shore. This cavern had once held another thriving village; now nothing was left but a few huts and delicately sculpted carvings. They ate a simple meal of dried meat, coarse cakes and fruit, talked for a time, and went to sleep. When they woke, they boarded the boat at once and continued their journey.

"Will we be going back to Ner Kes, then?" Svordo asked a little timidly.

"If that is where the Aryo is. If he is still besieging Ner Kes, I must help him take it; then we can return to Aishadan and I can become Pelshadan's apprentice."

"You've learned Burrower magic well enough to drive away that demon in the caves. Isn't that enough?"

"Nothing like enough. My mother has much to teach me also."

"I don't like the thought of being among the Badakhar again. Least of all among their lords and magicians."

Calindor smiled. "Are you enjoying freedom?"

"Yes. Now you mention it, yes, I am, even in this dark world of caves and tunnels."

"Life among the Badakhar has its own kind of darkness," Calindor said. "But we may not have to endure it for long."

"I'm worried about that possibility too."

Not long after, they entered a cave where coldfire already glowed, illuminating a great yellow pillar. On the shore stood a tall woman dressed in a hooded cloak. She welcomed them as they stepped from the boat.

"I am Sidimon. The Protector sent me news of you. I honor you for your gifts to us. Will you rest here for a time?"

"Thank you, no," said Calindor. He felt a little abashed by her; she was a beautiful woman, about his mother's age, and her dark eyes met his with confidence. He could see why she had been named Proud. "We wish to reach the surface as soon as we may."

"Then come with me."

The route was simpler than it had been at the southern entrance; here were no ladders, just a simple, well-worn path that climbed gradually through a narrowing cavern. At its end was a sand-floored chamber, its walls carved with spell glyphs to help conceal the exit to the surface.

"Here is the gate," said Sidimon. "When you come out, you will find yourself in a thicket of willow near the top of a canyon. Turn left and go gently through the thicket. The canyon will take you down to a creek; follow it north. Where it merges with a much larger river you will find the road to Ner Kes and Aishadan." She paused. "May you walk with Callia beside you at every step."

"And may you walk with Callia also," Calindor said. He clasped her hand for a moment, then turned and stepped out into a hot, insect-buzzing afternoon.

Eleven

Their path led north through thinly wooded low hills. The terrain reminded Calindor of the journey in Sveit's slave wagons; but now the rains were long past, and the hills lay brown and dry under the sun.

They made good progress. Though the ground was rough, generations of animals had worn paths along the creek; Calindor and Svordo followed them, walking easily in their strong new Gulyaji boots. Neither farmers nor herders seemed to use this land; it was eroded and rocky, supporting little but scrub pine and willow. They saw no one all that day, but heard distant wolves at night.

Late in the morning of the following day they came to a burned-out farmstead, little more than a couple of huts and a corral. Three dead Nerkesar lay in the mud—two little girls and an infant boy. Calindor saw sword wounds on them: the long, deep slashes of sabers swung from the height of a horse. No one else, alive or dead, was in any of the buildings. All the livestock were gone as well.

"The Aishadanar have been here not long ago," he said to Svordo as they walked on. "The farmer must have hoped he was too far from the road to attract attention. Now his children have paid for his gamble."

"Will the Aishadan cavalry attack us the same way?"

Calindor said nothing for a time as he walked quickly beside the creek. He thumped the staff of Tenglekur against a stone. "I almost hope they do," he muttered at last.

Late that afternoon, after passing several other destroyed farms, they came to the road and turned east. The signs of heavy traffic were everywhere: abandoned wagons, a bloated and stinking dead horse, the road itself churned to a strip of mud and excrement.

Following the road around a hillside, they came suddenly to a waystation—a crude cabin of fresh-cut logs inside a palisade, sheltering perhaps twenty cavalrymen and as many slaves and freemen. Beside the cabin, within a simpler palisade, stood a sizable corral with well over thirty horses.

A guard, seated on a chestnut mare, gaped at them in surprise.

"*Tala venigala!*" he barked in Cantarean. "Come here!"

"We speak Badakhi," Calindor answered, walking steadily toward the guard. His sword hung from his belt, clearly visible. "I need to speak to your commanding officer."

The guard, a gawky young fellow in new leather armor, grinned nastily and lowered his lance until it pointed straight at Calindor.

"Watch how you talk, slave boy. Where'd you get those clothes and that sword—steal them from your master?"

"My master is my father, the Aryo Albohar. I am his son Dheribi. Now take me to your commander."

Frowning and uncertain, the guard pulled his horse out of their way. "In the cabin. His name's Demazakh, and he'll cook you over a slow fire if you're lying."

Demazakh! His cavalry trainer, too old for combat but a good man for securing the army's supply lines. Calindor quickened his steps, forcing Svordo almost to a trot.

"Trainer Demazakh!" Calindor shouted.

The old horseman appeared in the cabin doorway, his sword in one hand. He stared at Calindor in amazement, but did not reject the hand extended to him.

"We're well met, trainer. I have much to tell you, and much to ask of you."

"You were sold into slavery," Demazakh said slowly.

"A trick. The Aryo wished me to spy out the defenses of Ner Kes. This slave and I escaped from the city some time ago, and now I must rejoin the Aryo. Is the army besieging the city?"

"It is. Here, come in, Dheribi, and have some supper. It's hard fare, but you've eaten harder."

The old warrior accepted his story—escape from Ner Kes as the Veik died at the hands of the possessed Parsur, weeks spent roaming the plains and hills, and final attainment of the road. The other men in the station listened in awe, but not entirely with respect; Calindor knew they would consider him degraded for even pretending to be a slave, whatever the purpose. And he was still the son of a Cantarean slave.

But they offered no questions or criticisms—only grinned and offered him a jug of medh and some honey cakes. Svordo sat happily ignored at one side, as he had predicted he would be.

Demazakh told Calindor of the failed spell and the men who had died two days before. Listening, Calindor felt a chill of fear: surely it was the jenji that had broken the spell on the river and slain the horsemen. But along with the fear he felt a pleasant arrogance: he had driven a monster from the caves of Bayo Bealar, defied Mekhpur himself. The jenji was not invincible.

"You must stay the night, and rest," Demazakh said, and grinned. "We're bringing in some slave girls—nice young ones, not even any fuzz on 'em yet."

Calindor paused for an instant, tempted by the thought of killing all the men in the cabin and knowing he could do it. Then he shook his head. "I have no time. I must reach the Aryo as soon as possible."

The men nodded. That was the attitude of a loyal warrior.

"Then we'll find you a couple of horses. None of ours are very good—the best are all up at the siege—but they'll get you to Ner Kes before noon tomorrow. And I'll give you a messenger's pennant, so you're not stopped at every waystation."

"I thank you, trainer."

Calindor hesitated a moment, knowing himself at the edge of a dangerous choice. He took it.

"I have something I must tell you in private," he murmured to Demazakh. The trainer nodded and led him out of the cabin to the fence around the corral.

"What is it, boy?" he asked, smiling.

Holding up his left hand, Calindor drew it across Demazakh's wrinkled face. The old warrior's eyes lost their focus.

"Hear me and obey, Demazakh. You will send the slave girls back to the farms where you found them. You will not touch them, nor allow any of your men to touch them."

"I hear and obey," Demazakh whispered. Calindor drew his hand across the man's face again, and his eyes sparkled once more.

"Well, let's get you saddled up and send you on your way."

Demazakh roared cheerfully at the stable-slaves until two fine mares were saddled and led out for Calindor and Svordo. The other warriors gathered to see them off.

"Good riding to you, Dheribi!" Demazakh said. "May we meet again soon."

"I hope so, trainer. Farewell!"

Demazakh tied a long red-and-white messenger's pennant to one of the reins of Calindor's mare. A few minutes later they were on their way. Svordo bounced miserably on the saddle of his mount, more concerned to keep upright than to guide her. But he did not complain, and Calindor did not push them into more than a trot.

Not until they were a thousand strides from the waystation did Calindor let himself think about what he had done—cast a spell on a man's soul. The Protector had not spoken of it, but Calindor had seen the pages in the book and had remembered. Even among the ancient Gulyaji, such a spell was rarely accomplished. And everyone had heard the tale of Vodan, the old Veik of Halamor, who had tried and failed to enchant his Aryo's daughter.

Perhaps, he thought, it spoke well for Demazakh: a Cantarean spell on a man's soul could work only to make him do what he truly wished to do. The old trainer had not really wished to sport with little slave girls. If he had, perhaps the spell would have driven him insane, like the Aryo's daughter—and the Veik Vodan himself.

Except for two long rests, they rode all night under a moon almost full. The air was chill and smelled of smoke and charred wood; all along the road stood the burned-out ruins of houses and upermannar estates.

"What if the Nerkesar ambush us?" Svordo wondered softly when they stopped to rest and water the horses.

"They won't. The land is empty."

"You know this for certain?"

"Yes." He had chewed some of the herbs he had used in the little cave before his struggle with the demon, and his focus had sharpened and widened. The effect would not last long, he knew, but it showed him all that lay around them for perhaps five thousand strides. And all that lay around them was desolation.

Well past midmorning they came again to the Hemarei Valley. Patrols were frequent, but Calindor displayed the messenger's pennant; no one stopped them.

The Aryo's headquarters was easy to see from the road—a man-tall palisade of sharpened logs around a cluster of big tents on a rise overlooking both road and river. Mounted guards challenged them at the gate through the compound palisade, but recognized Calindor and let them pass.

Dismounting, Calindor and Svordo led their horses along a dusty path to the white tent of the Aryo, where a flagstaff bore the golden-swastika banner of Aishadan. In the shade of the awning outside the entrance, the Aryo sat with his senior upermannar. Calindor recognized Vulkvo, who stared at the newcomers and then muttered something to Albohar.

The Aryo turned round and saw the two men approaching. He squinted, then swore happily and bolted out of his chair.

"I thank the Firelord for this favor!" Albohar strode across the distance between himself and Calindor, and embraced him. Calindor recognized the familiar smell of the Aryo, and felt tears sting his eyes.

"You are well, Aryo?"

"Better now than I was a moment ago!" Albohar gripped Calindor's shoulders and pushed him back, studying him. "Well, you've toughened up since the spring, haven't you? I'd not like to face you hand to hand and alone. Maybe I should have more of my young bucks flogged and sold into slavery." He laughed, and affectionately slapped Calindor's shoulder. "Come in and tell me where you've been."

Calindor brought Svordo into the tent as well, explaining that he was a slave taken in the escape from Ner Kes. "He's been useful, and I mean to keep him."

"By all means, he's yours. Now—eat something while I send for Snegh and the others. We need to know what you've learned."

Potiari and Dvoi were pale and weak; they slumped in their chairs, seemingly unmindful of the warriors around them in the Aryo's tent. Calindor sat next to Dvoi. Across the fire on the other side of the tent were Albohar and Eskel, leaning intently forward.

"The wall is misspelled," Calindor said. "The Nerkesar magicians did not invoke the Sterkar properly. I can bring it down."

"Any fool can see the wall is misspelled," Potiari snapped. "But Powers of Earth are stupid and hard to invoke."

"I can invoke them."

"He can invoke them, oh yes." Potiari sneered, nodding at Dvoi. The two magicians giggled.

"If I fail, no man of Aishadan will die from my failure."

Potiari frowned and said nothing. Dvoi wearily closed his eyes.

"But I would bring down the wall as a distraction," Calindor went on. "The Aryo Parsur had us build a tunnel under the wall, a bolt-hole. It runs straight to his stronghold. A hundred men or so could seize the stronghold before the Nerkesar even knew it was under attack."

He saw the warriors sit straighter, saw Eskel's eyes narrow. Albohar chuckled.

"A bolt-hole," he repeated. "And built by Parsur's worst enemy. A good tale this will be for the singers! Dheribi, you fill your father's heart with joy. Come, look at this map. Show us where the tunnel is. And then we'll decide who shall go through it."

"I shall go first," Calindor said.

Dvoi's pale eyes blinked open. "But you are disspelling the wall."

"What of it? I'll bring down the wall and then join the men in the tunnel."

Potiari spoke: "You will be in no condition, young man, to do anything else. Bringing down the walls will leave you exhausted for a fortnight. Maybe longer."

"I do not think so."

"Dheribi can do anything," Eskel murmured. "Isn't that true, Dheribi?"

"Not entirely." Calindor looked into Eskel's eyes, and the prince glanced away. "But what I say I can do, I can do."

Potiari laughed unpleasantly. "You wave that staff about, but you have shown us nothing so far. Prove your abilities, young magician."

With a gesture and a whisper, Calindor suffocated the fire burning in the middle of the tent, and then replaced it with blue-glowing coldfire. He stood, walked to Potiari, and said: "Give me your hand."

The older man's hand was chill and damp. Calindor murmured a spell of healing and felt energy move through him into Potiari. The effect was sudden: Potiari gasped, stood up and cried out.

"I am well! I am hale again."

Calindor took Dvoi's hand, and revived him as well. Then he put out the coldfire and called back the ordinary flames in the blackened wood. By the orange light, the warriors' faces looked like masks.

"Well," said the Aryo, and cleared his throat. "I thank the Firelord for sending you back to us, Dheribi. You are the answer to our prayers."

As usual, Bherasha prepared a simple breakfast; the apprentices ate in the kitchen, while she carried trays to Pelshadan and then to Pelkhven. The magician this morning was silent and irritable; Pelkhven was silent also, and sat very still in a chair by the window of her room.

"Is something the matter, my lady? May I do anything to help?"

The older woman shook her head and then summoned a faint smile.

"Yes, something is the matter, Bherasha, but it is not your concern. Thank you."

"I hope it isn't bad news from Ner Kes."

"The news is bad, but that's not what worries me. Sit down for a moment, Bherasha, there on the bed will do."

Bherasha did as she was told, while Pelkhven sat near her with the tray across her lap. Her breakfast porridge cooled unnoticed.

"I have made a bad bargain with the master of this house," she said softly. "When my son returns, the Veik will teach him the lore of the Badakhar, but in return I have had to teach Pelshadan something of . . . our own lore."

Bherasha's voice was almost inaudible: "You are a witch, my lady."

"Yes, and a betrayer of witches. How many of us have died rather than give up our secrets to the Badakhar? And now I give him all he asks for."

"I have never met a witch before. But my mother used to tell me tales of the Siragi Aibela and the wonders they could do in the olden days. My mother said the Badakhar could never learn our magic because they could never learn to love Callia."

Tilcalli smiled sadly at the mention of her clan, and nodded. "I hoped that was true, when the Veik bound me to him. But he has learned, even if he has not understood. He is like a farmer who knows he should water his crops, but not when he should stop watering." She thought for a moment and then said: "Or even why he should grow crops at all."

"What do you think he will do with his new lore, my lady?"

Tilcalli opened her mouth to speak, and paused. Her dark eyes gleamed with tears. "I am afraid he will kill my son, and then kill all our people in the mountains. I am afraid that we will never again walk free across the Big Prairie.''

Later that morning Bherasha accompanied Tilcalli to the market. The day was warm and dry, the air thick with the aroma of the bakeries and the reek of the sewers. In the market square slaves and freewomen jostled one another around the vendors' booths.

''Not much to buy these days,'' Bherasha said. ''And the prices are high.''

''They ruin their own fields and wonder why they grow poor,'' Tilcalli murmured in Cantarean. ''Look at these poor apples, and the meat isn't fit for dogs. Well, we will make do with vegetables and eggs. And the next time someone has a couple of decent chickens here, we'll buy them and build a henhouse in the yard.''

''I don't think the magicians would remember to feed them,'' Bherasha said with a smile, and Tilcalli found herself smiling back, cheered by the girl's giggle.

A man in a yellow tunic, his face shadowed by a wide-brimmed leather hat, stepped up behind Tilcalli. Bherasha glanced up, saw that it was a Badakh, and quickly looked away rather than meet his gaze. But she had seen his eyes; without hesitating she gripped Tilcalli's wrist and pulled her roughly to one side.

The man's knife caught in the folds of Tilcalli's robe, a finger's width from her ribs.

''Murderer! Murderer!'' Bherasha screamed. ''He's trying to kill my mistress! Stop him!''

The man swore and broke away, shoving himself through the crowd and into a nearby alley. Vendors began to hammer on little brass gongs, summoning the arekakhar. In all the hubbub Tilcalli stood as if confused. After a moment Bherasha, still holding her mistress's wrist, drew her back through the marketplace toward the house of Pelshadan.

''Did you see the man?'' Tilcalli asked.

''Just a little, my lady. I saw murder in his eyes. I am sorry to have pulled you like that.''

''I thank you. But how could you tell his intent?''

''I have seen that look in many Badakhar, when they mean to kill or rape. Like the one your son slew outside the beer hall.''

''Blaidakh, yes.'' Tilcalli was surprised to realize she had forgotten Blaidakh for months now. ''How strange . . . I always expected an attack with magic. A simple knife seemed too easy.''

They were in their own street now, hastening over the cobblestones. "You have saved my life, Bherasha."

"No more than you would have done for me, my lady, I'm sure."

The older woman shook her hand. "I'd not have noticed anything amiss until it was too late." She pounded on the door and Minukhi let them in.

"Is the Veik busy?" she asked.

"He studies in his room."

"I must see him at once." She embraced Bherasha and then went upstairs alone.

Pelshadan frowned when he heard the story.

"It might have been a cutpurse," he said. "But it was not. Blaidakh's father Aghwesi might want some kind of revenge, but he is with the army—and anyway, upermannar do not feud with slave women, least of all the Aryo's property. It was an attack from Ghelasha."

"I know," Tilcalli said. "She hates and fears me."

"But you are a slave, nothing more. The Aryo has coupled with a score like you."

"I bore him a son before she did. Dheribi is only a half-breed, but he is still the Aryo's eldest son."

Pelshadan nodded, stroking his short white beard. "And she knows nothing of your magician's skills."

"I would have been denounced and posted if she even suspected."

"Well. For now, I will have you stay within these walls. Bherasha and Minukhi can go to the market. I do not intend to lose you to an assassin's knife when you have much yet to teach me."

Tilcalli glanced around the Veik's chamber. She had lived almost half her life in captivity, she thought; this house was as good a prison as any.

"As the Veik wills it," she murmured, looking down. She told herself that when she had recovered from the shock of the attack she would think of some way to control Pelshadan. Some way.

Twelve

Calindor, Albohar, and Snegh rode briskly through a trampled field.

Potiari and Dvoi rode a respectful few paces behind. Night was falling; already the days were growing shorter. The two warriors and three magicians were trotting eastward across a dusty field not far inside the siege line. To their right stood the Aishadanar tents. To their left, abandoned fields and demolished buildings stretched for perhaps a hundred and fifty strides to the southern curve of the wall around Ner Kes. They were well out of bowshot, but occasionally an archer on the wall launched a shaft at them.

"With the wind behind him he might have made us jump," Calindor said as an arrow thudded into the dirt forty strides to their left. The other magicians chuckled nervously. Albohar and Snegh said nothing.

Calindor paused. They were directly opposite the main gate into the city. "This is where I will stand when I disspell the wall," he said. "It will come down for about fifty strides on either side of the gate."

"We will have a strong force ready to charge in," Albohar said. "Both horse and foot. We'll keep them busy."

"Then I must ride farther east," Calindor went on. "Across the downstream bridge and around to the northeast of the city."

They traversed the distance in silence, and came at last to a pile of rubble like many others: bricks and splintered beams from a cluster of wrecked houses. Calindor did not stop.

"They're watching us from the wall," he said, "and I don't want them to think we know about the tunnel. But it's right here, under the ruins. The Aryo Parsur, before he was possessed, wanted to be sure he could escape if need be."

131

"And here is where our real blow must fall," Albohar said.

"Yes, Aryo. After I have brought the wall down, I will ride here and join the attackers. By that time the battle will be on around the main gate, and the defenders will not be thinking about anything else. When we seize the Kes, the Nerkesar will lose heart and surrender."

"I hope it works," said Albohar softly.

"It will work, Aryo."

This is not the time for you to join us, Calihalingol said. The sun blazed down on her wrinkled face. *You have much left to do in Sotalar.*

I know. Tilcalli sat beside the Silent River, content to enjoy the sun and her great-grandmother's company for a little while. *But it is very hard now. First the creature from the Black World, and then Pelshadan, and now this—and I cannot even be sure that Dheribi is safe.*

He is safe, or he would be here with me.

Great-grandmother, why is it that only the Siragi Aibela come to the Open Dream? What becomes of all the other Cantareans?

That is one of Callia's mysteries. When I finally tire of the sunshine and silence here, I will go over the mountains in your parents' footsteps and perhaps there I will find the others. Or perhaps not.

This is a time when I wish I knew nothing of magic. I wish I had simply grown up and married Dragasa and had his babies and let someone else contend with the Badakhar.

Calihalingol put an arm around Tilcalli's shoulders. *You did have Dragasa's baby. Your son is the one who truly contends with the Badakhar. And with himself,* she added.

Tilcalli embraced her great-grandmother and let herself fall back into Sotalar.

Pelshadan stood beside her bed, staring down at her with half-crazed eyes.

"I felt that, whatever it was. What did you do? Where did you go?"

She said nothing for a long time. Then: "Where you cannot go."

He laughed, a deep and unpleasant sound. "I wonder."

The eastern sky was brightening fast, and in the still air Calindor could hear the distant tramp of boots on the wall of Ner Kes as the night guards were relieved.

He sat on a three-legged stool between two tents in the siege line, with Svordo holding a horse's reins close by. Farther back, Calindor could hear the random noises of three squadrons and several hundred foot soldiers: the snorts of horses, the coughing and spitting of men, the occasional clink of iron against iron.

The disspelling was complex but not truly hard; he simply had to remember each step and perform it correctly. A wrong word, a mistimed gesture could not only leave the walls standing; it could alert the jenji and any other magicians in the city, and perhaps provoke counterspells.

Calindor looked north across the scorched and trampled terrain to the wall. It stood black against the paling sky; here and there, torches burned on its battlements.

He clasped the staff of Tenglekur with both hands. Most of its secrets were still hidden from him, but it sharpened his focus and calmed his thoughts.

Now the wall, though it lay in darkness, was as bright to his vision as if it were made of blocks of glass illumined by fire. He saw the Sterkar twisting restlessly in their stones, yearning for freedom. When he called them by their deep names, the Sterkar paused. The air of early dawn fell still, and no bird sang.

Calindor spoke to the Sterkar in the long, murmuring syllables the Protector had taught him, freeing them from the crude spells of the Nerkesar magicians. Once more the magic rushed through him, like white water through a narrow falls, so that he swayed and gasped in its might.

The stones cried out, a shout of Powers unbound. He saw them flow like water back into the earth, gleaming and bright to the focused eye. Behind him, Calindor faintly heard Potiari and Dvoi scream as they too glimpsed the sudden cascade of the liberated Sterkar, and felt the power of Calindor's invocation.

Along a stretch of a hundred strides, the wall and its main gate sagged like a curtain, sagged and groaned and fell. It made little noise, only a low rumble and a thump. Dust swirled up in its place, and the startled shouts of the Nerkesar.

Calindor stood and turned. Behind the magicians and Svordo stood Vulkvo, armored for battle. The light was stronger now, and the upermanna's face was visible. His expression was a mixture of awe and blood thirst.

"The city is yours," Calindor said.

Vulkvo seemed not to understand at first; he stroked his grizzled beard while looking over Calindor's shoulder at the ruined wall. Then he chuckled softly.

"That's a useful trick, boy." He spun to face the horsemen and infantry arrayed a few strides away. "All right, you men! Saddles! Shoulder pikes!"

He swung up into his own saddle, took his helmet from the pommel, and drew his sword. It flashed blue and pink in the dawn.

"At the trot—forward!"

Calindor was already climbing into the saddle of his own mount, a strong brown mare. Svordo handed up the reins.

"Good luck," he said.

Calindor thought of the jenji waiting at the end of the tunnel, and smiled nervously. Then he guided the mare eastward along the siege line, feeling his old sword with its amethyst pommel slapping against his leg. His father had brought it on the campaign, and had returned it to him last night. Calindor liked it no more than he ever had.

The men in the siege line were all in noisy motion, shouting and stamping and banging swords against shields. Small groups of horsemen cantered out of the line and then swung back again. This too was part of the plan: the Nerkesar would have to watch every side of the city, and so could not throw all their men into the defense of the fallen rampart.

The turmoil also concealed Calindor's ride in the brightening morning. He reached the ruined house that hid the tunnel entrance; as intended, two squadrons were making a feint toward the wall, and the dust they churned up helped conceal the ruins from the defenders.

Calindor dismounted, blinking in the dust, and found only ten horsemen stationed near the ruin. One was Eskel. He looked impassively down at Calindor.

"My father and his men have already gone into the tunnel," Eskel said. "He commanded me to stay here. Something about the importance of the succession."

"He couldn't have! How many have gone with him?"

"A hundred."

"The jenji will destroy them."

"The what?" Eskel frowned.

"The deivushibi, the small god that possesses Parsur. I *told* him to wait for me." He pushed his sword back and fought the temptation to throw it away. Then he withdrew the staff of Tenglekur from a sling across his shoulder. It might still withhold most of its secrets, but it would give him something to fight with.

Without another word he strode down a short flight of steps and into a doorway. More steps lay beyond, descending into darkness. The air was chill and sharp with the stink of smoke: the raiders had carried torches to light their way.

Calindor called up coldfire, and walked swiftly down the stairs under a bright, pale blue circle of light. The steps were as he remembered them, roughly carved and hastily set in mortar. When they ended, the tunnel stretched out into darkness, just wide enough for two men abreast and too low for Calindor to walk upright.

He extinguished the coldfire. An enemy in the tunnel could use it to shoot an arrow at him, and his excitement had sharpened his focus so that the tunnel's path lay clear before him even in the darkness.

He thought ahead to the confrontation that must await him. The spell would have to be a Sending, and he would have to hope that it would work on a jenji as it had on the creature in the far caves.

And if it does not? he asked himself.

He broke into a jog, the head of the staff extended before him. Soon he was sweating despite the chill, amazed that underfed slaves could have built so long a tunnel in so short a time.

The Sterkar in the staff knew where they were; Calindor felt them stir as he passed under the city wall and drew closer to the citadel. Yet the tunnel was far too deep for any sound from the surface to reach it. He hurried on, expecting at every moment to sense Albohar's warriors returning in defeated disarray.

He came to another flight of stairs, this one extending upward. The smell of anxious men was strong here, and more than one had paused to empty his bladder or bowels before going on. The stairs ran first in one direction, then in another. Here and there they gave access to dusty cellars and storerooms, but always they led up into the Aryo's stronghold.

In darkness he sensed a dead man in a doorway ahead: a soldier or slave, surprised by the raiders. Now down the stairs came the noise of battle. Calindor felt himself shivering. His pride, his arrogance had brought him into the lair of a monster. A few days with the ancient book of the Protector, and he thought himself a Veik of the Cantareans; perhaps in the next few moments he would find himself just another young fool, blundering into death like Blaidakh or the dead man in the doorway.

Light stung his eyes. The stairs had leveled off in a narrow hallway, at the far end of which a door stood open to a larger room that must have windows. He was far above the part of the tunnel he had helped to dig; yet he suspected the escape route must start in the Aryo's own quarters or nearby.

Pausing at the edge of the doorway, Calindor let his focus swing out. The room was empty; he darted into it, his staff held in both hands like a battlepole.

It was a bedchamber, ornately furnished yet dusty and neglected. The white-plastered walls were stained and streaked with blood—most of it old, some very new. A wide bed stood in one corner, with a richly embroidered quilt thrown across it. Opposite, two narrow windows showed a cloudless late-summer morning sky above a broad terrace.

Between the windows was a doorway where two men lay still, their Nerkesar chain mail drenched red. From beyond, the clash of arms was louder.

Calindor stepped through the doorway and found himself on the terrace, overlooked on three sides by the second story of the fortress; the fourth side looked south across the city and river. Among the men fighting on the terrace, Calindor saw no more than thirty Aishadanar and twenty Nerkesar. The raiders held most of the area, and were pushing its defenders against the walls. The rest of the raiding party must still be inside the Kes.

He strode quickly to the parapet overlooking the city. The collapsed wall was half-hidden in dust and smoke, but he could see that the defenders were fighting bitterly to turn away the attack of Vulkvo's squadrons and foot soldiers. No one seemed to have noticed yet that their central stronghold was about to fall.

Albohar burst out of another doorway, his sword running red and his eyes bright. He saw Calindor and beckoned him to his side.

"It's gone flawlessly!" the Aryo shouted. "We'll hold the Kes before noon, and the whole city by nightfall. My men are still hunting Parsur, but I'll bet the deivushibi has left him dead. As soon as we know for sure, I'll fire the fortress and join Vulkvo's men."

"Aryo—you should not have gone into the tunnel without me."

"Nonsense, boy." Albohar's pale eyes were bright with battle fever. "We had no time to wait for you. Every moment we gave them was a chance to recover. Look, everything's gone well."

He swung his sword in a broad arc, taking in the terrace and the fortress. Suddenly he froze.

Stepping delicately from a window to the terrace flagstones was a slim young man in tight trousers and a loose blouse. He was unarmored and unhelmed, but carried a fine sword in one hand. Calindor shivered again: it was Parsur, still possessed.

A glimpse into the jenji's empty eyes made Calindor's tongue thicken; he tried to recall the words of the Sending, and could not. The jenji's gaze swept over him like a winter wind at midnight. Then something flickered in those eyes, a glint perhaps of recognition and even amusement.

It remembers me, Calindor thought.

Now the jenji entered the battle, ignoring the beleaguered Nerkesar and stepping lightly as a dancer through the ranks of the invaders. He seemed never to hurry, but no warrior was quick enough to oppose him; the jenji's fine, slender sword swept and thrust, and warriors fell dying.

Smiling, the jenji fought its way toward Albohar and Calindor. The Aryo seemed not to recognize what it was, or to care; his lips skinned back from his teeth, and his sword came up. Calindor glanced at Albohar and despaired: the Aryo himself had caused this jenji to possess Parsur, yet he prepared for battle as if with a human foe.

"Halt!" Calindor cried. His voice was no more than a rasping whisper. The jenji ignored him. Calindor raised the staff of Tenglekur, feeling its Powers writhe under his fingers. "I command you to halt!"

Another Aishadan warrior, blood spurting from an eye, fell to a quick thrust from the jenji. The jenji was close now. Calindor swung the staff like a battlepole and felt a shock of agony from his hands to his throat as the staff struck the jenji's shoulder. But the jenji paused; its dead eyes met Calindor's.

At last the words of the Sending came back to his mind, and Calindor uttered them with slow precision. The jenji half-smiled, and began to step forward; then it paused. Its features seemed to tremble. Calindor kept on with the spell, feeling a strange pressure from the jenji as it resisted what it did not want to resist.

Albohar roared and lunged forward, sword extended. The jenji parried and riposted—clumsily, yet accurately enough. The tip of its sword pierced the chain mail under the Aryo's ribs. Albohar gasped and recoiled; the jenji did not follow up.

"Now I command you to return!" Calindor shouted. The jenji hesitated, still half-smiling, and shook its head. Calindor felt the magic raging through him, and knew it was not enough to free the jenji. But it was enough to slow the creature's reflexes.

With a wordless snarl he cast down the staff and drew his sword. The jenji raised its own sword with dreamy slowness; Calindor knocked it aside and slashed at his enemy's neck. The blade struck with the strength of muscle and magic combined.

The jenji's head tumbled in a gush of blood to the pavement, while the body swayed and then fell back. Calindor watched the head roll slowly over, its eyelids blinking and lips twitching.

Then the dead eyes looked up and met his, and the jenji's mouth smiled. The lips moved in silent words that Calindor could read:

We will meet again, you and I.

Calindor stepped back; dizziness swept him as the magic ceased its roaring thrust through him. Blood trickled down his sword and dripped on the flagstones.

One of the younger upermannar took up Parsur's head by the hair and sauntered down a staircase with it. Calindor, from the edge of the terrace, watched the warrior unbolt a door and leave the Kes. In a narrow lane below the terrace a cluster of Nerkesar warriors burst around a corner and, seeing a lone enemy before them, charged.

The warrior held up Parsur's head and shook it at them.

"Come and honor your Aryo!" he bawled. His attackers paused, cried out, and turned away.

Calindor leaned wearily against the battlement. Had anyone brandished that head at him, he too might have fled screaming. He half-envied the young warrior's stupid courage.

"Look to the Aryo," he said. Albohar had sagged onto a stone bench, holding one hand to his wounded chest. His face had gone gray. Snegh was already at Albohar's side, murmuring in his ear.

"He says it's nothing, a scratch," Snegh said as Calindor approached. But his eyes met Calindor's with a different message.

"Be on my feet in a moment," Albohar whispered. "Someone get me water, or better still wine."

Calindor squatted before him, watching the Sterkar move restlessly within the Aryo's body. Gently but firmly he pulled Albohar's hand away and then rolled the mail shirt above the wound.

The wound was scarcely visible, a thin slit between two ribs, but Calindor saw a terrible magic at work within it. This was not something his healing spells could touch; he suspected the jenji had put much of its own power into the sword. *And what could I have done to the jenji if it had kept its powers intact?*

"Bear him inside," Calindor said. "Find a bed, and water. Give him no wine."

"No wine? What fool's medicine is this?" Albohar demanded.

Calindor gripped the older man's shoulders and looked into his eyes. Something almost like madness looked back, but it had nothing of magic about it.

"You went into the tunnel without waiting for me," he said softly to the Aryo. "You attacked the deivushibi as if it were just another warrior. Aryo, you cannot play with your life and kingdom like that."

Albohar grinned and wheezed. ". . . Sound like my father's old advisers, and your beard's not yet grown."

Other men took up the Aryo and bore him into the chamber that had been Parsur's. Albohar groaned as they gently lowered him to the bed. His eyes seemed to lose focus.

Snegh drew Calindor aside. "Something's wrong with that wound, boy."

"The deivushibi's sword was ensorcelled. My father has been grievously hurt, but not mortally."

"Ah, that's good to hear. What can you do? How soon can you have him back on his feet?"

Calindor shook his head. "I don't know. It will take a long time. Pelshadan may know better than I how to cure it."

"Ah, Pelshadan, who called the deivushibi down on Parsur in the first place," Snegh said bitterly. "I worried about it, but your father wouldn't listen."

Calindor said nothing, but watched Albohar pant and sweat.

Eskel, impatient, had entered the tunnel and emerged into the bedchamber with his escort at his heels. The prince looked briefly surprised to see his father wounded; then his features settled into impassivity while Snegh explained what had happened.

"Snegh, see that the Kes is taken quickly," he commanded. "I don't think we need to worry about a counterattack—Vulkvo has the upper hand. When the Nerkesar fall back toward the Kes, have some men ready to stop them as they come close to the fortress walls."

"Yes," Snegh answered. Calindor noted how quickly the

prince had taken over, and how readily even senior commanders accepted him.

"And see to it that no one starts any fires," Eskel went on. "Not our men, and not the Nerkesar. This city is too valuable to throw away."

He seemed to notice Calindor for the first time. "Well, it wasn't quite the painless victory you promised us, Dheribi."

"No victory is painless, Prince."

"Will my father recover?"

Calindor glanced at the Aryo, who had fallen into a shallow doze. "I hope so. But Pelshadan should look after him."

"Pelshadan's a magician, not a healer."

"The Aryo's wound is ensorcelled. Pelshadan may know how to lift the spell."

"Mm. Can my father be moved?"

"Yes."

"Then see to it."

The sack of Ner Kes continued as five squadrons left at dawn the next day. They were the escort for a small caravan of wagons bearing Albohar and his attendants. Calindor and Svordo rode beside the Aryo's wagon, ignoring the drizzle that fell from a gray sky. Behind them the air over the city looked oddly clear thanks to Eskel's order that all fires be extinguished.

As they passed the meadows behind the siege line, Calindor saw the horses of Aishadan feeding on great stacks of hay taken from the barns of the slain Aryo and his upermannar. The horses would eat well until it was time for their masters to take them home, he reflected, and the wiser upermannar would ensure that part of their booty was simple fodder. But by winter any remaining livestock in Ner Kes would surely be dead—slaughtered before starvation made them not worth butchering. The city would be a long time recovering.

For the Badakhar in Ner Kes it would be tolerable: the upermannar and freemen had sworn new vows to Albohar, in effect becoming subjects of Aishadan. Within their estates and workshops they would be as free as ever, if poorer. For the Cantarean slaves, Calindor knew, the peace would be one of sharper hunger and harder toil.

The squadrons moved no faster than the Aryo's wagons, but they rarely paused. Calindor stayed close to Albohar, sometimes in the wagon, sometimes riding beside it. At night he changed the dressings on the wound, and applied a poultice of three herbs the Protector had told him about. Albohar was drowsy, and could not be roused to full awareness, but seemed comfortable.

As they sat beside a campfire that night, Svordo murmured to Calindor: "Have you noticed how the warriors stare at you?"

"No. Wait, yes. And they speak very politely."

"They're afraid of you, a little. I heard some say the war would have been lost without you."

"Nonsense."

"They say their horses' fodder would have lasted only a few more days. Some think we have a big escort to get rid of mouths to feed, even with all the plunder of Ner Kes."

Calindor said nothing, but realized it was true. Albohar had gambled on a quick invasion and victory, and had nearly lost. Perhaps Ghelasha and Eskel would now have to leave him and Tilcalli in peace. And perhaps he could even use his new prestige to do something to improve the lives of the slaves in Aishadan. The thought cheered him as he curled up in his cloak and went to sleep.

Next day the party paused at the waystation where Demazakh commanded. The old trainer was there, already aware of how the battle had gone, and full of concern for his Aryo. Calindor and Svordo stayed in the background, letting the squadron commanders bark orders and make plans. They wandered into the cabin where Demazakh had fed them just a few days before, and found various men—free craftsmen and traders—sitting about with tankards of beer.

"Damn me if it isn't Dherhar!" rasped a familiar voice. "And Svordo too!"

Calindor turned his head and saw Sveit, hunched over the table with a half-empty tankard in front of him. The slave trader looked gaunt and pale; his face seemed to have sagged. Calindor needed only one look to see that Sveit's stomach cancer was far advanced.

"Come and join us, young warrior," Sveit invited, lifting his tankard with a shaking hand. "I hope you bear me no ill will for my part in the Aryo's plans."

"None." Calindor sat down on a bench opposite, while the others eagerly eavesdropped. "But how did you know of his plans?"

"Ah, only this day have I learned. I bought you in good faith as just another house slave gone bad. But when they talked of how a young warrior was whipped and enslaved so that he might spy out the defenses of Ner Kes, I thought at once of you. You were no ordinary house slave, were you?'' He laughed and then winced. ''If I drink more of this filthy northern excuse for beer, my guts will punish me worse than ever. This stuff makes me shit blood.'' But he lifted the tankard to his lips.

Calindor marveled at how simple the slave trader's disease seemed, compared to Albohar's wound. ''Come here, Sveit, and stand beside me.''

''As you wish.'' Grunting, he pushed himself upright and sidled round the end of the table. Calindor put his hands on Sveit's tunic, a finely made but dirty example of good Kormannalendh weaving. The flesh beneath it was thin on the bones, except for a slight pot belly: the cancer itself, swelling rapidly.

Calindor murmured a healing spell, and felt the Sterkar within Sveit's flesh take on new energy and balance. Another phrase stopped the pain.

''What have you done to me?'' Sveit's voice was soft and hoarse. His eyes were wide with surprise.

''You have a tumor in your stomach. Now it will shrink and disappear.''

''How—a tumor—''

''It would soon have killed you.''

''I must repay you, magician. The pain is gone!'' Sveit clutched Calindor's hands, while the other traders and freemen gawked. ''How can I repay you?''

Calindor freed himself from the man's grip. ''Stop trading in slaves. That is payment enough for me.''

Sveit looked appalled; Calindor could almost read the man's warring thoughts as he sought an escape from his promise. Then Sveit shrugged and shook his head, smiling. ''Let Mekhpur hear me, you drive as hard a bargain as the pimps of Halamor. What am I to do with the six lads with me now, if I can't sell them?''

''Give them to me.''

Sveit's eyes met Calindor's, and then looked down. ''A hard bargain indeed.'' He swigged again from his tankard. ''Actually, this beer isn't bad at all. Well, then, it's done. The lads are yours, and may you get more work out of them than I ever could.''

Thirteen

"Men laugh at magicians for wanting only to learn more magic," Calindor said to Svordo the night before they were due to arrive in Aishadan. "Perhaps we deserve it. But when you see how it works, what it can do, the beauty of it—when you can feel it running through you—"

They were sitting at a small campfire, a little apart from the guards around the Aryo's wagon but close enough to respond if Albohar were to call. Calindor watched the Pursterkar, the Powers of Fire, dancing joyfully in the flames.

"You begin to forget everything else," he went on. He gripped the staff of Tenglekur, which rested on his crossed legs. "I can feel the Powers in this staff, but I cannot make them do my bidding. And I yearn to."

"What would you have the Powers do?" Svordo asked.

"Win back Cantarea." Calindor laughed softly. "But I must keep reminding myself of that. It would be almost enough simply to learn what it is in this staff. And then to learn something more."

Next day they rode through country that seemed as scorched and bare as Ner Kes. Listless slaves were harvesting hay and barley and wheat, though the land yielded little. Cattle and sheep were few and closely guarded by armed herders. Along the creek beds, bands of freemen huddled in lean-tos in clouds of flies. In normal times they would be working for their local upermannar; now they had no work, and sent their scrawny children up to beg food from the cavalry. The only people who looked well fed were the estate guards who patrolled the fields and orchards.

"I wonder what the Aryo would say if he could see this,"

Svordo mumbled as they passed yet another settlement of homeless freemen.

"He would plan another war," Calindor said.

That afternoon, while thunderstorms growled on the horizon, the Aryo and his guards entered Aishadan. Ghelasha had sent word that he was to be brought directly to the Arekaryo Kes, where Pelshadan would be waiting.

No triumph had been arranged, but the quickest route from the Ner Kes road led through the freemen's town and the walled town; the streets were crowded with women, old men and children, and with slaves. The arekakhar prowled along the gutters, swinging their bludgeons and occasionally clubbing someone who stepped off the sidewalks.

Calindor, riding beside the Aryo's wagon, enjoyed the familiar stink of the city. But he watched the crowds with surprise that soon turned to alarm.

The two squadrons riding as the vanguard enjoyed ragged cheers from the freemen and even from the slaves. But as the Aryo's wagon rolled by, the crowds fell silent. None looked long at the wagon; the bystanders looked instead at Calindor. He heard them murmur: *Dheribi, the magician, the Aryo's bastard, the one who slew the deivushibi, whipped and enslaved, the magician.*

Sooner than offend the Aishadanar with the sight of a slave on horseback, Svordo had dismounted; he walked beside Calindor along with the six young slaves Sveit had given up. Hearing the crowds, Svordo muttered: "You're a hero, my lord."

"Hush." Calindor saw no hero worship in the eyes of the Badakhar, only curiosity and contempt and a little fear. He was still an oddity to them, a slave on horseback as the old saying held. And in the eyes of the Cantarean slaves he saw wariness: they must see him as only another kind of arekakh, a slave with too much power. Freemen and slaves alike looked gaunt and shabby, more concerned with their bellies than the troubles of royalty.

At the South Gate of the Kes the vanguard squadrons halted; the Aryo's wagon carried on, with a small retinue of riders including Calindor and Svordo. Hooves and ironshod wheels rang and clattered on the cobblestones of the main courtyard, where Ghelasha stood waiting in a plain white gown. Slaves stood behind her. At her command they hastened forward to bear the Aryo indoors. She followed close behind.

Calindor dismounted; Svordo took the horse's reins.

"I'll find the stables," he said. "And a bed and meal for all these fellows." He tilted his head toward the six slaves, who were clearly upset to be so close to the rulers of Aishadan. "Perhaps even a proper bed, when I let people know who our master is. You had better look to the Aryo."

"If the Aryasha permits me," Calindor answered quietly. Ghelasha had given him neither look nor word.

He walked into the Kes, imagining the familiar corridors, and halted. The sense of a malign presence was strong, stronger than that time months ago when he had felt it first. For a moment he hesitated, then strode ahead past the guards.

The halls echoed with the keening of slaves as they saw their master borne unconscious through the Kes. Calindor followed, certain that Ghelasha would want the Aryo in her apartment.

Her guards barred him at the doorway, but the door was open and Pelshadan stood close inside. The Veik growled an order and the guards stepped away.

The wide apartment was crowded with Ghelasha's slaves and attendants, as well as several magicians and warriors. Pelshadan drew Calindor into a corner, away from the noisy crowd around the Aryo's bed.

"I am glad to see you, Dheribi. News of your successes has preceded you."

"I only wish I had kept the deivushibi from wounding the Aryo."

Pelshadan's grizzled face was unreadable. "An ensorcelled wound, Ghelasha tells me."

Briefly, in a murmur, Calindor described the battle on the terrace and the wounding of Albohar. Pelshadan listened intently, one magician learning from another.

"It sounds bad," he said at last. "But let us examine the Aryo and see what may be done." He guided Calindor to Ghelasha's side.

"My lady—with your gracious permission, we would examine our master's wound."

Her beautiful face, framed in thick yellow tresses, was a mask of cold wrath that seemed to Calindor to be aimed at the world in general. She glanced briefly at him and then stepped aside.

"All of you get back," she commanded the others in the chamber. "Give the magician room."

Pelshadan and Calindor bowed, ignoring the insult of her use of the singular noun. Then they turned to Albohar. Speaking softly, Calindor summarized the Aryo's condition during the eight days' journey from Ner Kes.

"You tried no healing spells?"

"I know none that would work against a spell such as this, Veik."

"Yet you supposedly healed a man of a stomach cancer."

How had the magician heard about Sveit so quickly? "That was a simple matter compared to this."

Calindor gently lifted the dressing and poultice from the Aryo's chest, and pointed to the discolored flesh around the wound.

"You see the reddish bruising, and the white discharge from the wound. They are the signs of a direct contact between human flesh and metal under a powerful spell."

"Indeed? Who taught you that?"

". . . A teacher."

Pelshadan looked sardonically at him, and seemed suddenly to notice Calindor's staff. "Tenglekur. You studied under the Veik of Ner Kes."

"I saw him die," Calindor answered carefully. "But he did not teach me the proper use of his staff."

"Remarkable! When we have more time, you must tell me how you came to be his pupil!" Smiling, Pelshadan reached into a small leather pouch hanging from his belt, and drew out a bronze container no larger than his thumb. Removing its lid, he took up a pinch of brown powder.

"Your first lesson begins," the Veik murmured. "This is demonsbane." He rubbed thumb and forefinger over the Aryo's wound, letting the powder sift down. A musky scent filled the air. Pelshadan frowned and placed his hand lightly over the wound. Involuntarily, he gasped, snatching his hand away.

Calindor put his own hand over the Aryo's chest; it felt as it had for days, hot and infested with dangerous Sterkar.

"I think you sense the Powers in the wound, Veik. I am sorry; I should have warned you."

"You did, Dheribi, you did. I did not take you seriously enough. Demonsbane is useless against a spell this strong. Well, well. My lady—"

Ghelasha had been standing well within earshot. Now she stepped forward, hands clasped over her midriff.

"I must speak with you in private, if I may."

She turned and brusquely waved the bystanders out of the room. When the last had gone she faced Pelshadan.

"The Aryo's condition is much more serious than I had imagined. Dealing with it will take weeks if not months, and we will have little energy left for any other exercise of magic."

Ghelasha's eyes did not blink, but they narrowed. "You said dealing with it, not curing it."

"My lady, you heard me well. I can promise no cure though I may hope for one. For now we must simply learn the depth and nature of the spell in the Aryo's wound, and do all we can to weaken it. I must tell you that without Dheribi I would have little hope at all."

She looked at Calindor, her lips twisted in distaste. "Because he is a greater magician than yourself?"

The Veik fiddled with a strand of his hair, his eyes fixed on the Aryo. "In a sense, yes, my lady. He has much to learn, true, but we know of his power. He is a magician who . . . does not tire. We may well need to cast spell after spell to heal your lord of his wound—and neither I nor my other apprentices could do so."

"I will believe what I see. Do whatever must be done, Veik."

Pelshadan was suddenly all business. "Then we shall need this apartment and two adjoining rooms on either side as quarters. No, four rooms on either side—I must move my whole household here. We shall need access to the Aryo at all times, and the power to bar all others from this room if needed."

"Including myself and the Aryibi?" Ghelasha shot back.

"Obviously, my lady, you and your son may visit our lord when you please. But at some times even you would serve our lord best by remaining outside this chamber."

Calindor wondered about Ghelasha's mention of Eskel. The prince was still in Ner Kes; did she expect him back soon? It would make sense if he did return: the kingdom was in an uneasy state while the Aryo lay ill. Now that the war was over, the upermannar would soon return to quarreling among themselves over water rights, strayed livestock, the ownership of slaves. The freemen's town would seethe with unrest as tradesmen and artisans faced a hard winter with little work, and the slaves in the mines and fields would bear still greater burdens. With the Aryo unable to rule, Aishadan needed a regent; Eskel was old enough to take the post.

But Eskel in power would be a deadly menace, Calindor reflected. The prince and his mother had long resented both him and Tilcalli, and might well seize the opportunity to rid themselves of two upstart slaves.

Glancing at Ghelasha, Calindor thought he sensed the true source of her anger: through Albohar and his skills she had exerted great power, but Eskel was still untried and doubtful. She could govern him, no doubt, but could he govern Aishadan?

He spent the afternoon listening to Pelshadan discourse on the greater and lesser spells of healing—interesting, he thought, though useless against Albohar's condition. The various attendants and slaves were gone, and Ghelasha herself had retired to other chambers.

An uneasy peace lay over the Kes; Calindor sensed it, but was not reassured by it. The halls and courtyards were too quiet, and it was a relief when a thunderstorm broke over the city just before sunset. Amid the crash and glare, he heard the scuffle of footsteps in the corridor: Pelshadan's household had arrived.

"Veik, may I go to see my mother?"

Looking annoyed at being interrupted, Pelshadan nodded. Calindor hurried out.

Slaves in the next room were making up beds and setting up a table. Tilcalli and Bherasha worked with them, their robes still dripping water from the storm they had just escaped.

"I greet you, Mother."

Turning, she saw Calindor in the doorway and ran to him, smiling. She looked older, he thought, and smaller, but her eyes were as bright as always, and her smile as sweet.

"You're well," she murmured, urgently hugging him. Then she turned to the other slaves. "All of you—leave us for a time. Bherasha, wait in the corridor to see if the Veik wishes anything." Tilcalli drew her son to a chair. "Come, sit with me a moment."

They sat companionably together, interrupted only when a slave brought a bowl of stew and a flagon of beer. Calindor thought it was like the old days, like the evening when he had shared dinner with her before going to meet Blaidakh. They spoke in Cantarean, as softly as two slaves fearing to be overheard. She listened to his tale, asking a question now and then. When he had finished, Tilcalli nodded.

"So the Gulyaji still have some magic. They were old rivals of ours, the Sanpala clan, and they kept their secrets well. They have given you great gifts and honor, Dheribi."

"They gave me a new name also."

Her face hardened. "*I* was to give you your deep name. This Protector of the Gulyaji presumed too much."

"It is—"

Her fingers were on his lips. "Do not say it in this place."

"You feel it also?"

She nodded. "Enough of that. Whatever they taught you, it was not enough. I have much to teach you, and little time."

Calindor's days were filled with close observation of the Aryo's condition and with memorization of Pelshadan's lore. At night he sat with his mother, learning the spells of the Siragi Aibela. She taught him the methods of entrancement that should take him into the Open Dream, but he could not reach it.

"Something in you holds you here," she told him. "It broke when they flogged you, but it has healed itself again. Sometimes it happens."

"Can it be overcome?" he asked.

"My great-grandmother thinks the pain freed you before. Perhaps you will need to suffer again."

"Perhaps," he said, and spoke of other things.

In return for her lessons he taught her Burrowers' magic.

"They are like another branch of the same tree," Tilcalli said one night when the candles had burned low and the Kes was silent. "The Sanpala clan found their own way to strengthen Callia. But the Badakhar have a very different magic."

"I begin to see how different," he answered. "Pelshadan is a good teacher, but his magic bothers me. It is all force and leverage. The spells work, but they make me feel—uncomfortable. Unhappy with myself."

"Are you learning anything that you might use for Callia?"

He shook his head. "Some counterspells, but little else. So much of it is destructive. Spells to bring storms and floods, spells to spark fires, spells to . . ." He had been about to say, "spells to invoke jenji," but held his tongue.

Tilcalli picked up a candle stub to light her way to the room she shared with Bherasha across the hall.

"At some point you will see the principle of their magic," she said. "Then you will be able to devise new spells of your own, to ward off those of the Veikar."

"Could I devise a Sending for them?" he said sardonically.

She surprised him: "Perhaps. I do not think they belong in this world, any more than that creature you fought in the caves. Their magic itself tells me that, and the harm they do to Callia. But if you hope to gain full knowledge of our magic, you must go into the Open Dream again."

He remembered the vision of that silent, beautiful land, of his mother and the old woman and the man who walked away from them. And he remembered the bite of the whip.

The next day Pelshadan took the staff of Tenglekur in his hands. His fingers stroked its dark, smooth surface; his eyes looked deep into it.

"Great Powers indeed," he muttered. "Some have been contained here for centuries. Ah, they are beautiful. Here, Dheribi." Reluctantly he handed back the staff. "These are the Invocations you must use to gain control over them." Pelshadan took up a quill pen and a sheet of vellum. Quickly but carefully he wrote a long passage in Badakhi. "Speak the Invocations only when you have need of the Sterkar," he said. "This unlocks them. Next must come the right Commandment, or they will turn on you."

Calindor studied the phrases, feeling their power. He glanced at Pelshadan's own staff, which leaned against a wall far from the Aryo's bed. "And is this how you unlock your own staff?"

"The Invocations are different; the principle is the same. But my staff was enchanted long ago by the Veik Khausipas. He devised it so that its owner might never hold it. That is why it rests here. Minukhi put it against the wall."

"And you may never hold it, Veik?"

The magician looked away, and Calindor saw a ripple of distrust in the magician's eyes. *He doesn't want to teach me everything. He doesn't want me to hold an advantage over him.*

Like his teacher he rubbed the staff of Tenglekur, rehearsing the phrases of the Invocations and the Commandments. They would enable him to create a protective aura, to hurl fire and ward against it, to summon storms and demons.

The pleasure of knowing how was not quite as great as he had imagined. The Sterkar sensed his knowledge and clustered within the wood under his hands. Calindor's skin prickled with heightened awareness, and with that came sharper knowledge of the presence within Arekaryo Kes. It rested, tranquil and aware, and it waited.

After three days' attendance on Albohar, Calindor gained the Veik's permission to leave the fortress for a few hours. Though the fall was well advanced, this day was warm and sunny—a dragon's-wind day, the slaves called it, though the true dragon's wind of winter was still weeks away.

"Come with me?" he asked Tilcalli, who sat mending Pelshadan's winter leggings. "Let us go for a walk and enjoy the sun."

"Very well. Bherasha, you come with us. You haven't been outside this gloomy place in days."

Bherasha put down her own sewing. "Yes, my lady. I shall be glad to."

They walked together through the Kes, past the little compound where Tilcalli and he had lived for years, and out a narrow gate into the walled town. Others were out enjoying the sunny morning as well, crowding the streets and market squares.

"For once they have grain enough," Bherasha said as they walked past Fountain Market. To Calindor she seemed oddly alert, her dark eyes restlessly sweeping the crowds.

"The plunder of Ner Kes," he said with a faint smile. "At least the war has bought us an easier winter."

"Not the Cantareans," his mother murmured. He nodded.

They walked north, beyond the walled town and the freemen's quarter until the houses thinned out and open fields lay yellow under the sun. Tilcalli said little; Calindor would have liked to talk with Bherasha, but felt shy and awkward. What could you say to a tall and comely young woman for whom you had killed a man? In any case, she seemed more interested in the late-blooming flowers beside the path, and the honking geese flying south.

"I have much to tell you that I did not want to say within the Aryo's walls," Tilcalli said after a long silence. She sat on a boulder facing the sun. Calindor squatted opposite her, while Bherasha knelt in the yellow grass at Tilcalli's feet. The sun was warm, the breeze cool.

"Pelshadan knows I am a witch," she said. Calindor felt dizzy: her words threw a shadow no sunlight could dispel. "Some other Veik sent a flying demon to attack him, and I sent it away. He knew it must have been I who had done it, and he struck a bargain with me. That he would teach you his skills if I would teach him mine."

"You have taught him the spells of the Siragi Aibela?" Calindor's voice was no louder than the breeze in the dead grass.

"Some. Not as much as you have learned, and he rejects much of what I tell him. You said his magic is all force and leverage, and you were right. He does not understand any other kind."

"But you are in terrible danger."

She nodded and then, unexpectedly, laughed. "I have been

in terrible danger ever since Albohar came raiding up the river and I cast a spell on him. Pelshadan is dangerous, yes, but so are all of them.''

"Someone tried to stab my lady in the market," Bherasha said. "While you were away at the war."

"What?"

"Ghelasha," Tilcalli said. "I don't think she will try again, not while the Aryo lies ill."

"Not while I'm here," Bherasha said angrily, and Calindor understood her vigilance in the Fountain Market.

"It's not important," Tilcalli said, touching Bherasha's shoulder and smiling. "The important thing is that you know how dangerous Pelshadan may be. He says he wants only more knowledge of magic, but I do not trust him. When he thinks he knows all he can learn from me, he will turn on us. You must be prepared for that."

"I will try to be. But what must I do when Pelshadan is not a danger? You told me I was to make the Cantareans strong again, so that Callia would be strong and even the Badakhar would walk in beauty. How am I to do this?"

Her eyes met his. "I do not know, Dheribi. I only hope."

"Hope? Has this all been a gamble?" He stood up suddenly, fists clenched at his sides. "You wanted a magician who would know both our spells and theirs, so you let yourself be enslaved. Now I am learning what you wanted, yet you *hope* it will help Callia, you *hope* it will help Cantarea?"

She sat submissively beneath his anger, eyes downcast. Then she looked up. "Your great-great-grandmother, Calihalingol, had a dream before she died. She dreamt that Callia had fallen asleep, and was herself tormented by bad dreams. After a long time a son of the Siragi Aibela came and sat beside her, with the robes of a magician and a Badakh sword at his belt. He tried to rouse her, but failed. Then Badakhar warriors came, and attacked the magician. He feared he would die, and cried out to Callia. She woke at last and rescued him.

"All her life Calihalingol thought about that dream. When she died she did not forget it, but waited. When I was a girl, the first time I went into the Open Dream she greeted me and told me what she wished me to do. And I did it."

"So I am to save Callia, and Callia is to save me. And that is what a ghost wishes."

Her eyes looked up and met his. "No. That is what Callia wishes."

Surly and grim, Calindor walked with them back into the city. People on the street recognized him and saw his anger; they stepped hurriedly out of his way. Tilcalli and Bherasha followed close behind, saying nothing.

They climbed the hill toward the Kes. A squad of arekakhar suddenly poured into the street, ordering horsecarts into the alleys and shoving pedestrians onto the sidewalks. Calindor paused and turned to make sure that Tilcalli and Bherasha were close by and out of reach of the arekakhar's clubs. Down the hill, cheering and chanting broke out.

"What is it?" Bherasha asked.

The chanting grew louder, a cry of welcome: *"Eskel! Eskel! Eskel!"*

Fourteen

The Arekaryo Kes, which had seemed hushed since the return of Albohar, was now busy again. Couriers rode out, bearing messages to the upermannar: Eskel was calling a Great Gathering for the first day of Eleventh Month, just three weeks away.

"Of course," Pelshadan said when a servant brought the news. He was sitting comfortably beside the sleeping Aryo. Calindor sat nearby, with one of the Veik's books on his lap. The autumn day was fine and clear, and late-morning sunshine gleamed through the little glass panes of the windows.

"Of course," Pelshadan said again when the servant had left. "He must make himself Aryako, regent of the kingdom, or we will not get through the next year."

"How is that, Veik?"

Pelshadan's pale eyes seemed focused far beyond the windows. Two fingers twirled a strand of white hair. "We've upset the balance. We weren't supposed to conquer Ner Kes, only defeat Parsur, gain some tribute and weaken him. Then the Aryo dreamed of taking the whole kingdom over, and he succeeded—more thanks to you than to me. Now the other kingdoms are rightly alarmed. Ghrirei and Halamor will soon patch up their quarrel and look for a pretext to attack us next spring. Kormannalendh may join them. Rumors have it that the harvests are bad in all the kingdoms, so our enemies will have all the more reason to make war on us. If we don't have a strong ruler, they'll do to us what we did to the Nerkesar."

He sighed. "The first plan was much simpler. Build up the army with plunder from Ner Kes. Make Ghrirei an ally, then pick off Halamor and Kormannalendh in a quick campaign next summer. Now Ghrirei must see us only as an enemy."

"But the Aryasha is from Ghrirei, Veik."

" 'Your daughter in your enemy's tent is your enemy,' " Pelshadan quoted. "Well, it can't be helped, and Eskel is wise to act quickly."

He stood up, smacking his lips, and inspected the Aryo's wound. Albohar slept; he rarely woke, and then only to sip a little water or broth. He had not spoken since Ner Kes.

Calindor returned to his book, but his thoughts were of Eskel. The Aryibi was intelligent. If he was already preparing to battle his foreign enemies, he must also plan to eliminate his domestic ones. And his mother, Ghelasha, would help him in those plans.

He put the book down. "May I leave for a while, Veik?"

"If you like. I sense no change in him."

Calindor strode through the fortress's corridors with a warrior's quick step, ignoring Pelshadan's endless reminders about the slow pace that should reflect a magician's dignity. In the stables he found Svordo busying himself with the horses. Gheli, Calindor's favorite from the old days, nuzzled him and took an apple from his hand.

"Come out with me into the paddock," Calindor said. He brought Gheli from her stable and led her into the sunshine. No one else was exercising horses at the moment. Calindor kept the mare on a long rein and started her trotting in circles around him and Svordo.

"When you came into the stable I thought the Aryo had died," Svordo said. "You looked that grim. Then I thought, no, if the Aryo's dead then you'd have brought your mother and we'd have saddled up to make a run for it."

Calindor laughed, cheered by both Gheli's grace and Svordo's company. "Not quite that bad. But Eskel's calling a Mod, and once he has the power of the Aryo he'll probably try to arrange an accident for me."

"So? Can't you arrange an accident for him first?"

"It's more than my own survival I'm thinking about. If Eskel dies, then the succession is wide open. I can think of five or six upermannar, Albohar's cousins, who might make a claim. A civil war would put us at the mercy of the other kingdoms. And the first to suffer would be the slaves."

"Then enchant Eskel so that he won't fear you."

"So you think me that powerful!" He had not told Svordo about the enchanting of Demazakh; in memory it now seemed almost dreamlike, an event too unlikely to have been real.

"Yes, I think you that powerful."

"To enchant another man's soul, you must stand close to him, mingle your breath with his. Eskel would never let me that close. Even if he did, his mother would have me slain in any case."

"So what should you do?"

"I think I must conquer Aishadan for myself."

Svordo gaped at him. "And how will you do that?"

Calindor watched the mare trot contentedly in the sunshine. "I will rally the slaves and revolt."

Svordo said nothing for a time. Then he said: "Have you been out of the Kes since you returned?"

"Only once, with my mother and Bherasha."

"Come with me tomorrow."

The solid-brown tunic and cloak of a senior apprentice magician had seemed natural within the Kes; in the narrow lanes of the walled town and the freemen's town, Calindor felt oddly self-conscious. He sensed the stares: the sidelong glances of the slaves, the cold contempt of the arekakhar, the gawking scrutiny of the Badakhar. People made way for him and Svordo, who trailed him like a properly obedient slave.

In the walled town, where the upermannar kept their city homes, each house presented the usual blank brick face to the street. Guards lounged in the barred gateways, but from behind the walls Calindor could hear the usual household noises—cooks squawking, stewards bellowing, and the occasional wail of a slave being beaten.

Farther down the hill in the freemen's town, the houses were smaller, usually built around three sides of a square with the open side facing the street. The courtyards were the freemen's places of business, where they forged armor, turned wooden shafts on simple lathes, threw pots, and wove wool. Here the slaves were more visible. Some shuffled along the streets under great sacks of coal or reeking piles of hides. But most sat apathetically in their masters' courtyards or doorways, as idle as their masters themselves.

Though it was well before noon, Calindor saw many Badakhar tradesmen drinking to pass the time. Those already drunk were roaring at their slaves, or beating them while grinning companions looked on. One smith had posted a slave, leaving him to dangle in the courtyard by a cold furnace. The slave, a boy of perhaps twelve or thirteen, was far gone: his tongue protruded, black and dry, and his swollen hands had turned purple above the iron cuffs. Flies crawled over him as they did over the sides of beef in the market.

The Badakhar in the street swaggered as they always had; Calindor recognized Ner Kes cloth on many a warrior and his wife. But the markets were strange, with booths offering gold and silver trinkets while the millers casually spilled as much flour as they sold. It was plunder from Ner Kes, he realized, and the Badakhar never prized anything won in battle or made by slaves.

Many townspeople wandered among the vendors, but few seemed ready to buy. Children swarmed from booth to booth, thin and quick and ready to steal whatever a vendor did not guard. They begged alms from passersby, and shoved their grubby hands at Calindor. He had nothing to give them; they moved on, cheerfully cursing him for a mad magician.

Perhaps I am, he reflected. The Cantareans he passed seemed passive, only half-awake; he sensed no anger in them, only anxiety about food and warmth and the whims of their masters. Perhaps the miners would be different. They at least worked on their own, deep in the tunnels where the Badakhar feared to go.

They walked farther east until they came to the slopes of Aishadan Hill. Here the slaves were still busy; coal was always needed, especially now when the nights grew cold. The Badakh guards looked curiously at the apprentice magician and his slave but did not stop them. Calindor led Svordo up a trail through the slag to the mouth of one of the shafts.

An overseer met them, nervously smacking his knout against the side of his leg.

"What may I do for you, magician?"

"My master, the Veik Pelshadan sent me. He wishes me to watch the slaves for a time."

The overseer shrugged, accepting the strange ways of magicians. "I'll ask you not to slow the slaves, or talk with them."

Calindor nodded. Without speaking further, he stood by the overseer while Svordo stationed himself a few steps behind.

The men, women and children who emerged from the shaft were gaunt and black, their legs and arms deeply scarred. Each bore a sack of coal, supported by a headstrap. Even the children's hair had been worn away by their straps. They squinted uncomfortably in the daylight after the gloom of the mine, and kept their eyes on the trail.

They walked in a cloud of dull sorrow, as visible to Calindor as the coal dust ground into their skins. Most bore oozing or bleeding wounds, and many had lost fingers or toes. He saw their hunger, their thirst and their fear. It made him shiver with recollection of the snowy morning of the Trame Mod when he had felt the bite of the whip.

But he sensed no anger, no bitterness. A child of ten lurched past, staggering under a load almost as big as herself, and Calindor felt her pride in carrying so much.

Now he himself felt a kind of dull sorrow, for he knew that these slaves would not revolt—not even if he filled the sky with magician's illusions. They had the power to bring Aishadan to its knees, if only they chose to barricade themselves in the mines and refuse to bring out any more coal. But they would do no such thing.

And why should they, he asked himself. He could not supply them with the food and water for a long siege; he could not ask them to starve so that others might be free.

He stayed for only a little while, then said farewell to the overseer and headed quickly down the hill with Svordo close behind.

"You knew what I would see," he muttered to Svordo when they were back in the streets of the freemen's town. Svordo said nothing, but smiled.

That night he lay not far from the Aryo, whose breath was quick and shallow. A fall rain hissed on the terrace not far below, and guards' boots splashed through puddles in the darkness.

Calindor lay on a hard plank bed, watching the Sterkar glide up and down the staff of Tenglekur.

A word, a phrase would free them to do his bidding. He could bring down lightning to shatter the slate roofs of the Kes, call up storms to lash this city as he himself had been lashed. Let the upermannar draw their swords against him; the swords would glow red-hot.

Power and leverage: Badakh magic was not gentle. But it worked. It had worked against the ancient magicians of the Siragi Aibela and the Sanpala in the days of the Slave Wars. For all their lore, they had been driven out of Cantarea like dry leaves in the wind. And the wind had sprung from the staffs and spells of the Veikar.

His mother, caught up in her own magic, had dreamed that some blend of the two would restore Callia. He respected her courage; she had risked her life for many years to see him become Pelshadan's apprentice. But she had been wrong. If Callia and her people were to walk in beauty across a green Cantarea once more, the Badakhar—at least their rulers—must fall.

The Sterkar glided and turned like fish in a tranquil pond.

He had learned enough to know how great his ignorance was. The Protector had taught him much but not everything he knew. And Pelshadan had given him only a glimpse of the power hidden in the spells of the Veikar. But Calindor could sense his own strength. He could call up power greater than any Veik could imagine, and go on without weariness. He was not Minukhi, to be exhausted by a couple of illusions.

The jenji had not expected him to use his sword. Pelshadan and Eskel and Ghelasha did not expect him to attack them single-handed. If he was careful, and chose his moment, he might well wrest back at least this bitter kingdom for the Menmannar and the Gulyaji.

Smiling, his hand curled around the staff, he fell asleep.

The six slaves whom Sveit had given to Calindor had turned out to be useful. They were all young men, tall and lean and toughened by outdoor work. Tilcalli had taken charge of them, and used them for housekeeping and running errands. At first they had been abashed at working and living within the apartments of the Aryasha, where Albohar still lay. Now they were accustomed to it, and moved through the halls of the Kes as easily as they had once wandered the meadows of their last master.

On a frosty morning, Tilcalli summoned the oldest of them. His name was Moro, a common slave name; it meant Fool, but she had seen at once the glint of good sense in his deep-set eyes.

"We need some herbs and spices from the Veik's house," she told him. "And the whole house will need a good sweeping and dusting—hardly anyone's been in it for weeks. Go with Bherasha this morning, help her clean the place, and return before dark."

"Yes, my lady." Moro glanced at Bherasha, who was already pulling on her dark-gray cloak. Tilcalli understood the look.

"Bherasha, find the boy a cloak as well. He'll freeze in that tunic alone."

"My lady is most kind," Moro said.

"Nonsense. I'm simply looking after my son's property."

Calindor looked in from the corridor. He was carrying a cup of mint tea that steamed in the chill air.

"Good morning, Dheribi," his mother said. "Please ask the Veik if he needs anything from his house. Bherasha and Moro are just leaving to do some tidying up there."

"I will ask him."

He took the tea to Albohar, who was dimly awake. The Aryo took a couple of sips, smiled vaguely, and dozed off. Pelshadan, his bald crown covered with a woolen skullcap, sat by the fire and twisted his fingers in his beard.

"From the house? I need nothing. But I can think of a book you should have. It is on the shelf by my bed, bound in yellow leather. It is called *On Deep Names*. Tell the slaves to bring it back—no. You should go yourself, and get the book yourself. Make sure they clean only the first and second floors, and that they do not go up to the third floor. Do you understand? No one is to go up to the third floor."

"Yes, Veik. I will be back before dark."

"See that you are."

Calindor was glad to be out of the Kes again. With the coming of cold weather it had become a dark and smelly warren, full of smoke and mold. Even Aishadan's narrow streets and slippery cobbles were better than the Kes's echoing corridors, and the wind from the north was clean as well as cold.

Bherasha and Moro walked behind him, keeping pace with his long strides and saying nothing. When they came to the narrow alley where Pelshadan's house stood, Bherasha drew a key from her beltpurse and unlocked the door.

"I've never been in here before," Calindor said. "When I was a boy I used to hear all kinds of tales about what a strange place it was."

"I have worked in stranger houses," Bherasha said. "Please wait until I've found my flint and steel and we'll have some light."

"Don't bother." Calindor let the door swing shut behind them, and called up coldfire. A disc of blue light, wider than a man's extended arms, shimmered against the ceiling. Moro gasped.

"It's all right, Moro," Bherasha said with a smile. "After all, the young master is a great magician."

"When we are alone, call me Dheribi. I am not your master."

She looked at him, meeting his eyes for the first time. "As you wish, Dheribi. Well—now to work. Moro, lay a fire in the kitchen. Then I'll need some water. We have this floor and the next one to clean."

"The Veik's chamber is upstairs?" Calindor asked.

"At the back." She hurried off into the kitchen. Calindor created another disc of coldfire in that little room, and she cheerfully called her thanks.

He smiled as he went up the narrow staircase. She was an intriguing young woman, accepting magic as just another fact of life—something that might help or hinder the practical business of cooking and cleaning. About magicians themselves she seemed equally matter-of-fact: their quirks and obsessions stirred neither fear nor contempt. He had seen, since his return to Aishadan, how much his mother relied on her to administer the impromptu household that had sprung up around the Aryo's bed.

The door to the Veik's chamber was shut but not locked. Calindor tested it, then pushed it slowly open. The air was chill and musty, the floor pale gray with dust on which mice had left their tiny footprints. He went to the window and drew aside the curtain, admitting a little light.

The room was lined with shelves and cabinets, but it did not take long to find the book Pelshadan had named. Calindor browsed a while through other books, finding odd bits of interest but nothing that might repay deeper study.

How trivially the Badakhar used their magic! A spell to turn an enemy's stomach sour. A spell to taint the meat of an enemy's livestock. A spell to enhance sexual potency in old men. A spell to ward off whore's pox, and another to conceal the genital scars if the first spell failed.

Yet they could also call down lightning and torrent, or dry up a roaring stream. They could bring demons out of the earth, or out of the deeps of the night sky. They could imprison a Pursterk in a blade of steel so that it would never rust or lose its killing edge.

And they used these powers too for trivial reasons: to decide which murderer should be Aryo, to decide which magician should be the murderer's chief assistant, to decide which of the murderer's friends and clansmen should enjoy the toil of the Cantareans who had once lived at peace in this land. They sought power for nothing good or great, only to deny it to others.

Putting back one of the Veik's books, he took up *On Deep Names* and left the room. Perhaps, while Bherasha and Moro cleaned the house he could find a quiet corner in which to read. He looked into the other rooms on the floor, recognizing his mother's at once by the residual aura.

One door he found by the spell that concealed it from ordinary eyes and made it seem only a bare wall. It was much like the spells the Gulyaji used to protect the entrances to the Underland. Anyone trying to open it would feel as if his hand had burst into flames. But it was not a difficult spell to counter, he knew: both the Protector and Pelshadan had taught him ways to do so. The Veik had warned him that no one was to go to the topmost floor, but he felt drawn by the intensity of the spells that shimmered up there.

The old man keeps enough secrets from me, Calindor thought. Let's see what he hides in his attic.

He broke the spell without difficulty and pushed the door open. Beyond it, a flight of stairs climbed to the right.

Calindor stepped through, turned, and began to climb the stairs. The darkness was intense, reminding him of the far caves of the Gulyaji. He called up coldfire on the palm of his left hand, and cast it in a pale-blue beam ahead of him.

The third floor was a single room under the roofbeams. Calindor stood in the middle, the only place where he need not crouch under the sloping ceiling, and swung his upraised hand from left to right. Nothing: only dust and cobwebs. He turned to examine the part of the room behind the stairs.

A face glared back at him, eyelids collapsed over empty sockets, lips skinned back over grinning teeth.

Calindor took an unwilled step back. He called forth more coldfire and saw that the face was that of a corpse: a young woman, naked and mummified, hanging from the roofbeam by a chain around her wrists. On the floor beneath her dangling feet, dust lay thin over a complex pattern of red and yellow swastikas and hexagons. Just below her left breast, the handle of a knife protruded. Very little blood had escaped the wound.

"Peace upon your soul," he murmured. "I give you rest."

He could sense the magic tightly bound into the pattern beneath the dead woman's feet. And he knew why she had died: to call a jenji from the Black World and send it to possess the Aryo Parsur Seggas of Ner Kes.

Calindor moved his hand, throwing the beam of coldfire beyond the dangling corpse. At the far end of the room, a row of similar mummies stood facing him. Their yellow, withered arms rose above their heads as if in greeting. Their faces gaped with unheard screams.

"And to all of you," he said hoarsely, "to all of you, peace."

Slowly he descended the stairs, leaving the corpses in darkness once more. He shut the door, restored its spell, and went into Pelshadan's room. For a time he stood at the window, looking over the little yard behind the house.

"There you are," Bherasha said. "Moro was up here a moment ago and said he couldn't find you. We're going to sweep and mop the floor, if it's no trouble to you."

"None."

She looked at him, suddenly concerned. "Are you well, Dheribi? You seem—"

"I am well. Only thinking about many things. I will go downstairs and await you there."

"We won't be long."

She smiled at him, and he felt his spirits lift a little. Bherasha's soul was strong within her, and lent strength to any who needed it. Today he felt very much in need of it.

Pelshadan was still the same: pale-eyed, fingers restlessly stroking his beard or twisting the white hair that grew around his bald scalp. But now Calindor saw those long-fingered hands differently, imagining them curled around the handle of the dagger as it sank deep into a slave woman's heart.

The two magicians sat as usual at the Aryo's side, listening to his rasping breath. Pelshadan recited a simple spell, one to keep disease away from the Aryo. Calindor committed it to memory as the Veik spoke, and then turned to *On Deep Names*. But he could not focus on the old-fashioned calligraphy.

The presence in the Kes was stronger. He could feel it, as he had felt the being in the far caves, but this was a greater, colder entity. It was waiting for something, and he did not want to challenge it.

Was it the jenji in another form? Again he saw Parsur's head, the lips writhing in that mocking promise. Perhaps—but he suspected it was more powerful than any jenji. It was everywhere and nowhere; in his errands around the Kes, he seemed neither to approach it nor escape it. Pelshadan seemed unaware of it, and Tilcalli would not let him even discuss it. Whatever the presence might be, she sensed it and feared it.

All the more reason, he decided, to strike soon—to bring down this citadel as he had brought down the wall of Ner Kes.

A new plan was growing in his mind. If anarchy broke out in Aishadan, the Cantarean slaves would be the first to suffer. But if he could destroy Eskel, Ghelasha, and enough of the upermannar, perhaps he could lead the Cantareans up the river into the safety of the Menmannar villages. In those endless mountains and forests, they could learn freedom again while he learned still more magic. Eventually he might lead a Cantarean army out onto the prairie, to overthrow the other kingdoms—

It was a comforting thought. He imagined the great cities and fortresses of the Badakhar falling like rotted trees, the Badakhar themselves fleeing eastward into the unknown lands from which they had come. And then the careful, loving restoration of Callia's green domain.

Pelshadan was staring at him. "Daydreaming? A magician daydreaming when he might be learning great magic? Dheribi, you amaze me."

"I'm sorry, Veik. I must think carefully about what I read."

The old man snorted amusedly and stretched himself out on a cot by the glowing coal fire. "You have all night to read. I will question you on it in the morning. Rouse me only if the Aryo seems distressed."

"Very well, Veik."

The room was quiet; Albohar's hoarse breath and Pelshadan's snores mingled with the rush of the wind outside. With a murmured invocation, Calindor created a disc of coldfire in his palm again, and by its light he resumed reading the book. As he persisted, the lore took hold of his imagination; the spells and enchantments sang in his mind. But at length he recalled how coldfire in his hand had illuminated the sightless horror in the face of the dead woman.

The dawn seemed long in coming.

Fifteen

Aishadan had felt frost for many nights, but not yet snow. On the day of the Mod, the Gathering Field was dry and dusty; the tents of the upermannar flapped in the morning breeze. Smoke from a hundred fires mingled with the dust. Slaves hurried to and from the riverbank with great leather buckets: the upermannar might drink beer or medh, but their hundreds of horses needed water.

Calindor stood beside Pelshadan's tent, not far from that of the Aryo. He watched as the upermannar gradually congregated in their accustomed places around the field. For some reason he remembered earlier Mods far better than the one last spring; the whipping seemed as much a dream as the vision that had followed it of Tilcalli and the old woman and the man beside the river.

Many of the upermannar's tents seemed new, cut from good fabric. Probably plunder from Ner Kes, Calindor thought. The lords and their families were finely dressed as well, strutting in new boots and soft buckskin coats lined with mink. The green cloaks of their rank were new, well-woven and bright. But their attendants were patched and ragged, and looked ill-fed; their slaves were gaunt and shivering in threadbare tunics.

He gripped the staff of Tenglekur, enjoying the movement of the Sterkar. Soon, soon, he promised them. I will free you soon, at least for a little time.

The sky was clear, the sun rising above the southeast horizon. He squinted at it and thought about how he would invoke lightning to strike among the upermannar. While they fell stunned or dying, he would rally the slaves, lead them over the bridge into the city, and destroy the garrisons. He would bring down the citadel after rescuing Tilcalli and the other slaves in the Kes.

Then, with lightning and floods guarding their rear, they would all march southwest up the river. At length they would come to the villages of the Menmannar, and find shelter there.

The Badakhar, left in the ruins of Aishadan, would be too busy surviving to try to recapture their slaves. Within days, the Aryos of Ghrirei and Halamor would invade and sack the kingdom. Let them enjoy what spoils they might; soon enough he would be back, with a Cantarean army and the magicians of the Siragi Aibela, to wrest all the prairie away from the Badakhar.

Like the working out of a complex spell, it would come to pass; that he knew, and the knowledge gave him a strange serenity. He glanced north, over the tents, to the squat turrets of the Arekaryo Kes across the river. It had been his home, but he would bring it down in fire and rejoice in the act. Perhaps he could bury also the presence that had been lurking there so long.

A herald, splendid in red cloak and white tunic and trousers, entered the Aryo's tent and soon emerged bearing a silver-headed spear.

"My lords!" he bellowed. "I ask the kindness of your silence. The son of our beloved Aryo, the Aryibi Eskel, conqueror of Ner Kes, has words for you. I ask the kindness of your silence."

Calindor clicked his tongue in contemptuous amusement. So Eskel was now conqueror of Ner Kes, when he had simply stood by the tunnel at his father's command.

The cheerful rumble of conversation died away. On the edge of the field, horses whinnied. Eskel stepped from the tent, dressed in a black leather cloak that fell almost to his knees. Beneath it he wore fine chain mail and baggy white trousers tucked into black boots. His moustache was almost invisible against his pale face, and his beard scarcely showed, but his red lips were as vivid as a woman's. Not far behind him was Ghelasha, dressed with plain elegance in a pale wool cloak over a dark gown.

Calindor turned and drew open the flap of Pelshadan's tent. "Veik—the Aryibi is about to speak."

"Very well." Pelshadan stepped out into the morning sunlight, his hood pulled up against the chill. Rather than look at Eskel he stared off into the distance, one hand nervously twirling a strand of hair. "I'll be glad when this is over. Once I've recovered from the purification, I have some new ideas about treating the Aryo—" He mumbled on while Eskel stepped forward and raised his hands.

"Let Mekhpur hear me! I declare this Gathering called!"

Eskel shouted. "Let the Veik purify this field and all who stand upon it."

Pelshadan stepped forward. Behind came Dvoi and Potiari, who had been at Ner Kes, and Calindor. Last came Bherasha, bearing Pelshadan's staff, and Minukhi, his endless tears gleaming upon his scarred face.

Calindor wondered at the staff: he recalled from other Gatherings that a slave was supposed to carry a censer, not the Veik's staff. Perhaps some minor change in the ceremony was needed for an unusual meeting like this.

The procession of magicians walked slowly around the edge of the field, while Pelshadan cast his spells of purification. The watching upermannar and warriors were hushed; Calindor felt their eyes on him, as fearful and contemptuous as on the day he had ridden back into Aishadan.

As Pelshadan circled the field he began to gasp and cough. By the time the procession returned to the Veik's tent he was exhausted. Bherasha and Minukhi wanted to carry him inside, but he insisted on sitting beneath the awning of the tent.

"This is important," he whispered. "I want to hear what he says."

His servants acquiesced, and stood close behind him.

Calindor turned to face Eskel. "My lord, the field is purified," he called out.

"I thank Pelshadan and through him our lord Mekhpur. This Gathering is well begun!" The upermannar and their warriors cheered again, brandishing their swords, while their women held their arms above their heads and cried out in shrill wails. "And now I again invoke the Firelord, that I may do justice in his honored name."

The prince had memorized all the ancient phrases, Calindor reflected. But how would he appeal for the status of Aryako? Aishadan had never known a regent, and few other Badakhar kingdoms had needed one. Probably Ghelasha had invented something, while negotiating quietly with the upermannar to ensure that they did not humiliate her son by rejecting him.

"My lords," Eskel shouted, "we are met in hard times. Our victory over Ner Kes was a great one, and we paid a great price. My father the Aryo lies ill and all the spells of the magicians have availed him nothing. We have gained plunder, and gifts for Mekhpur beyond counting. As my father intended, our Veik shall render these gifts to Mekhpur, and ask in exchange the blessing of land ever fertile, herds ever growing, and warriors ever victorious. We of Aishadan shall seek what Mekhpur has denied all others—rule over all the kingdoms of the prairie.''

The upermannar uttered a low roar of approval.

''And I shall beseech the Firelord for still greater gifts,'' Eskel went on. ''We shall rule as well over the mountains and forests of the Menmannar, and make them our slaves. We shall go west beyond the mountains, into the lands of the dragons, and exterminate them. We shall make this Trame Modatun, this Gathering Field, the center of the world!''

His listeners cheered again, and swords gleamed in the autumn sunshine.

''This was my father's dream, and mine. I think it is yours as well. If we are to honor Mekhpur as my father Albohar intended, someone must sit in his saddle until he recovers his strength. I ask that you make me Aryako, Regent of Aishadan, until that happy day.''

The upermannar and their warriors were silent. At last one stepped forward; Calindor recognized Aghwesi of Vidhumen, the father of Blaidakh, the old man who had demanded greater vengeance than Albohar had been prepared to grant.

''Aryibi!'' the old upermanna bellowed. ''We must now debate this request. I ask in all respect that you withdraw to your tent until we have decided how to respond.''

''I obey in all respect, honored cousin.'' Eskel turned and went inside the Aryo's tent, with his mother close behind.

Calindor stayed close to Pelshadan, watching the other magicians as they ministered to the old man. It was just as well that the Veik was exhausted from the purification; he would be unable to attempt a defense against Calindor's magic. Calindor thought of the dead slaves hanging in Pelshadan's house, and thought that it would not be hard to kill the man who had taught him so much.

The upermannar, meanwhile, had clustered around Aghwesi in little knots of debaters. The talk was lively, interrupted by hoarse laughter. Before long Aghwesi raised a hand for silence.

''Herald! Send for the Aryibi Eskel.'' The herald obeyed, though Eskel himself must surely have heard the command.

Calindor took a deep breath. *Focus*. This would be the moment when the evil dreams of Eskel, Aghwesi, and all their people would be cast down. Let Eskel savor that first moment of triumph, and then let him fall beneath lightning from a clear sky.

The prince stood bareheaded before the crowded upermannar, facing Aghwesi. The old man, still in mourning gray, stepped toward him. The scar on his forehead, where he had slashed himself after Blaidakh's death, was a bright red.

"We grant you your request, Aryibi, on certain conditions. First, that tribute to Mekhpur be rendered within three days."

"I accept."

"Second, that the upermannar select your councillors from among their wisest and most experienced."

"I accept."

"Thirdly, that the slave bastard Dheribi be seized and slain forthwith, along with his mother the witch Pelkhven."

All turned to look at Calindor, standing motionless by Pelshadan's tent. A roar of agreement went up; when it died away, Eskel's high voice rang out: "I accept this condition also."

Calindor laughed bitterly and raised the staff of Tenglekur. *Focus.* He shouted out the words Pelshadan had written for him, the spells that would free the Sterkar and bring down destruction on Aishadan. Even as he spoke, he felt the Sterkar leap and twist within the staff, sensing their freedom. And he felt magic pour through him, filling him with a terrible energy.

The upermannar had hesitated at the sight of the upraised staff, but Eskel had only sneered. Calindor came to the last words of the spell and pointed the staff to the sky.

He sensed the Sterkar pouring forth, a shimmer of pale blue against the autumn sun, but in the same moment he felt something leave the staff and wrap itself around his neck. It was an entity he did not know, a being of malice. It filled Calindor's throat with an icy chill.

He gasped, and recalled a Sending to drive it away from him. But he could not speak. The entity had taken his voice, and with it his power to utter spells.

"And the fourth condition, my lord," Aghwesi cried out in a shaking voice, "is that I be given the honor of slaying him who slew my son."

"This too I grant gladly," Eskel replied. He folded his arms and smiled at Calindor as Aghwesi drew his sword and strode through the crowd toward Pelshadan's tent.

"Mekhpur loves justice," a voice rasped behind him. Calindor spun and saw Pelshadan standing close by. He leaned heavily on Dvoi and Potiari, and his pale eyes looked into Calindor's for the first time.

"Now Mekhpur sees justice done," the Veik went on.

"Justice for a treacherous slave who plotted against his masters."

Aghwesi was almost upon him, while the other upermannar and their warriors crowded close behind. Calindor could no longer see Eskel and Ghelasha. Aghwesi's sword glinted and shimmered.

Focus!

If I cannot speak, I can still fight, Calindor thought. And I am Badakh enough to go down fighting.

Tenglekur's staff was empty, a mere stick, yet it could still serve as a warpole. Calindor looked at Aghwesi, saw the anguished joy in the old man's eyes, and leaped forward with the staff extended like a lance.

The head of the staff struck the old upermanna in the chest and stopped him where he stood. Then the staff swung with a hum and cracked against Aghwesi's skull just above the left ear. His sword fell to the dust; Calindor was about to reach for it when a hard hand clutched his shoulder.

"You will not evade the Firelord's justice," the Veik said. He began another chant, a minor spell still within his half-exhausted powers. But Calindor knew it would impose stillness upon him long enough for one of the Badakhar to kill him.

Before the Veik could finish it, Bherasha stepped forward, Pelshadan's staff resting on her shoulder like a flail; its goldsheathed head gleamed. Her eyes were bright with rage. Without hesitating, she brought the staff down with all her strength on Pelshadan's head.

The Veik fell forward before his attendants could catch him. Freed of Pelshadan's grip, Calindor stepped back. The upermannar, startled by the attack, paused for a moment.

"Quickly!" Bherasha cried, and pulled him away from the crowd. They ran past the tent, across a narrow open space to a corral where scores of horses stood tethered.

The Badakhar were close behind them now, roaring with anger. As Bherasha drew Calindor past the first line of horses, she struck at some of the beasts with Pelshadan's staff. Frightened already by the howls of the Badakhar, the horses reared and plunged. Others caught their panic, and hauled frantically against their tethers. The corral was suddenly a storm of dust and kicking hooves.

Bherasha gripped one horse's tether, undid it, and tried to calm the horse. Shuddering, the horse tried to break away; Calindor seized its reins with old practice and authority, and it halted. He swung up onto its back and pulled Bherasha after him. She still held the staff, and in his state of enhanced focus he could see the Sterkar pulsing within it.

Focus. Riding bareback would not be easy, least of all with Bherasha clinging to him, but it could be done. He guided the horse through the dusty tumult of the corral, away from the crowd that still tried to make its way among the frightened horses. If he could get clear, perhaps he could manage to reach the river and then to escape upstream along the bank. But that way was closed: he knew he must return to the Kes and bring Tilcalli out. Aghwesi had called her a witch. They would slaughter her at once.

Now they were clear of the corral, and Calindor kicked the horse into a trot. Bherasha clung to him with one hand, the other gripping the staff of Pelshadan.

"Faster!" she shouted. "Don't worry about me!"

The horse was well trained: at a gentle tap of Calindor's foot, it went to a gallop. Calindor tugged on the reins, guiding it toward the road that ran to the bridge. When they reached it he looked over his shoulder and saw several Badakhar warriors already mounted and spurring hard to overtake them.

Also riding close behind was Minukhi, clinging to a black gelding. When he saw Calindor look at him, his scarred face contorted into a grin.

"Go on, go on!" Minukhi shouted. "I'm coming with you."

The small sorcerer must be mad, Calindor thought. He could do them no good, and himself much harm.

The bridge was looming close ahead, guarded by four pikemen. They gaped at the riders bearing down upon them, but reacted too slowly to bar the way. Calindor and Bherasha clattered onto the bridge. Close behind was Minukhi, who suddenly reined in his horse.

He truly is mad, Calindor thought. Or he's thought better about this.

The pursuers were within an easy spearcast of Minukhi when a gigantic dragon suddenly appeared on the road before them. It loomed three times a man's height, its gray-green scales gleaming in the sun, and its clawed forelimbs extended hungrily toward the pursuers.

Horses and riders alike recoiled from the monster, and the pursuit halted in a welter of fallen warriors and panicked mounts. Minukhi kicked his own horse back to a gallop and thundered across the bridge. He overtook Calindor and Bherasha and gave them a strange, tearstained smile.

"That was the best dragon I ever made!" he called.

The two horses raced up through the city, past frowning arekakhar and puzzled freemen. The guards at the gates of the Kes stared in surprise at them; they had expected no one back from the Mod until late in the day.

"Can you speak?" Bherasha asked as they dismounted in the main courtyard. Calindor tried and failed. The being that gripped his throat would not release him. He took her by the arm, with Minukhi close behind, and hurried them inside.

"What do you need here?" Minukhi asked. "A weapon?" Calindor shook his head; they were past swordplay now. "Clothing? Boots?" He nodded. "Your mother!"

Calindor nodded again. They were half-running down a corridor toward the apartments where Albohar and Pelshadan's retinue had been established. He felt the presence in the Kes more strongly than ever; was this what it had been waiting for?

They met Moro outside Tilcalli's room. Bherasha shoved past him.

"My lady—they mean to kill you and your son! The Veik cast a spell to silence Dheribi, and they would have slain him. We have no time—we must escape the city."

Tilcalli looked up from her mending, alarm in her eyes. It faded almost at once. She stood, and went to her son. Her hand went to his throat; she gasped.

"This is an evil thing he has done."

"Bherasha struck him with his own staff," Minukhi said, his voice shrill with excitement. Tilcalli saw Pelshadan's staff in Bherasha's grip, and nodded almost absentmindedly.

"Dheribi—do you know how we might escape from here?" she asked.

Calindor nodded. He pointed to Moro, who stood staring in the doorway, and then raised five more fingers.

"You want all the slaves." He raised one more finger and pointed to his black hair. "And you want Svordo!" Tilcalli said. "Moro—get the others. Bring them here at once."

Moro had scarcely turned to go before Tilcalli had stripped off her light gown. Naked, she went to the clothing shelves and pulled on linen undergarments and woolen trousers and tunic.

"Girl, are you warm enough? Take this cloak as well. And these sandals should fit you well enough." She looked at Calindor. "Your magician's robe is worse than useless now. Get rid of it. Put these on instead.'' Tilcalli tossed him a coarse black tunic and trousers, much mended but serviceable. "And now I must go next door for a moment."

They stood aside as she passed through the doorway and down the hall to Albohar's room. Calindor followed her. A young apprentice magician, newly taken on, was attending the Aryo. He looked up and smiled uncertainly.

"It's all right," Tilcalli said, smiling back. "I simply need to see that the Aryo is comfortable." She looked at him and murmured under her breath; Calindor knew it for a spell of protection.

"Very well," she said briskly. "Thank you, young man. You're taking good care of the Aryo. Now we must go."

Svordo, Moro and the others were in the hall. Svordo carried a bundle on his shoulder; he reached into it and pulled out a sheathed sword.

"I can't use this thing, but perhaps you can," he said, tossing it to Calindor. "Moro says you can't speak. Is that true? Well, no matter. He says you also know a way out of here."

Calindor hung the sword over his shoulder by its long strap, wondering where and how Svordo had acquired it. He had risked death to steal the weapon; it would surely do them no good now. Well, no matter.

He led them back down the corridor, down a spiral staircase, and ever deeper into the basements of the Kes. They saw no one, and heard nothing. This was a long-abandoned part of the fortress, used for storage. Calindor had often played down here when he was little, exploring with a stub of candle. Now he had no light, only his focus. It guided him through narrow halls, across musty storerooms, and down steps slippery with mold. Behind him came Tilcalli, then Bherasha and the six slaves, then Minukhi and Svordo.

The presence was closer now. They were not approaching it, but it seemed to be closing in on them from all around. He sensed its malicious amusement, and its contempt. Abruptly Calindor halted, swayed, and caught himself.

The presence was Mekhpur, the Firelord, the god of the Badakhar.

His mother gripped his hand. "Don't be afraid. He doesn't know your deep name. He can't hurt you. Don't be afraid."

But Calindor felt his strength leaving him; his legs trembled, and his breath whistled in his throat. Though the air was chill, sweat burst from his skin. He yearned to cry out, and could not.

As if from far away, he heard his mother chanting. It was a Sending, a powerful spell, and he could feel it gathering force around them. But it seemed absurd: a Sending, against Mekhpur himself?

The presence drew closer, loomed over him. It scarcely seemed to notice Tilcalli and the others; its interest was in him, him alone. He felt its intelligence, its malevolence, its power. He opened his mouth to cry out, and felt a terrible agony flame through him.

Sixteen

He lay sprawled on long grass under a bright blue sky. An old woman squatted beside him, dressed in a finely embroidered tunic and trousers. Her face was deeply wrinkled, but her eyes were as clear and dark as a young girl's. She smiled at him.

So, great-great-grandson! You return at last to the Open Dream. I am Calihalingol. She spoke without speaking; he heard without hearing.

He sat up slowly, feeling the grass beneath his hands. Before him, only a few steps away, a river ran deep and slow between its grassy banks. Beyond it were meadows, low hills, a few trees, and the sky. The air was warm.

I saw you before, with my mother. And a man. I was—up there. He pointed to the cloudless sky.

We saw you as a hawk. I have waited ever since for you to return. You have been a very difficult boy. She giggled as silently as she spoke. *You are too impatient to find the easy way here. You must be in pain before you can break away from the world. You are in pain now.*

Memory flooded back. *The Firelord himself attacked me. Tilcalli tried to send him away. And then I was here.*

That evil god of the Badakhar? Yes, he would fear you and try to harm you. But he has not killed you. You will return to Sotalar.

I must go at once! Tilcalli, Bherasha, the others—they all need me. Pelshadan took my voice from me. We were escaping to the mountains. We were in the fortress. I must go.

The old woman rocked back on her hams, laughing. Even in the silence of the Open Dream, her laughter eased his soul. He knew her name meant Woman Who Laughs, and understood why.

Do not worry about them. The Firelord does not care about them, only about you, because only you can harm him. And he does not know about the Open Dream. To him you now seem dead or dying. Your mother and your friends are of no interest to him. Come, come with me.

She rose to her feet in a single graceful movement, reached down and took his hand to help him up. He looked around and saw the village where the ancestors of the Siragi Aibela danced the past and future, and beyond the village the far mountains.

Calihalingol led him away from the Silent River, into the village. It was a collection of simple huts, deerskins pulled over arched poles. As he drew nearer, he saw that in some of the huts the poles were actually great curves of ivory: the tusks of giant beasts. Though he had never seen a Menmannar village, he felt he had lived in this place all his life, and known the people who walked and danced and held out their hands in greeting.

Some had dwelt by the Silent River far longer than Calihalingol; they remembered a Cantarea empty of all but a few wandering clans. Others had fought in the Slave Wars, hurling their magic against that of the Veikar. Most had come only recently to the Open Dream, and recalled the battles when the Badakhar had come to found Aishadan and had driven them far up the river.

All made him welcome, and drew him into their dances and songs. In the unchanging noon light, Calindor learned the steps and chants, and felt something loosen within himself. With Calihalingol holding one hand, and a great-uncle the other, he danced and sang and felt his soul grow straight.

When they did not dance, they sat within the huts, or walked along the river. All had something to tell him. An old man, Halasindor, spoke of the long-gone times when the mammoths and great cats had roamed Cantarea.

We were new in Sotalar then, and did not know the spells to call only the beasts that wished to die. We took too much, and Callia grieved for her lost children. Slowly we learned, and won her forgiveness.

Calindor, sitting close beside him in the old man's hut, was puzzled. *You say we were new to Sotalar. Had Callia just created us?*

No. We came from another world. No one knows how or why, only that long ago we walked out of that world and under a rainbow into this one. Some think Callia called us to her because she wanted eyes to see herself with, and thoughts to think. But the Badakhar come from another world also, and the gods and jenji, and surely Callia did not bring them here. Halasindor smiled and shrugged. *However we came, we came. We learned Callia's ways, and lived happily within her beauty. Come, let me show you a way to make the grass grow thick and tall.*

And they went out into the valley of the Silent River, and Calindor learned new spells to quicken life and fill the soil with fertility.

Calihalingol taught him also: spells to cleanse streams, spells to make trees grow straight and strong, spells to turn the trees' wood into simple and beautiful tools and utensils. He learned how to heal deep wounds, and how to save a child from stillbirth.

These are great spells, he told her, *but they will not serve against the Badakhar. How shall I use Cantarean magic against them?*

She laughed. *You still lie enchanted in Sotalar,* she replied. *Until the spell is removed you shall be mute and you will cast no spells with human magic. When you can speak again, perhaps you will see a way to use this magic.*

These are beautiful spells, but they cannot harm the Badakhar.

We do not want to harm them, child. We want them only to stop harming Callia.

You sound just like my mother. Perhaps I am too much of a Badakh to understand.

And perhaps I am too much a Cantarean to understand you. But I know that Callia wanted you to go among the Badakhar. You have done her will, and you are doing it now. Come with me.

She led him far out of the village, away from the river. At last they stood upon a grassy ridge, looking far across a forested plain to the mountains.

When we Siragi Aibela die, she told him, *we come to stay in the Open Dream. But at last we tire of this place, and walk into the forest to seek the mountains. No one ever returns. Perhaps those who go are serving Callia also. She is great, and she has not told us all her secrets. Still, we wait beside the river until we too wish to go to the mountains, and we serve our descendants by teaching them the old ways, the old spells. If we did not, our descendants would perish. Their mountain land is beautiful, yes, but it is hard and ungiving. If we did not show them how to encourage the crops to grow, the game to draw near, all our children would die.*

Calindor looked at the distant dark outline of the mountains. *It is a powerful magic, I know. But it cannot overcome the Badakhar.*

His great-great-grandmother looked displeased with him. *It is sanshandata: greenmagic. Nothing in Sotalar can live without it. That is why the land dies under the feet of the Badakhar. This is why you will accomplish nothing without it.*

You said I would cast no human spells. What other spells are there, great-great-grandmother?

She sang a soft, sibilant phrase, and wild roses burst into tiny pink blooms at their feet.

Callia is greater than we know. We do her bidding whether we know it or not. Come, Calindor, and let us dance again by the river.

He had not told her his deep name. But he was not surprised that she knew it.

Eskel sat in the Hearing Hall, in the Aryo's chair. The room smelled of candlewax, and coal fires glowed in four large braziers. But the night air still held a chill.

"So they have escaped." His voice was flat.

His father's old companion Snegh knelt before him in dusty riding clothes.

"Not yet, Aryako. We have horsemen out on both sides of the Vesparushrei, and longboats following as well. We will find them."

Eskel glanced around the room. Other upermannar also knelt on the hard floor, veterans of Ner Kes and many other campaigns. They looked angry and embarrassed, as well they should. They had let Dheribi and the others escape twice—once from Gathering Field and then from the Arekaryo Kes itself. Their incompetence had turned the Mod into a fiasco.

"Are you sure that when you do find them, Snegh, they will not overpower you and your men? That girl, the Veik's cook, knows how to use a warpole."

Snegh endured the sarcasm in silence.

"When you do find them," Eskel went on, "slay them at once. Bring back their heads, every one. And bring back the staff of Pelshadan."

"It will be done, Aryako."

"You are all dismissed."

Slowly they rose, bowed, and left the Hearing Hall. Apart from the guards at the door, Eskel sat alone for a long time. Then he called for Pelshadan.

The magician arrived promptly; no doubt he had been waiting for this summons, Eskel thought. Pelshadan looked weary and half-crazed. One finger kept curling a long strand of hair, and his pale eyes seemed almost blind. A black wool cap, worn against the cold, half-concealed his bandaged scalp.

"Your spell failed."

"Failed? Aryako, it succeeded. Greatly succeeded, yes. The greatest magician of our time, silenced by his own words!" The Veik's chuckle turned into a gasping laugh. "As I told you, he used the spell I wrote for him, not knowing it would free all the Sterkar in his staff. Not knowing at all."

"He escaped."

"Only thanks to my slave's treachery, Aryako. Only that."

"And now you've lost your own staff."

"Yes, yes. A grievous loss. It must be kept a secret, a close secret, or the Veikar of Halamor and Ghrirei will send new spells against me. Against us. And we must recover the staff. We must, Aryako."

With elbows on the arms of his chair, and fingers steepled before his face, Eskel studied the old man. "What if we do not?"

Pelshadan began to sway from side to side. "Then I am doomed. But so are you. The other Veikar hate and fear me, and they will strike me down. When I go, my spells of protection go also. The Veikar will reach you, Aryako. Yes, they will reach you."

Eskel kept his face calm, but felt a slow nausea rising from his stomach. *Perhaps they will send a deivushibi to possess me, as Parsur was possessed.*

"What if it should fall into the hands of the Menmannar?"

"Little matter—they know almost nothing of our magic, except Dheribi. And the staff will avail him nothing. The spell of silence is not one easily broken."

"But it can be broken?"

"Oh yes, yes, Aryako, eventually."

"And when it does, Dheribi will unlock the secrets of your staff?"

"Perhaps, perhaps—" The older man's face looked stricken. "Or he might destroy it."

"So. You tell me that if Dheribi reaches the Menmannar with your staff, we face a serious threat."

Pelshadan rocked back, laughing. "No, Aryako, we face the Black World! We face damnation!"

Eskel dismissed the magician, then left the Hearing Hall for his mother's quarters. She had taken an apartment on the floor below her old one, close to Albohar yet not too close. Ghelasha greeted him with a bow and a worried smile.

He slammed the door behind him. "How could my father achieve what he did, when all his helpers are fools?"

Ghelasha laughed without mirth. "He had me, for one thing. Come and sit, Eskel. Give me the news."

Over a mug of medh he told her about the still-uncaught fugitives, and about the danger in the loss of Pelshadan's staff.

"If he is right," Eskel said, "then we shall not conquer the other kingdoms—they will conquer us, and throw our bones in the river."

"They will do no such thing because they will not dare to," Ghelasha snapped. She pulled her fine wool robe close about her. "Here is what you must do. First, announce that the fugitives have been caught and slain. Kill a few slaves and put their heads up outside the Kes. Then hold a feast of celebration, and make sure that Pelshadan is seen with a slave bearing his staff."

"But his staff is *gone*, mother!"

"Eskel—" Her voice was calm and controlled. "The heads will be the wrong heads. The staff will be a copy. It does not matter, as long as word goes to our enemies that we are strong and not to be trifled with."

"Meanwhile Dheribi and his bitch-mother will be safe in the mountains with the real staff."

"Thirdly," Ghelasha said softly, "you will send an army up the river to pursue Dheribi. It will go out one squadron at a time, to attract no attention, and it will not come back until it has captured Dheribi and the staff."

"Mother, it's almost winter. Snow has fallen already in the foothills."

"What of it? If Aishadanar can't fight in the snow, they don't deserve to rule."

"Pelshadan says the spell on Dheribi's voice can't last forever. The Menmannar magicians will eventually lift it. What then, when he brings all his magic against us?"

"Pelshadan stopped him before he could summon magic at

the Gathering. Your warriors will stop him also. So you will have to be quick, Eskel.''

He nodded and drained his mug. "Yes," he sighed, putting down the mug with a slight tremble in his hand. "Yes, very quick."

Calindor did not know how long the dance went on in the silent, endless noon. But at last Calihalingol and the others smiled and kissed him, faded and disappeared, and he felt chill air on his face. The sunshine was gone; he blinked and saw stars glinting through thin cloud. Water splashed close by, and men grunted.

His throat was cold and clamped.

Calindor sat up, and felt his balance shift suddenly: he was in a longboat, on the Vesparushrei.

"He's awake," Bherasha said softly. "Dheribi, are you all right?"

He felt her hand on his forehead; he tried to speak, and felt tears sting his eyes. He nodded, hearing his breath rasp in his throat.

His focus showed him more than his eyes could. He was lying near the stern of the longboat, wrapped in a coarse blanket. Behind him was Bherasha, and behind her, steering the longboat, was Tilcalli. In front of him Svordo, Minukhi, Moro and the other five slaves sat at the oars, rowing steadily against the current. They had been at it for a long time, and he sensed their weariness.

Svordo and Minukhi were the sternmost pair of rowers. Without breaking his rhythm, Svordo said: "Still can't speak, eh? That's bad luck. Perhaps some of the Menmannar magicians can break the spell. At least we got you out. Thought you were dead at first, but Bherasha and your mother wouldn't leave you."

"Your mother cast a great spell," Bherasha said. "It drove away whatever it was that attacked you, and then we carried you and your mother out of the castle and down to the river."

Yes, Calindor thought. She would have been helpless after a spell of such power, though he suspected it had not truly driven Mekhpur away; Calihalingol was likely right when she said the Firelord thought him dead or dying.

"It was a near thing," Svordo went on. "Got down to the river and found this boat in one of the Aryo's sheds. A few others too, but we broke their hulls. The boys here had to learn how to row."

"They chased us along the riverbank," Minukhi said, leaning forward and hauling back. "All the day. They thought we would have to come ashore at nightfall, but we didn't. Your mother could hardly sit up, but she saw the course we should take.''

Calindor nodded and reached back to touch Tilcalli's hand. He sensed her weariness, but also her hard determination. She had put herself in her enemies' hands for twenty years, he reflected; she would not be frightened by a river in the night.

Gradually the rest of the story came out: they had rowed all that first night, then hidden at dawn in a gully full of bushes. Badakhar riders had come close, but had not found them; at dusk they had pushed the boat back into the river and continued upstream. So they had gone, day after night, for a long time now.

Now the sixth night was almost over. Tilcalli estimated they would be two more days before they reached Tanshadabela, Two Stream Village. Once it had been far upstream from other Cantarean settlements, but now, she said, it was the easternmost; the others had long since been abandoned. The scanty supplies they had managed to steal from the Kes were gone now. They would find little to feed them until Tanshadabela—a few fish, perhaps, or camas roots.

Calindor shrugged. Despite his long trance he felt no hunger, only cold, weariness and an unending ache in his throat.

Bherasha, sitting close beside him, lifted something from the bottom of the hull. ''I brought this,'' she said shyly. ''But I can't give it to you, because it can't be held by its owner.''

It was the staff of Pelshadan.

By the light of a single candle, Pelshadan sat beside the sleeping Aryo. Albohar was growing gaunt, he saw: cheekbones stood out above the beard, the nose was beaklike, the eyes more deep-set.

''Well, Aryo,'' Pelshadan murmured, rocking back and forth in his chair. ''We are fallen on evil days, you and I. Perhaps I should not have slain that slave and called up the deivushibi for Parsur. Perhaps I should have slain Bherasha and Minukhi instead, and you should have slain your bastard son. Then I would have my staff, Aryo, and you would have your senses. You would be planning next year's war, and I would be reading old lore to help bring down death on your foes, and all would be well. Instead you lie dying and I await some new visitor from the Black World.''

He cackled softly. ''Perhaps we'll go together, Aryo, and tear at one another's vitals for all eternity. Or perhaps we will simply go into the darkness alone, and lie there forever. Forever. Forever.''

Seventeen

Calindor dozed and woke while the night wore on. His focus showed him the river and its banks, and the spruces and lodgepole pines that stretched far into the distance. He sensed bears and owls, and wolves standing by the water. All watched the longboat go by, a shadow in moonlight.

The rowers said little, and said it softly. Calindor knew they feared Badakhar riders, but he knew also that none were close. The Badakhar were used to the prairie, not to these forested hills; they would not risk their horses in the darkness. But at first light they would resume the hunt, and would soon catch up. The fugitives would have to hide again, waiting for night as their pursuers waited for day.

If he could speak but a few words, he could enchant this longboat and send it skimming upstream like the boats of the Gulyaji. Instead the rowers must toil for hours, hungry and afraid. He smiled at his own wish. After all, if could speak he would have brought Eskel and all of Aishadan down in ruin and slaughter, and he would never have ventured into the Open Dream.

To destroy the Badakhar was not the answer; he thought he understood that much of what Calihalingol and the others had taught him in the endless noon. Death and violence did weaken Callia; had he slaughtered the upermannar and destroyed the Arekaryo Kes, he would have next faced still more slaughter as the other Badakhar kingdoms came against him. Even if he could win against them and their Veikar, Cantarea would have been left a smoking wasteland.

But what now can I do? Am I to hide among the Menmannar? When I win back my powers, am I only to defend the mountains and leave the prairie to the Badakhar? He thought of the magic he had learned in the Open Dream: it was beautiful, but it would not stop Badakhar warriors. Nor would it change their hearts, make them give freedom to their slaves, urge them to ride back east across the land they had ruined to their forgotten home.

Callia, what can I do now?

Eskel had summoned Snegh and Vulkvo to his rooms in the Kes. The hour was late; none but sentries walked the corridors. The fortress was cold and dark, but a cheerful fire burned in Eskel's hearth. Though he might have had any number of slaves to attend on them, Eskel served them medh with his own hands; the three men were alone.

"You are my father's oldest friends, and mine." Eskel smiled at Snegh. "I think my earliest memory is of pulling your beard."

Snegh chuckled. "I can still feel it, Aryako."

"My father trusted you, and I trust you. I must have your best advice, and your strongest support."

"You shall have them." Vulkvo grunted. Snegh nodded, his narrow eyes fixed curiously on Eskel.

"We must assemble a sizable army for a raid up the river— within the next few days. And we must do it in secret."

He was pleased to see surprise but no hesitation in their expressions.

"If you will it, Aryako," said Snegh. "How many, and where?"

"And why?" added Vulkvo.

"Two thousand men, a quarter of them mounted. They're going up the Vesparushrei to capture the fugitives."

Vulkvo rubbed his hands and held them out to the fire. "Search parties are still out looking for them, Aryako. Surely they'll bring them back in a day or two."

"I doubt that they will. The longboats have already come back—they can't find the safe channels now at low water. The horsemen don't know the country. Dheribi may not be able to speak, but he still has his tricks. His mother is a great witch, as Pelshadan has told me. If they get away into the mountains we shall have to fight our way to them."

"If you wish it, then we shall go after them," said Vulkvo. "But surely a small raiding party would have better luck. Just as when your father led us up the river. Five or six stout fellows could follow them, track them down, and bring back their heads."

"We need more than their heads. In fact, tomorrow I will

announce their capture, and someone's heads will go on display. We need the staff of Pelshadan.''

Snegh looked baffled, but Vulkvo turned pale and gently put down his mug.

"So it *was* taken!" he whispered. "I heard rumors, but no more than that. Now I see why we must act in haste. The other Veikar—do they know the staff is gone?"

"If you have heard rumors, so will they," Eskel said. "They will tell their masters, and their masters will bid them test Pelshadan a little. When they find him defenseless, they will strike with all their strength."

The older men nodded, calmly assessing their new position.

"The men must be assembled in secret," Eskel said. "Gather them in small groups, no more than squadron-size, and send them up the river."

"We still have some men coming back from Ner Kes," Vulkvo murmured. "We might divert them around Aishadan, get them upriver."

"I leave that to you. And I ask that you both lead this raid. You know the country."

"As you will, Aryako," Snegh said. "But not many have been up the Vesparushrei in a long time. I hear the old villages are gone now. The Menmannar have moved deeper into the mountains. It may be that Dheribi will go far west of the village where we caught his mother."

"I know you will go wherever you need to," Eskel said. "And I know you will come back with Dheribi's head and the staff of Pelshadan."

By dawn the rowers were exhausted. Tilcalli steered the longboat into a marsh thick with reeds; using their oars as poles, Moro and Svordo pushed the craft through the reeds.

"We'll stay here," Tilcalli said softly. "We're not far from solid ground, but if the riders come we'll see them long before they reach us." She pointed to the woods rising not far away beyond the reeds.

"The men need something to eat," Bherasha said. "They've had nothing for two days and more."

"No more have we. Do you know how to find camas root?"

"Yes. My mother showed me when I was a little girl in the country."

"It's better boiled than raw, but we can't risk a fire. The two of us will go. The men are too tired, and I don't want them crashing about making noise."

Calindor tapped himself on the chest. Tilcalli looked at him. "You want to go as well?"

He pointed to his mother and wagged a finger in negation.

"Ah—you want me to stay here? And rest? Well, perhaps so." Tilcalli looked past him to the other men, who sat slumped over their oars. In the growing light they were gaunt and weary. To Calindor, his mother looked even more exhausted. "We will stay here for now. Bherasha and Dheribi are going in search of food." She smiled faintly at them, her eyes dull with weariness. "Be back soon."

Without ceremony Bherasha stripped off her skirt and slung it over her shoulder. Then she gripped an oar and used it to steady herself as she stepped out of the longboat and into the water. It rose almost to her waist, soaking the bottom of her tunic. Calindor pulled off his trousers, shivering a little as the morning chill bit through his tunic. Holding his sword in one hand, he went over the side and felt cold mud ooze around his feet.

Bherasha reached back into the longboat and retrieved the staff of Pelshadan, using it to probe the water ahead of her. Calindor felt surprise that she would so casually use a powerful instrument. Well, she had been practical enough to use it as a club; this was little different. Perhaps the Sterkar within the staff would enjoy the experience.

Silently they waded through the yellow reeds. Overhead the sky was filled with pink and orange clouds. A bird chirped somewhere. From far away, the honking cries of migrating geese sang in the stillness, and a moment later they came into view above the treetops: a lopsided V, and then another, heading south with powerful wingbeats.

Despite the cold, Calindor felt a strange and tranquil joy. The marsh around them was alive, from the mud to the sky. He sensed the fish curiously gathering around his legs, the water beetles skimming over the surface, an owl dozing in its hollow tree. If the Badakhar had ruined the prairie, they had not yet harmed the forests here in the west.

He stepped out of the water onto a slippery clay bank and helped Bherasha up. The strength of her grip somehow surprised him.

"Callia is strong here," Bherasha murmured; Calindor nodded. He held up a hand to make her pause, and let his focus sweep the woods and bogs around them. Bherasha looked worried.

"Is all well?"

He nodded. No Badakhar were near.

Yet they moved silently across an old deer trail and up into a grove of quaking aspens, stepping carefully through the debris of twigs and branches on the forest floor. While Bherasha scanned the ground, Calindor's gaze moved restlessly through the woods. The deer trail worried him: the longboat was visible from it, and Badakh riders would surely find the trail as they moved upstream.

Bherasha paused now and then to dig in the earth with the staff, each time retrieving a long, narrow root. These she carried in her skirt, using it as a sack. Sometimes she found another plant and stored it also: an herb, a moss, a pod of seeds. Calindor recognized most of them from his mother's tutelage; they were useful in healing a wound or restoring strength.

Restore my voice!

But he knew of nothing that could expel the evil, mindless being that gripped his throat.

The morning was long; clouds gathered overhead, and the air was bitterly cold. With their legs bare and their clothes wet, they shivered constantly. But Bherasha would not quit in her search.

At last, irritably, Calindor joined with her. When she found the withered stem of a camas, he pushed her aside and dug for it with the blade of his sword. The work went faster then, and soon he was searching on his own. Once, when he caught Bherasha's eye, she seemed to be smiling at him; he wondered why.

A fine, cold drizzle began to fall. Bherasha looked at the roots they had gathered, nodded, and led the way back toward the marsh. Calindor found himself admiring Bherasha's legs: they were long and graceful, even spattered with mud and clay and prickled with gooseflesh. She walked lightly on the uneven ground, and her long black hair swayed between her shoulderblades. Once she reached up to steady herself against a tree trunk, and he saw in her arm the strength he had felt in her hand.

If she had not struck at Pelshadan, I would be dead now. He wished he could speak to thank her, and wished also to touch her arms and draw some of their strength to his own.

Softly, a horse's iron-shod hoof struck a stone not far away.

Without his willing it, he reached out and gripped her shoulder. She had heard it, also, and stood as still as the lodgepole around them. Calindor cursed himself for a fool: he had focused on the girl's body before him and ignored everything else. How long had the Badakhar been approaching? How many?

Now he swept the region again, so intensely that a Veik would have shuddered under the impact. Tilcalli and Minukhi would sense his concern, he knew, and alert the rowers. If the Badakhar had a magician anywhere near, he, too, would feel the scan and be warned.

It was a single rider, moving parallel to the river and approaching the marsh. He would follow the deer trail along the edge of the marsh, just as Calindor had feared. When he saw the longboat he would turn and quietly rejoin his companions. Then they would slip on foot into the marsh, get within bowshot, and kill everyone in the boat.

Perhaps not: Tilcalli was too exhausted to focus well, but she could not have missed his own focus. She might well move the longboat deeper into the marsh, where it would be harder to see. But he could not take that chance. The rider would have to be killed before he could summon help.

The ground before them declined a little through a grove of quaking aspen, their white trunks dull under the overcast. The deer trail was just beyond the grove. The Badakh would be coming up from the left, and would soon see the marsh and the longboat.

All this he had thought in the instant that he gripped Bherasha's shoulder. Now she turned to face him, a question in her eyes.

He pointed to her, then down to the trail just visible among the white trunks, then to the right. She nodded, but he could feel her fear. He pointed to himself and then to his sword. Bherasha nodded again.

Calindor could feel her fear, and the courage that overrode it. He touched her face with his hands and kissed her gently. She kissed him back, drew a single quick breath, and stepped quickly down through the trees to the trail.

Just as she reached it, the rider appeared: a big man, brown-bearded, wearing a leather cape with a high collar. Bherasha looked at him. She dropped her bag of roots, but not the staff of Pelshadan, and ran up the trail. The rider's white gelding broke into a trot.

Good—the Badakh's attention was all on Bherasha's flashing legs. He looked neither right nor left, and hunched a little to avoid overhanging branches.

Calindor sprang up and raced down the hill, sword in hand. He remembered old Demazakh's lessons about fighting on foot against a mounted enemy: "Cripple the bastard's horse, or scare it." But the horse was no enemy, only another kind of slave.

He was almost at the trail, no longer screened by branches, and the horse and rider were only a few paces away. The rider saw him at last, saw the glint of steel in Calindor's hand, and reached for his own sword.

Calindor pivoted slightly to the left, toward the horse's hind-quarters, and reached out with his left hand for the rider's cape. Just as he ran into the horse his fingers closed around the greasy leather.

The white gelding shied, and the cape snapped taut as Calindor spun away. He felt a sudden shock as the horse's right hind hoof struck his leg a glancing blow, but he did not let go of the cape.

With a grunt the rider toppled out of his saddle—but not out of his right stirrup. Deep in focus, Calindor could sense the snap of the man's femur.

Hanging from the stirrup, the rider kept his head. "Fsst! Fsst!" he whispered: the cavalryman's command to make his horse halt in its tracks. The gelding obeyed; the rider freed himself and rolled over to face Calindor. His sword wavered slightly, his face was pale, but he was clearly ready to fight.

Calindor stepped forward. It would not be a pretty fight, but it would be quick. He did not want a lot of blade-banging; the sound of a fight might carry to the Badakh's comrades.

Movement caught his eye and he looked up to see Bherasha not far down the trail. She met his gaze and shook her head urgently. Calindor hesitated. In a moment the warrior would gather his wits and cry out for help. What did Bherasha mean?

She ran lightly down the trail, unseen by the crippled warrior, and with a graceful swing brought the gold head of the staff against the Badakh's wrist. His sword flew into the sparse grass beside the trail.

Bherasha pointed the gold-tipped staff at the warrior and glared at him. "Badakh!" Her voice was a low growl. "I am a witch of the Menmannar. If you speak or move, I will blast your soul into the Black World and send your body walking empty through the woods until the beasts find it."

For the first time fear shone in the warrior's close-set blue eyes. He obeyed her, ignoring Calindor's sword just an arm's length from his throat.

"Bind him and gag him," Bherasha said in Cantarean. "We must bring him with us."

Calindor gaped at her. She frowned at him, almost as fiercely as she had glared at the Badakh.

"I said Callia is strong here," she whispered. "This is no place to slay even a Badakh. We can't leave him, so we must bring him along. Use the belt from my skirt. Gag him with his scarf."

Shaking his head, Calindor obeyed. The girl was right. A slaying here would affront Callia, and he should have realized it. But who would have expected her to disarm the man, and then to lie so well that Calindor himself had felt a trickle of alarm run down his spine?

When he had finished, Bherasha went over to the white gelding and slapped its flank. "Tsa, tsa!" she commanded it, and it trotted obediently up the trail.

"Now we have to get him and the roots out to the boat," she said. "Can you carry him over your shoulder?"

Calindor smiled and shook his head. The man far outweighed him. Instead, he gripped him by the armpits and dragged him off the trail toward the marsh. The warrior groaned for a moment and then fell silent. A brave man, Calindor thought; his leg must be in agony.

He pulled his prisoner down into the marsh and dragged him through the reeds. At times only the man's head and shoulders stayed above water. Behind them came Bherasha, carrying the roots on her shoulder and gripping both the staff and the warrior's sword. Calindor wondered why she was smiling.

Tilcalli and the others were briefly surprised by the sight of the prisoner. Moro and Svordo climbed out of the longboat and helped to lift the Badakh into it. Then they steadied the boat while Tilcalli stepped forward to examine him.

"It's a clean break," she murmured after a while. "If I were not so tired, I could put a spell of healing on it and he would be walking in a couple of days. As it is, he will have to go untended until we reach home."

For a moment Calindor, standing in the icy water, thought she meant Aishadan; then he realized it was Two Stream Village she was talking about, Tanshadabela. For the first time he fully understood that she was not really of Aishadan, not a Cantarean slave, but a free woman of the Menmannar.

"Tilcalli—was I wrong to bring him here?" Bherasha asked.

She looked at her and smiled. "No. You were right."

Calindor pulled himself into the longboat and pulled his robe over his cold-numbed legs. *She was right*, he thought, *but he's still a danger to us all.*

Svordo and Moro pushed the longboat into another part of the marsh, where the reeds grew taller and the boat could not be seen from dry land. The other Cantareans bound their prisoner and gagged him; in the stillness of that late autumn day, a single shout could carry a long way.

Tilcalli contrived a rough splint from a spare oar, and bound it round the Badakh's leg. He murmured a little behind his gag, but scarcely moved. Meanwhile Bherasha used the captive's sword to peel and grate camas roots. When she had cut them into a double-handful of white shreds, she passed them on to a Cantarean. Each man nodded politely and ate with full attention, letting no scrap escape.

Calindor waited until everyone else had eaten. He found the shredded roots bland but crisp, and they filled his long-empty stomach. But he wished he had thought to ransack the Badakh's saddlebags before they had sent the gelding on its way.

When everyone had eaten, they all huddled under blankets or robes in the longboat. The air was still and cold; the only noises were the occasional cry of a bird and the buzz of an insect. Calindor sat in the stern, with Bherasha sitting between his knees. He enjoyed the heat of her body, and the smell of her hair. In his focus she was a staff of light and strength; he wished he could speak to tell her so.

She leaned back against him, and he put his arms around her shoulders. Her cheek against his was cool and smooth. Calindor drew a long breath and let it out, feeling suddenly at peace.

Not long after, he sensed more riders and gestured to Tilcalli; she nodded and glanced at the captive. The others shifted uncomfortably and looked about at the reeds surrounding them. Soon they heard horns: the Badakhar were signalling to one another. Calindor looked down the longboat to where the prisoner lay; he did not move. The riders were skirting the marsh, unwilling to venture into it whether on foot or on horseback. But they were moving upstream; tonight the fugitives would have to row for a long time to get beyond their pursuers.

At twilight they poled the longboat back through the reeds into the river. In darkness they started to row upstream, while Calindor held the tiller. A fine drizzle began to fall, and through it they could see the campfires of the Badakhar on both banks of the river.

Tilcalli caught her breath, and then whispered to Calindor: "On the right bank—they are camped in the ruins of Bena Mipala. It was a large village, and now it is empty."

Calindor could see firelight reflecting from log walls that must once have been whitewashed. Bena Mipala must have been one of the villages often raided by the Aishadanar in the old days, but it had endured; now it was deserted though no raiders had come in many years. He wondered why.

They rowed on, stopping once on an islet to empty bowels and bladders. If Svordo, Moro and the others were uncomfortable, they gave no sign of it. Some of them even giggled softly over someone's joke. They helped their prisoner out also, pulled down his trousers for him, and giggled some more.

Tilcalli went up to him when he was finished and removed his gag. She gave him a little water, which he drank thirstily.

"What is your name?"

He would not answer, but lay in the darkness on the dead grass, breathing hard.

"I do not want to shame you by striking you," she said. "But I will if you do not speak to me. What is your name?"

"Pervidhu."

She nodded, sudden recognition in her face. "I have seen you before. You are from Vidhumen—Aghwesi's manor?"

"I am his nephew."

"Your family and ours have intertwined our lives," Tilcalli said; to Calindor she sounded almost amused. "Tell me, Pervidhu, nephew of Aghwesi, how many are riding after us?"

"I don't know. A lot. Enough to catch you."

Tilcalli laughed softly, amusedly, but Calindor felt a chill in it; he suspected Pervidhu felt it even more. "*You* were enough to catch us, and now look at you. I hope we won't be caught again. We won't have room in the boat for any more of you."

Pervidhu snorted, laughed, and then sucked in his breath with a gasp of pain.

"You can always strap us to logs and pull us along behind you," he wheezed.

Tilcalli clapped her hands and giggled; so did Bherasha. "A Badakh who can joke! Now I am truly glad that Dheribi didn't kill you. Listen to me. In a day or two I will have the strength to heal your leg. Until then you will be in pain. And I must add to your pain by keeping your hands tied. You are a funny man, but I don't trust you."

"Why do you keep me alive, then?"

"Callia wants you alive, even if you want her dead."

"Who is Callia?"

"Our goddess. She wants us alive also. So until you learn better, we must keep you bound."

"Then I will be bound for a long time."

"If you wish it." Tilcalli turned away and said to the others: "Put him back in the boat."

By dawn they were truly exhausted, and most were shivering uncontrollably. A cold wind was blowing from the north; it smelled of snow. The river here was wide, and its valley wider still. Enormous mountains rose in the distance, their slopes forested only a little way before the trees yielded to bare stone and snow. The banks of the river were treeless also, a long chain of dunes dotted with willow bushes.

They passed another abandoned village, which Tilcalli said was called Sedi Argudun. Its stockade had fallen in places, exposing cabins whose roofs had collapsed. Tilcalli looked grim until the ruins were lost in the distance.

After a time she told Calindor to steer for a narrow point that jutted out from the river's left bank. Its upstream side was thick with dry driftwood, and if the Badakhar should see the smoke of a fire, they in turn would be visible at a good distance.

Bherasha made a little fire in the lee of a weathered gray log, while the men gathered driftwood for both the fire and a shelter. The rough lean-to they built looked almost as accidental as the rest of the driftwood. Under it they huddled together, shuddering as they put their hands and feet out to the warmth. Calindor glanced at Pervidhu, who lay among them silent and abstracted, his blue eyes glazed with unexpressed pain.

While Bherasha and Tilcalli scraped the rest of the roots, the men talked softly among themselves: of their blisters, of the chance of snow, of the likelihood of the Badakhar overtaking them. Their breath puffed out in little white clouds that mingled with the smoke of the fire. Calindor envied them: exhausted and hungry though they were, yet they could speak and share their thoughts with one another. He could only feel the cold grip of the being in his throat.

"We should be getting on into a hiding place for the day," Minukhi said when they had finished eating.

"No," Tilcalli answered. "We will go on. Tanshadabela is not far. Better to risk the Badakhar now than to wait until night and then row on empty stomachs."

They looked at her with misery in their eyes, but no resentment. Moro put another log on the fire, and everyone basked in the extra heat. Minukhi wiped his tears and drew a rag over his lidless eyes.

"We'll go when the log is ashes," he said, and went to sleep leaning against Calindor.

The drizzle had turned to snow by the time they returned to the longboat. It fell in wet flakes, first scattered and then thickly. The mountains disappeared in grayness.

The oarsmen rowed steadily but with little strength. The river was shallow here, running fast and cold over stones and sandbars. Calindor found he must use his focus to find the safest course through the many braided channels, but his eyes kept turning to the glimpses of the mountains that appeared when the flurries died away. The mountainsides were great masses of upheaved stone, gray or black or brown, rising vertically or almost so in ranges like waves on a stormy lake. What power, he wondered, had raised this land while Cantarea lay undisturbed?

He sensed the arrow only a moment before it smashed through the hull near his right knee.

Instantly he steered to the left even as his focus reached out and found the Badakhar. They were near the crest of a long dune on the river's left bank, six of them, and close enough that he could see one of them drawing his bow for another shot.

Svordo saw the shaft of the arrow jutting through the hull and swore. "They've found us! Come on, put some muscle into it. Dheribi, can you put us over against the far bank?"

He shook his head. To the south the river's right bank was a long stretch of dunes, mudflats and streams. They might put the boat ashore and try to run for it, but they would likely find themselves caught on some islet between shallow but impassable torrents. And the Badakhar were doubtless on both sides of the river.

"That's an old friend of mine, I'll bet," said Pervidhu hoarsely. "Name's Gaupi. At Ner Kes he could shoot farther than anyone else. And hit his man too."

Calindor looked to his left and saw another band of horsemen moving easily along, keeping pace with the boat. Tilcalli followed his gaze and saw them also.

"Keep rowing," she said. "Tanshadabela is close." Then she turned to Bherasha, who sat just behind her and in front of Calindor. "I must go into trance. Hold me up."

Another arrow fell into the water nearby as Tilcalli leaned

back against Bherasha and closed her eyes. Calindor growled through his teeth. Why would she want to go into the Open Dream? Could Calihalingol save them from Gaupi's arrows?

Two arrows rose from the second group of riders, the ones on the right bank. The archers were not as good, and their companions across the river yelped in derision. Their voices carried clearly across the water, making them seem even closer.

"All right, boys," said Svordo. "We're picking up the pace. Row. Row. Row."

Now the Badakhar on both sides of the river had come down to the water's edge. Walking their horses, they easily kept pace with the boat as it struggled against the current.

"Ho, Gaupi!" a man called out from the right bank. So Pervidhu had guessed right, Calindor thought. *"A wager. First man to score a kill gets a barrel of medh."*

"Done. And five barrels if it's Dheribi or his mother."

"Row. Row. Row," Svordo growled.

The Badakhar seemed in no hurry. From time to time, one archer or another would launch a shaft. Through his focus, Calindor could see it rise, foretell its fall. The first two were ill-aimed; the next was not. He jerked the tiller sharply to the right, making Svordo stare at him in amazement as the longboat lost way. Then the arrow, from Gaupi's side, hissed into the water between two oars.

"Thank you, Dheribi," Svordo said. "Someone would have won the barrel at my expense."

Let them only think it was bad luck, Calindor thought. If they realized he could foresee the flight of a single arrow, they would begin to shoot five or six at once. He would not be able to dodge them all.

Painfully, the rowers fought against the current. Gasping, streaked with sweat that steamed through their tunics, the Cantareans pulled at their oars. Moro panted: "Perhaps—turn around—go with the river—outrun them."

"Can't," Svordo answered. "More men downstream—follow us easy—finish us off. Row. Row. Row."

All that long morning they rowed. For a short time the river's width put them out of range; a little later they were dodging shaft after shaft. Calindor felt like laughing. If the Badakhar hadn't made their bet, they would have tired of this game by now and put a cloud of arrows into their target. Kill or cripple even a couple of the rowers, and they would all be lost.

The rowers were tiring. Calindor could see it in their faces, in their shuddering arms, in the blood that oozed from their blistered hands. The longboat was making little headway, and snow was falling again. Soon the archers would lose patience. A single volley of arrows would kill enough of the rowers to send the boat drifting back downstream.

He swung the boat sharply to the right to evade an arrow from Gaupi's band. Ahead, the land was changing. The dunes were giving way to steep gravel banks with trees growing right down to the edge. Fallen trunks blocked what little room there might be between land and water.

Good—the riders would have to climb and then work their way through the trees to gain a clear shot. Their height would give them an extra advantage, perhaps, but they might find it harder to keep up even with the boat's slow pace.

"Row . . . Row . . ." Svordo's voice was a dry rasp. *They can't keep going long,* Calindor thought. Cold, ill-fed, exhausted, still they tugged at their oars.

Tilcalli gasped and sat up. Bherasha gripped her shoulder, steadying her. Pervidhu, sitting up in the prow of the longboat, uttered an unwilled groan of fear when Tilcalli's eyes met his.

She twisted around to see Calindor. "Dheribi! Is anyone hurt? No? Good. Keep rowing, keep rowing. They are sending help."

"Who is sending help?" Bherasha asked.

"Tanshadabela."

"But how do they know we're here?"

"The Open Dream. I spoke to my husband in the Open Dream."

Bherasha glanced over her shoulder to meet Calindor's gaze. She looked frightened and confused; he smiled and reached forward to touch her arm.

The arrows had ceased for a time; the riders on the right bank were lost in the trees, and those on the left were well out of range. The snow fell harder, flying on a chill wind out of the mountains. They passed two or three small islands, large enough to support a few spruce and lodgepoles, and Calindor dreamed of going ashore to rest for a time. They would be safe from arrows, they could have a fire, a rest—

No. Only shallow rivulets separated the islands from the shore; the Badakhar would cross them easily and put the fugitives to death without trouble. Calindor gripped the pommel of his sword for a moment, knowing himself too weary to fight strong men on horseback. He blinked away the snow that clung to his eyelashes.

For what seemed a long time, they saw no riders at all. Ahead, the river curved around a long, wooded benchland at the foot of a mountain just visible through the snow. The steep banks gentled into a broad and grassy valley.

"Steer for the left bank," Tilcalli murmured. "They will be coming down the trail."

"It's very open," Bherasha said, pointing across the water to broad brown meadows now half-crusted with snow. "The Badakhar will see them coming."

"Good. The Badakhar will turn and run without a fight."

"Maybe they have turned back already," Bherasha said. "I haven't seen them for a long time."

Calindor tapped her shoulder and shook his head. They were still there, moving through the trees. Soon they would reach the meadow and quickly catch up. And they would not be eager to run from a fight with a few Menmannar, not when the prize was almost within their grasp. He glanced down at the staff of Pelshadan, lying close to Bherasha's hand. The Veik would be terrified until he retrieved it.

Now his focus sensed others: men and horses, moving from the west along the river. The rescuers were near, but beyond them was something else—a presence that reminded him somehow of the lost caverns that even the Gulyaji had never explored. He shuddered with something more than the icy wind.

They were coming close to the shore now, close enough to see the trail winding across the meadow through the dead grass and clumps of willow. If Gaupi and his men caught up now, the longboat would be at almost point-blank range; the fugitives would be able to see the archers' eyes.

"Put us ashore," Tilcalli commanded. "The men have no more strength."

He could see that she was right. Even Svordo could barely tug at his oar, and the others were even weaker. They would have to get to shore and join the Menmannar as quickly as possible.

The longboat's bottom grated on the rounded stones of the shoreline. Calindor stood, stepped out into the icy water, and helped Tilcalli and Bherasha out. Svordo and Moro and the others sat motionless for a moment, and then lurched out of the boat. Clumsily, they staggered over the rocks and onto the bank.

"Do you leave me to freeze?" Pervidhu called.

"We leave you to your companions," Tilcalli said. "We cannot carry you, but they will soon be here."

"Well, they'll have a good laugh carrying me. I thank you all for my life, and for your hospitality." The Badakh grinned wryly through his beard and waved his bound hands in ironic salute. Then he settled himself, eyes fixed on the woods downstream where his rescuers must soon emerge.

Clinging to one another, the fugitives hobbled across the meadow toward the trail. Calindor walked at the rear, glancing over his shoulder. The Badakhar were close, close—and so were the Menmannar and the strange being that followed them.

He had never been so cold, not even on the day of the Gathering when they had whipped him in the snow. His legs were gray, his trousers soaked with slush. The others were no better off, and some of the rowers seemed barely able to stand.

Gaupi and the other five archers emerged from the woods, saw them, and spurred their horses to a gallop. The hoofbeats seemed to come from far away, muted by the snow and the sandy soil. But the riders would be upon them in moments, and they would lay no more wagers.

More hoofbeats sounded, from the west, and Calindor turned to see a column of riders moving at a trot along the trail. Their horses were smaller than the Badakhar's, sturdy and shaggy; the riders wore white buckskin and fur cloaks.

"Only five of them—only five!" Bherasha said. "Tilcalli, are there more?"

Tilcalli seemed startled, as if she had suddenly realized something, and turned to Calindor. "Dheribi—are more coming?"

He nodded and held up a single finger.

She turned to Minukhi, who was holding Moro about the shoulders. "Have your powers recovered? Can you create an illusion?"

"No. I cannot."

"Then let us keep on toward my husband and his friends. I must ask him why he brought so few to aid us." And she began to plod steadily across the snow-crusted meadow while the Badakhar rode closer.

The pursuers were within easy bowshot now, but they had put their bows away; swords' steel glinted in the grayness. Calindor drew his own sword. Perhaps he could get one or two, occupy them while the others reached the Menmannar.

They too were close, riding hard with bows in their hands and their reins looped about the pommels of their saddles. Calindor felt his heart rise at the sight of them, at the beauty of their movement and their long black hair flying in the wind. *One of those men must be my father,* he thought absently. *But I will never live to speak with him.*

A cry filled the winter air: a roar, a scream, a metallic shriek. The horses of the Badakhar echoed it with frantic whinnies, and Calindor saw Gaupi and his men suddenly struggle to control their rearing mounts. Some of the men cried out also, and they were close enough for Calindor to see the fear in their faces.

He spun back to the Menmannar, and saw that they had paused. Racing past them was a creature whose crested head was a little higher than those of the Manmannar horsemen. It ran on two legs, long and terribly clawed. Its forelegs it extended, clawed as well, and its long, narrow muzzle grinned with fangs. The mass of its torso and head was balanced by a ridged tail. Its scaled body was green and gold; its eyes were black and bright with a fierce intelligence.

No horse could match the creature's speed. It ran lightly and with grace, as if this was what it had been made for.

"Dragasa!" Tilcalli screamed, and Calindor understood why: it was his father's name, but it was also the name of the creature.

Dragon.

Eighteen

One man—perhaps it was Gaupi—controlled his horse long enough to shoot an arrow. Its path was true, but the dragon snatched it from the air as a man might catch a slow mosquito. It roared again, and now the Badakhar could restrain their mounts no more. The terrified horses spun and ran, while their riders cast away their bows and quivers.

With almost dreamlike ease the dragon overtook the rearmost, reached out, and delicately raked the horse's hindquarters. The frightened beast lunged forward, its rider clinging for his life.

Calindor saw that the dragon could catch and slay them all, but instead it turned and glided back across the snowy meadow. The Badakhar disappeared into the woods, but the horses' whinnies still pierced the snowy air.

Now, after a brief glance at Pervidhu in the longboat, the dragon approached the fugitives. Moro and the others stood in a cluster, unmoving. Tilcalli and Bherasha pulled closer to Calindor, as if to protect him.

Minukhi fell to his knees in the snow, his arms extended. "A dragon! And no illusion. I got it right! Pelshadan always criticized my dragons, but I got it right."

The dragon paused before them. Balanced easily with its tail extended, it lowered its great head to study each person in turn. *This must be how a beetle feels before a bird,* Calindor thought. Fear and joy battled in him. If they must be this creature's prey, at least they would fall to a great predator. In the Underland he had suddenly dreamed of seeking the dragons; now he had found one.

Its smooth snout, pierced by two thin nostrils, probed close, sniffing him and the others. Its breath was hot, pluming in drifts of steam, and the snowflakes that fell on its green-and-gold flanks melted at once. The scales that covered it were as fine as a garter snake's, yet through his focus Calindor could sense that they were tougher than the finest Staldhuno steel.

He sensed also that it too possessed a focus, far greater than his own, and was using it to examine the fugitives. Tilcalli, Minukhi, and Calindor himself—those with a talent for magic—staggered a little as the dragon's focus swept them.

Then the great beast settled back on its haunches, and its long, crested tail swept the snow. The Menmannar riders approached slowly, stopped, and dismounted.

Their leader was a tall man, his long black hair streaked with gray and held at the nape by a silver clasp. He wore a cloak of sable over white buckskin tunic and trousers, and fur-topped boots of black leather. At his waist hung a short, straight sword with an unadorned grip.

"I greet you, my husband," said Tilcalli softly.

"I greet you, my wife." But Dragasa's eyes were dark with anger.

"This is your son."

Dragasa's eyes, as black and bright as the dragon's, fell on him. A faint smile tugged at the older man's lips, and Calindor realized his father felt shy. *And he is my father—we have the same nose, the same chin!*

"Come here." Dragasa beckoned to him, and Calindor obeyed. Dragasa took his hands, felt them, then looked into his son's eyes. He touched Calindor's throat and frowned.

"This is bad. I have never felt such a presence as this one." He stepped back and raised a hand to summon the dragon, which had retreated to give room to the Menmannar. It glided forward and looked down at Dragasa.

"We call this dragon Obordur," he said to Tilcalli and the others. "They have no language as we have, and no names, so we must give them names. She is a very wise being." He turned to the dragon as Calindor felt something like a focus wash over him. But this was different: it was like standing beside a roaring waterfall and hearing a man's faint voice almost lost in the thunder. Dragasa's was the voice; the thunder was Obordur.

In the tales of his childhood, Calindor thought, dragons always spoke to men. That was how they cast their terrible spells. Yet here was a real dragon, possessing enormous power yet without speech. Magic without language seemed a contradiction in terms, but the dragon was no contradiction: she was a point of harmony with herself and the world.

The dragon extended one long foreclaw; the talon retracted almost like a cat's, and a soft pad touched Calindor on his collarbone. The cold grip on his throat seemed suddenly tighter, and he gasped. The thunder went on, silent yet deafening, and then stopped abruptly.

Dragasa looked disappointed. "I had hopes she could break the spell, but even a dragon's touch cannot cure everything."

Calindor recognized the saying from his childhood, something Tilcalli and the palace slaves used to tell one another.

"Time enough to heal him when we are rested and strong again," Tilcalli said. "Come—take us home."

Dragasa nodded, but Calindor could see anger still glittering in his father's eyes. "It is not far. Will you ride?" He gestured to his horse.

"No—just let me walk beside you, if you will let me."

"As you wish."

They had begun to plod across the crusted snow when a rasping voice called out behind them: "Am I to guard your boat, or may I paddle it home to Aishadan?"

Pervidhu was peeping over the prow of the longboat, evidently unafraid of Menmannar and dragon alike. Tilcalli found the strength to laugh; when she translated what he had said, Dragasa and the other men laughed also.

"He is our prisoner," Tilcalli explained. "We will have to bring him along as well. His leg is broken, so someone will have to carry him."

Dragasa nodded. "We'll make a litter, and carry him between the horses."

He and his men quickly improvised a litter out of oars and a blanket, and hoisted Pervidhu out of the longboat. Lashing the ends of the oars to the pommels of their saddles, they carried the Badakh slowly but easily across the meadow. Behind them trailed the rest of the fugitives, with Obordur prowling now at the head of the column, now at the rear. The dragon seemed patient with the humans' slow pace, and still curious about the newcomers; she leaned over Dragasa and his horse to study Pervidhu, who cried out in one spasm of fear and then fell silent.

The trail curved round a low hill and ran through stands of aspen and pine. Calindor saw his mother look around with eyes that seemed to notice everything, and he suddenly realized that this must be the trail that Albohar and the others had used in their raid long ago. *But not so long ago for Tilcalli,* he thought.

They crossed another meadow, on a bluff overlooking the

river, and from Dragasa and Tilcalli alike he sensed anguish. He sensed as well that they too knew one another's feelings, and Calindor felt the anguish begin to fade. Tilcalli stopped, turned to Dragasa, and put her arms around him. In turn he embraced her, and both wept as he stroked her hair.

Standing a few paces behind them, Calindor felt their painful joy, and his own as well. He was more Badakh than Cantarean by upbringing, and now felt himself neither. Had his mother not let herself be captured, he would have grown up in these mountains, known these trails, learned from his parents about a whole world. So that he might save her people, Tilcalli had made him someone else. His true self was lost, as lost as the years when he should have had a family and a place here.

Svordo caught his eye. He looked as out of place here as Calindor felt, yet he grinned and stepped closer.

"If you hadn't told me to run, back in Ner Kes, I'd still be in a nice snug barracks there instead of freezing in these mountains. Well, who knows where we'll end up before we're through?"

Calindor smiled back, shamed by Svordo's good humor. When Tilcalli had finished weeping, and turned with Dragasa back toward the village, he followed with a lighter heart.

Tanshadabela, Two Stream Village, took its name from its site: it stood on a bluff overlooking the river where it curved northeastward around the foot of a mountain, and where a smaller stream merged with it. The Vesparushrei was gray with glacial silt, and turbulent in its flow; the tributary was a cold, dark green that quickly merged and was lost without trace. In the curve of the river stood several wooded islets, and more forests rose on the right bank beyond. Through the thickening snow, Calindor could just make out the bulk of great mountains on either side of the river.

The village itself was not large—perhaps thirty small cabins, a few barns, a larger building in the center. A stockade ringed the village, but to Calindor it looked like a flimsy barrier against the warriors who had stormed Ner Kes.

The trail led to the stockade through small fields fenced with stones. Calindor could sense how poor the soil was here, and how much greenmagic had been used to keep grain growing in it.

People were coming forth to greet them, bearing fur cloaks and steaming bowls of soup. They crowded around the fugitives, draping the cloaks over their shoulders and offering each one a bowl almost too hot to hold. Calindor nodded his thanks and drank deep, suddenly aware of his hunger. The soup, almost thick enough to be a stew, revived him without appeasing his appetite.

They entered the village, and different families took charge of each fugitive; some took charge as well of Pervidhu, bearing him into the largest building with promises to tend to his leg. Obordur went alone into a barnlike building nearby.

Calindor followed Tilcalli and Dragasa into a cabin not far from the stockade. It reminded him, oddly, of the Protector's hut in the cavern of the Gulyaji. Three small rooms were heated by a single fireplace built of stone and mortar, with an opening into each room. The interior walls were rough-cut planks, the floor of dirt covered with goatskins. A ladder led from the front room to a small loft. Windows were narrow vertical slits, sealed with strips of translucent hide.

"Sit," Dragasa commanded, gesturing to a narrow bed covered with sheepskins. Calindor and Tilcalli obeyed while he built up the fire. Soon the room was blissfully warm; Calindor put out his hands to the heat, yet found himself shivering hard.

Dragasa had opened a beautifully crafted cabinet, and was setting out food: cheese, hard bread, a squat stoneware jug full of dark beer. Saying little, he served them and watched them eat.

"If you wish more, you have only to ask," he said as Tilcalli put her wooden plate aside.

"I will only make myself ill if I eat too much. Thank you."

"Do not thank me. This is your house. Everything you see is yours."

"I—I know. But it will take me time to get used to it again. It seems much bigger than I remember."

"Our old cabin is gone. I built this one six years ago. My ancestors told me you would come back some day, so I made it large."

She said nothing for a time, while the fire crackled and hissed. "We have much to tell each other."

He nodded, his face impassive in the firelight. "And to tell our son."

Tilcalli leaned over and put her arm around Calindor, who still shivered. "I think you will find him a true dragon's son."

Dragasa looked into Calindor's eyes. "Yes. I think you are right. Here, it's growing late. Come and dress properly, and then come with me to the Meeting Hall. The people will want to know everything.''

In his father's white buckskin trousers and tunic, with a cloak of fisher pelts, Calindor felt uncomfortably elegant. So, it seemed, did most of the other fugitives. The slaves whom Sveit had given him were constantly looking down at themselves, or at one another, unable to believe anyone would give them such finery. Bherasha, in a fine wool skirt that fell to her ankles, and a buckskin tunic ornamented with porcupine quills, looked beautiful; Calindor saw a number of young men eyeing her. Only Svordo and Tilcalli seemed at ease in their new clothes, while Minukhi stubbornly wore his original cloak and robe.

They had gathered with the rest of the village, perhaps a hundred men, women and children, in the large building in the center of Tanshadabela. The Meeting Hall's interior was a single large room; on each long wall, three rows of benches rose like steps. They faced a narrow floor strewn with sand. At either end of the building, fires burned on great hearths between tall wooden pillars, carved in images of bear and wolf and dragon.

In one of the adjoining rooms, someone said, the Badakh prisoner was being tended. He was reportedly cheerful and very hungry. Tilcalli replied that she would begin to heal his leg in the morning, if her powers had returned to her. Hearing her, Calindor kept his face still.

Obordur was not there; she could hardly have fitted through the doors. But Calindor, sitting with his parents in the first row of benches, could sense her nearby.

An old woman stood on the sandy floor, wearing a long cloak of blue-dyed wool; this, Dragasa murmured to Calindor, was Tulucuingol, Keeper of the House, who guided the people's debates and mediated their quarrels.

''I ask for your hearing,'' the old woman said softly, and the murmur of the adults and children ceased.

''Our sister Tilcalli has returned with her son from the lands of the Badakhar,'' Tulucuingol said. ''We all rejoice in them, and in those who brought them home to us.''

The Cantareans clapped their hands, a custom that seemed strange to Calindor. Minukhi twitched a little, and wiped his streaming eyes.

''I ask you, Tilcalli, to tell us of your journeys, and how you came back to us.''

Tilcalli stood. ''I thank you, Tulucuingol, for your welcome. I look around this room and I rejoice to see so many beloved kin and friends, and so many new children." She paused, then drew breath and began to speak: of Calihalingol's dream, of the long years in Aishadan, of Dheribi's upbringing and exile and return, of his tutelage under Pelshadan and the escape from the Gathering Field.

"He was born to the Siragi Aibela on both sides," she said. "Not often do members of the same clan marry, and some people questioned our wisdom. But we were in love, and I dreamed of a child who would wield great magic for Callia. My great-grandmother Calihalingol gave me the dream, and told me I must raise that child to learn the lore of our enemies as well.

"Calihalingol was wise, and my son has indeed learned more magic than anyone in our clan. He knows much of our magic, and of the Badakhar, and even of the Sanpala Gulyaji, our long-lost cousins. The Firelord, the evil god of the Badakhar, attacked him and could not kill him."

Calindor stared at the sandy floor: his mother, not he, had driven Mekhpur back.

"But he has been treacherously enchanted, robbed of his speech and of his powers," Tilcalli went on. "If we can remove the Gariba that grips his throat, and restore his voice, he will stand as the greatest magician Cantarea has ever known."

She fell silent. A woman in the benches opposite stood up and received Tulucuingol's permission to speak.

"I was one of those who questioned your wisdom when you married Dragasa," she said. "I did not know that your great-grandmother guided you in your steps, Tilcalli, and I am sorry for the hard words I spoke in those days. Now I ask you if this enchantment may indeed be lifted from your son by our magic, when it was put upon him by a Badakh magician."

"Perhaps. I hope that when the wisest of the Siragi Aibela have seen him, and sensed the Gariba that holds his voice, they will find a way to break the spell." She hesitated. "You have befriended a dragon, and perhaps she can help also."

A pulse of the dragon's focus flashed through the room, making Tilcalli stiffen and gasp; so too did Calindor, Dragasa, Minukhi and a few others.

"I sense she follows my words," Tilcalli went on after a moment. "But I cannot understand her. I humbly hope that she may grant us her aid and wisdom, and let my son regain the powers he has dedicated to Callia."

Again Obordur's focus filled the hall, but this time it was aimed directly at Calindor. He stood, looked fearfully at his mother and father, and then slowly walked out of the Meeting Hall.

The dragon was waiting for him in the barn.

She squatted on her powerful hind legs, with her forelegs held close to her golden body. A dim yellow-orange circle of light hung suspended without support near the rafters of the high-walled room, something perhaps like coldfire. Obordur's breath rasped in her nostrils, and her eyes fixed on his.

I greet you again, Calindor thought. *Do you understand me, Obordur?*

The dragon lashed her tail and nodded her great head.

Can you heal me? Oh heal me, Obordur!

Something rocked him, made him put out an arm to keep his balance. He felt he looked at himself in a wall of mirrors, and thought: *Myself? Am I to heal myself?*

In the multiple images of himself, the eyes grew large and bright; Calindor hesitated, and then understood. *I am to look within myself.*

Again energy surged out from the dragon, and he caught something like amusement in it. Slowly he sat, legs crossed beneath him. The muscles still ached from the long days in the boat, but he ignored the discomfort and sought a deeper focus.

Strange, to look at himself as he had become used to looking at the world around him. He saw his own Gariba, the powers that lived in him and through him, as well as the alien power that had invaded his throat. Even it had a shimmering beauty, a joy in its own existence for all that it was cold and malign to its host.

Deeper he went, into chambers of his own soul that he had not known existed. He saw rage there, and love and fear and arrogance and wonder. Deeper still, and found an opening: a gap that led outside himself, to a place, a state of being, an otherness that made him shudder and fall back upon the straw.

Dimly he saw Obordur's fangs glinting in the golden light, as if the dragon smiled.

That is what you wished me to find? An emptiness?

Irritably the dragon lashed her tail, throwing clouds of straw into the air. Calindor shivered under her displeasure. He turned fearfully back to the opening within himself, looked beyond it—

It was like one of the passages between the great caverns of the Gulyaji, Calindor thought, a place where a river might gain force by sheer compression and plunge on with unstoppable speed.

Ah—I see, Obordur. I see.

Beyond it lay magic, glowing and coiling with undreamable energies in another realm. Even through that tiny opening, it revealed enough of itself to dazzle and frighten and exalt him. It was through this gap in his soul that it had poured, making him the vehicle of its energy and will as the edge of a sword carries and focuses the power of its wielder's arm.

But I cannot call it up. I cannot speak. Free me of the Gariba, let me call the magic and save my people.

Obordur lost interest in him. He felt her attention leave him, and did not know if he was glad or miserable. Yet he knew he had been dismissed. Slowly he stood up and walked out of the barn.

New snow was falling, gleaming in the yellow light that spilled from the barn door. Nearby, Bherasha stood with the staff of Pelshadan in her hand. He saw the Powers moving in it, more clearly than ever, yet he knew himself as helpless as ever to master them.

Something in his face made Bherasha step quickly to him, and put her arm around him. He held her and burst into tears, weeping in whispers.

I know what Obordur has shown me. But what does she mean?

Nineteen

Snegh's riders had fashioned rough lean-tos in the ruins of the Menmannar village. He remembered rowing past it in the dark, all those years ago, when it had smelled of smoke and cooking, and women's laughter had trilled across the river. Snegh had known then that if the Menmannar had seen them, they would have died in a cloud of arrows, but he had feared nothing. Now the village was only rotting timbers and fallen stones, and it made him uneasy.

He and his vanguard squadrons had paused here for two days now, waiting for the rest of the army to catch up. Scouts had gone out in search of the original pursuers, but had found no one. The fugitives must have rowed hard to get so far up the river, Snegh thought. Perhaps they had indeed reached that same village far upstream.

He sat before a smoky fire in a lean-to overlooking the river. Snow was falling steadily now, and building up in places. A few more days and ice would begin to reach across the river, and then to thicken.

This was a bad time to bring so many horses and men into forested country, Snegh thought. Like Ner Kes all over again, an endless struggle for food. Eskel had been generous with supplies, but horses must carry much of their own fodder in this winter country. That limited their range; if he could not find the fugitives within a few more days, he would have to send much of the army home and go on into the mountains with just a handful of fighting riders and a long string of pack animals.

Vulkvo came crunching across the snow, calling Snegh's name, and then filled the entrance to the lean-to. Behind him was a lean man whose beard did not entirely conceal the scars on his face. Nor could he conceal the terror in his eyes.

"This is Gaupi," Vulkvo grunted, pulling the man in to sit by the fire. "Give him some medh and some of that jerky. He's had a hard ride and tells a hard story."

Snegh passed a jug of medh and watched as Gaupi swigged it.

"We nearly had them," Gaupi whispered. "They'd come ashore just a little way ahead of us, and we should have taken them easy. Some Menmannar appeared, four or five, nothing we couldn't have handled. And then the dragon came."

Snegh coughed, snorted and spat into the fire. "A dragon? Just another small sorcerer's trick. That renegade Minukhi, the one with the eyes, he made a dragon when they escaped."

Gaupi looked into Snegh's eyes. "You may go and look at the wounds on my horse's croup, and tell me that a small sorcerer put them there. This was no illusion. Let Mekhpur hear me, I saw a dragon and nearly fed it."

The archer's fear was real, and contagious. Snegh glanced at Vulkvo and saw his own sudden alarm mirrored in his comrade's eyes. Witches and magicians were bad enough, riding in winter into Menmannar country was bad enough, but now a dragon stood between them and the fugitives.

"The old tales tell of many slain dragons," he said brusquely. "Now we'll have another such tale."

Vulkvo laughed without amusement. "My granny always told me it took a great warrior and a strong Veik to kill a dragon."

"We should have brought your granny along to share her lore with us. Dragon or no dragon, we go forward when the last squadrons reach us."

Snow trimmed the roofs and merlons of the Arekaryo Kes, and fell lightly through the gray air. Ghelasha pulled her fur cloak closer around her as she walked through the icy corridors to the Hearing Hall. The whole fortress stank of coal smoke and decay, she thought. Too many people cooped up too long inside closed windows, closed rooms.

The Hearing Hall was still crowded with petitioners; they bowed and made way for her, smiling and murmuring. A slave hurried to bring her a chair beside the hearth, not far from where her son sat on the Aryo's throne.

Eskel rose in respect, greeted her, and resumed his seat. The petitioner she had interrupted seemed rattled, and lost the train of his argument. Eskel nodded impatiently, said: "I will look into it," and waved him away.

Ghelasha watched Eskel with interest, and the petitioners as well. He was handling the chores of office with some skill, and showed no sign of puffing himself up. Good—many a fine warrior had undone himself and his kingdom by thinking only of the battlefield and not of the storehouses and smithies. And no Aryo was ever rich enough or strong enough.

The petitioners were the usual mix of upermannar and freemen, seeking exemption from taxes, a job for a son, an apprenticeship for a cousin, grazing rights for themselves. They looked sleeker and better fed than they had last spring at the Gathering, Ghelasha thought. Ner Kes had put fat on their ribs and fur on their backs, enough to get them through the winter.

"Aryako," said one big smith, a famous stalmagh, "I ask for eight new slaves and enough grain to feed them until spring. If I do not have them—"

"New slaves?" Eskel interrupted. "Why? You must have twenty already, toiling in your smithy."

"Twenty-two, Aryako, but most are weak and useless, unable to carry any weight. I've branded two and posted one to smarten up the rest, but it's no use. They're sick, fuddled with hunger, and no good to me. Meanwhile I have much work that you have graciously bestowed on me."

"The slaves are dying like poisoned rats this winter," Eskel muttered. "Half the ones we brought back from Ner Kes are in the river already. The Nerkesar deserved to lose if they couldn't look after their slaves any better than that."

"Indeed, Aryako, you speak the truth. Yet if I can have but six, six good strapping males, next spring you will have swords and armor in great number and of finest quality."

"I can let you have four, and three barrels of grain."

The stalmagh frowned for an instant, then smiled. "Aryako, I am deeply grateful for your generosity. I humbly thank you and wish you much joy."

Hooded by her yellow hair, Ghelasha allowed herself a longer frown than the smith had risked. If the slaves were dying off like that, Aishadan would be ill-equipped for the wars and trading of the spring. But it was dangerous to pamper them, to feed them up and keep them too comfortable. They grew fat and lazy, got their women pregnant, and did less work than ever. The trick was to keep them hungry enough to think only of their next meal and what they must do to deserve it. Three barrels of grain would be enough for a month or more, but if the smith overfed his new slaves he would be back where he'd started in no time.

Other petitioners approached the Aryako while Ghelasha sat silently. They all confirmed the image she had gained from other hearings, from the whispers of the slaves and the looks of the freemen in the markets: the upermannar and the richer freemen were doing well, but the poor and enslaved were suffering badly.

Well, let them, so long as they lived to serve the Aryako in his spring battles.

At last the petitioners were gone and the Hearing Hall was empty except for the two of them and a few guards. Ghelasha smiled at her son.

"You handle them well. And you look as stern as your father did."

"I do what I must. Have you heard anything more from Snegh and Vulkvo?"

"I? They do not report to me."

"Then their servants do." Eskel smiled faintly. "Let them just send word that they have the staff, and I can plan for the spring with a light heart."

"I have spoken with Pelshadan."

"Does he say anything worth listening to these days?"

"He is a Veik and a Skalkaz afi Mekhpur, a servant of the Firelord," she reproved him quietly. "He knows the perils we face."

"Has he been—tested?"

"He thinks so. Perhaps they were only dreams, but he thinks they were more than that. We have done well to stop the rumors, but it only needs one snot-nosed child to prattle in the wrong place."

"What of his assistants, Dvoi and the other fellow? Potiari?"

"They are caring well for him, and for your father. You should come to see him, Eskel."

"I am pressed with business. I will try."

She knew better. Albohar was a wraith now, his beard half-white and his skin pulled tight over his bones. The wound in his chest had blackened his whole torso, and stank of some awful fetor. No one visited the Aryo without good reason to.

"What I meant," Eskel went on, "was whether the Veik's helpers might take over for him. Protect him."

"They tell me they cannot, and I know they are right." She felt a sudden horrifying urge to wring her hands and to wish out loud that the filthy slave girl had fallen dead before striking Pelshadan. Fear was the worst feeling in the world, she hated it, yet it clung like the stink from the Kes's latrines.

Eskel shrugged and smiled as brightly as a girl. "Then we can only hope for Snegh and Vulkvo to bring back the staff."

"And what if they fail? What then?"

"Then we are doomed."

She glared at him. "And you can speak of doom so calmly?"

Something like contempt glittered in his eyes, making her feel he had suddenly changed from her son into something else—a strange and powerful male, immune to her, blind to her.

"Every man who goes into battle knows what he risks, Mother. We have been in battle ever since that slave bastard killed Blaidakh." Eskel rubbed the thin beard sprouting on his chin. "But I will win this battle. I will win."

Dragasa's cabin was too small for the three of them. Calindor slept ill that first night, listening to them whisper in the next room. He could have focused closely enough to hear each word, but they deserved some privacy and they would have detected his attention as easily as if he had walked in and climbed into bed with them.

So he dozed and thought and worried, and in the morning went shivering out into a blue-gray dawn. The sky was lightening behind the great mountains to the east, and the peaks to the west glowed with the promise of a new day under clear skies. Yet a few stars still gleamed overhead.

His feet crunched in the snow; the cold made his nose run. He passed the cabin where Bherasha slept, and the one where Svordo and Moro snored. The others were scattered around the village, with Pervidhu back in the Meeting Hall. Today Tilcalli hoped to restore his leg.

Calindor came to the dragon's barn. The door opened easily, and warm air steamed around him. Inside was dark and rich with the dragon's scent.

I greet you, Obordur. I seek only a quiet shelter. May I share this place with you for a little while?

The dragon stirred a little, flicking her crested tail through the straw. He realized she was building him a bed at her side, and bowed in gratitude. Pulling his new fur robes around him, he lay down in the straw and felt Obordur's heat close by. *I thank you.*

Her only reply was a long rumbling sigh, and then silence. Calindor felt a strange contentment, much like the moment when he had rested close to Bherasha, and closed his eyes.

* * *

He seemed to hang in the air like a hawk, but now he did not look down on the Silent River and the sunny fields of the Open Dream. Now he glided over sharp-edged mountains, and knew somehow that they were the mountains around Tanshadabela in an earlier age.

The valley of the Vesparushrei looked deeper and narrower, and the forests were different: the trees were strangely fronded, their thick trunks rising to the sun through a humid haze. Beneath the trees small creatures darted from shade to shade, or pursued one another through marshy meadows. Others, slightly larger, moved more deliberately. Calindor recognized them not from their appearance but their Gariba: these beings had once explored the caverns beyond even the reach of the Gulyaji, and had left their traces for him to find in the silent dark of the Underland. They did not look much like dragons; they were too small, too slow and gentle, and their muzzles were blunt. Yet they moved with dragons' grace, and their eyes saw the world with dragons' sharpness.

The valley receded southward between great mountain ranges that trapped thunderstorms on their peaks. Calindor soared and sank, rejoicing in the richness of Callia's youth. He saw herds of great scaled beasts, trudging in formation around their young as they moved in search of new pastures. Sometimes the dragons' ancestors hunted them, but more often they seemed like human herders guiding their cattle to safe country.

How long ago was this, and how long had the valley lain hot and green under the hazy sky? Nothing told him. But a breeze seemed to catch him, turn him around, and when he looked down again the mountains glittered with the thick blue-white crust of ancient ice.

The many-fronded trees were gone, and the scaled herds. Glaciers groaned down the mountainsides, merging into a crevassed mass in the valley. Each tongue of ice followed an ancient stream bed or avalanche chute, but the land was not utterly overwhelmed. On steep ridges, green terraces faced the sun and stone houses defied the wind.

Calindor saw magic at work. And on those ridges he saw the dragons, as proud and terrible as Obordur. They tended their patches of green, little memories of ancient luxuriance, and put up their walls and spells against the ice. Tall they were, fierce and hot, their golden flanks steaming in the chill air. To them the glacier at their feet was no more than a road, and they raced upon it with joy in their own strength.

They knew the Gariba; some among the dragons were like Veikar, masters of magic wielding staffs and bidding the Powers without word or chant. They roved far, east onto the prairie and west to the plateaus and ranges that fell at last into a great sea. All of Sotalar was theirs; they held the world in easy mastery.

Again the wind caught him, drove him toward a sunrise cloaked in storm clouds. He sensed a kind of opening somewhere in the storm, and a presence: vast, intelligent, and strange, a being as great as Callia yet utterly different. Then it was gone. Lightning walked across the prairie in the dawn; when it had passed, a little band of humans huddled by an icebound lake. They looked about themselves with surprise and fear, like people roused from sleep and finding themselves in a strange place. They were roughly dressed in furs and skins, and the just-risen sun gleamed on their spearheads of fine-chipped flint.

Calindor wished he could cry out a greeting to them, for they looked so much like his ancestors in the Open Dream. But his voice was still gripped by the Power that had hidden in the staff of Tenglekur.

The band of hunters did not long stand still. One among them pointed to a nearby hill, led them there, and in its lee began to dig a shelter by a spring. Others loped off to the south, moving with the easy strides of men accustomed to run all day. Calindor saw their prey before they did: a herd of great beasts, not scaly but furred and tusked, with strange noses like snakes. The hunters laughed and sang at the sight of them, knowing their prey even if the land seemed strange.

Again the wind took him, and again. The land looked less bleak now; the glaciers gleamed only on the highest shoulders of the mountains in the west. The smoke of the hunters' fires rose in a hundred places, and the bones and hides of their prey made their houses.

Where were the dragons who had once run free across the prairie? Calindor saw them retreat into their mountains and valleys, casting wordless spells to bar the intruders. Yet the hunters had their magic also, and pushed west in search of the great tusked animals. Few did they find, and when those were slain they found no more. The dragons held to their high fortresses, and gave the hunters new lore: seeds and young plants, long nurtured on the green terraces above the ice. These the newcomers planted in the rich black soil of the prairie, and in the ever-warmer summers the plants grew well.

Now the prairie was truly the Cantarea of the old songs and

legends, a land of villages and green fields marked by long lines of trees shading simple trails. Now Callia grew strong again, and men lived at peace in her beauty. The dragons came down from their redoubts, roving across the fields in hundreds and taking honor from the Cantareans.

The dragons might be without speech, but they were not without wisdom. They had sensed that strange presence in the dawn storm, recognized it as an entity as great as Callia. They had seen that the first hunters, whatever unknown world they might come from, could be a gift to Callia as well as a threat. The dragons had served her well as their tutors. The Cantareans learned much from the dreams the dragons sent.

On the horizons of the prairie, other storms sometimes flashed and receded. Calindor knew that when they passed, more humans found themselves gazing at a different world from that they had last slept in. But they moved in other directions—south into high plateaus and endless grasslands, southwest into mountains and deserts, north to the treeless lands and east to forests that seemed afire in cold autumn days. With them came strange new animals: sheep, goats, cattle and horses, dogs and scuttling rats. These sometimes escaped their masters, lived wild on the land and came at last to the lands of the Cantareans. With the dragons' wisdom the Cantareans learned the ways of these new beasts, and made a place for them in Callia's land.

East of Cantarea, far to the east, the prairie lost itself in a maze of lakes and trees, and beyond them true forest began. Here lived other people, small tribes who hunted and fished as the Cantareans themselves sometimes still did. Calindor soared over their villages, simpler than Tanshadabela but still homes to eager children and quick-footed, laughing men and women. The smokes of their fires rose in thin tendrils beyond the treetops, reaching for the sky.

Now among them came a new people, few in numbers but mounted on tough ponies and driving herds of cattle through the forest in search of upland pastures. Calindor felt hatred and grudging admiration contend within him: these were the ancient Badakhar, strangely dressed, with simple weapons of bronze and tents of oxhide painted with swastikas. For all their rough simplicity he saw their lives burn fiercely in them, almost as brightly as the Sterkar they worshipped.

Like the Sterkar, these nomads were unreflective, so closely in tune with themselves and their beasts that they scarcely seemed to think. When they came upon a village of the hunters they destroyed it as casually as the Powers of Air might bring down an old tree.

Soon Calindor saw them enter the empty eastern reaches of the prairie, and watched them flourish there for a time. Their tribes multiplied even while they warred on one another. Their herds grew great, and darkened the plain with their numbers. Soon they could no longer move easily in search of new grass; each tribe found some other, with its thousands of cattle and goats, in occupation of every pasture.

Some tribes, beaten in war, retreated to the eastern forests and burned them to make new grassland. But their herds sickened and the tribes turned west again with weapons sharpened by desperation.

Yes, Calindor thought, the pattern was set even then: devour the land, leave it desert, and move on to take someone else's. If your eastern neighbors attacked you, fight them off or grant them passage to the lands still farther west. Then, when your own land failed, move west against them. So the tribes had moved across Cantarea, until they had come at last upon the Cantareans themselves.

The villages of Cantarea were not to be sacked and forgotten like those of the eastern forest-dwellers. Here the Badakhar found magicians as capable as their own, and a people with many strange and clever arts. A cautious friendship grew between the two peoples, and a regular trade. For a generation or more, Cantareans and Badakhar shared a broad stripe of land across the prairie.

The nomads saw much to like in the villagers' life; the Badakhar freemen came to share that life, or to found their own villages where stalmaghar discovered the spells that shaped iron and then steel. The upermannar, clinging proudly to their old roving life, found themselves depending on the tools and weapons the villagers forged, and on the cloth the weavers made so easily on their great, immovable looms.

Calindor glided over a crude village by a muddy river where an upermanna had built himself a Kes and made himself the first Aryo. He protected the village's freemen, and in turn they gave him wealth and weapons. The Aryo conquered or recruited his nomad neighbors, and held the first kingdom in his fist.

But he and his sons, and the others who imitated them, could not make the grass grow again, or sweeten the waters where the herds had passed. The kingdoms fought one another, grew, and fought again. Always the day came when they must abandon salt-crusted pastures and fields, and move deeper west into Cantarea.

The Badakhar villages became towns, and then cities, smoking from hundreds of chimneys. The freemen were too few to do the work the upermannar disdained, and always the Aryos warred against one another. They took the herdsmen from their herds, the tanners and weavers from their shops, the stalmaghar from their forges—all to wield pike and sword against the other Aryos' armies.

Now Calindor wished he could cry as he circled above the burning villages of the Cantareans. He watched the Slave Wars, as the Badakhar struck west in search of captives to toil in the fields and mines and mills. The Cantareans knew little of war, but they fought back with spell and arrow alike. They knew the harm they did to Callia yet they could not prevent themselves. And for a time they held off the attacks of the slave raiders.

Then, amid the fires of burning villages, something else appeared. It was a being, a Power of Powers, a force of darkness that the Badakhar soon worshipped. It was Mekhpur, Great Fire, the Firelord. Calindor saw it as he had seen the Gariba of the dragons' ancestors, and recognized it as the presence that had lurked in the Arekaryo Kes. This was the being that Tilcalli had somehow driven off.

It was as alien to Sotalar as Cantareans and Badakhar were; like them, it had somehow crossed the gulf between the worlds through some will or force even greater than itself—perhaps even by the same being that had brought men here. He sensed from afar its rage and hatred of all it saw and touched. It yearned for its own world, the Black World, yet it was trapped in Sotalar.

When first it appeared to the Veikar, the magicians had dreaded it. Yet Mekhpur granted them knowledge none had ever dreamed of, and enticed them with visions of knowledge greater still. They became its servants, doing its bidding in exchange for secrets of magic. In turn the Veikar gave strength to their Aryos.

Calindor saw the Slave Wars end as the last villages of the Cantareans fell to the Veikar's enchantments. He saw the Sanpala clan retreat to the caves, and the Siragi Aibela to the mountains. Mekhpur sent no armies in pursuit. It seemed content with the great land it had won for the Badakhar.

And now he saw the dragons' last retreat into the far west. Long ago they had changed their shape, grown claws and fangs as adornment and tools; but their souls were still those of the small and gentle herders who had roamed this valley long ago. They had no love of war; they took no pleasure in battle or in imposing their will. Sooner than betray themselves and Callia, they had abandoned Cantarea and the mountains to humankind. They loved their steep coasts, the rain-gray forests and fierce white rivers, but still they yearned for their lost home.

Then why have you come back to Tanshadabela? he asked in his sleep. But the dragon gave no reply.

He roused himself. The night was over; when he got to his feet and shuffled outside to find the nearest latrine, he saw dawn rising red behind the mountains. The air was dry, clear and cold. The snow squeaked under his feet. Tanshadabela was very quiet.

Calindor left the latrine and walked to the edge of the bluff. Below, the two streams fought their unequal struggle under a scaly, broken crust of ice floes. The tumult of the water was muted; in summer, he thought, the rivers would thunder over the stones in their beds. He wondered if he would ever see the Vesparushrei in flood here, as he had so often from the terraces of Arekaryo Kes.

The thought surprised him; why should he not see the river in summer?

The dragon's visions came back to him. He saw the land again as it had been in far distant times, and as it was today. The dragons' ancestors had walked the banks of this river, when it had run deeper beneath taller mountains. That river was buried now, buried deep under the stones and soil worn from the peaks. This river too would vanish some day. The mountains that reared so proudly against the reddening sky would vanish, reduce themselves to mere hills, to prairie. And other creatures would walk beside it, dreaming their own dreams and knowing nothing of all who had gone before.

Calindor felt himself in Callia's embrace. Tears stung his eyes, ran down his cheeks. The mountains, the river—they were as insubstantial as the brief flutters of his breath in the cold. He himself was nothing, a momentary shaping of matter and dream; he could glimpse only the smallest part of Callia's beauty and love.

You have made me for yourself as you have made the mountains and the river, he called to her. *They adorn you and serve you as the dragons do. Let me serve you also.*

The sky was turning blue now, a clear and cloudless blue. But within himself he sensed another kind of light: hazy, yellow, humid—the light of ancient Sotalar, the light by which the dragons first saw the world, the light by which they worked their magic.

He looked down at the river, turbulently flowing amid the tumbled ice, and saw the ice melt at his silent command. The Gariba of Water sang loudly in their sudden freedom, swelling the river. The Vesparushrei foamed over stones, rose hissing over long-abandoned channels, and hurried on to the northeast. To Aishadan.

Shivering, Calindor pulled his fur coat closer about him. A magic without words seemed an impossibility, yet now he possessed it. No—if anything, it possessed him, resided in him until it chose to go elsewhere.

Obordur. He turned from the river, hastened back to the great barn. She had given him more than visions. She had lent him this strange and ancient power. It seemed to grow within him, growing greater, vaster as he walked quickly through the snow. Abruptly he paused, hands pressed to his chest. Something was happening to him, something in his soul that made his flesh ache in sympathy. *Am I becoming a dragon?* No. But the gap, the opening to the realm where magic was everything—that gap was changing, growing, shaping itself as a stalmagh might shape a blade in the forge.

He fell to his knees, breath rasping in his throat, and tried to call Bherasha. No sound came. Crawling, he pulled himself toward the barn, seeing the Gariba in the crusted snow drink warmth from his hands.

After what seemed a long time he reached the door and tugged it wide enough to allow himself entry. The room smelled of straw and smoke and dragon. But Obordur was gone.

Twenty

Snow fell from a white sky.

First it fell in fine, dry flakes that vanished as they touched the earth. But the wind from the north turned colder, freezing the soil, and now the snow blew and rippled like dust. On Aishadan Kleir, the black slagheaps turned slowly white. The black slates on the roofs of Arekaryo Kes turned white also, and the red-and-gold banners fluttered and cracked in the strengthening wind. Ice spread itself along the gutters in the freemen's town, and the slaves of the stalmaghar counted themselves lucky to be toiling near the forges.

Ghelasha drew a fur robe about her, pulling its broad collar up around her ears, and walked out onto the terrace. Its flagstones were already covered; the snow squeaked under her shoes.

Full winter, she thought, and still the staff is gone. Pelshadan half-mad, his apprentices chanting and whining their empty spells. Eskel trying to do everything himself—judge, tax collector, war leader. Our best warriors off in the wilderness, and no news in how many days now? And that bastard slave with his whore mother, plotting against us, plotting and scheming—

She leaned against the battlement, peered through the crenel at the rooftops of the lower Kes and beyond them to the river. The far bank was lost in the snow. Even the bridge was scarcely visible. The dark surface of the Vesparushrei was mottled with ice floes. Once she had looked forward to the freezing of the river, to the ice games, the sledge races and fishing. Now it meant only cold, inaction, a dull waiting. Waiting for what? Some evil Veik's spell, or the revolt of some upermanna thinking to make himself stronger at the expense of a young prince and his dying father?

Albohar. She had not entered her old apartment, where he

221

still lay, in many days. He no longer looked like a man, only a skull crudely sheathed in yellowing parchment. The stench of his wound repelled all but Dvoi and Potiari, and they were too often obliged to tend their master. Pelshadan, the Veik, the Skalkaz afi Mekhpur, she thought scornfully. Curled up in a corner of his room, blankets pulled around him, rocking back and forth and muttering under his breath: Bring me my staff, bring me my staff.

The wind stung tears from her eyes, and she rubbed them angrily away. This time last year all had been well. Albohar had been hale and fit, eager for her in bed and on fire with his dreams of conquest. A year ago Eskel had given her his ear, learned from her, planned with her. The slave whore and her bastard whelp had been an annoyance, not a mortal threat. And Pelshadan had been a true Veik.

She watched small dark figures trudge through the thickening snow. The streets were almost empty, save for a few freemen's children and the ever-present arekakhar. The children played; the arekakhar guarded. A few traders walked beside their horses over the slippery cobblestones, while their private guards marched beside the sledges.

Her face ached with the cold, but she would not go back inside to the smoky darkness of the Kes. Faintly, muffled by the snow, she heard a horn blare in the distance. It must be coming from the garrison at the north end of the bridge. The horn sounded again, and she could hear men shouting in faint, far voices. A messenger? A brawl? Perhaps a riot in the freemen's town, a rising in the slave huts?

The alarm died away. But before long she saw three warriors riding recklessly up the snowy streets toward the Kes, and she saw the messenger's banner fluttering from the leader's lance.

At last! She drew in a deep breath, savoring the ache of icy air on her teeth, and hastened back inside.

Others had also heard the horn, and had gone to meet the riders. Ghelasha walked serenely through the corridors to the Hearing Hall, knowing that the messengers would be waiting there for the Aryako.

So they were, warming their hands by the fire while melted snow dripped from their furs and boots to puddle on the floor. They bowed in greeting as she entered.

"Have you been given hot medh? Any food?"

"Not yet, my lady Aryasha," said the leader. "The steward

has sent for some, and he tells us your noble son will soon be here."

She was already reading his face, and dreading its message.

"You are not from Snegh and Vulkvo. You do not bring the heads of Dheribi and Pelkhven, or the staff of Pelshadan."

"No, my lady. We come from Staldhuno."

"With grim news."

"That must await the Aryako, my lady."

"Tell me."

"I must tell the Aryako first, my—"

Her nails raked his face; he gasped and stepped back a pace before composing himself.

"Tell me, you pig's turd, or I'll cut your guts out myself!"

"My lady mother, step away from that man."

Eskel was in the doorway, his face pink with cold. But anger flared in his eyes, and she obeyed him sullenly.

"I welcome you," Eskel said, striding across the room to his seat. Slaves hastened in behind him with buckets of coal, and fed the fires. But the Hearing Hall remained chill and dim.

"I would wait on your news until you were refreshed," Eskel said softly, "but I suspect you would rather tell me first. So do so."

"My lord." The leader of the messengers ignored the red stripes of blood that lost themselves in his beard. "Staldhuno has fallen."

"Fallen? To what?"

"To an army, my lord, from Halamor, and Ghrirei, and even Kormannalendh. Our enemies have invaded Aishadan. They are marching on the city as I speak."

Dragasa had lived alone so long he seemed almost to resent Tilcalli's efforts to prepare breakfast. Smiling but firm, he waved her into a chair by the table. Bherasha, who had been invited to share the meal, was sitting nearby with Calindor; the two women exchanged slightly exasperated looks.

Meanwhile Dragasa swung a copper pot over the fire to heat water for tea, and while it came to a boil he mixed a kind of batter of flour, water, honey and spices. This he poured into a deep-sided pan, crudely made of iron; the pot went over the coals of the fire, to bake into hardcake.

"I am not surprised that Obordur has gone," he said as he poured tea into fine stoneware mugs. "She came without warning, not long before you arrived."

"Have dragons ever come here before?" asked Bherasha.

"People have sometimes seen them, far down the valley. But no, they have never come into Tanshadabela until now." He smiled, a little sadly. "We were very worried when she came. It seemed like a portent from Callia, a message from the Open Dream—" He shrugged and sipped his tea. "She knew you were coming," he said to Calindor. "The message was for you, not for us. And it was a great message."

Calindor nodded awkwardly. His silence had become oddly comfortable now, less a burden than an emulation of Obordur's stillness. He was resigned to it but knew that others still wished to speak to him and be spoken to. That too would come eventually, he thought, if events allowed. And if events turned out badly, he would be dead and speaking with his ancestors in the silent language of the Open Dream.

The aroma of the hardcake filled the cabin. Dragasa hooked a handle onto the pan and lifted it from the fire. It rested on a slab of stone while he tipped it over, freeing the cake. Breaking off steaming chunks, he handed them to the others.

"It's delicious," Tilcalli said. "Even better than my mother's."

Calindor thought it good also, but saw that Dragasa's thoughts were not on cooking. His father tossed a hot lump of cake from hand to hand until it cooled.

"I think the Badakhar will come back," he said quietly. "They pursued you this far. They will come back."

Tilcalli frowned. "Even if they fear the dragon?"

"I think they fear our son even more. They fear what he might be able to do, especially with that staff." He nodded to where it leaned against the wall, not far from the fireplace. "And we are few. In a fight we might be able to put thirty men in arms, and twenty women. The rest of us are too young, or too old."

"I don't understand," Bherasha said. "When Pervidhu found us, I knew it would be wrong to kill him. Yet you talk of fighting. I thought Callia doesn't like fighting and killing."

"You are right," said Dragasa. "It hurts her, weakens her, but sometimes we must fight. When we hunt we seek the animals that wish to die, and we give them back to Callia. But when we ourselves are hunted, and do not wish to die, we must sometimes fight and kill. And one of those times is coming soon."

He and Tilcalli grunted, shifting in their chairs, as Calindor projected his focus. He was seeking enemies, and found none—

at least not within half a day's march. Not far beyond that range he sensed someone, perhaps many, who did not move. He nodded, pointing northeastward, and Dragasa grimly nodded back.

"Your focus is almost as strong as Obordur's," his father said. "I wish you would let us know when you plan to use it." Calindor nodded, embarrassed.

"So the Badakhar haven't gone away,"Dragasa went on. "We will have to talk about it. Perhaps we can move the children and old people deeper into the valleys, but it will be hard. The snows are upon us." Then, as if dismissing the subject altogether, he picked up a small harp, tuned it, and began to play old tunes.

Tilcalli laughed and began to sing the words. The music soon drew visitors, neighbors bringing small gifts of cake or meat or tea. They stayed to sing and talk; Tilcalli knew all the older people, and between songs she spoke with them about life in Aishadan and in Tanshadabela.

Calindor and Bherasha listened politely, but at last he took her arm and led her outside.

"How they all chatter!" she whispered when they were outside in the sun-bright day. The air was sharp and cold, the snow brittle underfoot. "In Aishadan slaves never talk if the Badakhar are anywhere close. Here everyone gossips and jokes and sings."

He raised his eyebrows inquiringly.

"Oh, I don't mind it," she answered. "It's wonderful to hear Cantareans talking so freely. Like that habit they have of making noise with their hands. I just have to get used to it. To being free."

Smiling, they walked around the village. Calindor found it much as his mother had often described it, but plainer and harsher. Twenty years ago, he thought, this place had been far upriver from the Badakhar. Now it was the nearest village to Aishadan, and the people knew it. They had not had a fight, not even a raid since Albohar's, but they knew that some day a fight would come and could not be escaped. That knowledge had led to them build their cabins of thicker logs, to strengthen the stockade, and to stockpile food and firewood.

The people themselves were both like and unlike the slaves of the Badakhar: they looked the same, yet the people of the mountains stood straight, and met one another's eyes. They wore beautifully ornamented clothes, and the women braided their long black hair with yarns of many colors. Calindor saw how gracefully they worked, doing more in a few moments than most slaves would do in a morning. Here a man chopped wood, swinging his ax with fluid ease and making the wood sing as it split. There a woman carried water in copper buckets hanging from a shoulder yoke; she moved across the slick, trampled snow with a dancer's grace, singing as she went and smiling at Calindor and Bherasha.

"I like this place," Bherasha said, looking around at the snow-mantled cabins and above the stockade at the looming, brilliant mountains. Calindor nodded. This might be a hard place, but it was worth defending.

Missing Obordur, he went with Bherasha to the barn. They found Pervidhu sitting in the sunshine on a bench by the door. His broken leg was resplinted and jutted out before him.

"Well," Pervidhu drawled. "Have you come for a chat, Dheribi?"

Calindor smiled. The idea of a Badakh with a sense of humor was funny in itself, quite apart from his jokes.

"Why have they put you here?" Bherasha asked.

"That old woman who runs the meeting hall, Tulu-something, she put me in here soon as the dragon left. I don't know much of your slave-talk, but she seemed to think I smell bad."

"You do. How is your leg?"

"Hurts a bit. I still can't walk on it."

Calindor smiled again. He squatted in the straw, smelling the dragon rather than Pervidhu's stink, and drew aside the red wool blanket that covered him. Then, dizzy, he reached out to steady himself against Bherasha.

His focus had changed again, changed in some deep and subtle way. When he had seen Sveit's cancer, it had seemed clear enough, and healing it had been only a matter of encouraging Sveit's body to do what it wished to do. Now he saw the first particles of rot in Pervidhu's leg, the death eating its way through blood clots and torn flesh. The infection was still too small to be seen with ordinary eyes, even if a knife had laid open the leg from knee to ankle. But Calindor could see it, foretell its progress, and he knew that an ordinary spell of healing could not help. Tilcalli or Dragasa or the Protector of the Gulyaji might have knitted bone and ligament, but the infection would have escaped them.

This insight was Obordur's gift, he knew, part of what she had granted him through her visions. And he thought he knew why. Just as he could see the pattern and purpose of Pervidhu's flesh and bone, she had seen something in human society that must be cleansed and healed. She had chosen him to be her means.

The dizziness passed. Pervidhu and Bherasha were looking at him in surprise. Calindor folded his legs under himself and reached out to touch Pervidhu's splinted leg.

Obordur, dragon mother, you wished me to learn this, and to heal this enemy. I obey your wish.

He felt wordless force burst through him, through his fingertips, a flood of strange Gariba rejoicing in the new world he had opened to them.

Pervidhu's face went pale as snow above his beard, and his blue eyes bulged. Breath hissed in his throat; one scarred hand gripped Calindor's shoulder with startling force.

Calindor saw the broken bones knit themselves, merge into wholeness; the clots dissolved, the ligaments grew strong. Through Pervidhu's veins the Gariba swarmed, filling the warrior's body with a new strength and vigor.

Color returned to his face; he let go of Calindor's shoulder.

"What have you done to me?" Pervidhu asked quietly. Calindor got to his feet, bent, and undid the splint. He pulled the warrior up from his straw bed.

"Doesn't hurt anymore. Can I walk on it?" Calindor nodded. Pervidhu took a tentative step, then another, and suddenly threw himself into a somersault. He stood up again, grinning.

"They say some Badakh women still practice healing, but they've never healed a broken leg this fast. I'm in your debt, hemamagh!"

Blood magician. Is that what I am now? Is that what she's made me?

Snegh sat before a fire too small to give off much smoke—or heat. The camp was on the lower slopes of a pyramid-shaped mountain an hour's march north of the Menmannar village; he could see the roofs of some of the larger buildings, and watch smoke rise into the crystalline air. But the intervening woods prevented a clear view.

"The place could have more dragons than fleas," he growled to Vulkvo. "But you couldn't tell from here. We've got to get closer."

Vulkvo frowned. "Hard to do. We don't know the terrain that well, and anyone going close will leave tracks in this snow." He shook his head and squatted closer to the fire. "Cold, miserable country—the Menmannar deserve to live in this waste-land. This is why civilized people don't fight in the winter.''

''If we don't fight, we'll have to quit,'' Snegh said. ''And if we quit, the Aryako will wonder if we're the men we used to be.''

Vulkvo snorted. ''We're not, and a good thing too. I think about how we came up this river with Albohar when we were boys, and I shudder. Mekhpur must look after young fools.''

''Then he's looking after most of our men. Even with all the stories about the dragon, they're still ready to fight.''

''All the more reason for us to use some common sense. We'd be mad to charge in, not even knowing the layout of the village, with a dragon and a lot of magicians lying in wait for us.'' Vulkvo shielded his eyes against the glare of the sun, low in the south between two mountains. ''The river's going to ice over soon. Maybe we could get across before it does, look at the village from the far bank, and then make our plans.''

''Take five good men with you,'' Snegh said. ''If you go quickly, you can reach the river and get across before dark in that longboat they left on the shore. Then come back by noon tomorrow, and we'll work out a plan. By the day after tomorrow I want the Veik's staff, and the heads of those magicians.''

''It's like one great feast,'' Svordo marveled. He and Calindor and the ex-slaves had been wandering all afternoon from one house to another, enjoying food and drink. The villagers danced and sang and told jokes, while Svordo, Moro and the others happily ate. Even Pervidhu was welcome, and while he could not speak more than a few words of Cantarean he seemed content to eat and drink like the others.

Calindor thought the Menmannar must have been wary at first, unready to welcome the fugitives fully. Now, after only a couple of days, Tanshadabela had opened itself to them. Their mugs were always full of strong cider, and every cabin was full of the rich smells of soups and stews and new-baked bread. Girls danced intricate steps, laughing at the newcomers' clumsy efforts to follow; young men and women asked earnestly about life in Aishadan, and about the great wars the Badakhar fought among themselves. They listened to Svordo's and Moro's tales of slavery with a fascinated horror, while the elders shook their heads and clicked their tongues. They glanced warily at Pervidhu, who pretended to ignore them.

"If they ever come against us," one youth said solemnly, "we'll fight them as we did in the old days."

Svordo laughed. "You may, but I intend to run like a rabbit."

"No," said Bherasha. "The boy is right. If they come—when they come—we will have to fight them. Because they will never stop pursuing us while we have the Veik's staff and while Dheribi and Tilcalli are alive."

"Then why allow one of them to wander freely here?" a young woman demanded.

Bherasha smiled, but looked embarrassed. "I think Callia wants him here. That's why we didn't kill him when we could have, and why she made it easy for Dheribi to heal him."

And they all looked at Calindor as cautiously as they had Pervidhu. Many had seen the Badakh's leg, and known how badly hurt he was; to see him walking about was a marvel in itself.

Calindor enjoyed the deflection of interest from himself to Pervidhu. Bherasha was right—the Badakhar would return. He could sense a few of them already, not far to the north, as well as others downriver to the northeast. But he did not think the people of Tanshadabela could withstand a serious attack. The boys and girls might talk bravely of war, but they lacked all training. Even the oldest men had memories only of skirmishes with raiding parties like Albohar's; the Badakh warriors out in the woods must be fresh from Ner Kes.

Somehow, then, the Badakhar must be kept from attacking the village. He thought about how he had melted the ice on the river; did he have other powers hidden in his new dragonlore? No: only a sense of something new, something growing, waiting its time like a seed in the soil of early spring. Should he then go out with Dragasa, Svordo, a few of the more able men and women of the village, and try to drive off the Badakhar? If they could slay the leaders, perhaps the rest would retreat.

He shook his head wearily. No, they would not retreat. They might be worried about the dragon, but they would only choose a new leader and continue the attack. If the weather grew any colder, they might even decide that taking the village was the only way to survive, and fight all the harder.

"Is something the matter, Dheribi?" asked Bherasha. She was sitting beside him on a bench near the fireplace. Around them, people stood or sat in a cheerful cloud of talk and laughter and song.

He shook his head, then nodded. Glancing at the door, he

stood up; she followed him, thanking their host and promising to return soon.

Outside the evening air was sharp with cold; somewhere in the distance a tree cracked as frost burst its heart. The cabin was near the bluff overlooking the river, but the water made little noise; ice had formed again in a thickening crust.

"Do you want to go for a walk? Or go back to your father's cabin?"

He shook his head and took her through the narrow lanes with no goal in mind, wishing only for her company and an answer to his worries. She seemed to understand, and walked along companionably. Their footsteps crunched in the hard-frozen snow.

After a time, however, Bherasha began to shiver. "I think I'd better get back to my host's cabin," she murmured.

Instead he guided her to the barn. It was chilly inside, and very dark, but it still smelled reassuringly of Obordur. Perhaps, Calindor thought, she has more to teach me. He walked about the barn, uncaring of the darkness until he bumped into a pillar. Then, without even thinking about it he brought forth coldfire. But it was not the blue light of the Gulyaji; this was a warm yellow-orange, and it gave out heat as well.

"Oh—how beautiful," Bherasha cried. She gazed in wonder at the sphere hanging in the air above Calindor's head: a globe the size of his fist, almost too bright to look at. "Did you make it?" He nodded, feeling embarrassed. Bherasha smiled, her skin a rich brown in the light. "It's like—like the sun on a warm spring day. I wish you had made it when we were freezing on the river."

He shrugged and pointed to the flattened pile of straw where the dragon had lain.

"I know, I know—the dragon taught you how, didn't she? What a wonder, to make heat and light wherever you wish." She held up her hands, warming them. The sphere (what would you call it, Calindor wondered—dragonfire?) drifted slowly about the barn as if caught on some gentle breath of air. Its heat made the plank walls glisten as frost melted; the straw warmed also, giving off a stronger scent of dragon.

As the dragonfire floated away, Bherasha did not lower her hands. Instead she turned and put them on Calindor's shoulders. Her smile faded.

"I used to be glad I was a magician's slave," she said softly. "Because magicians don't care about women. At least Badakh magicians don't. And now—now I care about a magician, the greatest of them all. And I hope you care about me, Dheribi, as your father cares about Tilcalli.''

Her strong arms went around his neck; she pulled herself up to his lips and kissed him. He no longer smelled Obordur, only the dizzying perfume of Bherasha's hair and skin.

With the second kiss Bherasha giggled and hooked one foot behind Calindor's ankle. They topped into the straw. Shadows rippled as the dragonfire sphere bobbed and turned.

After a time the barn door opened and Tilcalli stepped in. She looked with surprise at the sphere, which had risen into the rafters, and then at Calindor and Bherasha lying in the straw under his fur coat.

"Well, it was about time," Tilcalli said. "Since you two look so comfortable, perhaps you might stay here for the night." She looked at Calindor with a smile much like Bherasha's. "Then your father and I can have some time to ourselves in that tiny cabin. Good night."

When Tilcalli had quietly closed the door, Bherasha hugged him and laughed. Feeling her body close to his, he hugged her back. *Strange,* he thought, *how much this feels like magic moving through me.*

Twenty-one

Pelshadan woke suddenly as gray light began to glow in the cracks of the shutters. The Aryo's sickroom was chilly, though slaves had piled coal on the fire sometime during the night. The air held the stink of Albohar's wound. The Aryo lay still, his chest rising and falling almost imperceptibly beneath a heavy sheepskin blanket.

Pelshadan slowly rose from his pallet against the wall. He pulled his robe tighter around him, and sucked thoughtfully on a strand of his hair.

I can do nothing to help you, Aryo, or to help your people. I can only watch you all die, until it is my turn as well.

The stink was unusually bad—or he was more aware of it. Distantly, he realized he was more conscious of his surroundings than he had been in a long time. His mind seemed clearer than usual; perhaps it was the cold. He debated whether to open the shutters to let in clean air, or to pile more coal on the fire.

He would do each in turn. Shuffling across the darkened room past the Aryo's bed, he unlatched the shutters and pushed open one window. Icy air struck his face like a slap.

Far off to the southeast, the sun had almost risen; red clouds glowed in a clear sky. The distant horizon marked a boundary between two realms of dark and darker blue. Frost prickled on the windowsill beneath the Veik's hands. The river below was a band of mottled white and gray. It seemed to have frozen over completely during the night—or at any rate since Pelshadan had last troubled to notice.

The invaders—yes, he remembered hearing about them though the news had not seemed important then. They were in the land, but not yet encamped within sight. Someone had mentioned in his hearing that they were more numerous than anyone had imagined possible, and better equipped. Last summer Aishadan had squandered its riches to gain those of Ner Kes. Meanwhile the Aryos of Halamor and Ghrirei had quietly allied themselves, and saved themselves the costs of raids and skirmishes. They had foreseen Aishadan's triumph, and the threat it would soon pose to themselves. Last summer they had sent that evil presence from the Black World against him, but they had not trusted entirely to magic.

But to attack in winter! What a gamble, worthy of immortal fame in the longchants of the bards! The cold and snow, which ought to have hindered them, gave them instead an easy road. The frontier garrisons had huddled indoors, imagining no danger, and had died by their firesides.

The invaders had been subtle: they had slaughtered the upermannar and their families, yes, and seized every sack of grain, every cow, every jar of pickled vegetables. But they had not slain the freemen or abducted the slaves. Those they had sent in long columns, fleeing toward Aishadan for refuge and food.

Making our own people into leeches upon us. As well send rats into our granaries.

But they had sent no more magic against Aishadan, unless this bitter cold was a weatherspell greater than any he had ever known. Since their first delicate probes, weeks ago, the Veikar of Halamor and Ghrirei and Kormannalendh had done nothing. They must know his weakness; they would not be deceived by the frozen heads fixed above the main gate of the Kes, or by the lies that Eskel had noised about—that Pelshadan was in full possession of his powers, that he was preparing devastating counterspells to spread plague and madness among the invaders.

They'll wait, he thought as he latched the shutter tight and turned back to the room. *They'll wait until they stand on the far bank of the river, and then they will hurl spells at me. And I will have no defense against them—not even the protection of that slave witch.*

He sensed the protective aura that Dvoi had put around the Arekaryo Kes, and which had cost him many days of exhaustion. It was a good spell, proof against many attacks, but it could not withstand the assault that two or three Veikar could inflict upon it. And when the people saw blue flames jetting from the windows and chimneys of the Kes, and knew that their rulers were slain, they would offer little resistance as the invaders came trotting across the bridge.

But perhaps something might yet be done. Perhaps the Veik

of Aishadan might show his adversaries he was not yet completely undone.

"Dvoi."

The round-faced young magician had been sleeping nearby, in the room once occupied by Pelkhven and Bherasha. He roused himself, snorted, and spat heavily on the floor. His eyes still had the empty look of a magician drained of power. "What is it, master?"

"Go and sit with the Aryo for a time. I have duties to attend to."

Dvoi looked puzzled. "What duties, master?"

Pelshadan slapped him, without much energy. "Do you interrogate a Veik? Look to the Aryo until I return."

Pelshadan shuffled out of the room and down the corridor. The Kes was coming awake, but it seemed strange to him: he had taken little notice of events since the theft of the staff, and while he had known of the invasion he had not troubled to think through the implications.

Now armed guards stood in every stairway, and heavy frames of logs leaned against walls. Pelshadan had passed several of them before he realized what they were—barricades, ready to be hauled into place across corridors to slow the progress of invaders within the Kes itself. Did Eskel think the city's defenses that weak?

The fortress was dim and cold; the loudest noises were the tramp of booted feet and the occasional shouted command. Pelshadan made his way past stumbling slaves and angry soldiers until he came to the Hearing Hall. It was empty at this early hour; the guards at the door let him enter. Inside, slaves were building up the fires to prepare the hall for the Aryako's later arrival.

"Leave me for a time," he commanded. "I have business here before the Aryako comes."

Without a word they bowed and scuttled out. Pelshadan wrinkled his nose. They smelled of sickness and hunger, as bad as freemen's slaves. No doubt, in the alarm over the invasion, the slaves' feeding had been neglected.

No matter; he put the thought aside as trivial and turned to face a small altar, a stone shelf built into a niche close to the left side of the throne. On the shelf stood a small sphere of gold, set on a base of polished bloodstone carved with swastikas. Pelshadan knelt before it, placing his hands on either side of the sphere.

"O Mekhpur," he said softly, "I call upon you out of my very great need. Out of my need I call upon you, Lord of the Badakhar, Lord of the Sterkar, Deivush of this world."

For a time nothing happened. Then a breeze stirred the air, making the coal fires smoke, and the cold deepened. Pelshadan saw his breath flutter white above the gold sphere. The Firelord's presence was strong, stronger even than last summer when Pelshadan had gone into his attic to ask for the deivushibi, the small god, to be sent against Parsur Seggas of Ner Kes.

Shuddering, the Veik gripped the bloodstone base to keep himself from slumping to the floor. "O Mekhpur—you have guarded us and made us strong. We have given you blood and tribute, and we ask of you only green fields and clean water for our herds, and victory in war. Now our enemies assail us, Lord. My powers are almost gone, O Mekhpur, yet still I would serve you. Give me again the strength of my staff. Give me again power over the Sterkar, that I may defend my Aryo and his people. And ask of me what price you wish."

He felt light-headed as he ended the prayer. This was an invocation rarely made, an appeal that might pitch him instantly into the Black World like the legendary Veik Megnash. A moment passed, and then another. And then came the Firelord's demand, wordless yet insistent and inarguable.

"I obey, Lord." Grinning, Pelshadan struggled upright and half-ran, half-tottered to the door. The guards stared at him.

"Give me your dagger," he commanded the nearer one. "Quickly, quickly, Mekhpur himself awaits!"

The guard drew his dagger and handed it over without a word. Pelshadan looked about. Three young slaves were approaching, bearing sacks of grain on their backs. Pelshadan stopped one and pushed her burden to the floor. "Come!" he said, grasping her thin wrist.

She obeyed, letting him pull her into the Hearing Hall. He felt the Sterkar pulsing in her flesh, and thought with anguish of his lost staff. Standing before the altar, he pulled her coarse smock from her. The girl was perhaps fifteen or sixteen, almost as tall as Pelshadan but very thin. Pubic hair shadowed her groin, but he could tell she had not yet begun her menses. Good. She kept her eyes downcast, as she should, and stood shivering in the cold.

The presence of Mekhpur was stronger now, almost visible. Pelshadan gripped the girl's black hair and pulled, drawing her chin up. In that moment she looked at him, her soul in her eyes.

He drew the dagger's edge across her throat.

As always he marveled at how easily, obediently, flesh opened at the touch of steel. Blood gushed out in great pulses, steaming on the altar and painting her breasts. Red bubbles thickened to a froth around her wound as her last breaths left her. Pelshadan felt her Sterkar burst free to be seized and devoured by Mekhpur.

"Ah," said Pelshadan as the girl sagged to her knees. He sensed the Firelord's pleasure, and trembled with joy. As if from a great distance he felt the girl's fingers gripping his wrists and then sliding away as she fell to the floor. Blood still pumped from her throat, but more slowly. When he looked down, he no longer saw her soul in her eyes.

"May this gift please you, Lord," he whispered. "And may you restore my powers."

Yes, he could still feel Mekhpur's pleasure, but more than that: beyond the pleasure was a desolation, an emptiness so dreadful that Pelshadan staggered, slipping in the slave's blood.

Blood. What a paltry sacrifice she now seemed. What pathetic gifts they had always rendered to Mekhpur. One might slaughter every slave in Aishadan, in all the Five Kingdoms, and be no nearer assuaging that desolation in the Firelord's heart. Why had Mekhpur chosen to reveal it now, after all the countless sacrifices over the centuries?

Because the same desolation lies within me, he told himself.

The presence of Mekhpur seemed to withdraw a little, but it left something of itself behind. No—not quite itself, but a different entity. It was not as mighty as Mekhpur, but it had its power. It was the desolation made aware of itself, the desolation given will. Pelshadan recognized it as it drew closer to him. He opened his mouth to scream, but had no time.

It was the deivushibi he had sent to possess Parsur Seggas, the deivushibi that Dheribi had slain. Now, as easily as the knife had sunk into the girl's flesh, the deivushibi sank into the mind and soul of Pelshadan and made them nothing.

Dragasa had found an old, little-used cabin for Calindor and Bherasha. Its fireplace was good; a few logs kept the one room comfortable all night. But in the early morning after their second night in it, Calindor woke feeling chilled. Beside him Bherasha stirred, shivered, and drew closer to him. He smiled and pulled their blankets tighter around them. Then he let his focus sweep far around the village.

The Badakhar were still there. A few had crossed to the right bank of the river, and were camped among the trees opposite the bluff on which Tanshadabela stood. The main body was a half-day's hard ride to the northeast, clustered in the lee of a rocky hill. They must be cold and angry, he thought, impatient to attack but afraid of what they might find.

Why did you leave, Obordur? If you had stayed we would have been safe here. Even the Badakhar would have turned back sooner than face you.

Did she want the Cantareans to stand and fight, or to flee upriver to the other villages? Why would she have rescued the fugitives, only to abandon them?

He felt the pulse of another focus, and recognized it as his father's. It was a kind of summons, but not to visit him; it was a summons to the Open Dream.

Calindor shivered, not entirely from the cold. Before, he had gone into the Dream only through great pain or fear. Now he knew the way, but the memories remained of those earlier journeys—especially of the suffocating, terrifying presence of Mekhpur.

Well, I must go again. Slowly, hesitantly, he put himself into trance. The icy cabin faded, Bherasha faded, and he stood on the banks of the Silent River under an endless noon.

Calihalingol was dancing with the other ancestors on the edge of the village, but she broke off when she saw him, and hurried to greet him. When she was a few steps away, her expression changed; the welcoming smile faded a little. Calindor turned and saw Dragasa standing beside him, his dark face grim.

I greet you both. I have long looked forward to this meeting, when father and son would stand together in the Open Dream.

Dragasa looked unmoved. *Old woman, ancestress, I do not greet you fondly. You hatched your plans without me, and used Tilcalli and me as an angler uses bait upon a hook. But I have need of you, and need of this place.*

Calihalingol smiled girlishly, almost flirtatiously, and gestured to the grassy bank above the river. *Come, sit with me. Whatever I can do to help you, I shall do.*

Dragasa sat cross-legged, hands on his knees, facing the old woman. Calindor sat with his father on his left and his great-great-grandmother on his right. Even in that place of endless peace, he felt their wills clash like the first faint rumble of thunder on a clear summer's day.

The Badakhar fled from the dragon, Dragasa began, *but they have come back and the dragon has left. Soon the Badakhar will attack us, to slay us and seize the staff of the Badakh magician. We cannot fight them—they are too many. But we cannot flee; the snow is thick and the cold deepens with every hour.*

The snow . . . I miss the snow, Dragasa. Perhaps that is what some of us seek when we leave the river and go to the mountains. They yearn for the snow. And she looked across the river meadows and the village to the mountains gleaming on the far horizon.

Dragasa smiled without gladness. *We have enough for them all. Listen to me, old woman! Our people, your grandchildren, may all be dead within a day or two. We of the Siragi Aibela will come here, but what of the others? Their lives are sweet, but they have no Open Dream. I will not see them die until they are ready to join Callia.*

Calihalingol nodded, moving her lips as if chewing something, but said nothing. She looked at Calindor. *Have you asked your son, Dragasa?*

How can I ask him, when he cannot speak? He has written his warnings, but we cannot take counsel in Sotalar where he is mute.

Ask him now. Call him by his name. You know it.

Dragasa looked at his son as if for the first time. *Yes, You are . . . The One Who Goes Away. Calindor. Your mother said she was angry with the Gulyaji for giving you your deep name, and she would not tell it to me out of fear of Mekhpur. But she was wrong. Our deep names come from Callia, and she has given you a name to protect you from him. When he seeks to grasp you, you are not there.*

Yes, I am Calindor. And at last I can speak to you, as son to father, as warrior to warrior, as magician to magician. And I say to you that I love and honor you as I love and honor my mother.

Dragasa nodded, smiling now with something like happiness on his lips. *So do I love and honor you.*

After that he said nothing for a long time, while the river slowly flowed past and the sun hung unmoving in the cloudless sky. The ancestors resumed their dance, dancing the past and future.

And what else would you say to me, Calindor my son?

That I must go away, when I have scarcely arrived.

Where can you? The winter has just begun, and already it lies hard upon us. And wherever you go, there the Badakhar

*will pursue you. If you go up the river, to Belosti or Galivela,
they will hunt you down.*

*I will not go up the river. As you say, they would only pursue
me, and first they would destroy Tanshadabela.*

Then where, Calindor?

Back down the river. Back to Aishadan.

Dragasa put out a hand to him, touched his arm with strange
gentleness while the old woman nodded and squinted at the
ripples on the river. Calindor put his hand over his father's hand.

I will have no peace, Father, until I have faced Mekhpur.

Twenty-two

Vulkvo and his scouting party returned from across the river in the night, making their way by moonlight to the observation camp north of the Menmannar village. By the time they reached the camp, dawn was a dull gray glow behind the mountains.

"I'm glad you're all back safe," Snegh said. He sent Vulkvo's men off to warm themselves with hot tea and porridge. "What did you see?"

Vulkvo was a dark shape, hunched close to the fire that reflected oddly in his eyes. "It's what we didn't see that was important."

With his scabbard he drew a line in the snow near the fire. Adding two branching lines, he made what looked like the footprint of a gigantic bird. At the end of each line he placed dots where claws might have left their tracks. The footprint was three times the length of his own.

"Just like the letter *darkiped*," he said to Snegh. "A whole string of them, running south along the far riverbank, with a good two swords' lengths between them." He pointed to the dots. "The claw marks were deep enough to put most of your hand in."

Snegh looked chilled by more than early-morning cold. "So the letter really does mean dragon's foot," he whispered. "And you've seen its tracks."

"Going away. But not coming back."

"Could it have come back another way?"

"For all I know, it's flown to Aishadan. But I think it's left the Menmannar, and I'm ready to go against them while I can. If we stay out here much longer, we'll have to start killing the

240

horses. Kill the horses, and Mekhpur knows how we'd get home."

Snegh nodded and put his hands out to the little fire burning before the lean-to. He looked up at the dawn sky. "Clouding over. I can smell more snow on the way."

Vulkvo nodded. "If we're going to attack, we'd better do it soon."

"Call a messenger, and send him to the main camp. We'll want all but fifty men up here by noon." Snegh put a stick on the fire. "That way we'll win or die before the sun is gone. I'm too old for night battles, least of all against magicians."

"No!"

Tilcalli stood by the fireplace, fists clenched at her sides. The others, crowded into the cabin's main room, seemed to wince under her anger. Dragasa had summoned them all: Bherasha, Svordo, Minukhi, Sveit's former slaves—only Pervidhu was not there. Calindor stood by the fireplace also, facing his mother across the hearth.

"No," she said again. "He cannot go back to Aishadan. He will *not* go back. We might as well have stayed and died there, and saved Eskel and Ghelasha the trouble of hunting us."

Calindor glowered into the fire, his hands jammed in the pockets in the front of his buckskin tunic.

"Calindor came here for what he needed," Dragasa said quietly. He was sitting in a far corner, arms folded across his chest. "He didn't need a hiding place. He needed what Obordur gave him. But his new powers are no use to us. If the Badakhar attack, we can throw some magic at them—but not enough to drive them off. Give them a day, or two at the most, and they will make this village a ruin. But if Calindor leaves, and they see him leave, they will follow him back to Aishadan."

"Very brave," Tilcalli snapped. "So the village saves itself at his expense."

Bherasha spoke: "If he goes, I will go with him."

"Then you're as great a fool as he is," Tilcalli shot back, speaking in Badakhi. "Is freedom so heavy you can't bear it any longer?"

Dragasa, not knowing the language, looked mystified; the others all understood Tilcalli's sarcastic pun on Bherasha's name, which simply meant "bearer."

Bherasha shook her head. "I must bear what he cannot," she

murmured in Cantarean, looking at the staff that had once been Pelshadan's. It leaned against the wall beside her.

"I will not allow it," Tilcalli said bluntly. "Dragasa, you say that in the Open Dream our son told you he must face Mekhpur. He faced the Firelord before, and it nearly cost him his life—and mine as well. We did not go through that horror only so he could return to it. No, I will not allow it."

Dragasa stood up, his face dark with wrath. "You will not allow it? And who allowed you to go to Aishadan all those years ago, with our son just quickening in your belly? Who allowed you to desert me, to rob me of Calindor? Who judged you fit to go among the Badakhar to gamble with the future of our people?"

Her eyes flashed with shock, and she reached out to touch the stone chimney as if for support. Dragasa stepped forward, and those near him flinched as if they feared a blow.

"Listen to me, Tilcalli my wife. You are a great magician of the Siragi Aibela, and the bravest woman I have ever known. But you have lived too long among the enemy. You have forgotten that no Cantarean is bound to do another's bidding. You speak of Calindor as if he were some toddler venturing too close to the fire. Look at him!"

Tilcalli did, and Calindor saw fear and uncertainty in his mother's eyes.

"He is greater than any other magician of the Siragi Aibela, greater than the magicians of the Gulyaji, greater than the magicians of the Badakhar. If he chooses now to go to face Mekhpur, I would not stop him even if I could—no more than I would dare to command Obordur. Look, look at your son, Tilcalli." His voice softened. "He is a kinsman to dragons."

She shook her head, and her eyes filled with tears. "I fear for him. I fear so much for him."

Dragasa took her in his arms, but she stood stiffly within his embrace.

"Callia," he whispered. "Callia shaped us all so that we would create Calindor. Does the bow fear for the arrow?"

She said nothing, but rested her head on his shoulder. No one spoke for a long time. Then Minukhi cleared his throat.

"I don't understand all this Cantarean chatter," he said, wiping his streaming eyes, "but I'll go with Dheribi if he'll have me."

"And I," said Svordo. Moro and the others nodded.

Calindor smiled and shook his head. He put a hand on Svordo's shoulder. They had saved his life more than once; now they would endanger themselves to no purpose. They must stay here. If he could overcome Mekhpur, they would meet again in joy. If the Firelord should win, at least his companions would be spared.

"How will you go?" Dragasa asked. Calindor mimicked paddling. "But the river is icing over." Calindor shrugged and smiled.

"If it's to be only the two of them, the Badakh longboat is too big," Tilcalli said expressionlessly. "They'll need a canoe."

"I have one," Dragasa said. "When will you go, Calindor?"

Calindor made a fist and flicked his fingers upward; Dragasa looked confused by the Badakh gesture.

"He means now, right away," Svordo explained.

"Then we'd better get the canoe and some supplies for it," Dragasa said. "You've picked hard weather for a river journey."

No, I have not picked it, he thought. *I have been picked.*

Dragasa led them from the cabin, through the village to a shed just inside the gate on the riverbank. Inside it, canoes hung upside-down on racks.

"This one is mine," Dragasa said, touching a long, sleek craft. It had been carved from a single log, shaped with loving skill and strengthened with spells. Its hull seemed no thicker than a sword blade, yet Calindor could feel the Gariba that dwelt within it and gave it strength.

As he helped his father carry it outside, he paused.

"What is it?" Dragasa asked.

Calindor sent out his focus, remembering too late that he should have warned his parents first. Both of them, and Minukhi, staggered under the force of it.

Yes, the warning had been right: the Badakhar were coming. He could almost count them among the trees. They were riding slowly, their horses' hooves punching through the crusted snow. Soon they would be here, and their numbers would be too great for the people of Tanshadabela to withstand.

Dragasa read his son's expression. "How much time do we have?"

Calindor pointed to the sun, low above the mountains to the south, then swept his hand to the right, westward.

"Another two hours? Very well. You can get away from the village, but how will you get the canoe through the ice?" Dragasa pointed through the gate to the river at the foot of the bluff. Floes were bumping together, riding up on one another, welding themselves to the banks. Open water was already a narrow maze of channels and gaps. Soon the entire surface of the Vesparush-rei would ice over. Calindor knew how he would deal with that, but it would take too long to explain. Instead he only shrugged and smiled.

They carried the canoe to a launching ramp, slid it down to the riverbank, and left it lying in the snow. Dragasa, Calindor and the others began clambering up and down the ramp, carrying blankets and sacks of food. The canoe was narrow, yet it held a surprisingly large cargo.

Most of the village had come down to the bank to see them go. Tulucuingol spoke in murmurs with Tilcalli for a few moments, and then said: "Bravely you came to us, bravely you leave us. May you return soon, our son and daughter, and live long in peace with us."

The villagers clapped in approval; the Dragasa raised a hand for silence.

"The Badakhar are coming," he said, his words fluttering in white frost from his lips. "We will hold them off while we can. Calindor, I thank you for your courage. You and Bherasha risk your lives for people you have never known."

"As you risked yours for us," Bherasha said. She embraced Dragasa, and then Tilcalli.

"Are you sure you don't want us to go with you?" Svordo asked. "We will, you know. The canoe's big enough."

Calindor smiled and shook his head. Then he beckoned to Pervidhu, who stood on the edge of the crowd. The Badakh strode forward as if on parade, the sheepskin collar of his jacket pulled up to his ears.

"Haven't you seen enough of this river in winter?" he asked. "And what's all this jabber? Something about Badakhar coming?"

Calindor nodded, gesturing to the north and northeast. Then he took Pervidhu's arm and led him through the crowd to a stamped-down path that led along the edge of the bluff outside the wall—and away to the northeast. Bherasha and Tilcalli followed. After a few paces, Calindor gave Pervidhu a little shove, as if to send him on his way.

"What is this?" the Badakh demanded. "Sending me away? Have I worn out my welcome?"

"Go to your comrades," Tilcalli said. "Tell them that my son and the staff are returning to Aishadan."

"He's crazy." Pervidhu's nose was running in the cold; he

wiped it with a gloved hand and then spoke directly to Calindor. "They couldn't hit the longboat on the way up, but now you'll never be able to stay out of bowshot. They'll kill you and the girl before you're even out of sight of this place."

"We will see," Bherasha answered.

"In any case," Tilcalli said, "Tanshadabela no longer welcomes you. You must go to your own people."

Pervidhu still looked at Calindor, who smiled faintly in reply. "Well, hemamagh, you did me a bad turn when you broke my leg, and a good turn when you healed it. I reckon we're even. If you want to die to protect your people, I can understand that. You're more of a Badakh warrior than you'd like to admit." He put out a hand. "Good luck to you. I won't ask Mekhpur to look after you. He'll do that without my advice."

They shook hands, and Pervidhu turned without another word. He plodded up the pathway through the snow and into the trees.

"That was why Callia wanted him alive," Bherasha said, her eyes wide.

Tilcalli nodded. "Perhaps so. Now you must go, and quickly."

They returned to the ramp, and again the people clapped. Bherasha let Dragasa guide her into the front of the canoe; she carefully slid the staff of Pelshadan between the hull and the bundled supplies on which she was to sit. He handed her a paddle.

"The spell on this paddle will give you strength," he said. She took it from him and held his hand for a moment. Calindor, settling himself in the stern, saw her eyes gleam as she looked at Dragasa and then at the village, the river and the mountains. *Look well, Bherasha,* he thought. *We may never see them again.*

The wind was quickening, striking exposed skin like a fist. Calindor took another paddle from his mother, and gripped her shoulders as she kissed him. Then Dragasa gripped his hand.

"Our love goes with you. Some day soon you will come back, and we will speak together, I to you and you to me."

Calindor nodded. Dragasa and Svordo gripped the gunwales of the canoe and pushed it forward into a narrow strip of green-black water between the bank and the nearest floe.

Thrusting his paddle once, twice, Calindor called upon the spell that had warmed the barn. With startling speed it erupted from him: the strange orange dragonfire formed an arc in the path of the canoe, perhaps ten strides ahead. Within that arc the ice steamed, shattered, and melted.

The people of Tanshadabela cried out in wonder as Calindor steered the canoe into open water. With every stroke of his paddle the dragonfire moved ahead, clearing a path through the icy river.

As the current took them, Calindor looked once over his shoulder. The people were already going back inside the stockade, preparing for an onslaught they could not survive.

Eskel walked wearily to his horse, standing not far from the north end of the Bridge of Alekakh spanning the Vesparushrei. The assault by the Kormannalendhar cavalry had been just another probe, a test of Aishadan's defenses and will. The besiegers had paid—fifteen riders and six of their mounts, plus another twenty or so warriors wounded. But it had cost him six good men and eight horses he could ill afford.

This is what we're reduced to—counting every man, every arrow. Was this what it was like for the Nerkesar when we stood outside their gates?

The snow was trampled into a pink ice, but another flurry had started; soon the bridge and the roads leading to it would be white again. He pulled himself up into the saddle and looked south.

All along the south bank of the Vesparushrei, the invaders had dug in. The little garrison at the far end of the bridge was now their headquarters. Gathering Field was crowded with their tents. The villages along the south bank housed the upermannar of Ghrirei, Halamor and Kormannalendh. The mansions of Aishadan's upermannar were plundered and burned.

At least they haven't crossed the river yet. When it freezes—

When it froze completely, the Vesparushrei would expose the whole southern flank of the city. Then these desperate massacres at the bridge would be needless; the invaders would come across wherever they chose. The barricades that the slaves were now building at the water's edge would not slow them for long. Somewhere along the riverfront the invaders would hack their way through, and then fight street by street through the city to the Kes.

He tugged his horse's reins and rode it through the thickening snow. His bodyguard, six tough warriors, fell in around him. Everywhere, slaves were out shoveling and sweeping, while the arekakhar swung their clubs at any who worked too slowly. They were trying to keep the streets clear so that horses and wagons could get through. But the city was trying to fight while half-paralyzed.

Eskel felt thick-witted with exhaustion. A hot meal, a few mugs of medh, and a change into dry clothes would revive him. Instead of checking the defenses along the riverfront, he turned up the street leading to the Kes. The bodyguards seemed cheered by the thought of a few moments' rest.

Sentries at the gate saluted him; their captain stepped close.

"Your honored mother, the Aryasha, wishes urgently to speak with you, Aryako." He nodded absently and rode into the first courtyard; stablehands took the horses and the men walked into the Kes.

Slaves murmured over him as they stripped his wet clothes from him and dressed him in warm wool trousers and a fur-lined buckskin tunic. He stood shuddering before the coal fire in his apartment, holding a cup of warm medh with hands that shook uncontrollably. Only after draining the cup and calling for another would he sit at table. And only after devouring a whole roast chicken did he send for Ghelasha.

She came dressed in a fine hooded robe of black ermine and white wool. Her blue eyes blazed with unusual brightness, he thought, and she moved with a nervous quickness he had not seen in her in a long time.

"We have good news at last," she said, embracing him. "The Skalkaz is well again."

"Pelshadan? He's mad."

"No longer! He sacrificed a slave to Mekhpur, and his powers are restored."

"I heard about the slave yesterday, but not that he was any the better for it."

"He says he went into a meditative trance in his room, next to Albohar, and woke only this morning. He came to speak with me at once, since you were out in the city. Oh, Eskel, we have a chance! He says he doesn't need the staff to turn back the invasion."

"Where is he now?"

"Tending to your father, and awaiting your summons. Shall I send for him?"

"At once."

The Veik appeared in Eskel's doorway soon after. Eskel had not seen him in days, and stared in surprise. Pelshadan was still gaunt, but he stood erect and walked with an even tread. His pale blue eyes met Eskel's without shifting or blinking.

"My lord Aryako, I am grateful for your summons," the old man said. His voice was as firm and cold as his gaze. "I believe

Mekhpur has answered our prayers. He has tested us as the stalmagh tests his steel. Now we are ready to be forged into the weapon of his will.''

"The invaders are within two bowshots of us," Eskel said. "How shall we overcome them and drive them out of Aishadan?"

"I know a great and terrible weather spell. It will bring down still more bitter cold upon our enemies. They will freeze to death in their saddles, or in their tents."

"What of our own people? They will freeze as well."

Pelshadan shrugged. "Some of the slaves, perhaps, if they have no shelter. But our people will be warned to stay by their firesides. Our god Mekhpur is Firelord; through fire they shall be saved, and through absence of fire shall the invaders perish."

Something about Pelshadan bothered Eskel, but he could not tell what it was. "How soon can this spell be done, Veik?"

"The preparations are complex, Aryako. Five or six days."

"Five or six days! Why not five or six years? Veik, did you not hear me? They are across the river. They test the bridge again and again. When the river freezes over, they will be at our throats. And that will be in a day or two, three at most."

Pelshadan looked unworried. "If the warriors of Aishadan deserve rule over the Five Kingdoms, they can hold off the invaders for another day or two."

Eskel looked at his mother, whose eyes were fixed on Pelshadan. Never had Eskel seen such yearning in them, such fear.

"Begin your preparations at once, Veik. I shall rally the warriors and prepare them for what they must face."

"I am honored by the trust you place in me, Aryako. I will not disappoint you."

The Veik left as quickly as he had come. Ghelasha turned to her son and smiled.

"Isn't it wonderful, Eskel! Mekhpur is testing us, and we have not been found wanting. Now all those dogs across the river will freeze into stones, and you shall be Mekhatar Aryo, Greatest King of all the kingdoms."

"If the Firelord wills it. I must go now. Make sure the Veik and his magicians have all that they need."

Pulling on his cloak, he kissed his mother and strode from the room. What was it about Pelshadan that had seemed so strange? Eskel was almost to the courtyard when it came to him: the Veik had not twitched, had not fiddled with his long hair. A kind of stillness had filled him. A good thing, too, Eskel thought. Watching the tics and twitches of most magicians was tiring in itself.

He went out again into the cold, grinning at his waiting bodyguards. They smiled back, uncertain but encouraged by their master's cheer.

As the riders moved through the trees, Snegh considered how the Menmannar would defend themselves. The palisade around the village would not be a serious problem. Fire could breach it, or improvised battering rams. From across the river, Vulkvo had studied the gates and found them also vulnerable. The defenders would be using bows and arrows and spears—dangerous, but not impossible for attackers in armor and tough leather. No doubt the Menmannar would have some nasty surprises as well, pits and snares and traps. Maybe even a dragon, though Snegh doubted it.

No, the worst threat would be magic. Maybe Dheribi was crippled by the spell Pelshadan had put on him, but the witch woman Pelkhven might have powers no one had suspected. The renegade small sorcerer, the one with the burned face, had created a good illusion of a dragon when the fugitives were escaping from Gathering Field; he might well be restored enough to deceive men and horses again. Other magicians might also be lying in wait.

"Remember," he had told his men as they gathered for the onslaught, "the greater the magic, the less the magician can sustain it. If they make it snow harder, it won't last long. If they create illusions, the really frightening ones won't last long either. More likely they'll lay little spells—strange noises behind us, cramps to make our muscles ache, smells to frighten the horses. Just you keep going. The sooner we're inside that village, the sooner we'll see the magicians' heads come loose. And the sooner we'll be home by a hot fire." They had nodded, sitting hunched in their saddles while the snow stung their faces.

Surely this cold was natural, not a work of magic; Snegh recalled that the Menmannar knew little of the Sterkar of air and water. But if they had a real weather magician defending them, this fight would go hard.

The Badakhar rode now through open woods, along trails the Menmannar must have used for generations—ever since they had fled from the Slave Wars. The land made Snegh uncomfortable: how could they live among all these trees and not cut them down? Surely their smithies and hearths needed fuel, their cabins needed timber, their crops and livestock needed new fields. Yet they left this land deserted, almost untouched, like a sack of gold left lying in the marketplace.

And how could anyone fight in this terrain, with no visibility, no way to get a clear bowshot or to charge on horseback? Well, he and his men would have plenty to brag about when they got home. Only in the oldest longchants had warriors fought in such conditions. Perhaps they would compose a longchant about him: *The Forest-Battler Snegh*. That had a pleasant sound to it.

Snow fell in a sudden, heavy flurry; Snegh looked to left and right, and saw only the nearest riders. The forest had disappeared in a swirl of white. He sat up in his saddle. Was this natural weather or a spell of some kind? Up ahead, he thought he saw motion on the very edge of visibility: Menmannar, or illusions? The wind picked up, moaning in the trees; then it died down but the moaning went on.

Snegh's horse snorted and hesitated, smelling fear on the wind. Snegh himself could smell it, bringing back memories of countless battles, and a memory of this country on a late summer's evening long ago. Had it been this very trail they had come down, giggling and half-drunk with medh? Had it been his own fear he had smelled, or that of the others? Or was it the smell of the woman Albohar had so proudly, foolishly carried away on his shoulders?

Whatever its source, the smell filled the air. He heard other horses whinny, the jingle of harness as riders fought to control their mounts. Yes, this was surely a spell, a trick to frighten them off. He drew his sword and growled deep in his throat. Let them send their dragon if they liked—he would not be driven away.

They came through the trees, most of the riders still struggling with their horses, and into a broad meadow that Snegh recognized at once. Yes, yes, this was where the girl and her horse had been, this was where Albohar had cut her off and pulled her from the horse. The village was just beyond.

The flurry had died away and the air was relatively clear under a dark sky. At the far side of the meadow, a man stood between two lodgepole pines, dressed in Badakh coat and trousers. So they'd killed someone and robbed his body; this sentry would pay with his life for that.

Snegh whistled, a low, birdlike call that carried well. It meant a charge. Even if the sentry raised an alarm, the Badakhar would be at the village within moments. The horses knew the signal as well as the men, and training took over even with the stink of fear still hanging over them. The first line of horsemen broke into a trot; the hoofbeats in the snow sounded to Snegh like white water racing over stones in a riverbed, and he drew his sword with a kind of grim elation. The sentry would be his first kill of the day, but not the last.

Walking almost casually, the sentry came forward out of the trees and into the snowy meadow. He was waving as if in greeting, while the warriors rumbled closer. *What a fool*, Snegh thought. *Does he think us traders bringing gifts?*

The sentry pulled off his leather cap and waved it. His yellow hair and beard glinted even in the gray snowlight.

"Ghe sleu!" the man shouted in Badakhi, his voice almost lost in the thunder of the charge. "Go slow!"

Snegh stared. Was this another trick, another enchantment, another illusion from that small sorcerer with the burned face? The man looked real enough, with real snow sticking in his hair and on his sheepskin jacket. *If it's a trick, it's a good one. Charge through it? Or stop? Is this one of Vulkvo's scouts, or a renegade?*

In the same instant that he decided, Snegh whistled again and pulled on his horse's reins. The Badakh man stopped and raised both hands above his head in greeting. Snegh slowed his mount to a walk and approached the man. Across the meadow, the other riders paused. When he had come close enough to the man to kill him with a sword thrust, Snegh looked down at him.

"Who are you?"

"Pervidhu of Vidhumen. And you're Lord Snegh. I was one of the lead scouts hunting for the slave magicians. They took me prisoner."

"And you've escaped?"

Pervidhu shook his head. "They threw me out of their village. Told me to tell you that Dheribi is heading back down the river with the Veik's staff."

Snegh brought his sword's point under Pervidhu's chin. "What proof do you have?"

Pervidhu shook his head and grinned. "I saw him and his girl paddling down the river not long ago. They must have gone right past you as you were coming through the woods. If you'd seen them, you'd have all the proof you needed. He's melting the ice on the river as he goes."

"Downriver. Where?"

"Back to Aishadan, my lord. Back to Aishadan."

Twenty-three

Three Halamori warriors escorted Potiari from the south end of the bridge to the garrison now occupied by the besiegers. To the anxious magician this seemed more like enemy territory than Ner Kes ever had. The invaders who swarmed through the garrison's corridors and rooms were warriors like those of Aishadan, but with differences. The Halamorar wore their long hair in many little braids. The Kormannalendhar spoke in an uncouth, whining accent. And the men of Ghrirei waxed their beards and moustaches into spikes. But they all walked with warriors' swaggers, and Potiari saw death in their eyes.

The guards took him to the commandant's apartment, a large room with a low ceiling. Even with coal burning in the fireplace, the room was bitterly cold.

Standing before the fireplace was an upermanna in his fifties, short and stocky, with a close-cropped white beard. His bald scalp was thickly scarred, and the fringe of gray around it was twisted into a fringe of Halamori braids. They were woven around strips of blue and white ribbon—a sign of high rank in Halamor.

"I am Karman," he said. "Come in and sit by the fire."

Shivering, Potiari nodded and stepped forward to the chair by the hearth. The glow of the fire warmed his hands.

Karman preferred to stand. He was mantled in a fine sable cloak, but he had not troubled to cover his hairless head. Silently he handed Potiari a tall mug of hot tea sweetened with honey. Their eyes met for a moment, and Potiari decided the upermanna was well named: Karman in the Halamori dialect meant Hard Man, and this warrior was surely that.

"Thank you, my lord. I am the sorcerer Potiari. This drink

is most welcome." He tried not to spill it from his shaking hands. "The Aryako has sent me here to discuss certain matters of our common interest."

"Ah. Is he surrendering, then?"

"Not at all, my lord. The Aryako Eskel bids me advise you that he will in no way hinder your swift return to your homes."

A faint and humorless smile flicked across Karman's face. He stood with his back to the fire, looking down at Potiari.

"A generous offer. We will accept it as soon as we can afford to."

"My lord?"

"Are you coal-diggers all dull-witted? Why do you suppose we've come to make war on you in winter?"

"Why—to reduce Aishadan's might, my lord, and to catch us by surprise. As you have indeed."

"To reduce Aishadan's might," Karman repeated. "My lord sorcerer, do you know that the crops failed in Halamor and Ghrirei last fall? That the harvest in Kormannalendh was half last year's? The only thing that seems to grow well in our soil these days is salt. Yes, we knew you were growing too strong for our liking, but we knew also you'd sacked Ner Kes and brought home plunder to get you through the winter. So we'd no choice but to fall upon you before you'd eaten all your grain and meat. Otherwise we'd see famine by spring."

Potiari replied to Karman's bluntness with the singsong whine of a herald: "You will understand, my lord, that we love famine no more than you, and times have been hard here as well. Indeed, one motive of our great Aryo Albohar is to weld together all our kingdoms, so that we may give proper sacrifices to Mekhpur, and so persuade the Firelord to make our soil sweet again and to cleanse our streams."

"Mekhpur rewards those that reward themselves," Karman grunted. "Look you, sorcerer, I am too hard-pressed to trade lies with you all day. Even with all we've taken from your other towns and estates, we've sent home almost nothing to feed our people, nothing to feed our livestock. We will have the granaries of Aishadan, or we will die fighting for them. If your little Aryako really cares for his people, let him surrender his grain and cattle—we'll save him the trouble of slaughtering them. Then we'll trouble him no more, and he can spend the spring plotting all the revenge he likes."

Potiari forgot to sound like a herald, and spoke now in an incredulous whisper. "My lord Karman—what you ask is impossible. We would have mass starvation within days, and in the worst winter in living memory. No Aryo would tolerate such a humiliation.''

Karman nodded. "Nor survive it, if his upermannar decided he'd lost his grip. No doubt it's hard to have an Aryo who's dying and an Aryako scarcely bearded. But that's an internal matter for you northerners to settle among yourselves. We want your food and fodder, my friend Potiari, and we will have it at any cost.''

Potiari nodded and finished his tea. The room seemed colder still. "Very well, my lord. I will take your words to our Aryako and his advisers. But I should warn you that your sufferings so far will be as nothing compared to what our Veik has in store for you.''

The upermanna sneered. "Your Veik is helpless, a gibbering fool. Our own Veikar have tested him. They spare his life only out of pity for one of their own.''

Potiari laughed, a nervous cackle. "Pity for one of their own, my lord? No Veik ever knew a moment's pity for his fellows. And our Veik will waste no pity on you and your magicians. His powers are restored and magnified. Even now, he brings still worse cold and suffering upon your men and beasts. Those of you who die soon will be the lucky ones. By next Third Night, a cold will lie upon your armies that will freeze men in their boots. To draw breath will be like drinking fire. Only your immediate retreat will save you.''

Karman crossed his arms under his fur cloak. "A fine threat, well uttered. For a magician you carry yourself well, my friend. But we have our spells as well, and more trust in our Veikar than in yours. I thank you for your company and your advice. Now return to your masters, and tell them our terms: their food or their lives. Good day to you.''

The guards walked Potiari back to the bridge. He hastened across it, his boots slipping on the frozen mess of ice and blood. The river below, he noticed, was icing over quickly. Another day or two, especially as the Veik's spell began to take effect, and the Vesparushrei would be a solid mass of ice—solider, he reflected, than the ice on the river at Ner Kes which he and Dvoi had created at such cost and to so little gain.

At the north end of the bridge waited his own escort, men even grimmer in bearing than Karman. They would take him quickly back to the Kes, back to his master. He had the whole conversation fixed in his memory; he would relate it to Pelshadan, word for word. Then it would be out of his hands, and perhaps Pelshadan would give him leave to attend on Albohar. Sitting in that dark, frigid, stinking sickroom was better than staying in the company of the Veik.

Pelshadan was not as he had been. And whatever had caused the change frightened Potiari more than anything else ever had in his life.

The arc of dragonfire could melt the ice and turn it into a curtain of steam, but Bherasha and Calindor found it did not much warm them. A wind was blowing from the northeast, sweeping across the mountains and then down into the river valley. It struck the left side of the canoe with uncertain violence, sometimes hard enough to rock it. Snow flew on the wind, too fine and dry to stick.

They paddled steadily, fast enough to keep themselves warm without breaking into a sweat. Calindor admired the spells his father had put on the paddles; each stroke pushed the canoe ahead with surprising force. He admired also the gloves Dragasa had given them. They were lined with rabbit fur, their outsides sewn of supple hide and elegantly decorated with fine beadwork. He marveled at the wealth of the Menmannar—not just the beauty of the things they made, but the greatness of spirit that made them wish to create beauty and to give it away without a moment's hesitation.

The canoe itself was another such work of beauty: as he saw and felt how it took the water, Calindor felt a happiness almost as pure as that of the craft's Gariba. The Powers that Dragasa had sung into the canoe were eager to float, to play with the Gariba of the river.

And the river's Powers in turn rejoiced to be freed of the ice by the heat of dragonfire, to foam and curl around the canoe's hull and the enchanted paddles. Calindor watched them and smiled.

They all wish me to go where I go, he thought. *They feel Callia steering me back down this river. This river I have journeyed down before, quickening in my mother's womb.*

His focus was now so deep and strong that he felt himself in a dream without end. He saw the snow flying on the wind, and saw the mountains though they were hidden in the rising storm. He felt the quick stillness of each snowflake, and heard the long songs of the mountains as they rose and fell like the waves on a lake. He smelled the wild roses lost beneath the snow, and sensed the elk as they moved into deep thickets out of the reach of the wind.

Everything that was Callia's was alive, but the wind was not hers. He could tell it had been summoned, called by the Firelord to bring this cold to Cantarea.

Their speed was not great—perhaps a little faster than a man might run on bare ground. Calindor found he must steer carefully, looking ahead to the clearest way through the icebound river. Dragonfire could melt even the greatest rafts of ice, but to do so took time—and if the ice had built up over rock or driftwood, he must turn the canoe aside and seek an easier way.

Before long they came to the place where the longboat had come ashore. It was still there, but pulled higher up the bank and sheltered under a rough lean-to. The snow around it showed many footprints, now half-buried by the current flurry. The Badakhar must have used it in crossing the river, Calindor thought. It would not serve them well now; the open water behind the canoe soon froze over, giving no chance of pursuit.

But the longboat was still in sight when horsemen came down the trail that Obordur and the men of Tanshadabela had taken when they rescued the fugitives. These were Badakhar, moving slowly but steadily through the snow; red-and-gold banners of Aishadan flew from their upraised lances.

Bherasha saw them also, and glanced over her shoulder at Calindor with a grim smile: "Pervidhu must have reached them."

Calindor nodded. He hoped Pervidhu would get a good horse and plenty of food. He would have a long, cold ride home to Aishadan.

For the rest of the day hundreds of horsemen were usually in sight, moving along the left bank of the river. They made no effort to come down onto the river itself; the ice was thick enough in many places, but so uneven and slippery that no horse could keep its footing. Still less could a man. As long as the canoe stayed near the middle of the stream, or near the right bank, no archer could hope to come within range.

The snow stopped falling not long before dark. Bherasha turned to Calindor: "Should we stop for the night or go on? If we stop they'll surely try to cross the ice to us, or go on ahead to find an ambush."

Calindor shook his head. They might be toughened cavalry, but they had been out in the cold for a long time. They would prefer to stop and rest, and perhaps send scouts on downriver.

If they did not lose sight of the dragonfire, they would be content to wait at least until dawn.

He steered the canoe toward the shore on the right bank. Steep sand dunes stood here, scoured clear of snow by constant wind. Calindor and Bherasha dragged the canoe into the lee of a dune. Calindor put a ring of dragonfire around them, bright enough for the Aishadanar to see from the across the river.

Within the ring, the wind died down. Calindor made more dragonfire, a simple disk on the sand; it glowed as comfortingly as an ordinary campfire. Upon it he put a copper pot full of soup thick enough to be a stew. It had sat frozen in a larger pot, but now it quickly thawed and began to steam.

They sat in the shelter of the upturned canoe, thick blankets under them and furs over them. Bherasha sat close to him, an arm around his waist.

"Will we ever go back to Tanshadabela?" she murmured.

He nodded and smiled, though in his heart he was not sure. *I am The One Who Goes Away,* he thought. *Perhaps I will go away from Aishadan but never back up this river. Perhaps I will go away from Sotalar, to one of the other worlds. Wherever I go, unless it is to death or the Black World, I hope you come with me, Bherasha.*

When the soup was hot they drank it from finely hammered copper bowls and wiped up the last of it with lumps of bread. Then they sat warming themselves before the dragonfire while snowflakes drifted down into its light. Calindor played a little game with them as he once used to with dust motes, making them rise and turn in patterns: circles, spirals, wheels. In the orange light they glowed like sparks from a stalmagh's forge. Bherasha laughed as he encircled her with a ring of snowflakes, and he delighted in the happiness he saw in her eyes.

Once I played like this and I was a boy. Then I learned that my life was not my own, that I belonged to Cantarea, to Calihalingol, to Callia. What will I be if they ever release me? A boy again? A man? What kind of man? Shall I be like Dragasa, or like Albohar? No—they belong to others also. Maybe we all do. Maybe I am a fool to think I could belong to myself. Don't I want Bherasha with me always? Doesn't that make me belong to her?

He lay back on the blankets and drew Bherasha down with him. Her arms were strong around him, and the scent of her made him rejoice in the snowy darkness.

* * *

The Hearing Hall was far too cold to be used now. Much of the Kes was sealed off, and fires burned constantly in the remaining rooms. Slaves slipped on icy stairs as they brought sacks of coal up from the store rooms. When not needed, they huddled together in the hallways; a lucky few worked in the warm kitchens, helping to feed the ovens and prepare meals.

Eskel's chambers had become his headquarters. There he sat receiving messengers and his senior warriors. There his clerks scribbled awkwardly, trying to keep their inkwells from freezing as they wrote down his orders to the city's defenders.

This evening he had sent everyone away for a time, so that he could eat his supper alone. He sat at a table near the hearth, spooning up a horsemeat stew that had cooled quickly on its journey from the kitchens. The bread was a hard lump that scarcely absorbed the stew's scanty juices. The medh, at least, was good.

"Aryako—" He recognized his mother's voice at the door.

"Come in, my lady mother."

Ghelasha entered with a flourish of her long cloak, and sat without ceremony across the table from him. In the candlelight her eyes seemed huge.

"The cold grows harder by the hour," she whispered.

"Imagine how they like it out in those tents on Gathering Field," he answered with his mouth full of bread. "May Pelshadan make it colder still."

"I hear reports that our freemen are freezing to death in their homes. And that the slaves are fleeing their masters and sheltering in the mines."

Not only cold made Eskel shiver. He did not like the thought of those shafts and tunnels deep under the earth. "They will have to come out soon, or starve. When they come out, we'll post them all."

"And then who will do their work?"

"Whoever I choose! Why all these senseless questions? Have you come here only to annoy me at my table?"

"No—only to see you, and to see how you are."

"I am as you see me."

"So thin—I shall have the cooks flogged for feeding you so ill."

"I eat no better than my men. If I did, they would soon start thinking of who might better serve in my place. Have you seen the Veik?"

"No. I hear he keeps to his chambers, but sometimes walks the corridors in the dead of night."

"Whatever he does, his spell is winning this war for us."

"He has changed, Eskel. I fear him now, though I never did before."

Eskel laughed, though he knew what she meant and shared her fear. "He has made a pact with Mekhpur, and won great powers. Even calling down this spell of cold has not tired him. He is as strong as Dheribi. And if those damned soldiers of Snegh's ever get back with Dheribi's head and Pelshadan's staff, we will see even greater deeds."

"So you are content with Pelshadan?"

"Should I not be? Shall I ask his underlings to do as well as he has?"

"No, no. Only . . . he frightens me."

"I am sorry for it, my lady mother. I shall ask him to avoid you, if that will make you feel any better."

"Do not be harsh with me, Eskel." The tremor in her voice was so unusual that it took him a moment to realize she was on the edge of tears. "You have done so well in all our trials, and I would not burden you with more troubles. It is only that—that I have no one else but you."

He reached across the table and patted her hand. It felt cold. "You have all the people of Aishadan. You are their Aryasha, wife of their king. While they live, you need fear nothing."

Her eyes, wide and blue, seemed to look through him, toward the frosted window overlooking the icebound river. "I fear the Veik."

"May our enemies fear him also. Now I must ask you to leave. My officers will soon be here to report, and then I must go to see the men at the defenses."

Ghelasha composed herself and nodded. As she left the room, Eskel frowned. She was a woman of hardness and intelligence, of royal birth—a fit mate and mother for princes. If she was this close to snapping, how must lesser people feel after all these days of siege and cold and hunger?

Snegh was not sure if he had slept at all. His men had built huge bonfires last night, as soon as the magician had beached his canoe across the river. Crude walls of logs helped reflect some of the fires' heat, and shielded men and horses from the wind a little. But the cold had deepened further. Sleeping robes filled with ice and turned stiff. Horses groaned and shuddered, though their riders kept them well covered with blankets and close to the fires. Snegh had assigned four men to keep watch on the orange glow across the river; when their relief came in the middle of the night, the lookouts were crouched under blankets, frozen dead.

The second shift of lookouts had fared better, with two fires to keep them alive. Near dawn they sent a messenger to rouse Snegh.

"The magician is moving. That fire of his is down on the river again."

Snegh grunted, glad for a reason to get out of his icy sleeping robes. Freezing in the saddle was better than this inaction. He gave terse orders: a few men to ride ahead and alert the advance party, which had camped well ahead of the main body; a double ration of grain for the horses, and of horsemeat for the warriors; a party to butcher the horses that had died overnight, and another party to build cairns over the bodies of the men.

Vulkvo joined him soon. Frostbite had put white patches on his cheeks and nose, and his beard was crusted with ice.

"Sixty-one men dead in the night," he murmured, "and eighty-three horses. Perhaps we should have taken the Menmannar village after all."

"Not while our deadliest enemy is on his way to Aishadan." Snegh warmed his hands around a mug of tea. "What point in staying warm and dry if Dheribi is causing mischief back home?"

Vulkvo grunted, but his assent seemed halfhearted. Snegh worried: if even the leaders of this force were so discouraged, what of the men? They had come home weary from Ner Kes, and been sent off without rest into the unknown forests and mountains. Now they were chasing a single canoe back down the river, while men and horses died of cold. They remembered Dheribi's disspelling of the wall at Ner Kes, and they had heard something of his escape from Aishadan. Even so, they might find it hard to believe that the Aryo's half-breed son could be so dangerous as to warrant all this effort.

All the more reason, then, to catch and slay him, and then get home to Aishadan. Snegh thought of a hot feast, a roaring fire and a bed warmed by a couple of young slaves; yes, it would be good to be home.

Somewhere nearby, a tree cracked open as ice in its heart expanded and split it. It groaned and fell.

* * *

So now it is done, Calihalingol said. She had found a place in a grove of aspens where the grass grew thick and soft, and shade dappled the sunlight of the endless noon. Dragasa and Tilcalli sat on either side of her.

He has gone with the girl, Tilcalli said. *In three days, perhaps four, they will be back in Aishadan. If they do not freeze.*

A terrible cold lies over the mountains, Dragasa explained. *No one can remember a winter like it. Calindor has a spell from the dragons to melt the river ice, but it will be a hard journey.*

I remember cold. When it snowed, we made winter butter-flies. We would fall straight back into the snow, and wave our arms. When we got up, you could see the butterflies.

Tilcalli smiled. *Children still make butterflies, great-grandmother. But now it is so cold we have to keep the children indoors.*

And do you stay indoors also? And do you talk?

Tilcalli smiled. The old woman was not really lost in mem-ories of her childhood. *We talk. With our mouths and our bodies.*

I remember that also. Calihalingol laughed, sunlight flashing on her white hair. *Here we dance and sing and dream, and sometimes we hold one another, but our bodies do not talk as they did in life. Tell me what your bodies say.*

Dragasa stretched out in the grass, hands under his head. *They say, old woman, that we are glad to be together. They say we will not part again, no matter what old women may want in the Open Dream.*

Old women in the Open Dream will be glad to know that. She squinted, then looked up through the fluttering leaves that glowed green and yellow overhead. *Look—is it growing dark?*

No—but clouds are starting to cover the sun. Tilcalli an-swered.

I remember clouds also. They are not part of the Open Dream.

Let us go back to the village, great-grandmother. Tilcalli helped the old woman to her feet, and they walked out of the grove and down a path into the village. Clouds were forming, thick and dark, over the distant mountains. Only their fringes had yet reached far enough to obscure the sun.

In Sotalar, with a sky like that, I would expect a storm before long, said Dragasa.

Calihalingol looked solemn. *This is the sign of a storm in Sotalar. A storm so great that it reaches even here. My dear children—you must go home now. I feel Callia stirring.* Her

expression changed to a kind of surprise as they neared the
village. The ancestors of the Siragi Aibela had all stopped dancing. They too looked up at the thickening clouds.

Go home quickly. Quickly! Calihalingol embraced her great-
granddaughter, and faded even as she did so.

Tilcalli woke beside Dragasa in their bed. It was late at night.
The cabin creaked in the cold. She put her arms around her
husband, as much to comfort herself as him.

"A storm in the Open Dream," she whispered. "What is
happening, Dragasa?"

He said nothing, but his embrace told her of his love and fear.

Twenty-four

"They're coming," said Snegh. He was crouched behind an upturned slab of ice, well out from the shore. The sky was almost as white as the land and the river, and flakes whirled around in the strengthening gusts from the north. With him were five archers and a dozen warriors armed with swords and throwing spears.

Pervidhu was one of them; he had not drawn his sword, and leaned close to the upturned slab to find shelter from the wind.

"We're wasting our time," he muttered. "He'll turn our arrows into icicles or some such thing. Assuming he even lets us get within range of him."

"Be quiet," Snegh commanded.

"I'll be no such thing. Being quiet got me dragged out here away from a nice warm fire. We're all freezing to death for no good purpose. Trying to kill Dheribi is like ants trying to ambush a horse."

"You don't know what you're talking about," Snegh responded. "His head will come free of his shoulders like any other slave's."

Pervidhu's grin was almost a sneer. "Have you ever felt magic? I'll bet you haven't, or we'd be somewhere warmer than here. That witch's bastard can call Sterkar that no Veik has ever dreamed of. When he healed my leg I couldn't tell if I was dying or finally coming to life."

"How can he call Sterkar if he can't talk?" one of the other men asked.

"The same way he melts the damned ice. I think that dragon taught him some things. And if we start shooting arrows at him, he'll teach *us* more than we want to learn."

Snegh spun around, strode to Pervidhu in four long paces,

263

and punched him in the stomach. The young warrior staggered back but did not fall.

"The witch's bastard certainly put a spell on *you*," Snegh said calmly. "Now be quiet. And when we've hit them with the arrows, you come out with the rest of us and help take his head. Or would you rather donate your own?"

Pervidhu was gasping for breath. "I'll do—whatever I can—my lord Snegh." But his eyes still held contempt.

A distant horn sounded from the riverbank, signalling the approach of the canoe. Snegh stood up to glance through a gap in the ice, and saw the strange orange glow burning through a white mist of steam. The canoe was well within range already, but the archers would have to reveal themselves if they were to see their target. They would have to wait until the canoe came abreast of the ice slab; it would then be no more than twenty-five strides away.

Silently he gestured to his archers. They strung their bows and notched arrows. A minute passed, and then another. The wind strengthened, moaning, but the hiss and crackle of melting ice came clearly.

Then the glow was visible to the ambushers, and the canoe appeared a moment later. Snegh could see two figures in it, sitting close together in the stern of the canoe. Their faces were hidden under fur hoods.

"Shoot," Snegh said softly. This was almost point-blank range; the archers drew their bowstrings and let fly.

The shafts flew humming through the white air, and burst into flames—not just as fire arrows would, but along their whole length. In less time than it took Snegh to catch his breath, all five arrows were faint smears of ash, blowing away with the snow.

"Again!"

The archers obeyed, drawing new shafts from their quivers. But even as they rested them on their bows, the arrows exploded in fire. Crying out in fear, the men dropped their bows and watched the shafts burning and sputtering on the ice at their feet.

"Damn him for an evil magician!" Snegh bellowed. "Come on, let's take him with these!" And he brandished his curved steel sword. "Quick, while we can reach him."

He led a silent charge across the ice, slipping over its rough and treacherous surface toward the canoe. His men followed close behind, and Snegh could hear their breath whistle in their nostrils. Someone hurled a spear that arced over Snegh's head and fell harmlessly into the wake of the canoe.

Snegh saw the two fugitives now, sitting close together and looking directly at him. The girl was sitting in front, between the magician's knees, while he dipped a paddle easily into the steaming water. The melting ice had formed a strip of water scarcely wider than the canoe itself; Snegh would have no trouble reaching Dheribi with a single swift blow of his sword.

The magician smiled faintly, an expression that filled Snegh's heart with dread, yet he plodded on. As he raised his sword and drew closer, Snegh felt a pulse of heat caress his face. He looked up and saw his sword on fire.

No—not on fire, but glowing as red-hot as when some stalmagh had taken it from the forge. Snowflakes hissed as they touched it, and Snegh could feel the heat burning through his glove.

Let it burn me to the bone, so long as I get his head! Now he was right by the edge of the melted ice, close enough to grip Dheribi by the shoulder. His right hand was locked in agony around the sword's handle. Screaming, he swung the glowing blade.

It disintegrated into flaring, orange-white droplets that vanished sputtering and steaming into the ice. Releasing the handle, Snegh fell to his knees as pain overmastered him.

Dheribi's eyes met his again, and Snegh shuddered. Still he reached out with his scorched glove, trying to grip the gunwale of the canoe. Instead Dheribi seized his hand, stripped off the glove, and held the blistered, blackened hand in his own. Snegh cried out, a wail like a forlorn child's, and fell facedown.

The other warriors had paused; now they advanced again, cautiously, while the canoe glided on. Snegh was still wailing.

The girl pulled back her hood and waved, smiling.

"Hello, Pervidhu! We'll see you in Aishadan, perhaps!"

Pervidhu spluttered in laughing consternation. "If you're truly bound for Aishadan, perhaps I'd better go to Ghrirei or Halamor. What have you done to my commander?"

She did not answer, only waved again, while Dheribi sent the canoe ahead with quick strokes of his paddle. The snow thickened, and the strange flames faded to a blur. Then the canoe was gone.

Men helped Snegh to his feet. He seemed dazed but unhurt. He looked down at his bare right hand.

"Best get a new glove on that, my lord, before it's frostbitten," said one of the archers.

"Frostbitten? I could feel the blisters swell and burst. I could feel the flesh cooking to the bone." Snegh flexed his fingers. The men saw his hand unharmed, the hand of a warrior yet strangely smooth and uncallused.

Pervidhu reached out and touched Snegh's arm. Their eyes met.

"Now *you* have been touched by magic, my lord. He whom you sought to slay has healed you as he healed me."

Snegh clenched his hand into a fist against the cold.

"Let us get back to the camp, and get on the move," he mumbled. "We have a long ride before us."

The river had frozen.

Over Aishadan the sky was pale with the promise of more snow. The streets were drifted deep, except where men and horses had trampled narrow paths. Soot from ten thousand fires had settled on the snow; ice crystals turned the air to a milky haze.

Eskel and Pelshadan rode blanketed horses through the city, escorted by fifty foot-soldiers. The streets showed few signs of life, and many of death: frozen corpses crouched in doorways, or lay in the snow where others had flung them. All were slaves. The city would stink in the spring, Eskel thought. He would have to order a great pyre to be built in tribute to Mekhpur, and on it he would burn all the corpses.

Odd, how easy it was to look ahead to spring, to the easy tasks of victory. Easier than facing the troubles of today.

The patrol moved south toward the river, along a street whose foot was sealed off by a barricade of logs and ropes. Even though snow had softened it, Eskel knew it would slow any attackers long enough for archers and pikemen to finish them off. The defenders stood shivering by the doorway to a freeman's house, doubtless yearning to get back inside to a warm stove. But they gave him a brave enough cheer, and brandished their pikes. As freemen they had much to fight for, Eskel reflected, and the longchants were full of accounts of freemen who had died defending their upermannar and Aryos.

The cold was bitter, even within the heavy furs he wore; Eskel could feel little shards of ice, frozen sweat, lie unmelted on his skin. Yet Pelshadan, riding beside him, seemed scarcely to notice. No doubt the Veik must have some little magic to keep away the cold he had invoked. Yet it looked strange indeed to see him wearing only the lightest of gloves, and a simple wool cloak with the hood casually pulled up over his bald scalp.

"Your spell is working, Veik," Eskel said. "The invaders haven't moved, even though the river's frozen over."

"They will come, Aryako. The cold has slowed them, not stopped them. Cold will make them desperate, and desperate men are good fighters. But cold will weaken them also, and your people will have the advantage."

Your people? Eskel was struck by the phrase. He looked at Pelshadan, who met his gaze—another strange act, when magicians almost never looked into anyone's eyes.

"This battle, Aryako, is a minor one. The invaders are a nuisance and nothing more. Whoever dies fighting them will please Mekhpur, but the Firelord's concerns are elsewhere."

Eskel bit back a curse. "Veik, we fought Ner Kes to give gifts to Mekhpur. We fight the invaders for the same reason. If we cannot please him this way, how can we better win his favor?"

Pelshadan smiled faintly. "First prove yourselves worthy of serving him as masters of this city and this land. Then see what new tasks he will choose to grant you, and what new favors he will give."

"As you say, Veik." The patrol was moving down an alley to the next major street. Somewhere nearby a baby wailed; its cry seemed to Eskel as thin and cold as the new snow drifting across the hardened crust of the old. "And what is it that concerns Mekhpur more than this siege?"

"Dheribi is returning, and Mekhpur awaits him."

"Returning?" Eskel sat up in his saddle. "Did Snegh and Vulkvo catch him?"

"The Firelord tells me only that Dheribi returns, and with my staff."

"Then you will be truly unconquerable, Veik!"

"Yes, Aryako."

The patrol soon returned to the Arekaryo Kes, and Pelshadan took his leave. Eskel hastened to his apartment to warm himself with a fire and a flagon of medh. Even there, though, the air was so chill that he could see his breath as he stood not far from the glowing coals.

It occurred to him then that during the patrol he had looked at Pelshadan whenever the Veik spoke, and not once had he noticed the flutter of frozen breath from the old man's lips, nor seen frost cling to the old man's beard.

* * *

The riders in the vanguard reported that the fugitives had stopped for the night, camping some distance from the river in a grove of aspen. Snegh nodded absently at the news. How long had they been pursuing the canoe now? Three days? Five? Time had blurred into a permanent nightmare of cold. Last night the army had slept amid enormous bonfires, yet still almost fifty men were dead in the morning, and twenty-three horses. The horses had been butchered and roasted in the fires, and then the corpses had been hurled onto the coals; burying them under cairns would have taken too much time and energy.

"Two more days to Aishadan," Vulkvo calculated as he and Snegh rode out from camp at the head of the column. "Tomorrow we'll be back out of the wilderness, in settled country. The upermannar can shelter us; we won't lose so many men to the cold. And the night after that we'll be in Aishadan, snug in our own beds."

"Not if we haven't caught Dheribi by then."

Vulkvo smiled through cracked lips. "We *have* caught him, Snegh. We're simply herding him along."

That seemed a clever idea. "Yes—herding him along until he paddles right into the city and the guards take him." Snegh rubbed his gloved hands together, trying to create some warmth. His right hand, the one that had been both burned and healed by magic, was as vulnerable to cold as ever—perhaps more so, since it lacked calluses. How had Dheribi done that, without even speaking? What kind of magic was it that needed no speech?

A magic that would encourage him to return to the fortress of his enemies. Surely, though, the Veik who had stolen Dheribi's voice would be ready for him.

The column plodded on through the snow all morning, while scouts occasionally returned with reports on the canoe. It was moving at the same steady rate, melting its way through ice that now seemed thicker than anyone could remember. One scout said the canoe itself was below the level of the ice, and only the heads and shoulders of the fugitives were visible from shore. Snegh nodded and kept on, while others brought him news of men dying in the saddle, and horses falling dead.

The reports all seemed slightly absurd to Snegh, like pointless tales told only to interrupt his thoughts. He preferred to ride in silence, thinking of the long-gone days when he had been young, and had gone drinking and brawling with the young Aryibi Albohar, long ago before they had ever come up this accursed river.

Near noon the sky clouded over again. The landscape remained the same, countless lodgepole pines whose limbs slumped under the burden of snow. Now and then the trees parted on the right to show a stretch of the river: blankness, emptiness, with yet more trees beyond it.

Snegh dozed in the saddle and woke suddenly when a scout spoke to him urgently.

"My lord! My lord! We've reached settled land up ahead—a drovers' cottage on the lands of the upermanna Badpekash. The drovers say Aishadan lies besieged by a great army from Halamor."

"Besieged? In winter? I think not."

The scout shook his head. "It seems madness, my lord, but I think the drover spoke truly."

Slowly the import of the news sank in. He thought for a time while his horse paced steadily on. Then he called to Vulkvo, who rode nearby, and told him the news. Vulkvo swore through frost-crusted whiskers.

"Pass the word down the column," Snegh said. "We stop for a hot meal and then we ride without pause for Aishadan. If we cannot help our Aryako, we might as well die in the snow."

Calindor woke long before dawn. The sky had cleared again, and stars gleamed far overhead. He and Bherasha lay sheltered under the upturned canoe, and ringed by dragonfire, yet something had chilled him into wakefulness.

His focus swept out a circle that reached across the river: he sensed hundreds of mice in their burrows, a hibernating bear, a wolf pack drowsing in its dens, and the Badakhar clustered around their campfires.

They had ridden hard yesterday, almost as soon as they had reached the outmost farmsteads of Aishadan. Watching them from the canoe, Calindor had thought they seemed more eager to be home than to capture himself and Bherasha. Last night they had stopped in exhaustion at the estate of an upermanna. Its barns and sheds had not been enough shelter, and many had spent another night outside. Not all had survived. Calindor wished peace on the souls of the dead, but he knew their dying was not what had wakened him.

—There it was, in the northeast, far down the river toward the city. A being was coming toward them, moving fast, flying, and it was not of Sotalar. He remembered the Firelord's servant in the far caves of the Gulyaji; this creature was something like it. Perhaps it was like the creature that Tilcalli had sent away from Pelshadan.

Whatever it was, he recognized it as a tool of Mekhpur. It would test him, kill him if it could, and try as well to kill Bherasha. He could destroy it, but turned from the thought. For all its menace it was only a slave, torn by magic from its own world and sent to do the will of its master. Mekhpur would not expect it to live; he wanted only to see how Calindor killed it, and make his own plans accordingly.

Gently he shook Bherasha. She woke at once, eyes bright in the glow of the dragonfire. She made no sound, but followed Calindor in pulling on her trousers and tunic, slipping out of the sleeping furs, and silently loading the canoe. Lifting it out of the ring of dragonfire, they stepped back into a world of bitter cold. The riverbank was not steep; after a few steps they lowered the canoe to the snow and dragged it, squeaking, to the river ice.

Calindor sensed that the river had fallen sharply during the night, but its ice surface had remained anchored by the many rocks rising from the riverbed. Finding a rope of woven thongs, he tied it to the bow ring of the canoe. Then he sent a thought out to the Gariba in the ice, asking them to part.

Bherasha gasped as a black circle silently formed in the blue-gray surface of the ice. Out of the blackness came a soft moan as wind blew over the hole.

Calindor stepped into the hole, the canoe behind him. He glanced back and saw Bherasha gripping the stern seat, keeping the canoe from striking the edge of the hole. Behind her, dragonfire glowed around their campsite as if they still slept within it.

In five or six steps Calindor was under the ice. At first he had to hunch over, slipping on ice-crusted stones, but then the riverbed deepened and he could stand. Bherasha was barely visible, a dark outline against the faint glow from the dragonfire, but he sensed her fear. He made his way back to her, embraced her, and felt her warm breath on his face.

"Why?" she asked softly. "Are they coming to attack us again?"

He took her hand in his and pointed downriver, then up toward the sky.

"Something's coming. Something flying?"

He nodded, and then asked the Gariba to close up the hole they had made. Utter darkness fell.

"Dheribi, I'm afraid. The Black World must be like this. Please, whatever it is that's coming, let us meet it under the sky."

Again he embraced her. Then he lifted her up and gently placed her in the canoe. With a few tugs he got it clear of a rocky part of the riverbed, and onto smooth ice.

The river had fallen swiftly, and by half again the height of a tall man. Then it had frozen again, forming a tunnel of ice. Its walls were irregular, sometimes close together and sometimes very far. Beneath the floor, water still gurgled and rumbled in its confinement. But the ice muffled sounds, and the darkness was total.

Settling the rope over his shoulder, Calindor began to pull the canoe downstream. Though he could sense the tunnel through his focus, he created coldfire so that Bherasha too could see around her. The disk of blue light shimmered over his head, reminding him of the Underland. But this cavern was stranger than any of those the Gulyaji had dwelt within. Its uneven ceiling was shaped into swirling spikes pointing downriver, like a bed of river grass suddenly frozen. Frost had formed like fur on the ice, and sent back countless tiny glints from the disk of coldfire. In the far reaches of the tunnel, stray gleams reflected back like the eyes of forest creatures.

The ice beneath Calindor's boots was translucent, and he glimpsed the water still alive beneath it. The air was cold, though not quite as chill as it had been on the riverbank. The keel of the canoe scraped softly.

The creature of Mekhpur was closer now, but its course was less certain. Calindor sensed it swooping low over the river, then rising high again. Eventually it would see the coldfire glowing through the ice—or simply sense the magic behind the coldfire. What it would do after that, Calindor did not know. He did not think it strong enough to batter through the ice.

He felt the canoe sway as Bherasha climbed out of it.

"Let me help you pull," she said. "It's better than sitting back there like some upermanna's stupid wife in a wagon. Are we close to Aishadan?"

Calindor nodded as he gave her one end of the rope. They were close indeed. Last night he had expected to reach the city by late afternoon today, and if the tunnel was as clear as this all the way to the city, they would arrive only a few hours later.

And then what? He had no real plan, except to seek out Mekhpur and challenge him, try to drive him out of Sotalar and back to his own realm. That did not worry him; just as the flying creature did Mekhpur's will, so he did Callia's.

More changes were at work within him. Even as he helped guide the canoe around rocks, or ducked under icy stalactites, he felt something happening within his soul. He wondered if Gariba felt this way as magic shaped them into the edge of a sword, or into snowflakes.

After what seemed like a long time, the tunnel began to brighten: dawn had come, and a little light was reaching through the ice wherever wind had scoured away the snow. Calindor and Bherasha paused briefly to eat a few handfuls of nuts and dried fruits, and then went on. They had gone only a few steps when the tunnel darkened again.

"What is it?"

Calindor pointed upward. The creature must be enormous, and its great wings threw a long shadow. It knew they were under the ice, but it did not attempt to smash through. Instead, it settled onto the surface and began to follow them. The ice creaked a little, protesting the creature's weight.

The presence of Mekhpur suddenly intruded. For a dizzy moment Calindor thought himself back in the Kes, aware of something slipping through the shadows in distant corridors and unused chambers. He realized the Firelord was using the winged creature's eyes. The thought made him shudder as the cold could not.

"Shall we go on?" Bherasha asked. He nodded.

So they walked on, slipping sometimes as they pulled the canoe. Above them the creature followed, keeping its shadow between them and the sun. Calindor ignored it, pulling his focus in tight.

You are a fool going to a fool's death.

The voice in his mind was like that of the creature he had fought in the caves of the Gulyaji. Calindor did not reply.

The tunnel under the ice seemed to go on endlessly, a cavern of white and blue and black. Always the creature stayed close above. The voice in Calindor's head jeered at him. Perhaps Bherasha heard it too, or something like it; she muttered under her breath, and glared furiously in the blue glow of coldfire. Twice they stopped just long enough to eat. The faint light through the ice dimmed to darkness again. Night had fallen.

"Are we close?"

He took her gloved hand in his. Yes, they were close. He could feel Mekhpur himself near at hand, and sense the thousands of Aishadanar huddled in their houses. He sensed also thousands more, out in the open and close to the river, moving toward the ice. Who were they? Servants of Mekhpur? Their souls were Badakh, but they moved like strangers in the land. An invasion? Foreigners seeking shelter in Aishadan?

They would learn the answer soon enough, if it mattered. For now, it was time to rest. He sat wearily on an ice-crusted stone. If they were standing on the riverbank a few strides away, he knew they could have seen the torches burning on the battlements of Arekaryo Kes, and the bridge downriver.

"The creature is still above us, isn't it? I can feel it."

He put his arms around her. The Firelord was close by, but in no hurry. He would wait until morning. And until then, they could rest and sleep, sheltered by the frozen Gariba of the Vesparushrei.

Twenty-five

Pelshadan had kept to his chambers all night, while Eskel rode in and out of the Kes. The invaders would surely attack by first light, and he had much to do to prepare the city's defenses.

No one knew how many slaves were still alive; perhaps thousands had somehow slipped away into the mines, and the number lying dead in the streets was at least in the hundreds. Not one freeman's household in five had as much as a single healthy, fit slave. Even some of the arekakhar had vanished. Eskel wondered if they had actually sought shelter among their fellow-slaves. With their swastika-tattooed faces they could not conceal their identities; the slaves they had beaten and mutilated might not be forgiving.

The freemen and their families were huddled in their kitchens, trying to keep themselves warm and fed on little coal and less grain. Yet when he called on them they came, bundled in heavy robes and bearing pikes or axes. When this was over, Eskel promised to himself, he would mantle some of these men in the green robes of the upermannar—and give them the estates of those upermannar who had not come to the rescue of Aishadan, but stayed instead within their own walls.

The invaders had not troubled to conceal their strategy: they had concentrated their forces on the bridge and the riverbank nearby, and clearly intended to break into the city on a narrow front. They would fight their way westward through Aishadan, through the freemen's town and then the walled town; finally they would assault the gates of the Kes itself, rather than waste men in a direct attack on the steep sides of Aryofi Kleir from the opposite bank. Eskel had even thought of sending his own warriors across the frozen river west of the city, circling the invaders' left flank and falling on their rear. But he had too few men, and his one chance lay in fighting from shelter while the attackers froze in the open.

By the hour before dawn he had done all he could. He rode back up to the Kes for food and a last meeting with his mother. She was as unsleeping as he; he found her sitting by a fire in her rooms, sharpening a sword of strange design.

"My father gave us this as a wedding gift," she told her son. "Your father never had much use for Ghrirei steelcraft, and he put it aside. But now my cousin Badvai is Aryo of Ghrirei, and he may learn if his uncle's sword has held its edge."

"You will have to come out into the snow to find out, my lady mother. They will never get into the Kes."

Her eyes, cold as the sky, met his. "The rulers of Aishadan have always been confident men. We of Ghrirei always plan for the worst."

A soft knock sounded at the door. They turned and saw Pelshadan bowing, a gaunt figure in a hooded gray robe.

"They all come upon us now, Aryako—Aryasha."

"The invaders? Have they finally come out of their holes?" Eskel strode toward him, one hand instinctively going to his sword.

"They have begun to cross the river. They do not trust the ice to bear their horses, and they are wise. The river has fallen, and the ice is just a crust. So only foot-soldiers are coming across the river. The cavalry has concentrated at the Bridge of Alekakh."

"I must lead the defense."

Pelshadan did not move from the doorway. "The greater attack is yet to come, my lord. Dheribi has returned."

Eskel frowned. "A captive? Dead?"

"Neither. He and my slave Bherasha have come down the river on their own, it seems. Snegh's army has followed them, but now Snegh is riding straight to the city."

"Ha, is he indeed! Veik, you bring good news. With his men, we'll drive the invaders home to starve. My lady mother, we'll feast in victory tonight!"

Pelshadan seemed to smile in his beard. "Snegh has served you ill, Aryako. Dheribi is a greater danger than all the hosts at our gates. If Snegh had brought back Dheribi's head and my staff, Mekhpur would have been greatly pleased. He would have gladly granted all that you asked of him. Instead the Firelord must take matters into his own mighty hands."

"What do you mean?" Eskel shivered. "The slave bastard is only one man, magician or not. We'll slay him as soon as he shows his ugly face."

"He is already here, Aryako. And I do not think any blade in the Kes—even yours, my lady—would be more than a feather's edge to him."

"Then what of your own power, Veik? Are you not as great as he, or greater? You no longer tire; you have called down this great cold. Can you not stop Dheribi?"

"I will do what I can. And Mekhpur has other servants as well. But I do not underestimate our enemy."

"What can I give you to help fight him?"

"For now, nothing. Perhaps a few slaves in a little while, if the Firelord hungers."

"As many as you need. Every slave in the kingdom, if you wish. Where is Dheribi?"

"Under the ice, my lord."

"What?"

"Go to the window and tell me what you see on the river, Aryako."

Eskel obeyed. He rubbed the frost from the windowpane, but could still see nothing. Impatient, he struck the frame and the window broke away from its frozen hinges. Eskel squinted against the blast of cold and looked out at the frozen river and the snowy fields beyond.

Eastward, to his left, hundreds of soldiers were trudging across the ice, pausing at times to shoot arrows at defenders who were shooting back. The attackers made little sound, as if the effort of war cries was beyond them. Their shadows stretched far across the river in the light of the just-risen sun. As he watched, Eskel saw one man suddenly fall through the ice as if dropped through a trap door. In other places the ice had given way as well.

Just below, however, he saw no invaders at all—only a dark form on the ice, looking something like an enormous effigy of a bird. Then it moved and he realized it was no effigy but a living creature many times larger than a man. Its wings were like black banners, and its head was a beak that could bite a horse in half. Eskel felt dizzy.

"A bird—a giant bird," he muttered.

"A gheishauka, my lord," Pelshadan answered softly. "A ghost hawk from the Black World, sent by Mekhpur against Dheribi."

"And where is Dheribi then? I see only the—the thing."

"I said he is under the ice, Aryako. But I feel him preparing himself. Oh yes, he is coming. He is coming!"

The emptiness in Pelshadan's eyes was more frightening to Eskel than the winged beast below on the river ice. Eskel stepped back as the Veik came toward the window, then caught himself. He would not show fear before his mother and the Veik. To hide his fear he turned and looked again out the window, while Ghelasha stood at his shoulder.

The gheishauka was looking down at the ice, and Eskel realized something had begun to glow beneath the creature. Without warning, the ice erupted in a fountain of yellow fire, immediately before the gheishauka's head.

The black beast reared up, and the spreading of its wings made Eskel shudder. On the wind, a harsh cry rang out; Ghelasha echoed it with a gasp. The wind caught the creature's wings and lifted it from the ice; it struggled to hover close to the fountain of fire.

The gheishauka cried out again, snapped its great jaws and seemed to slash at the air with one taloned foot. Then it rose still higher, its beak pointed at the fountain of fire. The fire disappeared. A moment later, the gheishauka vanished also.

Eskel turned to stare at Pelshadan, who had not been close enough to the window to see what had happened. But he seemed to know anyway, and looked disturbed. The Veik even twisted a strand of his beard between two fingers, a habit Eskel had not seen in him since Pelshadan had regained his powers.

"Well, well," Pelshadan murmured. "He has cast away the gheishauka, as his mother did also, but he has used a magic I know not."

Eskel turned back to the window. Some dark object was now projecting from the hole in the ice where the fire had gushed forth. After a moment Eskel recognized it as the bow of a river craft, like a small longboat. A person in some kind of fur robe clambered up the craft's hull and out onto the ice. Another, slightly shorter, followed. The second one carried a staff or spear—

"The first one must be Dheribi," Eskel said tonelessly to his mother. "The second one is carrying the staff of Pelshadan. Am I right, Veik?"

"You are right, Aryako."

The two people pulled their boat out of the hole and began to drag it across the ice toward the foot of Aryofi Kleir, the hill on which the Kes stood. Eskel's eyes were keen; he could see now that their robes were rich Menmannar furs.

"He is coming back," Eskel said, "with just the slave bitch, against you, Veik, against all the warriors of Aishadan, against Mekhpur. Is he a fool about to die, or a monster about to slay us?"

"He is a fool, Aryako." Pelshadan's eyes seemed unfocused, vague, as if he were thinking of something far removed. "With your permission I shall meet him in the Hearing Hall."

"Meet him? May I not even attempt to slay him?"

"You would fail, Aryako. He is beyond the reach of the longest spear and the sharpest sword. We must fight him with weapons of magic. It will be dangerous. You and your mother should stay safely away."

Eskel laughed, almost merrily. "On this day, Veik, every breath I take may be my last. And I would not deserve to rule Aishadan if I dared not face its enemies. Come, my lady mother. Let us greet the witch's bastard."

"What of the invaders?" she asked. "Your men will be expecting to see you, to fight at your side."

"I will join them soon, or I will be dead." His eyes met hers; his mouth, though like a girl's, was hard. He offered her his arm, and led her from the room. Pelshadan followed close behind, his boots making no noise on the icy floor.

Snegh had no idea how many men were still in saddles, nor any idea how many of those were fit for battle. They had risen in the middle of the night for one last hard ride to the city, and now the steep walls and turrets of the Arekaryo Kes stood outlined against the blue-gray light of a clear winter dawn. In the distance, he could hear the staccato rattle of Halamori war drums, and a few faint cries.

"We're just in time," he mumbled to Vulkvo. "They must be storming the bridge. We'll go around the north side of Aryofi Kleir and through the freemen's town. The swine won't expect us."

"What if we interfere with the Aryako's plans?"

Snegh nodded and rubbed his face wearily. "Yes, yes. I'm not thinking clearly. Very well, then, we go around the Kes and wait. I'll go into the Kes and seek orders. Then we'll do whatever the Aryako wishes."

The horses were as exhausted as the warriors; they plodded through the hard-crusted snow and scarcely responded to their riders' whips that had opened frozen cuts on their flanks. The column wove its way through the few poor houses that clustered at the southwestern foot of the hill on which the Kes stood. Snegh saw no signs of life—no faces, no open doorways, not even smoke rising from the chimneys. The inhabitants had fled this part of the city. The steep sides of Aryofi Kleir helped defend the Kes, but not the houses at its base.

Further on they found a few more people, mostly women and children who said their men had gone to defend the city. But they did not seem overjoyed to see new defenders riding by; they only bowed and hastened inside to their fires. Snegh, swaying in his saddle, wished he might join them. To be warm, to eat, to sleep and sleep . . .

At the north gate of the Kes he found a dozen guards who gaped in wonder at the procession. Their commander shook his head at the hundreds of horses and riders.

"You are most welcome, Lord Snegh," he said, "but we cannot look after you and your men as you deserve. Most of our slaves have fled to the mines to escape the cold and the invaders. We have scarcely enough grain and meat to feed our garrison, but we will give you what we have, and find your men a warm place to rest until the Aryako decides where to use you."

"I thank you. My men need rest. But I must see the Aryako at once, to learn where he would use us."

"Of course. I believe he is in his apartment, preparing to go forth to lead the fight."

Snegh and Vulkvo dismounted and set out up the stairs and lanes to the Aryako's keep. The Kes seemed strange to Snegh, a mysterious warren of walls and corridors and little rooms full of darkness and sour smells. For all the danger in the forests, they seemed almost kindly compared to this place. The thought surprised him: he had grown up here, learned his first fighting skills here, spent countless nights in drunken revelry here with Albohar. It was more home to him than his own estate down the river, where he kept his unloved wife and their three sullen daughters. Yet now the Kes was an ugly and menacing pile of stone and brick, a fitter home for rats than for men.

A guard escorted Snegh and Vulkvo, quickly telling them about the invasion and siege. Snegh shook his head. Desperate men took desperate chances, as he had learned too well in these last few weeks.

A terrified old slave crossed their path; the escort grabbed the man and demanded to know where the Aryako was.

"He—he goes to the Hearing Hall, master. With his lady mother and the Veik."

The guard frowned. "The Hall is too cold to use."

"Yes, master. Yet he goes there. I am sent to bring more coal, master."

The guard sent him on his way with a casual shove. "Even the old ones are growing insolent. Soon as this is over, we need a lot of postings to remind them who's master here."

Snegh hawked and spat on the ice-slippery floor. "What's the matter, son, not enough bleeding and death lately to keep you happy?"

The guard gaped at him as if Snegh had suddenly begun reciting love poetry.

They came to the Hearing Hall, whose great doors were open wide despite the cold. Eskel sat upon the throne, with his mother standing near a brazier filled with glowing coals. Pelshadan the Veik stood by the shrine to Mekhpur.

The Aryako seemed more annoyed than pleased to see the two upermannar; he acknowledged their bows with a perfunctory wave.

"You have returned with Dheribi, it seems, yet not quite as I desired," Eskel said.

"No, my lord," said Snegh. "We failed in the task you gave us. But we have returned to defend the kingdom. Send us against your enemies wherever we can best serve you, and when the battle is won you may punish those of us who survive."

"Pelshadan tells me Dheribi is the greatest of my enemies, but not one you can harm. That seems true."

Snegh clenched his healed hand into a fist, and said nothing.

"Furthermore," Eskel went on, "Dheribi and Pelshadan's slave girl are coming into the Kes at this very moment. If the Veik cannot overcome Dheribi, the Firelord himself may have to do so."

Now Snegh swayed dizzily. ". . . The Firelord is here, my lord?"

"The Firelord is here and everywhere," Pelshadan said tonelessly. He drew a thin stylus of gold from a pocket within his robe, and upon the wall beside the shrine he drew a swastika. Many before him had done so also; the Veik had only to follow the grooves they had cut into the stone. Snegh recognized the first step in the Calling of the Firelord, a ritual often discussed but not performed except at the death of an Aryo or some equally grave crisis. He felt a sudden urge to vomit, as he had felt before battles when he had been a boy, and then all fear left him. As in a great battle, his fate was now out of his hands; he would only do his duty.

He wished his true lord Albohar were at his side.

Calindor and Bherasha climbed off the ice onto a dock scarcely visible beneath the snow. No one had used the dock since the last snowfall, but Calindor could sense the presence of warriors not far away. He tied the canoe to a mooring ring; perhaps they would not return to claim it, but the craft was too beautiful to abandon under the ice.

"This is where we escaped, when the Firelord nearly took you," Bherasha said quietly. "You were unconscious, and Svordo and Moro were carrying you. And I had to carry your mother after she drove the Firelord away. I was more frightened than I had ever been." She looked at him and smiled. "Until now."

He embraced her, kissed her and breathed in the scent of her. The ice, the black creature, the men fighting and dying not far away—even the vast bulk of the Kes seemed thin and insubstantial. Bherasha was real as nothing else could quite be. The Gariba that pulsed and burned in her were far greater than those within the staff she bore, the staff that now seemed little more than a child's toy.

His focus swept the Kes and found Pelshadan and the others in the Hearing Hall. *Very well,* he thought. *That will be as good a place as any.*

The door into the Kes was sheathed in iron and heavily barred. Calindor raised his hand; from his palm came a jet of dragonfire almost too bright to look upon. The door reddened, then glowed; the iron blazed white-hot and exploded in snapping sparks. Men's voices cried out in terror on the other side. Then the door burst inward.

Calindor stepped forward into smoky darkness. The men who had guarded the door had already fled. No one opposed his entry. He took Bherasha's hand and they walked together through the basements of the Kes.

The old chambers and corridors had been mysterious and exciting when he had been a boy playing in them. Now they seemed only shabby and dirty, filled not with treasures but with a forgotten clutter of ill-made furniture and cast-off clothing. The stairways led up through piles of spilled coal and broken earthenware; the air within the Kes was thick with the reek of ice-choked drains. The Aryos of Aishadan had built a palace to glorify themselves, but it was no more than a prison and they had always been its chief prisoners.

He sensed Mekhpur's presence, everywhere yet nowhere, powerful and hostile, yet Calindor felt only alertness and a detached tension. *Callia, you chose me and now you will use me. I am only as strong as you made me, and I will serve you as you wish me to.*

The stairs seemed to go on forever, but at last they came onto the main floor. The corridors here were deserted. Neither slaves nor warriors were visible, though Calindor could detect many on other floors. He detected Albohar as well, with Dvoi and Potiari tending him. The Aryo was on the edge of waking, breathing hard as if he dreamed himself in combat. The two magicians were muttering spells of protection, weaving them about the Aryo and themselves.

Calindor could feel himself moving through a web of magic; within it, the spells of Dvoi and Potiari were no more than a single short thread in a tapestry. But the web was not to protect the Kes from the invaders, or to shield its inhabitants from other magic. It was woven around Mekhpur, woven by Mekhpur to protect only Mekhpur.

The Firelord was afraid. He was still building defenses, armoring himself against two small enemies. Calindor smiled grimly and imagined Obordur walking with him, walking in him. The opening in his soul was wide. The world of magic pressed close.

In his focus Calindor saw spells laid across his path. Like the winged creature, their purpose was not to bar him but to provoke him. But he no longer cared what the Firelord knew or did not know. The time of tactics, of skirmishing, was over. The main forces were engaging; in a few minutes, Calindor thought, he would overthrow Mekhpur or fall before him.

Calindor broke the barrier spells with a gesture and a thought. The floor shifted beneath his feet, and ice crystals drifted down from the corridor ceiling. Somewhere deep in the fortress, foundations shifted with a soft rumble.

Bherasha looked at him. He took her hand; together they entered the Hearing Hall and saw the dull gleam of the golden swastika on the wall.

"Welcome back, Dheribi." Pelshadan's voice was soft, yet it carried the length of the Hall and seemed to reverberate under the high arched ceiling. The others in the room—Eskel, Ghelasha, Snegh and Vulkvo—said nothing.

Calindor paused, remembering the judgment that Albohar had passed upon him for the death of Blaidakh. This hall then had seemed just a room. Now he saw it as a charnel house. Not long ago a slave girl had died where Pelshadan now stood beside the Firelord's shrine. But she had not been the first. Hundreds had died here to appease the Firelord, sacrificed like the sunrise offerings of chickens and puppies that households made to ensure the prosperity of the Aryo. The souls of the slain filled the great room with silent torment, and beyond them were thousands more: those who had toiled and died to build this fortress of cruelty, those whose forgotten bones were the citadel's brick and mortar. They had known no joy in life nor peace in death, nor would they while the Arekaryo Kes still stood on the plains of Cantarea.

"I forgot; you do not speak." Pelshadan smiled. "You have prospered in adversity, Dheribi. You are an exemplar to us all."

Calindor looked at Pelshadan and saw the jenji staring back. He caught his breath. When Parsur Seggas's head had stopped rolling across the terrace in Ner Kes, the jenji had looked out of the dead Aryo's eyes and said: *We will meet again.* Now it had kept that promise, and once more moved through the world of Sotalar. But it did not belong here, it never would, and he knew its only true desire was for the silence of the void between the worlds.

"And Bherasha has returned my staff. I owe you thanks, girl."

She was silent for a moment. Then she said: "Whoever you are, whatever you are, you are not Pelshadan and this is not your staff. You owe me nothing."

Ghelasha looked startled; she glanced at Pelshadan and then turned back to Bherasha. "Slave, be still! You have dared to speak to the Skalkaz afi Mekhpur, the Veik Pelshadan."

"I served Pelshadan for six years. This is someone else. Can't you see it in his eyes?"

Calindor saw Snegh and Vulkvo shift restlessly. Eskel seemed scarcely to notice; he was watching Calindor only. But Ghelasha had begun to shudder. She clenched and unclenched one gloved hand around the scabbard of a sword.

"We have no time for a slave's idle accusations," Pelshadan said. "Dheribi, you seek to destroy Mekhpur. If you try you will yourself be destroyed. My master offers you something better."

Eskel pulled his eyes away from Calindor and stared in surprise at the Veik. "Are you bargaining with him? Destroy him! Kill him!"

Pelshadan ignored him. "Your power is beautiful in Mekhpur's eyes, Dheribi. You have gained knowledge no Badakh Veik ever dreamed of. Looking at you is like looking into the eye of the sun. You hurled the gheishauka back to its own world with magic strange even to the Firelord. Now you have a great choice before you. Attack Mekhpur, and be hurled yourself into eternal darkness and torment. Or serve him as the Aryo of Aryos, the Veik of Veikar, the ruler of the Five Kingdoms and all this world."

Eskel sprang to his feet, his breath white in the freezing air.

"Treason! Veik, how dare you bargain with this slave's bastard—offering him the Five Kingdoms—this throne—after all we have done to serve Mekhpur and to win power for Aishadan over this land—you would give it to this—"

The magician turned at last to look at the Aryako, and now, it seemed, Eskel at last saw what Pelshadan had become. "My master loves power, and Dheribi wields more power than any Aryo ever imagined. Together, Mekhpur and Dheribi could conquer everything in their path—all this world, and the worlds beyond as well. Dheribi, think of it. My master has favored these fools because he had nothing better to work with. He challenged the Mekhdeivush, the Great God Bha of the infinite aspects, and was cast out of his own world to exile here. Here he has dreamed for centuries of return and revenge, of true godhood over all the worlds. But he has needed strength, power, and all the Badakhar can give him is the strength of spilled blood. Give him your strength and he will give you his. All this world, and everyone in it, can be yours. You can make it what you wish—restore it to what it was before the Mekhdeivush sent the Badakhar into it from their own world. Can you imagine that, Dheribi? Can you imagine a world cleansed of the Badakhar, a world where the villages of Cantarea stand again in a green land?"

"Traitor! I'll feed Mekhpur your own blood, you—" Eskel drew his sword and strode away from the throne, toward the Veik. The jenji never took his eyes off Calindor, never moved, but Eskel suddenly crumpled to the floor. Ghelasha cried out; Snegh and Vulkvo sprang forward to the aid of the Aryako.

"You see how the Firelord casts away your enemy, Dheribi," said the jenji. "Be his first servant, and he will make all mankind yours to do with as you please."

Calindor did not move, nor did Bherasha. But with the jenji's words had come images as well: visions of Cantarea green and bright under a summer sun, cities of white towers rising from dense jungles in a hot land far away, great ships riding the swells of the sea far beyond the lands of the dragons. He saw armies riding to victory on distant battlefields, and the warriors were Cantarean and Badakhar under a blue banner with a green swastika. In the plazas of conquered cities, the people knelt before him and murmured his name.

But those were not the only visions. He seemed to hang in space high above a world unlike Sotalar, and to command its peoples and creatures. He saw the Black World, and found it bright. He saw a world that might have been Sotalar's twin, except that its Powers had forgotten themselves and could not hear the call of magic; and he knew somehow that it was this world that had been the first home of Cantareans and Badakhar and all the other human tribes of Sotalar.

And he looked upon a visage of terrible brightness and knew it was the Great God Bha, father and mother and maker of all the universes; and he saw himself reach out a hand and topple the Mekhdeivush into nothingness. Then he stood in the place of Bha, and it was his visage that gave light and life to all the worlds, to all the lesser gods.

"All this can be yours," Pelshadan said. "All your life you have done the bidding of others, Dheribi. All your life you have been no more than a means to an end chosen by others. Now you can choose for yourself. Do what others want of you, and die; or do what you wish, and become a Deivush yourself, walking among the worlds."

The visions faded though their beauty still glowed in his mind. He saw Pelshadan standing close before him, and looked into the jenji's eyes. They were as empty as they had been the first time, when the jenji had possessed the Aryo Parsur in Ner Kes, but now Calindor saw something else far back in their depths: he knew that Mekhpur was looking upon him out of the emptiness in the jenji, and he knew that the jenji too had once been a great magician. Once it too had seen visions of glory and power, and it had accepted the rule of the Firelord—

"Betrayer! Monster!"

Ghelasha had stepped forward, her sword unsheathed, and now she brought it down in a humming arc upon Pelshadan's hooded skull. Yet before it struck, something tore it from her hands and sent the blade spinning up into the air to embed itself in a rafter. Ghelasha was hurled backward until she smashed into the wall where the golden swastika glinted.

"Choose, Dheribi," Pelshadan whispered. "Choose."

Bherasha snarled and swung the staff at him just as she had once before. Against this weapon the jenji could not easily defend itself; it stepped back and with one raised hand it tried to deflect the blow. White light flared from the staff, driving the shadows from the corners of the Hall. In that light Calindor saw the faces of all who had died here, saw their wounds still fresh, and looked into their eyes.

You cannot avenge us, they said in voices as silent as those in the Open Dream. *But you can give us peace.*

Calindor raised his hand, and again dragonfire shot from his palm. It enveloped the jenji, turned from yellow to white and then to an intensity too powerful to see. When the fire ceased, the Hall darkened again.

The jenji was gone.

Eskel was sitting up, and Ghelasha struggled to her feet while Vulkvo helped her. The Aryasha's lips curled in a sneer.

"So you've won? And what have you won? A dead city about to be conquered and pillaged. You will be an Aryo in the ruins, you slave, and your reign will be shorter than this winter's day. Go ahead and slay us, and we will wait for you in hell."

Calindor scarcely heard her. The Kes was trembling again, its foundations shifting. But now it was for another reason. He turned and looked toward the gaping doors of the Hall.

Mekhpur appeared.

Twenty-six

"My lord father," Eskel whispered. For it was Albohar he saw arrayed in chain mail and a warrior's woolen cloak, standing in the entrance to the hall.

"Vella," cried Snegh, for he saw his beautiful first wife who had died long ago in childbirth.

"*Breitari!*" shouted Vulkvo, seeing his brother Sengvakh who had died in a skirmish with Halamor ten summers past.

Ghelasha said nothing, but edged back while the others stepped forward. She turned to look at Eskel, then back at the figure in the doorway who exactly resembled him, and her face turned to a mask of terror.

Bherasha reached out blindly to touch Calindor's arm. Only then did she turn away from the newcomer to look at him.

"*You* are the real Dheribi. And that is—"

He put an arm around her. For to him, the being in the doorway was Bherasha herself, dressed exactly as the real Bherasha was.

So that is what you choose, Mekhpur, he thought. *To be what each person loves most in the world. And in your service, out of love, the Badakhar destroy all that they touch, all that would sustain them if only they did not serve you.*

But this was no small-sorcerer's illusion, like Minukhi's dragons. Mekhpur as Bherasha was Bherasha herself, solid, her cheeks reddened by cold, her black hair falling thickly around her shoulders, her eyes full of love for him.

"You cannot harm me, Dheribi," said Mekhpur, speaking Badakhi in Bherasha's own voice. "Your dragon's tricks are no match for me."

The Firelord walked slowly into the Hearing Hall, and the air grew colder still. He stopped a few paces from Calindor and Bherasha.

"I can destroy you with a word, Dheribi, as I gave Pelshadan the Power that stole your voice. I can send you into the Black World, and bring you back as a deivushibi—what your people call a jenji. You would be my slave forever, like the one you met in the far caves, like the one who walked in Pelshadan's body.

"But that would sadden me, Dheribi. The jenji told you truly that I admire you. Your powers are great. You need only time and guidance to make yourself a god, a walker between the worlds. Together you and I could indeed overthrow Bha himself, and shape all the worlds to our desires. The jenji showed you only a little of what you could see, what you could be.

"Ah, Dheribi! How I would love to show you sunrise over the great prairies of Earth, where men first walked, and the stars at midnight in the sky of the Black World. Bha exiled me from there long ago, imprisoned me here and forgot me. But with you at my side we could break the fetters that hold us here, and all the universes would be ours. Only come with me. Only be mine, my own true friend and lover, and all this world shall be as you wish it."

Calindor said nothing but felt a kind of trembling; he could not tell if it was himself or the fortress that shook. Pain pierced his chest as if something were tearing itself loose inside him. Bherasha pressed closer against his side.

"Think," Mekhpur said softly. "Ever since you learned of your own Powers, you have known they were in the service of others. You have obeyed your mother, obeyed Albohar, obeyed Pelshadan, obeyed your mindless goddess—you have even obeyed a dragon. You should be master, yet you are everyone's slave. Come with me, and use your powers as you choose, not as others wish."

"He is you," she whispered. "Oh, Dheribi, he is *you*. He speaks your own soul's wishes."

Was she right? The same voice spoke before him and beside him; the same dark eyes implored him. Yes, Mekhpur understood him, knew how much he wished to wield for himself the power Callia had given him. With that power he could cast down the Badakhar, raise up the Cantareans, turn the big prairie rich and green again. He could call the dragons back to their ancient lands, lead the dying Gulyaji from their caverns back into the sunlight. All would be well again.

The room shimmered for a moment, and then disappeared.

He hovered on hawk's wings over the Silent River, and cried out in wonder and fear.

Snow was falling in the Open Dream. The green and sunny land lay dying. Trees had fallen under their burden of snow, and the village of the ancestors had disappeared in the drifts. The far mountains were lost in whirling whiteness.

Below him on the bank of the river stood Calihalingol, her arms upraised to him, her lips moving in a silent chant: *Callia, live! O Callia, live! O Callia, wake and live!*

Then he was back in the Hearing Hall of the Arekaryo Kes, swaying a little. The Firelord, with Bherasha's beautiful face, still stood before him. Her hands reached out to him; her smile filled his soul.

Calindor's breath was cold in his throat, and he sensed the other coldness of the being that still clung there within him. He considered all the magics he had learned: the brute leverage of the Badakhar, the subtle spells of the Gulyaji, the ancient enchantments of the Open Dream. None would serve him. Even if he could speak, and could invoke all the Powers, he could not stand against the will of the Firelord. All he had done in learning magics, he now saw, had been to widen the opening in his soul that linked him to the other world.

With a sudden furious motion, he tightened his grip on the real Bherasha's shoulder and flung her behind him. She fell to the icy floor with a despairing wail, still gripping the staff of Pelshadan.

In the next instant Calindor raised both his hands and threw dragonfire from them against the false image of Bherasha before him. Yellow-white flames gushed out, swirling around the Firelord. They burned away the Menmannar furs and robes, and then the flesh that had seemed so like Bherasha's. But the body of the Firelord did not blacken and die.

A hard smile came to Mekhpur's lips. Like a man casting off a garment, he dropped his guises and appeared now as a man, garbed in a Badakh chain-mail tunic and an upermanna's green cloak. He was far taller than Calindor, yet seemed squat and massive. His legs were thick with muscle and coarsely pelted. His head was a snouted horror, and his long arms ended not in hands but in sawtoothed pincers of horn. Calindor sensed that this appearance too was an illusion, an embodiment of his own fears, or Mekhpur's own mockery of the people who worshipped him; but still the apparition frightened him just as Minukhi's first dragon had, long ago in the beer hall. For it was the vision that Calihalingol had dreamed long ago before her death, and Calindor knew that he was the Cantarean in her dream.

"You have rejected me," Mekhpur said, speaking still in Bherasha's voice. "You throw your spells at me like a child in a tantrum, throwing its cup. I wish you had accepted me, Dheribi, for then your death would have been sweet with your own awareness of your mistake. You have robbed me of that pleasure, so I will console myself in other ways. You are young and strong, and I am in no hurry to kill you."

One pincer reached out and seized Calindor's throat. He felt its bitter coldness freeze his skin, felt its edges bite as they sank into the still-warm flesh beneath the skin.

Pain pierced him as he raised empty hands to try to push away that enormous arm. Vaguely he realized the Firelord had lifted him into the air, holding him as easily as a man holds a puppy. The pincer pressed deeper, and Calindor could now see only the grinning snout of Mekhpur in the center of a humming grayness.

Something burst within his throat as the pincer cut into it, and suddenly he could breathe again. He saw his own blood spurting, spattering on Mekhpur's huge forearm and freezing there. But not only his blood had spilled: the Power in his throat, the entity that had lurked in the staff of Pelshadan, was freed at last by the touch of the Firelord.

Calindor tasted blood, yet air could move through his wounded throat. He drew a deep breath and let it out in a cry that seemed no more than a whisper yet grew to a shout and then a roar:

"Callia, live! O Callia, wake and live! O Callia, come to us! I am Calindor, and I call you in the names of the Gariba and the dragons and the people and creatures of Sotalar. O Callia, wake and live!"

His heart seemed to explode. Mekhpur released him, and Calindor struck the floor and fell onto his back.

The gate in his soul to the world of magic was fully open now, and through it came something great and frightening. It was like the Gariba, but the greatest Gariba was no more than a raindrop compared to the deluge now about to burst over Sotalar. And while Gariba had powers without self-awareness, this being knew itself. He recognized it, knew it for what Calihalingol had called *sanshandata*—greenmagic, the unstoppable force of life seeking to create itself. Another name for it was Callia: Beauty.

It was bursting from him, tearing him apart yet leaving him untouched. In some corner of his consciousness, he realized he could never have controlled the force that had used him to reenter Sotalar. Unable to move, he lay staring up at the Firelord.

Bherasha arose, holding the staff of Pelshadan, and stood astride Calindor. She raised the staff in one hand until its gold-sheathed head pointed at Mekhpur.

"Fool!" Bherasha shouted, and hers was not the voice of a young woman but of a harsh wind blowing over bare stone. *"Fool! Bha exiled you because you chose cruelty and death when you had life and love. He sent you here to waken me, to rouse me from my long sleep. In my dreams I have shaped this man and woman, and now they shape me. You have thought that I would never waken, that you could devour me endlessly and that I would never rise against you. You have despised Callia as a goddess of love, a goddess of weakness. Now suffer the wrath of love outraged!"*

Blue-white light, hotter than dragonfire, mantled Bherasha's body. The air in the hall suddenly swirled into a cyclone of heat, filling the room with steam and stinging dust. From the tip of the staff, more fire erupted. It hurled Mekhpur's huge body back against a wall, and through the bricks into the snowbound garden beyond. Calindor saw the Firelord's writhing body vanish in a cloud of steam, and his cries were faint under the howling of a new-risen wind.

Bherasha pointed the staff upward, and the high vaulted ceiling of the Hearing Hall exploded in burning splinters. The beam of fire rose high into the cold black sky of a stormy morning. And the wind grew stronger still—not a winter wind, but a warm one, a dragon's wind. Still lying on the floor, Calindor saw the wind lift the red-and-gold swastika banners until they snapped furiously, and then rip them from their poles.

The snow and ice that lay heavy on the roofs of the Kes began to melt, to run first in trickles and then in freshets. The wind blew them away into spray, and tore at the exposed slates of the roofs. By ones and twos, and then by dozens, the slates broke away and spun into the air. Somewhere close by, a chimney toppled. The floor shuddered and would not cease trembling.

The light that had wrapped Bherasha now faded away. The staff of Pelshadan fell from her hand and broke on the floor like a rotted branch. She turned and knelt beside Calindor, herself again, and shouted in his ear over the roar of the wind: "Can you get up? We must get away. She will destroy all the Kes before she is done."

He took her hand and she pulled him to his feet. Ignoring the deafening wind, he embraced her for a long moment. He knew at last that he had been only the conduit, the stepping-stone. Through him Callia had walked into the body and soul of a slave girl, and through her Callia had awakened and struck down Mekhpur.

He put his lips to her ear. "You know my deep name. Now I give you yours. You are not the Bearer any more. You are Callia's Voice. Your name is Callishandal."

She pulled away from him, enough to look into his eyes, and smiled at him. In her own eyes he saw something new and strange, a glint like the movement of Gariba in a fast-running stream.

"She made me to open the way to Mekhpur," he said, "but she made you so that she might see and love Sotalar as humans do."

Callishandal laughed, and her voice was no longer the terrible hiss of Callia enraged. She kissed him quickly and took his hand.

"We must get everyone out of the Kes," she said. "Snegh! Vulkvo! Bring Eskel and Ghelasha, and hurry."

As if roused from sleep, the two warriors stumbled forward and turned to Eskel and his mother. Both seemed numbed, only half-aware of what was going on. Snegh took Eskel's arm, and Vulkvo put his arm around Ghelasha's trembling shoulders.

"Take them out the North Gate," Calindor said, shouting over the growing roar of the wind. The warriors nodded and hastened from the hall. As they passed through the doorway, Pervidhu appeared. His cloak was blowing around him, and he held his sword unsheathed. When his blue eyes fixed on Calindor and Callishandal, he grinned wryly.

"I thought you'd be at the bottom of this," he said, striding across the littered floor. A new gust of wind roared through the hall, throwing spray into their faces. Pervidhu squinted and swore. "What's happened here? Where are they taking the Aryako and Aryasha?"

Calindor pointed to the shattered wall. "Mekhpur is overthrown. Now Callia rules again."

Pervidhu glanced at the body lying in the mud and rubble of the garden. "Who's that?"

"I told you—Mekhpur." Calindor and Callishandal followed Pervidhu across the floor and looked down at the Firelord.

He was no longer a monstrous giant, but a man. He might have been young or old; his pale face was unlined, and his beard carried only flecks of gray. His naked body showed no wounds, yet his eyes stared sightlessly at the stormy sky. Lightning flared overhead, followed by a boom of thunder. Still more slates clattered down into the courtyard. One struck the Firelord's body and bounced off.

"So that's what we've been worshipping?" Pervidhu asked. "Looks like an ordinary man to me."

Calindor shook his head. Ordinary the body might seem, but it was not: Powers still moved in it, trapped like the Gariba in the staff of Pelshadan. The Firelord was overthrown, but he was not slain. Perhaps even Callia could not destroy him: despite the hot winds that now raged, and the torrents of water cascading into the garden from the roofs, frost was forming over Mekhpur's body, sheathing him in ice. Yet Calindor could see that once this had indeed been an ordinary man—a man of vast talent and intelligence, a man of great knowledge, but a man.

Lightning struck a turret overhead, and they ducked back as bricks cascaded into the courtyard. The floor was shuddering now, as if the whole Aryofi Kleir were trying to cast off the burden of the Kes.

Calindor turned to Pervidhu. "Find all the people you can, and send them out. And rescue the horses as well. I must go to Albohar."

The warrior nodded and sprinted from the ruined hall. Calindor and Callishandal hurried in another direction, toward the apartment where the Aryo had lain all these months. They found no one on the stairways or in the corridors; but Calindor sensed many people still in the fortress who were too frightened to seek their own safety.

The room that had once been Ghelasha's looked very different now. The only furniture left was the Aryo's bed, two plain wooden chairs, and a small table. In the chairs sat Dvoi and Potiari, their hands folded in their laps. They were staring at Albohar, who looked to Calindor like an old man on the brink of death. But he could see the Aryo's Powers still within him, made dormant by the poisoned wound the jenji had inflicted.

The dragon's wind howled through the blown-out windows into the room. The sky looked black, a mass of slowly turning clouds blasted by constant lightning.

"I greet you," Calindor said. The magicians rose, smiling faintly, and bowed.

"We sensed the battle you fought," Potiari said. "I congratulate you on your victory. I ask only that you slay us quickly and mercifully.''

"I have no wish to slay you. Pull back the Aryo's blankets.''

Blinking in surprise, as if the command was the last thing he had expected, Dvoi obeyed. Even in the turbulent air, the stench was foul. From throat to groin, Albohar's torso was a mass of blackened flesh oozing pus from a hundred lesions. His arms and legs were wasted sticks, and the strong bones of his face stood out under a thin sheath of skin.

Without hesitating, Calindor walked across the shuddering floor and placed his hands on the rotting flesh. The poison had worked deep into that flesh, but it could not escape Calindor's focus. Without lifting his hands, without speaking, he summoned a wisp of the torrent of magic still pouring out into Sotalar.

The room filled with golden light. Beneath Calindor's hands, Albohar's body seemed to soften, to blur into a glowing cocoon. Within it Calindor saw the Aryo's body as it was, as it had been, as it might be. He saw the ancestral Sterkar that dreamed within Albohar's flesh, waiting for some new birth, some new flesh; he saw the webwork of spells that had kept the Aryo from death.

He saw other spells as well, cast from Albohar's birth by Pelshadan and others. Yet what he had expected to find, he did not. No matter—he must attend to the urgent present, not to the past.

Then the light faded and the Aryo lay whole. He was still gaunt, but the necrotic flesh was healed and pale. He drew a deep breath, opened his eyes, and saw Calindor.

"Hello, Son. Have we taken Ner Kes?''

"Yes, Father.''

"Good. Good. I must rest.'' He fell quietly asleep.

"Quickly—dress him and wrap him well in blankets,'' said Callishandal. "We must get him outside.''

"But it's freezing out there,'' Dvoi protested.

"Can't you feel the wind? Look outside.''

The magicians went to the window, with Calindor and Callishandal close behind. They looked out on a world in torment.

Twenty-seven

Low black clouds stretched south to the limits of vision, whirling themselves into scores of tornadoes. The gray-green dimness flickered with hundreds of lightning bolts. A violent downpour of rain swept in across the river, blotting out the scene for a moment, and then passed on to the north. In its wake, the Vesparushrei's ice began to break up; the crash and boom of the ice were as loud as the thunder. Along the river-banks snow was melting fast, gushing into the channel. The attackers were in retreat, struggling to get back across the river to the relative safety of the right bank.

"Enough," said Calindor. "Let us get the Aryo to safety, if any remains." He carried Albohar in his arms, amazed at how little his burden weighed. Ahead went the two magicians; Callishandal walked at his side.

Water flooded the corridors of the Kes. Every ceiling poured water, and in places walls and ceilings had collapsed. The stairways were treacherously slippery as water ran foaming down them. The only light came from the near-constant lightning flashes that turned every window to a rectangle of blazing white.

They saw no one else, and Calindor sensed that Pervidhu had brought out all the remaining people and horses in the Kes. The fortress was still filled with Gariba of Water, Earth, Air and Fire. But they were in a tumult, especially those that held the walls and foundations: they sensed the energies pulsing and roaring around them, and yearned to break free. Only the Powers trapped within the body of Mekhpur were still.

At last they came to the North Gate, where Snegh's army was drawn up in the outer field as if for review. Men and horses alike waited unmoving under the rain and wind. Snegh, Vulkvo and Pervidhu stood in the lee of the Kes's outer wall, with Eskel and

Ghelasha huddled together under the arch of the gate. They all stared to see Albohar in Calindor's arms. Ghelasha cried out and reached to touch her husband's face.

"He will be well again," Calindor said to them, "if he survives this storm."

"I pray that he will," Snegh answered. "But he is no longer Aryo of Aishadan. You hold that title by right of conquest, Mekhmagh."

Mekhmagh: Great Magician. Would the Badakhar always prostrate themselves before strength, and punish weakness as an evil? Calindor felt a flash of anger at stubborn Badakh stupidity, then let it pass. They must find shelter, and soon.

He looked northeast across the city. Barely visible through driving rain was the gray-black mass of Aishadan Kleir.

"Lead your men to the mines. We will seek shelter there and hope that the storm soon ends."

Snegh and Vulkvo gaped at him, as if unable to believe what they had heard.

"But, Mekhmagh—we cannot go underground. Can you not calm this storm?" Vulkvo asked.

Calindor laughed in surprise before realizing that the others could not sense the magnitude of what they saw. "It is far beyond my powers. The Earth herself is wreaking vengeance, and she would brush me aside like an ant in an avalanche if I tried to stand in her way."

The Badakhar did not move; even Ghelasha looked at Calindor as if he had disappointed her.

"Look at the sky!" Calindor shouted. "Feel the wind! Even the most stupid slave knows the master's lash punishes wrongdoing. If you do not recognize punishment when it falls on you, your fate must be swift death. And for your crimes you will be lucky to escape death in any case. Do not turn to me, Badakhar, for rescue. Do not think I can save you from your folly."

"Then why take us with you to the mines?" Eskel said. "Why not let your goddess slay us where we stand?"

Calindor looked at the Aryako, whose eyes still held more anger and courage than fear.

"Albohar is not my true father, Eskel, and you are not my brother. Yet I grew up among your people; I am more Badakh than Cantarean. You were bad masters, bad masters of the land and its people. But once we lived together in peace and we must learn to do so again. We start now. Come—"

Thunder drowned out whatever else he wished to say. He

handed Albohar to Dvoi and Potiari, who wrapped him in blankets and carried him on their shoulders. Calindor walked away from the shelter of the wall and out into the field where the remnants of Snegh's army stood with their horses. The beasts were well trained, and did not start at the constant lightning strokes or at the sting of windblown rain. With Callishandal at his side, Calindor walked through their ranks, nodding to many he knew, and continued eastward toward Aishadan Kleir. Behind him followed Snegh and Vulkvo, then Eskel and Ghelasha and Pervidhu, and then Dvoi and Potiari bearing the Aryo. As they passed, the warriors fell into two files behind them, leading their horses.

The rain was falling harder now, and the wind struck at them with greater fury. Out of the black sky, tornado funnels groped downward; none had yet touched ground, but Calindor could see that many of them would. The procession entered the flooded streets of the walled town, finding some shelter in the lee of the townhouses of the upermannar. But in many places the houses had fallen, their roofs crushed in and their walls toppled. Bricks and logs had dammed the rushing waters at two places in the streets, forming deep pools of black water, and Calindor had to search with his focus for a safer route.

As the procession made its way through the ruined city, others joined it: Aishadanar soldiers, women and children, a few Cantareans, and even some of the invaders. Few of those still bore arms, and most were so drenched and muddy that they could scarcely be told from Aishadanar. Without speaking, they straggled out of lanes where corpses lay piled high, or limped out of wrecked houses. Their eyes, like those of the Aishadanar, were pale and unfocused.

They came down out of the walled town into the freemen's town, and Calindor looked out over the fallen rubble of a row of houses to the river and the Bridge of Alekakh. The rain had eased a little, though the wind was still fierce and hot. Where snow had lain thick over the banks of the Vesparushrei, now only streaks of white remained amid sudden lakes. The river itself was dark brown and white, and rising swiftly under its burden of ice floes and uprooted trees. All manner of debris was building up against the pilings of the bridge, where the invaders seemed to have broken through to the city.

Snegh stood behind Calindor. "They'll block our way to the mines, Mekhmagh. Shall I send our warriors against them, while you lead the rest to safety?"

"No. Only Callia chooses the living from the dead today. We go on."

Their route led them directly to the northern end of the bridge, through a little square dominated by the garrison. Calindor remembered riding through it many times, when his squadron had gone out behind Demazakh to train in the fields across the river. Now it was a pond, knee-deep in muddy water, and part of the south wall of the garrison tower had collapsed. Just beyond the tower, at the north end of the bridge, a few dozen Aishadanar warriors stubbornly resisted the pressure of hundreds of invaders. But the defenders could not last much longer; the invaders were fighting with mad desperation to reach solid ground. The Bridge of Alekakh was groaning and cracking under the sudden onslaught of flood-borne wreckage.

Calindor turned to Snegh. "Call those men back, before more die. Let the invaders through."

"As you command, Mekhmagh." Snegh snatched a horn from a herald nearby and sounded the call himself. The shrill notes were almost lost in the uproar of creaking timber and shouting men, but the defenders turned to see the procession across the square. They cheered, thinking that reinforcements had come, and broke away from their attackers in good order.

When the invaders saw the hundreds of warriors in the square, and more coming in all the time, they paused for a moment. Then the bridge swayed, and the invaders ran forward.

Perhaps three hundred reached the square when the bridge swayed and crumpled. Its great pilings snapped or fell beneath the unstoppable force of water and debris. The roar of the liberated flood shook the ground; the warriors still on the bridge vanished into the torrent. Calindor saw the river lunge forward like a vast snake. Overwhelming its banks, the flood swept away still more buildings: houses, stables, and barracks.

Lightning struck the garrison tower and demolished yet more of it. As the thunder died away, the remnants of the two armies waded across the flooded square toward each other. Calindor and Callishandal raised their hands in greeting as four upermannar approached.

"Put aside your swords," Calindor called out. "The war is over. Come with us to shelter."

"Who are you?" barked one of the invaders. His eyes were half-mad, and Calindor could see the turbulence in his soul. "A slave, by the look of you."

"None are slaves or masters now." He raised a hand and

threw dragonfire against their swords. The steel glowed red-hot, and the men cried out as they cast their swords into the water. Steam swirled up out of boiling bubbles. "You see no enemies here. We are all companions in peril. Come with us, or join your comrades in the river." Calindor turned and waded toward a lane that led up toward Aishadan Kleir and the mines.

The invaders stood motionless for a time, while the wind strengthened. Rain fell, sometimes cold and sometimes warm as blood. When Calindor glanced back, he saw the invaders had peacefully joined the long procession.

As they made their way into the slave town, the lane widened until they seemed to be climbing up a barren hillside. The slave huts had disintegrated under the blows of the storm; they were only scattered piles of stones and debris amid a broad cascade flowing rapidly down to the river. The nearest mine shaft, Calindor recalled, was well above the slave town. The slope was steepening. Footing was treacherous, and now the rain had become a constant chill downpour.

Callishandal looked up. The sky was writhing blackness, coiling and twisting into tornado funnels. Lightning leaped through the clouds and smashed into the earth. Thunder rolled and boomed until it became a constant noise, as steady as the roar of a waterfall. Callishandal turned to Calindor.

"What do you see?" she shouted. Calindor stopped while the Gariba of Water pulled frantically at his legs. Hailstones fell like an avalanche.

He saw Powers of Earth and Air, Fire and Water, contending in a battle no warrior could withstand. The Powers themselves were frightened by the wrath of Callia and fought one another as if to escape. But they had no escape; their whole being was in her and of her.

As is ours, Calindor thought, and began to feel despair. Taking Callishandal's hand, he bowed his head beneath the whirling hailstones. The thousands who followed were drenched and muddy and in pain, and he could sense their terror. Badakh warriors and Cantarean slaves alike all felt themselves at the end of life, at the end of the world.

The road to the mines was a torrent, knee-deep and filled with tumbling stones. The mountain itself was lost in white curtains of falling rain and hail. Less than a bowshot away, a tornado funnel touched earth; bricks and shattered boards flew into the air like startled birds. The funnel moved away, toward the dimly visible river, but Calindor knew more tornadoes would come. The judgment of Callia would fall on them all, Badakhar and Cantareans, humans and beasts.

At least we die together, he thought, and embraced Callishandal. He wept, feeling the strength of her arms around him.

Then the embrace was over and she was gripping his sodden robes. Her face was a mask of anger as she shouted at him over the tumult of the frightened Powers: "Go on! Go on! They trust us to save them. Go on!"

The lightning had lessened. Between its strokes he stood in shrieking darkness while hail whipped at his face. Was this what the Black World was like, an endless chaos of Powers in agonized damnation? Had Mekhpur brought a worse infection to Callia than the mere poisoning of her land?

If so, then the struggle to save her had only begun.

Calindor raised his hands to the storm and filled his mind with dragons' visions. He called on the Powers, and yellow-white light sprang up. It ran like a burning string around the long file of men and women who followed, and it hung in the air: no thicker than a hair, yet too bright to look upon. Within it the rain and hail no longer fell; the flood turned aside, leaving them standing on mud and stones. But all around them, the storm grew in fury.

The heat of the dragonfire added to that of the wind. Calindor cast aside his robes and stepped forward in only his buckskin trousers and sodden boots. Callishandal, too, threw away her robes, standing in trousers and a thin wool tunic. Together they climbed farther up the slope, their eyes on the slippery footing; Calindor rejoiced in the strength of her hand in his.

"This is the place you seek," a voice said amid the thunder. Calindor looked up. In the hillside, blue light glowed from a narrow opening. The light outlined a tall man whose pale robe was drenched and clinging to his spare frame; he seemed not to care. "I greet you, Calindor."

He spoke in Cantarean, strangely accented yet familiar. Lightning flared in three huge bolts overhead, and Calindor cried out in wonder when he saw the man's wrinkled face and white brows:

"Renjosudaldor! Protector!"

They embraced at the mouth of the tunnel. After a moment, the Protector broke away, smiling.

"Get your people to safety. They will find food and water, and shelter from the storm."

"How did you come here?"

"When the cold began to fall, we knew a great battle was coming. Some of us left the Bayo Bealar and came in secret to Aishadan, thinking to do what we could to serve Callia. We called the slaves to us, and kept them hidden. And now we welcome you once more to the Underland."

"I rejoice to see you, Renjosudaldor. You are an even greater magician than I thought, to hide so well under the Firelord's nose—and under mine." He turned to Callishandal. "Here is the Protector who sheltered Svordo and me when we fled from Ner Kes. And here, Protector, is Callishandal, who spoke today with the voice of Callia and cast down Mekhpur."

He took her hands in his own and sang a blessing on her. She embraced him as she would her own father.

Other Gulyaji had come from the tunnel entrance—almost casually, Silisihan waved to Calindor.

Snegh struggled up to the entrance and looked at the Gulyaji.

"Who are these people?" he asked Calindor.

"Burrowers. Don't look like that, Snegh! They're here to save us. Put your life in their hands, or stay out here."

His face pale, Snegh nodded and strode into the mine entrance. The others followed.

Calindor would not go inside until all who followed him were safe. During all the time, while the storm raged on, he stood at the tunnel mouth with Callishandal and Renjosudaldor beside him. Potiari and Dvoi, helped by Vulkvo, bore Albohar inside. Ghelasha and Eskel followed close behind, their eyes empty.

At the end of the procession came Pervidhu, leading six horses that had lost their riders. He was drenched and weary, yet he smiled when he saw Calindor.

"They'd better have room for the horses," he said.

"They have room."

"It can't smell any worse than that dragon's barn."

When the last stragglers were safe inside, Calindor looked out over Aishadan.

The clouds had lifted and broken a little, and the rain had stopped at last. But lightning still marched across the prairie and through the ruined city. By its light, Calindor saw the Vesparushrei far over its banks, rushing to the northeast under an almost solid mass of trees and broken ice. The camps of the invaders had vanished under water. Nothing remained of the Bridge of Alekakh, or of the buildings that had lined the banks of the river. On higher ground, the freemen's town and the

walled town were only rubble; here and there, fires set by lightning somehow burned despite the flood.

At the far end of the city, Aryofi Kleir rose against the red-
black sky. The towers and battlements of the Arekaryo Kes had
fallen, but here something had turned aside the dragon's wind.
The ruins of the fortress glittered white in lightning's glare: ice
mantled the Kes and ran well down the hillside.

"He is still there," the Protector said.

Calindor nodded. "Overthrown but not slain. Callia has imprisoned him, or his own evil has done it for her. He makes this
a twice-cursed place. No city will rise here again."

Clouds were parting in the west, allowing a few beams as
bright as dragonfire to pierce the storm. Calindor saw that yet
another tempest was sweeping up from the south, and it would
grind the ruins of Aishadan into still-finer dust. But the light of
the setting sun reminded him that the next storm would pass as
well. He thought of Tanshadabela, standing high above the
flooded river, and of his people there.

Soon, when Callia's rage had passed, he would return to the
mountains. Callishandal would go with him; together they would
welcome the turning seasons, explore the forests and peaks, and
sing with the people in the Meeting Hall. And then, he knew,
they would go on—westward, to the sea he had once seen in a
vision, where Callia sang in the waves' crash and in the endless
wind among the great trees.

In the shafts that Cantareans had cut into the ancient stone,
light now glowed: coldfire, rippling across walls and ceilings.
It shone on hundreds, thousands of people. The Badakhar huddled together, scarcely looking up; Calindor could feel their
terror. They shuddered almost without cease, though their sheer
numbers warmed the air.

Among them moved the Cantareans and the Gulyaji, tall and
slender, bringing small loaves of bread and leather buckets of
water or milk. They said little, but walked with the confidence
of masters in their own house. Calindor remembered the miners
he had visited short weeks ago, and marveled.

He and Callishandal walked deep into the mountain, through
crowded tunnels and echoing galleries. Everywhere the Cantareans greeted them with smiles and gentle embraces; a few Badakhar looked up and recognized him, but fear did not leave
their eyes.

At last Calindor paused and slumped against a stone bench

carved from the wall of a long gallery. Now it served as a barn for horses and cattle, with bales of hay piled up at either end. The livestock seemed unperturbed by the shimmer of coldfire or the echoes of hundreds of voices.

"Thank you for making me go on," he said to Callishandal. "I would have stopped and waited for Callia to take me back."

She sat beside him and put one arm around his shoulders.

"I would have stopped with you. But . . . she didn't want us yet. She spoke, not I."

He nodded, smiling faintly and enjoying the strong stink of the barn. He remembered the barn in Tanshadabela.

"If she wants us to live," he said, "then perhaps she will save enough of Cantarea for us to live upon." He stood up and took her hand. "Let us find Renjosudaldor again, and see if we can be of use. This will be a long night."

In the morning Pervidhu roused him where he and Callishandal lay sleeping deep in a tunnel. The Badakh was still filthy from the journey through the storm, but his blue eyes gleamed in coldfire light.

"Come quickly, Calindor. The storm is past."

Silently Calindor and Callishandal rose and stepped lightly up the tunnel, past the sleeping Badakhar and Cantareans. In another tunnel horses whinnied; perhaps, Calindor thought, they recognized the storm was over and yearned to be outside even if the land lay ruined.

At the mouth of the tunnel Pervidhu stopped and stood aside. Calindor and Callishandal walked out onto the hillside.

The storms were indeed gone; the dawn sky was streaked with the red rags the tempest had left behind. The sun, just risen, threw the clear light of a fine winter's day across Aishadan. The icy dome of the Kes glittered in sunlight above the ruined city.

"It's warm," Pervidhu said. "Warmer than yesterday, at any rate."

"Dragon's wind," Calindor answered. He looked across the muddy plain and felt an ache of sorrow. The land was destroyed. The floods had scoured the soil from the bedrock, or buried it in vast banks of gravel. Once orchards had grown behind the walls of the upermannar; now even the walls had vanished. The Gariba had reveled in their freedom, and this morning they slept like drunken carousers in a ruined tavern.

Callishandal pointed off to the southwest, across the still-swollen river. Something gleamed there, like a flame. Then it seemed to split in two, and then three, then many.

"The dragons have come back to Cantarea," said Calindor.

"Can they help us?" Pervidhu asked.

Calindor shook his head. "They taught our ancestors, and they have much still to teach us. But they cannot rescue us from this. They cannot make the land fruitful again. That is up to us."

He walked away from them, away from the mine entrance, and along the stony remnants of a trail. The slag heaps were deeply eroded, and water still ran through the gullies it had cut during the storm. The sun was surprisingly warm on his face, and the dragon's wind comforted him. After fifty steps or so, Calindor paused and looked again at the approaching dragons. What must they feel, looking at this land that once had been theirs and now lay dead?

I must give them something, Callia. Some sign that this world still lives.

He squatted on his haunches, looking at the Gariba in the torn soil and shattered rock of the hillside. In the crevice of a stone, he sensed a seed—better said, he sensed its desire for life. He called to it, and heard nothing but the roar of the wind in his ears and the trickle of running water. Again he called, and then a third time.

A fleck of green appeared in the gray soil packing the crevice. It grew, curled and straightened, and lifted itself from the stone like a tiny green flame. As Calindor watched, it rose until it was as long as his little finger. The dragon's wind bent it, but it straightened and seemed to grow stronger. Small though it was, alone though it might be on that blackened breast of a ruined land, Calindor saw Powers pulse within it that no sorcerer's staff could ever contain.

"Greenmagic," Calindor murmured. The words his mother had taught him in secret, long ago, came back: "Thanks to the Gariba Sotalara, the Powers of Earth, for this gift."

Standing, he turned back toward the mine entrance. The land of Aishadan still lay ravaged and empty. But in Calindor's vision a green shimmer pulsed just below the surface, eager to burst forth and make all things new. Callia could heal herself. And somehow, mankind must heal itself as well.

Epilogue

After the dappled shade of the woods, the midsummer afternoon sunlight was dazzling. Albohar reined in his horse for a moment and tugged his wide-brimmed hat a little lower over his eyes. Snegh and Vulkvo were close behind; Pervidhu as usual was straggling with the string of packhorses.

"It looks smaller than I remember," Albohar said.

The meadow stretched out before them, bounded on the north by lodgepoles and on the south by the steep bank of the river. On the far side, the woods were thinner than they had been twenty-two years before. Albohar could see some of the cabins of Tanshadabela, and heard the clang of a stalmagh at work.

Seven or eight horses were grazing at the north end of the meadow. They lifted their heads to look at the newcomers, then went back to their grass. Travelers were common these days.

"We came right through here," Albohar went on. "She was down there, walking toward that horse. We were all half-drunk, but I can remember every step we took. You and the others went out to cut her off, and I went straight for her. I remember thinking how smart she was to keep walking, not to try to run. She'd have frightened the horse away."

"She gave you a good fight," Snegh said with a smile.

"That she did."

"And I was angry with you, back at the longboat, when you wouldn't share her with the rest of us."

Albohar said nothing. Pervidhu and the three packhorses finally caught up with them. "Well, here we are," he remarked. "A pretty place when it's not snowbound."

Snegh and Vulkvo grunted and grinned.

They rode slowly through the meadow, following the trail into the trees and then into the village. Here the trail became a street running through loosely clustered cabins. Each cabin had its garden, dense with vegetables at this time of year. Menmannar were going about their business, and no one paid much attention to the newcomers. Indeed, quite a few other Badakhar walked along the street, or sat beside booths filled with trade goods.

"Now, this is new," said Pervidhu as they reached the center of the village. Where the dragon's barn had been, a large new cabin stood; like a Badakh freeman's house, it formed three sides of a square around a courtyard, and a stable was close behind it. "A proper inn, here in the wilderness. I vote we shelter here."

"Vote, vote, vote," Snegh said. "A man can't take a piss these days without his whole household voting on it."

"Then I will decide for us all," Albohar said, and swung gratefully from the saddle. A couple of young Menmannar, a boy and a girl, walked over to take the horses, but Pervidhu insisted on taking them into the stables.

The innkeeper came out on the porch; he was a rawboned young Cantarean with a quirky smile. When he recognized Albohar, his eyes widened in surprise. He jumped to his feet and bowed.

"My lord, this is a great honor!" he exclaimed in Badakhi. "But why did you not send word ahead? We would have prepared a feast for you and your companions. As it is we have little but a venison stew and a lot of Menmanna vegetables."

Albohar had first assumed the man was local Menmanna, but his speech gave him away as a Cantarean ex-slave. It was still awkward to talk civilly to such people, but easier than it had been. "That will serve us very well. That, and a keg of medh or beer."

"We brew a very fine beer, my lord. Please—come in out of the sun and rest. You've come to the right place. We have proper beds here, the best beds in Tanshadabela."

The men's boots thumped and squeaked on the floorboards as they tramped across the porch and on into a large common room. A few Badakhar and Menmannar sat drinking at tables, but none gave the newcomers more than a casual glance.

The innkeeper settled his new guests at a table near a window, looking out on the courtyard. In a moment he had tankards of foaming beer before each man; they drank thirstily and gratefully.

"Will you be wanting anything else for now, my lord?"

"A proper keg of this stuff," Albohar replied. His flagon was already half-empty.

"Very good, my lord. If you gentlemen wish anything else, simply call me." He bustled off into the kitchen.

Pervidhu came in from the stables. The four men sat and drank companionably for a time, until the innkeeper brought out bowls of stew and platters of unfamiliar vegetables and salads.

"I know you," Pervidhu said.

The innkeeper looked again at him. "Pervidhu! So this time you got here on your own! Welcome!"

They shook hands, and Pervidhu turned to his companions.

"This fellow is Svordo," he explained. "He's an old friend of Calindor's, one of the crew that rowed him up the river."

Albohar smiled. "Now I recognize you! You were with Dheribi when he came to Ner Kes during the siege. Later he told me more about you. I thank you for all you've done to care for him."

"He has done much more for me, my lord. Well, please don't let your stew cool on my account. Eat, and perhaps later we can talk."

They fell to their meal with an appetite. When even the third servings were gone, and washed down with more tankards of beer, Svordo emerged from the kitchen and took a seat at the table.

"What news from the prairie, my lords?" he asked.

"A good harvest," Pervidhu answered. "The farmers complain they lack enough hands to bring it in. And the price of a good horse is outrageous."

"So we hear. Some of the Menmannar are talking about taking some of their livestock down the river in the autumn."

"Let them come to Vidhumen first," Albohar said. "They'll get the best price."

"I hear it's quite a good-sized town now, Vidhumen. Though nothing like old Aishadan, of course."

"It serves us well enough," said Albohar. "Two thousand men and women, and a couple of hundred children."

"And you are the electman, they say, my lord."

"I am. Harder work than being an Aryo, but someone must speak for the town."

"He even got votes from some of the Cantareans," Vulkvo said proudly.

"Well, of course," Svordo said with a nod. "And is your visit here for business, my lord?"

"In part. I also came in search of Dheribi and Pelk—Tilcalli, his mother."

"Ah. Well, I don't know if they're here at the moment. But you might speak to Dragasa. He's our electman this year."

"Indeed," Albohar said. "Then I must certainly pay my respects. Where might I find him now?"

"His cabin is not far." Svordo gave brief directions.

Albohar stood up. "The rest of you stay here. I'll be just a little while."

He walked out into the village, marveling at the splendor of the mountains all around. Even now, in high summer, their peaks gleamed with snow. He felt an impulse to go wandering deeper into the mountains: all those years ago they had thought themselves bold explorers, yet they had barely entered this mysterious world of the Menmannar.

Svordo's directions brought him to a cabin much like the others. A tall man with graying hair was sitting at a simple table on the porch of the cabin, writing on parchment. He looked up as Albohar approached.

"Excuse me for interrupting. You are Dragasa?" Albohar asked in Cantarean.

"I am. You speak our language well."

"My father took pains to make sure I learned it. Now it serves me better than he expected. My name is Albohar." He extended his hand.

Dragasa smiled through his surprise, and took the hand. "Welcome to Tanshadabela! Come, sit down. May I offer you bread or beer?"

"Nothing, thank you." Albohar took the other chair on the porch. A squirrel ran up a nearby lodgepole pine, stared at him, and scampered down again. Gray jays perched on a branch, hoping perhaps for a crumb. "I came to see Dheribi and Pelkhven." This time he did not trouble to correct himself about their names.

"I am sorry. Calindor left for the west in the spring—"

"For the west?"

"The dragons asked him."

"Ah."

"And Tilcalli is visiting clan members upriver. She will be back in a month or so."

"Ah." Albohar fell silent for a time, and Dragasa said nothing more. "They are well?"

"Very well, yes. Marriage agrees with Calindor. His wife Callishandal went with him."

"And how does marriage agree with you?"

Dragasa looked sharply at his visitor. "We rarely talk of these matters outside the family."

"We *are* family, you and I. We shared a wife and son."

"Yes. And lost them both."

Albohar heard a quiet sorrow in Dragasa's voice. "Lost them more than once, you mean."

"I did not expect to keep my son. You know his deep name means One Who Goes Away. Callia made him for her own purposes. But Tilcalli." Dragasa leaned back in his chair, arms folded across his chest. "Tilcalli I thought would come back to me as she left me. I was wrong."

"She is no longer your wife?"

"Oh, we are married. We enjoy one another. My life is better because of her. But she is not the same. She could not be."

"None of us is the same," Albohar said hoarsely. "The world is a better place than it was, no doubt of that, but we are not the same. Except perhaps in one way."

"What is that?"

"The night I stole her from this place, she put a spell on me. She cast a spell on my soul, so that I would love her and our son—her son. I have come—" He hesitated, and looked away from Dragasa. "I have come to ask her to lift the spell, so that I can go on with my life."

Dragasa said nothing for a long time. Then he leaned forward, elbows on knees, and looked into Albohar's eyes.

"We both love her, you and I. So I will tell you something Calindor told me when they returned from Aishadan, after the storms. He did not tell Tilcalli or Callishandal, but he told me. When the Firelord was overthrown, and the storms had begun to destroy Aishadan, Calindor went to you and healed you of your wound."

"Yes."

"And when he did so he looked deep into your body and soul. He found there the traces of all the spells that magicians have cast upon you. But he found no trace of Tilcalli's spell."

Albohar frowned. "What of it?"

"Enchanting a human soul is a rare and difficult feat. Tilcalli had prepared for a long time to enchant yours, so that you would protect her when you took her with you. I knew nothing of this—

she had planned it all with her great-grandmother in the Open Dream.''

"I don't understand," Albohar said.

"That part doesn't matter. Calindor found that her spell had failed. She did not enchant your soul. She was lucky she did not drive you mad, or herself. But the spell failed."

"But—I *did* care for her. I did raise Dheribi as my son, and not as just another slave."

Dragasa smiled. "You fell in love with her by yourself. It happens. I fell in love with her the same way."

Albohar seemed to clench himself into stillness, while a breeze whispered through the treetops overhead. His voice was scarcely louder. "Then—am I doomed to love her forever?"

"We don't understand the Badakh idea of doom. Callia dreamed of all that we might do to save her, to waken her. Perhaps she caused you to love her; perhaps it was only chance. If you had not, who can tell what the world would be like today?"

Albohar stood up. "So I would be a fool to pursue her, to ask her to free me."

"Free people set themselves free. Until they choose freedom, Callia can do nothing for them."

"Would you choose to be free of her?"

"No."

Albohar thought for a time, elbows on his knees and palms pressed together before his face. At last he sighed and said: "I cannot think of a happy moment in my life when she was not there to make it so."

Dragasa nodded. "Yet you have your wife, your son—"

"And I love them, too. But I will always yearn for what I had, and lost, and will not have again."

Dragasa stood and again took Albohar's hand. Then the Badakh met his eyes.

"I thank you for what you have told me. You have shown me the greatest hospitality today. I hope someday you will come to Vidhumen so that I may return it."

"With Tilcalli?"

"With her or without her. I will not steal her from you again," he said with a crooked smile.

"You never stole her from me at all. She has never been any man's property."

"No." He sighed. "I must rejoin my companions. Perhaps

we can meet tomorrow, to talk about trade. We can offer good prices for horses.''

"I will be glad to. Until then, Albohar.''

Albohar walked back through the quiet village, enjoying both the warmth of the sun and the cool of the shade. The people he passed smiled at him and greeted him, and he replied with smiles.

He did not return directly to the inn, but walked on through the village. *She walked here,* he thought, *both when she was young and now in her middle age. These cabins, these gardens and trees have been part of her life, more a part than all the years in Aishadan. I was only an interruption in her life, but she was the core of mine.*

He came to the bluff overlooking the river. The mountains on the other side gleamed green and gold in the sun, their white peaks bright against the blue sky. Aspens glittered silver on islands in the stream; on one islet, two elk stepped delicately among the willow bushes.

Albohar looked down a flight of stone steps leading to a small dock on the water's edge. Here the smaller stream, clear and green, flowed into the turbid mainstream, and for a little time kept its own identity. But at last it disappeared, and the river ran on, gray-green with the silt of glaciers, past Tanshadabela, past Aishadan, past all Cantarea to an unknown sea.

About the Author

Crawford Kilian was born in New York City in 1941 and grew up in California and Mexico. After graduating from Columbia University in 1962 he returned to California, served in the U.S. Army, and worked as a technical writer-editor at the Lawrence Berkeley Laboratory.

In 1967 he and his wife Alice moved to Vancouver, British Columbia, where he has taught English at Capilano College since 1968. In 1983 the Kilians taught English at the Guangzhou Institute of Foreign Languages in the People's Republic of China.

Crawford Kilian's writing includes several science-fiction novels, among them *The Empire of Time*, *Icequake*, *Eyas*, and *Lifter*. In addition he has published children's books, an elementary social-studies text, and two nonfiction books—*School Wars: The Assault on B.C. Education* and *Go Do Some Great Thing: The Black Pioneers of British Columbia*. He is the regular education columnist for the Vancouver *Province* newspaper.

The Kilians live in North Vancouver with their daughters, Anna and Margaret.